# Snowfall at Catoctin Creek

## Catoctin Creek: Book 2

### Natalie Keller Reinert

Natalie Keller Reinert Books

Copyright © 2021 Natalie Keller Reinert

Cover Photo: pierivb/Depositphotos

Cover Designer: Natalie Keller Reinert

Interior Formatting: Natalie Keller Reinert

ISBN: 978-1-956575-09-5

# Books by Natalie Keller Reinert

*The Catoctin Creek Series*

*The Grabbing Mane Series*

*The Eventing Series*

*The Alex & Alexander Series*

*The Show Barn Blues Series*

The Hidden Horses of New York: A Novel

# Chapter 1

# Nikki

"**O**w, that's hot!"

Nikki dropped the pan with a resounding crash and rubbed at her burned fingers. What a rookie mistake! It was like she was new in the kitchen or something, instead of a veteran who had been working in the Blue Plate Diner since she was eighteen.

Since she was eighteen . . . Nikki began to run the math in her head between eighteen and thirty, then stopped herself.

*Oof. Don't think about how many years you've been doing this.*

She grabbed a couple of towels and picked up the pan she'd dropped, making another clatter as she set it back on the stainless steel countertop. The apple-cheeked cook working next to her paused slicing his onions just long enough to give Nikki a stone-faced glare. "Must you do that now?" he asked, injecting each word with venom.

Nikki held up her hands in surrender. "You're right, I shouldn't be in here on Thanksgiving eve. Sorry, Patrick. I just wanted to get a head start on these sweet potatoes for dinner tomorrow."

Patrick grunted and went back to his carrots.

At the other end of the cramped kitchen, Betty looked up from the silverware she was sluicing clean. A matron of sixty with a youthful face, Betty picked up kitchen shifts at the Blue Plate Diner because she liked to get out of the farmhouse where she'd been cleaning up after an army of children for decades—all of whom were off at school or in the Navy now. "Don't they need you out on the floor?" she asked.

Nikki forced a smile. No one needed her. Business was slow. "It's early yet, I think the girls have got it under control."

Betty shrugged and went back to her dishes.

Nikki sighed and looked around the tight kitchen. As usual, Patrick and Betty had the place running smoothly. From a dinner rush to a crawling afternoon slump, they knew how to pace themselves. The morning crew, Bobby and Michael, were the same. They'd been serving up the same dishes and washing the same plates since Nikki's Aunt Evelyn had run the Blue Plate. Nikki's job, for the past five years, had been to make sure she signed the purchase orders and make sure the paychecks went out on time.

No one seemed to know just how little she was needed here.

She hoped no one ever found out.

The only employees at the Blue Plate who actually needed managing were the dinner-shift servers. A revolving collection of teenagers with no good sense, her dinner waitresses could keep her hopping on a busy evening. And out on the floor, where she wasn't in Patrick's hair.

So to speak.

Nikki noticed his shoulders were still up near his ears and tried to apologize again. "I'll be more quiet. This is your kitchen."

Patrick snorted and ran a hand over his pink scalp. He'd never had much hair, but spending two decades in the steamy kitchen of a country diner had pretty much done in whatever he'd started with. Nikki wasn't sure how old Patrick actually was; she'd always thought of him as her aunt's contemporary, and Aunt Evelyn had moved to Arizona at the age of sixty, leaving Nikki the Blue Plate and a legacy she felt responsible for upholding.

The diner was a pillar of Catoctin Creek. An ugly mid-century brick pillar, with staring plate-glass windows around the dining room and country decor so old it had gone from cheesy to kitsch to museum collection, but a pillar nonetheless. The other eateries on Main Street, the soda fountain and the ice cream parlor and Mama Bella's Italian Ristorante, had all closed up years ago. Catoctin Creek's boom years were a hundred years in the rear-view mirror. The Blue Plate, Trout's Market, and the feed store were the only commerce left in town.

With that kind of failure rate, Nikki wasn't about to make any sudden moves and change the place. Or annoy the kitchen staff until they decided life was greener on the other side of retirement, like Aunt Evelyn had done. Nikki was fine with helping out on the floor. Talking to the restaurant patrons, most of whom she'd known for years from school or church or just living in such a tiny polka-dot of a town. But the cooking? Nikki loved to cook. *Adored* cooking. Spent hours in her apartment's kitchen tinkering with flavors, toying with textures. Working in the Blue Plate kitchen would suck her spirit dry.

Whipping up the same old pot roast, meatloaf, fried chicken, and pan-fried trout every night sounded like her worst nightmare. The gravy-forward country cooking was all delicious in its own way, tasting of Friday nights celebrating good grades, Sundays after church, and the occasional weeknight when both farm chores and work ran late and her mom couldn't beat the clock to get dinner on the table before bedtime. But Nikki's tastes—and her cooking habits—ran far more modern than anything on the Blue Plate menu.

So she had to behave herself in her staff's kitchen. Never give them any reason to walk out on her.

Not like Kevin.

Nikki ground her teeth and started looking for a spare few inches of counter. She needed to *work*. She couldn't stand here and think. If she had too much time on her hands, she'd fixate on Kevin all afternoon. She needed work.

Work, and an affirmation.

*You put too much stock in one guy, and now you need to get over him.*

Plain and simple, to the point. Nikki took a deep breath. She was new to affirmations, but she was very good at making action plans. And now she needed one.

*Action plan, Nikki.* What needed handling right now?

The sweet potatoes, of course. Tomorrow she was celebrating Thanksgiving at Notch Gap Farm with her best friend Rosemary, and Rosemary's husband Stephen, and she was responsible for the sweet potato casserole. She could make it at home in the morning, but the flavors would be better if it sat overnight. Plus, she needed the distraction.

Nikki shoved some loose curls of auburn hair beneath her white kerchief and tried again to give herself a little prep space in the shoebox kitchen. This time, Patrick obligingly moved a few feet out of her way, perhaps trying to avoid another flying pan if she burned herself a second time. Patrick: a silent, but astute man.

"Hey Nikki, you want some extra carrots to take to your dinner?" he asked, dumping the orange carrot coins into boiling water. "We got enough for the dinner rush and then some. They reheat just fine."

"No thanks. You take them," Nikki replied, smiling quickly. "You and Betty. I have a new recipe for carrots I'm going to try making tomorrow morning, before dinner."

Patrick shrugged, supremely indifferent to her special new recipes. "Don't know why you want to add anything special to carrots. They're fine with just some salt, maybe a little pepper. Sweet and savory, carrots."

"I know, you're right. I'm just feeling creative, I guess. Can't mess them up with a little honey, maybe some bourbon, right?"

Patrick grimaced in a way which suggested he found messing up carrots to be *all* too possible. He rubbed his hands on his grimy white shirt and leaned across the stove-top to nurse along some boiling green beans.

Privately, Nikki thought those boiled, squishy green beans were the most vile thing imaginable. The last time she'd eaten green beans, they'd been dressed in a vinaigrette and topped with feta cheese. Delicious. That had been in the privacy of her own home, of course. She was pretty sure if she put feta on the Blue Plate menu, her regulars would start a prayer circle for her soul. Green beans were boiled until soft, then heavily salted at the table. That was how they were eaten. Carrots? Pretty much the same.

Green beans and carrots: how drastically her taste buds had changed over the years! The Blue Plate served the classics she'd grown up on, the daughter of a truck-driver and a kindergarten teacher, and the granddaughter of farmers on both sides. As a child, nothing was better than snuggling into a corner booth of Aunt Evelyn's diner for a chicken drumstick, a scoop of mashed potatoes, and a pile of those soggy green beans. Then, as a teenager, one very impassioned home economics teacher had awakened her passion for blending flavors, and Nikki had been developing into what her mother described as a "total food snob" ever since.

Nikki had washed off the masher and begun the assault on her bowl of sweet potatoes when the door from the dining room swung open. Lauren, a recent high school grad whom Nikki had been grooming into her assistant manager, poked her sleek head into the kitchen. Her chocolate-brown hair was coiffed into a perfect bun, like a ballet dancer's. Nikki couldn't understand how the kids got their hair so smooth. Her own curls were like springs attached to her scalp. She'd love, just once, to have elegantly straight hair.

"Nikki, phone call," Lauren lilted. "I think it's your mom."

"Good grief," Nikki muttered, putting down the masher and forgetting all about her hair. "Now? She *knows* I'm at work."

"It's not busy out here," Lauren offered. "You can talk. No one else is calling."

"I am aware it isn't busy. That's why I'm making my sweet potato casserole now." Nikki sighed as she accepted the cordless phone, an old-fashioned model which usually lived on the restaurant's front podium along with the menus and the crayons for restless children. "Hello, Mom."

"Nikki! I'm *so* sorry to call you at dinner! But I just missed you so much. Everyone is here for Thanksgiving but you."

Ever since Nikki's mother had followed her sister to Arizona, she made a plaintive phone call to her distant daughter on major holidays. In between the bold-faced days on the calendar, Nikki initiated all of their phone calls. For much of the year, her mother seemed happy enough having Nikki's elder sister, aunt, and father all gathered together in the same clay-hued town. Nikki became an afterthought—out of sight, out of mind.

This was becoming her default position in life, she thought ruefully, perching the phone on her shoulder and cocking her neck to hold it there. She went back to mashing sweet potatoes with her freed hands. "I hope you all have a very nice Thanksgiving," she told her mother. "I'm thinking of you."

"You should be here. You couldn't close the diner or let someone else be in charge for a few days?"

"Now's not the time for the guilt, Mom," Nikki replied stonily. Steam rose from the potatoes, bathing her face. "It's too late to get a flight out there." Not that she'd ever considered going, of course. She still filled an essential role in the diner, even if it was largely signing off on requests or chasing down the dinner servers.

Who would run the Blue Plate if she went on a trip? Things *did* happen. There were ice storms, broken pipes, missing shipments, medical emergencies. Who would handle the unexpected? The stick-in-the-mud kitchen staff who never left their greasy kingdom? The flighty teenaged night-shift servers who didn't show up if they suddenly realized they had a paper to write, or snagged a last-minute date? The ancient, grizzled morning servers who wouldn't have stayed past three in the afternoon even if Nikki offered them a bonus in gold coins?

*Maybe Lauren?* Nikki reflected suddenly. Not yet. Lauren was too new at the management gig to be running this place with Nikki in another time zone.

No, the Blue Plate only closed on major holidays, and this rule wasn't changing anytime soon. Nikki left the place to Lauren on Sunday and Monday nights, but that was as far as she was willing to go right now. Someday, Lauren would take more weight onto her shoulders and let Nikki dabble in her own culinary dreams— and *perhaps* even take a vacation—but they weren't there yet.

Nikki's mother made a fussy sort of exhalation. "I get that you can't come *this* time, but for Christmas, Nikki, come on—"

"Maybe," Nikki said, knowing she wouldn't be able to go to Arizona for Christmas. "Maybe then."

When the call ended, she stood still for a long moment, looking into the depths of her sweet potato mash, before taking the phone back out to Lauren. The world on the other side of the swinging door was cozy and warm, a mile away from the cramped, fluorescent-lit kitchen.

She glanced around at the evening's early supper trade. A few early bird diners were settled comfortably in the booths along the windows, but most of the tables in the center of the dining room were still empty. Well, it was early yet—six o'clock was when the farmers began to finish up and head inside for a shower, and the commuters were just arriving back in Catoctin Creek after spending their day in city offices. Not that many of the newcomers to the area ate here, but the long-term residents who had turned from farming to steady indoor jobs still brought the family back to the diner where they'd eaten as kids. The dinner rush was generally from six-thirty to just before eight, when the *Open* sign on the door was flipped to *Closed.*

Or so a normal weekday's dinner service would run, anyway. On the day before Thanksgiving, all bets were off. Last-minute runs to the grocery store, long drives to grandma's house, or trips to the Caribbean—the Blue Plate would probably have a quiet night while the residents of Catoctin Creek prepared for the holiday in their own ways.

Lauren glanced up from her smartphone as Nikki dropped the landline phone back on its charger. The young woman ran a hand over her smooth hair, as if checking for flyaways. Nikki's wild hair had that effect on people. She looked over at Lauren, so slim under her loose black blouse and impossibly skinny jeans. Nikki was still pretty much rail-thin, so she didn't resent Lauren or the other skinny high school girls on the night staff, but the older women who worked the day shift couldn't stand them. Mom jeans and elastic-banded khakis were their favored uniforms for the hard work of pouring coffee and bussing syrupy plates. Nikki wondered if she'd ever make that switch herself. She stuck her thumb in the snug waist of her jeans, considering the fit. It still worked . . . for now.

*Thirty,* she thought. *Going on sixty.*

"So, is your mom doing okay?" Lauren asked.

"Yeah, just feeling guilty she left me here when she moved across the country to bask in the desert sun." Nikki shrugged and bared her teeth in an attempted grin. "The usual holiday phone call."

"That must be tough." Lauren dragged a damp towel across a laminated menu. "I can't even imagine. My entire family lives in Catoctin Creek. Well, except my brother. But he just lives in

Frederick. I'll probably move there, too, when I finally move out of my parents' house."

Nikki raised a slanting eyebrow. At least her eyebrows were good, slender and arching, dark to match her deep auburn hair. She didn't have any lines in her forehead yet, either. Little blessings. "A whole half-hour away? Really? Why so daring?"

Lauren laughed, abashed. "I know, I know. But why would I leave the area? My friend Kristi talks about going to D.C. or maybe New York for college . . . I just don't see it, personally. I like it up here. It's not crowded. And I like the mountains." She glanced out the front windows, as if they could see the hazy blue humps of the Catoctin Mountains looming behind the two-story buildings across Main Street. Sunset was long past, though. "This is a good place, you know? We just need more to do here."

Catoctin Creek *was* a good place. That was why Nikki stayed, too. Even though she had only inherited an old restaurant built in the sixties, and not an elegant red-brick Victorian with a turret and wrap-around porch like the house where Lauren had grown up, she could feel her roots here, tugging at her every time she chanced going too far away.

Though just a few cross-streets around the quiet commerce of Main Street, Catoctin Creek had the bones of a more memorable country town: a village of modest frame houses and a few aging mansions from nineteenth-century farmers who'd managed to make small fortunes. Sadly, most of the houses were falling into disrepair. Catoctin Creek had ceased to be a place where people raised their families. It was a place people left.

Those who didn't leave ate dinner at the Blue Plate and went quietly about their business. Nikki watched them pick at their plates of country-fried steak and their bowls of chicken noodle soup, and then gazed into the darkness outside, dreaming her own personal little fantasy: a big house with deep verandas, the kind of place where she could set up a restaurant very different from her little diner.

She knew exactly where she wanted to put her dream restaurant: the old Schubert place. The elegant Queen Anne sat at the edge of the little town, aloof on a sloping lawn above Main Street, shaded by stately elm trees. She had fond memories of that porch: she used to sneak onto it and ride on the porch swing when she was a kid. The elderly Schubert couple hadn't minded her, but her mother had swatted her a few times for using that swing without permission.

The Schuberts passed away a few years back and the house sat empty now. Nikki slipped onto the porch and peered inside from time to time. The enormous windows, stripped of their heavy curtains, gaped lonesomely, and sunlight slanted across dusty hardwood floors. She always reassured herself that the ceilings were still intact, no mice were nibbling at the wainscoting. Just in case she could somehow acquire a lease, or even buy the place—but that was impossible. The Schubert children had long since left Catoctin Creek, but as far as she knew, the house had never even gone on the market.

The bells on the restaurant door jingled as another elderly couple paid their bill and left. Nikki watched them shuffle to their car. Martin and Shelly Wolf, who had farmed north of town for years. Their fields were fallow now, their barn collapsing, but they still lived in their old wooden farmhouse, watching the seasons change around them.

"That's what happens when you don't leave," Nikki murmured.

"Is that good or bad?" Lauren asked.

"I can't say for sure."

"Seriously, though, *you* wouldn't leave Catoctin Creek, would you, Nikki?" Lauren asked. "I mean, I know your family did. But that must have been weird. Arizona." Lauren shook her head at the impossible oddity of it all.

Restless, Nikki picked up a menu and a wet towel from the bleach bucket. She might as well clean menus, keep her hands busy. "Well, no one exactly gave up the family homestead when they moved. The Mercer farm was sold a long time ago. My dad didn't want to be a farmer. And . . . I guess once it was gone, people didn't feel so rooted here. My parents figured they raised their family here, and that was enough. My aunt didn't have kids, so family wasn't even an issue for her. Nothing was really tying her down."

"But, are you going to raise *your* family here?"

"Where? In my apartment? That used to be the McKinley's garage? In fact, before that it was the McKinley's carriage house. My bed is in the old hay-loft." Nikki had always seen herself bringing up two kids, a boy and a girl, in a big house with shining hardwood floors and a wraparound porch—a house like the Schubert place. "I couldn't wedge a family into my place."

"I guess you could move," Lauren pointed out with a pert little snort, which was as close as she'd come to sarcasm on the clock.

"You going to make me say it, Lauren? I'm short on a mate to *make* the kids with, too."

Lauren laughed. "Okay, that's fair. But you're gorgeous and funny and run your own business. I'm sure you could find a guy who wants to have babies with you." She paused and glanced at Nikki speculatively. "Unless you're just looking for a sperm donor. In which case, what are you waiting for?"

Nikki heard Mrs. Babson choke on her green beans. "Okay, enough of this," she hissed. "I'm not looking for *anything*, as a matter of fact. Not a man, not a woman, and definitely not any children of my own."

"What do you want, then?" Lauren asked, undeterred. "I mean, I love working here, but we both get it's not my career. I realize you own the place, and that makes leaving hard, but don't you want something else?"

Nikki wondered when teenagers had gotten so concerned with other people's business. This new generation was way too in touch with feelings. Not just *their* feelings, either. They wanted to experience everyone else's feelings, too. Nikki would rather not think about her own feelings, and she definitely didn't want anyone else to notice them. This went for every hope and dream and sorrow she had, from her absent family to her frustrated cooking ambitions to that jerk, Kevin, who had gone back to New York City after Rosemary and Stephen's wedding and hadn't been back here since.

Him, most of all. On Nikki's list of frustrations, what could come higher than Kevin? Dancing with her at the wedding, kissing her softly on her lips, telling her she was beautiful.

Vanishing without a word.

It wasn't like Kevin had been hit by a bus or something, either. No, he was just fine! Stephen went to New York City for work occasionally and saw him there, but the last time she'd had the nerve to ask about him, Stephen had told Nikki that Kevin was, quote, "Pretty busy with work stuff." Nikki figured this answer meant he wasn't interested in her, after all.

Which was *fine*. She wasn't about to moon over some guy she barely knew, some guy she'd found hopelessly attractive because of his fox-colored hair and his kind eyes and his silly sense of humor. Sure, she liked redheads, and she was a sucker for a sweet and soft personality, but Nikki Mercer would not waste her time chasing a guy who lived three hours away and liked it that way.

"I'm doing fine as I am," she told Lauren. "And since it's still dead out here, I'm going back to the kitchen." She'd find something else to cook, or clean, if Patrick and Betty didn't chase her out first.

"Fine," Lauren retorted. "Don't tell me. But we both know you're looking for something better . . . even if you won't admit it out loud."

# Chapter 2

# Kevin

"Come on. Let me move in," Kevin wheedled, fixing Rosemary with a pleading look. His mother had always told him he had eyes which could beg like a basset hound. He was going to use that talent today. "Let me stay here forever and never go back to the mean old city."

Rosemary just shook her head and laughed at him before she bent over the oven again, checking her pies. The farmhouse kitchen smelled exactly as one would imagine it should on Thanksgiving eve: spicy and sweet, the air filled with cinnamon and caramelizing sugar. Kevin's own kitchen had never smelled this good. Granted, he rarely cooked anything more intoxicating than toast in it. The gleaming marble counters and stainless steel appliances of his condo with Midtown and East River views were more for showing off at parties than for actual cooking. The rare meal eaten at home came from delivery guys.

"Really, Rosemary, I'll shrivel up and die if I go back to New York City. My condo hates me. My job hates me. The entire city hates me."

Rosemary didn't turn around, but he could see her ears move. She was smiling. "I bet it's more likely the city doesn't think about you at all, right? Isn't that the problem with New York? It's nothing personal. It's not you—it's them. And no, you can't move in. That's final. I love you, but I'm not looking for a roommate, and neither is my husband."

*Cruel creature!* Kevin thought dramatically. He liked to be dramatic sometimes, in his head. Adding some old-fashioned verbiage to his mental monologue made his life, which never seemed to be moving on a trajectory of his choosing, feel more exciting. He wasn't actually dramatic, or exciting, in real life. He was a very normal guy—possibly too normal. In truth, his normality was the cause of all his problems, from career to love.

Rosemary wasn't actually cruel, of course. She was a sweetheart. Rosemary was his best friend Stephen's wife, a perfect gem of a human, and if she didn't want Kevin to move into her beautiful farmhouse with herself and Stephen, he'd respect her decision. But not without just a little moaning. She had to know he was dead serious about the whole thing: moving to Catoctin Creek, abandoning his New York life, starting all over again here. Hell, it had worked for Stephen. And he and Stephen were like brothers.

Ergo, it would work for him.

Kevin ran his hands through his red-gold hair, which was falling into his eyes as usual, and concentrated on smiling just as hard as he could at Rosemary until she turned around and saw his face.

She burst out laughing, and her dark hair came loose from its bun, swinging in front of her face. "Kevin, I have faith you can figure out this move without taking up my spare bedroom or eating me out of house and home. I already have eight horses doing that, plus Stephen. And he's honestly a bigger expense than I expected. Thank God he pays his own way."

"Stephen! Pah!" The drama was vocal this time. Kevin raked a hand through his hair. He needed a haircut again—he *always* needed a haircut, it seemed like. Then again, the drooping locks might give him a more sympathetic look—a kind of elegant, desperate poet, he hoped. His green eyes glittered at the idea. "Look here, Rosemary. Let's be real. Stephen eats like a bird. I'll eat like a *smaller* bird. And I'll pay your room and board—I'll pay for half the groceries."

"You're going to pay me? With what?" Rosemary turned her back on Kevin with a grin and a swish of her long paisley skirt. "You're wrong about Stephen, by the way. He eats more than you think."

Kevin subsided, watching her work at the uneven wooden countertops. She was dressed for a chilly day in a drafty house, wearing wool-lined house clogs, the aforementioned skirt, and a long sweater. Kevin thought she looked just like a good witch. A young, spritely good witch, who seduced her customers into her cottage with smiles and apple pies.

Well, she had certainly enchanted Stephen. What had started last winter as a little vacation fling—well, not exactly a vacation, as Stephen had come down to Maryland to settle his father's estate and get his detoured life back on track—had turned into a happy marriage. The two of them had been married since September. Hard to believe that pretty autumn day was nearly three months ago, and harder still to believe that was the last time Kevin had come down from the city.

For all of those months since he'd been dreaming of nothing but coming back to Catoctin Creek: the sunsets, the silence, the serenity, and the sweet vixen of a bride's best friend. *Nikki.* He was pretty sure Stephen had made the right choice in marrying a local girl and settling down on a farm in the middle of nowhere, even if their mutuals in New York City had lost their collective minds. Stephen's move had been the main subject at every dinner party, get-together, and after-work drink for weeks after the wedding announcement. Kevin had been faced with the unenviable task of explaining his best friend's escape from New York at dozens of gatherings.

But even with such intimate knowledge of Stephen's wooing and wedding, Kevin was not so certain he'd manage the same stunt. For one thing, Stephen had managed to find work which was almost entirely remote; he only had to go up to New York once or twice a month for client meetings, contract signings, that kind of thing. Kevin was still expected to show up at his office daily, or, at the very least, be ready at a moment's notice to cross the Queensborough Bridge and make it to Manhattan boardrooms for presentations and evaluations. Managing investments *sounded* like it should be a virtual job, but for some reason the gig seemed to require an awful lot of in-house work.

And of course, Stephen had seen no trouble in leasing out his prewar apartment just off Riverside Drive, even if it *was* a walk-up. Kevin, on the other hand, had paid new construction prices for a floor-to-ceiling view of Midtown from a skinny glass tower in Queens, but the building wasn't sold out yet, rendering his attempt to sell the apartment and the units he'd invested in completely futile. Why buy Kevin's lived-in spaces when an oligarch or an influencer or another investment banker could get something completely sterile and new?

To make matters worse, word had spread around NYC's real estate circles—which was to say *all* circles, as everyone talked incessantly about real estate—of the needle-slim building's single most nauseating flaw. High-floor views of the city were great; the motions of a tall tower in a strong wind were not. Even the silvery glow of the Citibank Building outside his windows each night seemed a cold comfort while his living room swayed ominously through summer storms and autumn gales. On gusty nights, Kevin clung to the cold marble counters and dreamed of the stable, solid earth of Catoctin Creek.

And here he was—for as long as he could manage it. Kevin leaned back in a creaking old kitchen chair and sighed. He loved the Notch Gap Farm kitchen, so old-fashioned and peaceful. Vintage wallpaper on the walls, creaking floorboards at his feet, a window of wavy old glass overlooking the pastures and the sloping foothills beneath Notch Gap at the far end. Rosemary moaned that the space hadn't been updated since her grandmother's day, but Kevin privately believed any improvements to the mismatched cupboards and cabinets would be criminal.

He watched her pick up a little tin box of recipe cards. "What are you going to make next, Rosemary?"

She'd already baked an apple pie and a pumpkin, and he had designs on whatever was coming out of that oven next. No one's stomach could withstand the delightful smells floating around that kitchen. He had eaten half a sub and an entire bag of potato chips on the drive down from New York, but ten seconds in Rosemary's kitchen and he felt like he hadn't eaten in days.

"I'm leaning towards green beans," Rosemary said, flicking through the yellowed cards. "They'll reheat well tomorrow."

"The green beans with crunchy onions on top?"

"No, those are gross."

"How can you think crunchy onions are gross? Does Stephen know this? Was it mentioned in the wedding vows?"

"Nikki says green bean casserole with crunchy onions is a crime against humanity *and* side-dishes," Rosemary replied, casting him an arch glance.

Kevin had been trying to keep Nikki out of his thoughts. A fool's errand, no doubt. With her wild coils of dark auburn hair, skinny legs, and a tightly wound personality which he found delightfully different from his own devil-may-care attitude, Nikki's presence was always a plus for him when he was visiting Notch Gap Farm. A *very* big plus.

At the wedding, they'd steamed up the downstairs bathroom. She'd seemed on the verge of inviting him back to her place—so he'd driven back to New York before she had time to make a move she'd ultimately regret. Nikki wasn't a one-nighter to him, a bridesmaid to bag while everyone was feeling the pinch of being single at a best friend's wedding. There was something special there, something he wasn't going to wreck by making an impulsive move.

Kevin hadn't gone home without a plan. He'd driven back to New York with nothing on his mind but the idea of returning to Catoctin Creek to properly court Nikki.

So he'd put his head down and worked like a dog for two months straight, doing everything he could to strengthen his position at work, only to be refused remote work yet again. He'd talked to every real estate agent representing property in western Queens. He'd cold-called headhunters. He'd even asked Stephen if there were openings on *his* team. He'd chased down every idea he could cook up in the attempt to make his life more portable, instead of being locked down in the city.

Because the simple truth was that he couldn't have Nikki if he couldn't stay in Catoctin Creek. She was just as devoted to this little town as Rosemary, and look where that had landed Stephen! He was outside checking the horses' water buckets right now. You'd never know the guy was an investment genius. He'd traded the Financial District for feeding horses, and there was no regret on his face when he came inside smelling of manure and mud.

Kevin wanted that. He wanted all of it: the girl and the town and the dirt under his fingernails. He wanted people to look up when he walked into a restaurant—even if that restaurant was only the Blue Plate, not a Soho bistro—and he wanted to sit down after a hard day's work and know he'd done something real with the hours he'd been allotted. Even remote work was losing its allure. The more he made money for other people, the more Kevin wished he wasn't.

Kevin couldn't seem to buy Stephen's kind of luck, the fortune which had granted him income, a loving wife, a meaningful life. He had done all that work, and stayed away from Nikki all that time, and nothing had come from any of it. No headhunters called him back. No real estate agents had managed to make his condo budge on the glutted luxury market. He was stuck.

The chief problem, of course, was that he wasn't good at his job. Not the way Stephen was, anyway. Stephen had managed to find dream work: lenient bosses, worthwhile clients, and virtual meetings. He'd gotten this kind of job because he was damn good at investments. Kevin was just doing the job he'd had since graduating from college, and ten years at a job might buy you forgiveness, but not mobility.

Still, he had a little in savings. He'd already pooled all his vacation time and taken leave from his job. Every realtor in New York City had the code to his condos. He was here to rip off the Band-Aid, start a new life, or die trying.

But if Rosemary would not let him stay here, he had to figure out a new place to crash.

And it was hard to focus when Nikki was on his mind.

Rosemary was still smiling at him, waiting for a reaction to her little bomb.

"I guess Nikki and I differ on green beans," Kevin said finally, leaving out the thousand and one thoughts which surfaced from just mentioning her name.

Rosemary pulled out an index card and studied the crabby old handwriting on it. "You know, Nikki asks about you all the time," she said breezily.

Kevin looked down at the tabletop and traced a knot in the wood grain with one finger. "She does, does she?" That was nice. It was nice to be asked after. Didn't mean anything. Didn't mean she wasn't mad at him for leaving, or that she wasn't seeing someone else. A nice farmer, perhaps, with a hundred acres and a mooing cow for each of them.

"She says we don't see enough of you down here. And I agree. You should visit more."

"Well, I was trying to work things out with the job, the condo, all of that. And it just wouldn't come together. That's why I asked you if I could stay here," he added. "I'm really not trying to be an imposition, I'm just trying to figure my life out so I can make some headway with Nikki. I can't do it from New York."

And she really was at the heart of all of this. There was no brand-new, sparkling Kevin without Nikki at his side. If she didn't want him, he might as well stay in Queens, up all night as his bed swayed in the wind, and keep making half-assed decisions at a job he didn't care about.

Rosemary pushed the recipe tin back to its spot beside the rooster-shaped cookie jar. She turned and faced Kevin, a serious expression replacing her usual serenity. "Kevin, are you going to do this for real, or just halfway? If this is the real thing, I'm sure Stephen would let you stay in the brick house. Just ask him."

Kevin considered the brick house. That's what they'd taken to calling the house Stephen had inherited from his father. The ugly little rancher sat on a hill about ten minutes away from Notch Gap Farm, with a big square of green lawn and a magnificent view of the Catoctin Mountains and Notch Gap, the dip where two mountains in the chain sat shoulder to shoulder. Stephen's father had enjoyed spectacular sunset views from that house, and Stephen had enjoyed them himself until he'd moved down to Notch Gap Farm just before the wedding. Now, the house sat empty, while Stephen tried to decide what to do with it.

Kevin considered the brick house's few charms. The view was sensational, the furnace worked, the location was remote but somewhat close to the farm, and Stephen had at least updated the furniture while he'd lived there. It wasn't quite as depressing as it had been the first time Kevin had stayed there, back when he'd first come to Catoctin Creek. The day he'd met Nikki.

The day he'd known, without really understanding it, that his life had changed.

Maybe there was a chance here. "You really think he'd let me stay there?"

"Of *course* he would. You're his best friend."

"He might want to rent it out, or sell it." In Kevin's experience, friendship came second to the demands of real estate. Stephen was still a New Yorker, after all.

"He hasn't decided yet. If you beat him to the punch, he'll say yes to you." Rosemary dug a casserole dish out of a cabinet with a deafening clatter. "I *know* he'd say yes to you. Even if he already had some idea about selling it. Go on, ask him when he comes in from the barn."

"You're probably right," Kevin mused. "If you convinced Stephen to help take care of your horses so you don't have to go out in the cold, I can convince him to let me stay in his empty house."

Rosemary laughed.

The front door opened and closed with a *thunk* of stuck wood. "I gotta fix that door," a voice mumbled from down the hall.

Rosemary winked at Kevin. "He doesn't know how to fix that door," she whispered.

"Neither do I," Kevin whispered back, grinning. "We're worthless city people."

"I can hear you," Stephen called. "Strange acoustics in this hallway."

"Whoops," Rosemary giggled, that charming little bubble of laughter of hers that had driven Stephen crazy when he was chasing her. Kevin remembered the way Stephen used to talk about her, like she was a siren and an angel all at once. He'd listened amiably enough; he was a nice enough guy to be happy for his friend . . . but he'd been envious, too. He wanted that feeling—the hungry, trembling rush of falling in love. When he looked at Nikki, he really believed he was almost there. She did something to him, something that might be the prelude to falling in love, as if he was slipping at the edge of a deep pool, half-hoping he'd just tumble in.

If he could just stay a while, he could find out what the water was like.

"Okay. I'm going to ask him," Kevin told Rosemary. "Wish me luck."

"What are we asking me?" Stephen appeared in the kitchen door, his face pink with cold. "It's freezing out there. Rosemary, I know you say it never snows before the New Year, but damn. Feels like a white Thanksgiving to me."

"No such thing," she said, turning back to her green beans. "Stephen, Kev has a question for you."

"If you'd like to fix the front door, you don't have to ask," Stephen declared. "Be my guest." He shrugged off his quilted plaid shirt, revealing a much more elegant French blue button-down beneath it. Kevin grinned. Stephen still sported his tailored office wear around the farmhouse like he was going to be called up in front of a boardroom at any moment. Kevin's own ensemble was much more country: he tugged on flannel shirts and jeans the moment he left New York.

Now he ran a finger along the soft cuff of his blue-and-white plaid shirt, nervously fingering a loose thread around the button. Of course Stephen would let him stay . . . it was just the asking that was hard. "I was wondering if you'd let me have the brick house for a little while—to stay in, I mean. To see if I can figure out something down here."

Stephen lifted an eyebrow. "To rent?"

"No. I can't rent it." It was painful to admit. The investment in Excelsior East had been a supposed slam dunk. He should have known by the stupid name it was a failure waiting to happen. "Not until one of the condos sells. I can't afford another payment. I have enough in savings to keep my mortgage paid, but that's it." His last year's bonus was still sitting in the bank, too. He could manage making payments on the condos without a job for another six months—and it just *had* to sell in the next six months, didn't it?

Stephen poured himself a cup of coffee. He gestured questioningly with the pot, and Kevin nodded. Rosemary handed down another mug from the cabinet. Kevin liked the way everything between them was a team effort, with no words required.

"But," Stephen began, setting the mugs down on the table. He rubbed at his stubbled chin. "Not that I don't want to help you, but, can I ask why?"

Rosemary slammed the refrigerator door with unnecessary force.

"It's okay," Kevin said. "I guess I thought you knew."

Stephen slid into the chair across from him. "I know you were trying to get out of the city. Any reason you can't wait another minute? At least until your condo sells, and you find another job?"

Kevin took a swallow of coffee, considering the question. He might have said a lot of things, like: *I'm terrible at my job and it's starting to show,* or, *I feel like I'm living someone else's version of life,* or even, *I just want to sleep through the night without dreaming I'm on a sinking ship.* He could have said all of those things, and they would have been true, if they would just make it past his cold lips.

But Stephen and Rosemary didn't need to hear all of that. It was a holiday, for heaven's sake. So Kevin smiled and said, "I just really need a fresh start right now. And I'd like to see more of Nikki."

Stephen nodded knowingly. "Well, fine. You can have it. I owe you one, taking a hit on the Long Pond investment like that. The least I can do is let you stay in the brick house."

Kevin drew in a shaky breath. "You don't have to worry about that," he managed to say. "We did the best thing we could with Long Pond."

Rosemary smiled over her shoulder at him. "You really did. Both of you. I know it didn't end the way you expected, but I appreciate it."

"I'm glad we saved the Kelbaugh farm," Stephen agreed. "But I promised Kev a huge return on that investment, and when we shifted gears from subdivision to boarding school, the *huge* part went away. Sometimes I think the *return* part is going to vanish, too. I had no idea it would take this long to get a deal through."

"There are a lot of moving parts," Rosemary said soothingly. "What's important is the contracts are signed and you'll get paid eventually and Long Pond will be a beautiful girls' school instead of a bunch of McMansions."

*And Stephen gets you as the perfect wife,* Kevin added privately. There was no way anything would have lasted between Rosemary and Stephen if his friend had gone ahead with his original plan to turn the farm next door into a subdivision. Rosemary loved Long Pond too much to see it flattened, even if the elderly couple who had lived there, and served as her surrogate family after her parents died, had used the sale money to move to Florida for a warm and sunny retirement.

"So that's settled," Stephen said. "You're moving in." He took a long pull of coffee. "I can't wait to see Nikki's reaction to that."

Rosemary flicked Stephen on the back of the head.

Kevin just leaned back in his chair, considering the next few days. He was pretty interested in Nikki's reaction, too.

Suddenly, he couldn't wait one more minute to see her.

# Chapter 3

# Nikki

Nikki's sweet potato casserole was assembled and settling in the fridge at last, but the night wasn't over yet. She leaned over the back counter, surveying the mostly empty dining room impatiently. Another hour until they closed up, and business was showing no sign of picking up. Maybe she *could* have closed for a long weekend and gone to Arizona. If they couldn't even draw a normal dinner rush on Thanksgiving eve, what should she expect for the rest of the holiday?

She supposed Saturday's business would tell her for sure, but so far this particular Wednesday was turning out to be the biggest dud of the year. Even the efficient Lauren was practically asleep, draped over the hostess stand with her glazed eyes locked onto her phone, waiting for one of the old-timers in the booths to summon her for more coffee. Headlights slowly picked out the upper corners of the dining room as cars rolled past on Main Street, taking late commuters home for their holiday weekend.

Nikki traced her fingers over the laminate countertop, wondering if this was the rest of her life, if this was every

Wednesday-before-Thanksgiving for the rest of her working days, until she finally got so fed up that she sold the diner and moved to Arizona herself. She considered life as a spinster in a desert town. Could she take up pottery, wear sandals year-round, grow succulents in a patch of rock garden in front of some faux-adobe house in a town where no one knew her name? Or would she move into the house next to her parents and continue squabbling with her sister at family dinner nights as if they'd just picked up and moved every aspect of their lives from Catoctin Creek to the desert?

Her lip curled slightly. The idea was not alluring. But neither was growing old and alone in the winter chill and summer humidity of western Maryland, watching a succession of high school girls fumble through their interviews, pocket their dollar tips, grow up, graduate, and move on—while she stayed in one place, unloved and unfulfilled, withering down to the very root.

*You have to get hold of yourself,* she warned herself. *The holidays aren't going to get any easier.* She had no excuse to turn this into some kind of Scottish moor melodrama. Sure, she'd been disappointed in her latest love affair. Sure, she had no prospects for future relationships. Sure, she lived in a garage apartment and paid rent to a former high school classmate. Sure, none of her dreams were ever going to come true . . .

*Oops, did it again.*

What would it take for her to rise above this funk? If Kevin hadn't come here and raised her hopes, and then just disappeared . . . Nikki's brow furrowed. She wondered how hard it would be to look up Kevin's New York apartment, drive up there, bang on his door, and just . . . just rough him up a little bit. Let him know he'd blown it. Teach him that his actions mattered. He couldn't just show up in a town, get a girl all revved up, and then disappear.

Suddenly, the bells on the door chimed, making both Lauren and Nikki jump. A gust of cold air rolled in around a tall, slim figure dressed in riding clothes: a long, vented coat; thick fleece breeches; a pair of muddy black field boots. Nikki knew who it was before she even saw his face—only one guy waltzed around Catoctin Creek dressed like a huntsman who'd lost his hounds. This was Sean Casey, the new riding instructor at her old classmate Caitlin's horse farm, Elmwood Equestrian Center.

*Caitlin picked this one for looks,* Nikki thought, as she did every time she saw Sean. She'd met the riding instructor in October, when Caitlin had brought him in for a first-day lunch. Nikki had been impressed from the moment she'd laid eyes on the kid: Sean had elegantly sunken cheeks and piercing green eyes under sandy eyebrows, a skeleton which apparently only existed to hold up his toned muscles, and a smile which could make a girl's knees go weak. He truly looked more like a riding apparel model than someone who actually rode horses for a living.

But Sean had an impressive resume for his field, with a background in big-time horse show circuits. Caitlin had gushed to Nikki about his experience, which she believed was perfect for her newly expanding business of putting wealthy, exurban children on her home-bred ponies.

Sean's thin cheeks had flushed as Caitlin went on about him, which made Nikki like him. Sure, he was too handsome for Catoctin Creek by half, but at least he had some humility—which was more than could be said for her grasping ex-schoolmate, Caitlin Tuttle.

Nikki decided to go and ask him how the lesson program was doing. She still found it hard to believe people were moving all the way out to Catoctin Creek when they had to drive into D.C. for work each day, but if Caitlin was seeing a surge in business from these hardcore commuter families, maybe someday Nikki would, too. If she could figure out how to get them in the door, anyway.

Nikki was halfway across the dining room before she realized something was wiggling in the riding instructor's arms. A fluffy paw pressed against his coat collar, and Nikki realized what was happening a split second after Lauren did. In a booth, an old man lifted his head and chuckled.

Lauren, ever the bold heroine of the picture, stepped right up and grabbed his arm. "Sean Casey, you can't bring a dog into a restaurant," she told him. "Take that thing back outside!"

"But he's cold," Sean protested. "He's been outside for who knows how long. And the heater in my car is busted."

"Take it back to your apartment, then!" Lauren looked to Nikki for support. "We have regulations to abide by. No pets. Not for any reason."

While it was true, there was no chance a rogue restaurant inspector would enter the Blue Plate Diner on the evening before Thanksgiving and start writing citations, Nikki appreciated Lauren's hard and fast respect for health and safety. "She's right," Nikki agreed. "Out you go."

Sean continued to protest, but Nikki waved him backwards with both hands until he was back outside, standing on the concrete stoop. He tucked his wool coat around the dog and looked at her reproachfully. Nikki had to admit it was absolutely freezing outside, and damp besides, but she kept her face stern.

"Why did you bring your dog out in the cold if your car's heater is broken?" She folded her arms across her chest, wishing she had on more than a cardigan. The wind was bone-chilling. If it wasn't far too early for snow in this part of Maryland, she'd have been looking up, ready to spot the first flakes flying on the breeze.

Sean squeezed the wriggling dog close and looked at Nikki like she was crazy. "He's not *my* dog. I found him on Old Frederick Road while I was on my way here. He was out wandering along the side of the road. He was going to get hit by a car. I couldn't *leave* him there."

Nikki sighed. "Sean, that's somebody's dog. You can't just pick up dogs in farm country. He has a home. Look at his coat! There's no way a dog this clean and shiny is a stray."

"I drove up the nearest farm lane and asked. It was Mrs. O'Reilly's place, and she said she'd never seen him before. There's no other lane or barn around that road for miles. He was definitely lost. What could I do?" Sean repeated, looking desperate. "I couldn't leave a dog by the side of a highway on a cold night. Could you?"

Nikki frowned. Kathleen O'Reilly raised Australian shepherds at the center of a vast farm, and this dog was some sort of fluffy yellow Labrador mix. Sean's story added up. "Okay. Maybe someone dumped him, then. But what do you want me to do with it? Why did you bring a dog to a restaurant? That should never be your first instinct. I could get fined out of existence."

Sean looked down at her with such puppy-dog eyes, the actual dog in his arms was barely any competition. "Because I can't take him back to Elmwood. Caitlin's pointers are crazy territorial. They'll tear this guy apart. Look how gentle he is! And you're about the only place in town that's open tonight. I thought maybe someone here might take him home, keep an eye on him."

Nikki considered this as the bells on the door rang. She stepped out of the way. The old man who had been drinking coffee in a booth, the one who had laughed, came through the door and looked at the dog for a moment.

"This looks like Ethel Beerbaum's dog," he said. "The Beerbaum place is catty-corner to the O'Reilly farm. The dog could have crossed the fields and ended up along Old Frederick Road. If he had nowhere else to go. Dunno why he would. It's a long walk."

Sean brightened. "Can we call her? Do you have her number?"

The old man shrugged. Nikki remembered his name suddenly: Wilbur Schultz. He wasn't a regular, but he came around every so often. "She died two weeks ago. Her grandkids were clearing the place out last week. They went back to—where was it, Denver?—this morning. I'd say they either gave this dog to someone, and it didn't keep, or they left the dog behind."

Nikki sighed. "Thank you, Mr. Schultz. It's probably the latter. They didn't mix with anyone while they were here. I was at the viewing and they just hung around in a corner, their backs to the room."

"Well, they weren't raised here," Mr. Schultz pointed out. "We were all strangers to them."

Sean was upset. "That doesn't give them the right to abandon a dog!"

"Well, of course not," Nikki said. "They probably figured country folk like us would just take it in. City people are always dumping dogs up here. Anyway, they're gone now, and the dog's here." She gave Sean an appraising glance. "You can call the humane society on Friday. They're probably closed tomorrow."

"Like I said, I can't take this guy." Sean clung to the dog, who whined and licked at his ear. "But someone here . . . surely someone would help out Ethel Beerbaum's old dog . . ."

"No one in there's taking a dog," Mr. Schultz said authoritatively. "Walt Routzahn is sitting over in the corner, but I think he's moving in with his kids. Mrs. Babson left a while ago, but she hates dogs, so that don't matter."

Sean looked at Mr. Schultz speculatively. The old man laughed, waved his hand, and hobbled down the steps. "My dog days are done," he called as he opened his car door. "A young man's game."

Nikki watched the old man climb into his car. "That's it for us. Betty has six cats and Patrick has an English bulldog that would eat this guy for breakfast. Lauren lives with her parents, she can't just bring a dog home. I'm sorry, Sean. It's not exactly adoption night at the Blue Plate."

Sean sighed extravagantly, and Nikki's eyes wandered down to the fluffy dog pressed against his chest. The dog wasn't exactly small, and Sean's arms had to be getting tired. As she gazed at the dog, it turned its head and fastened liquid dark eyes on hers.

What was it about making eye contact with a dog?

"Hey, good boy," she whispered gently.

The dog's tail thumped against Sean's leg.

Sean grinned, sensing triumph was near.

"Absolutely not," Nikki told him, taking a step back before she did something she regretted. "I don't have room for a dog in my apartment."

"He's not a big dog," Sean told her. "Look, he's a nice, medium-sized dog. Mostly Lab. He's just what you need. He probably has a nice deep voice for scaring away intruders. I'll bet he protected poor old Ethel Beerbaum against all sorts of danger."

Nikki put her hand on the door. She was beyond freezing. "Poor old Ethel kept a pistol in her purse. I saw it every time she paid her bill. Look, I have to get back to work. And you need to get that dog out of the wind. Go home. Smuggle him into your apartment for the night. Caitlin will understand."

"Oh, come on—" Sean was prepared to jump into one last epic plea, and Nikki was afraid she couldn't withstand it. Even if she just took the dog home over the holiday, it would upset all of her careful plans for the next day . . . and what if it was an adoption that hadn't taken right away? She'd had enough heartache this year to last her a lifetime. She didn't need someone banging on her door to claim a dog she'd fallen for.

The crunching sound of tires on gravel interrupted Sean's next plea. They both looked down the short flight of steps to the parking lot, where a nondescript beige sedan had just pulled up.

Nikki bit her lip. That was Stephen's old car, the one he'd inherited from his father.

Stephen *never* drove that car anymore.

Somehow, Nikki knew who it would be before the driver even opened the door. Her hand went to her mouth; then she forced it back down again. She *wouldn't* look surprised. She *wouldn't* look excited. She wouldn't even look *mad,* and that would be the biggest accomplishment of all . . . because she *was* mad.

She was furious.

She was raging.

She was . . . dying to see him. Nikki wished fervently that just once, just one stupid time, her heart could agree with her brain.

The car door opened, and a man in a black wool coat climbed out. He ran his hands through his red-gold hair, pushing it back from his eyes, but it just fell over his brow again. Her heart clambered eagerly into her throat and sat there, choking her, while her stomach filled up with an entire flock of butterflies.

*Kevin.*

She tightened her arms across her chest, pulling her sweater taut. She could hear her teeth grinding and all she could hope was that she didn't break anything. The dentist was closed for the holiday, too. Then she reached for the door. She'd go inside, meet him from behind the hostess stand, a woman of substance, a woman who owned her own restaurant, a woman who didn't need a man in her life. She'd lie and lie, and lie again, with every fiber of her being. She'd never let him see the hurt.

Her hand seemed to freeze to the door handle, and not because of the cold.

Kevin glanced up the stairs at Sean, arms full of dog, and then at Nikki, with her hand on the door, still in her arrested escape. His expression was broad and open, giving no hint that he might understand how he had hurt her, how he had made her feel unloved and unwanted. Nikki waited, her entire body tensed for a blow.

"Hi guys," Kevin said cheerfully. "Am I interrupting anything?"

# Chapter 4

# Kevin

Kevin had driven all the way from Notch Gap Farm hoping he wouldn't come across a scene just like this.

Well, excluding the dog. Over the past three months he had pictured, with quiet desperation, Nikki enjoying the company of any number of good-looking men. Even men as good-looking as this chiseled-jaw specimen looking down at him? Maybe not. This guy was, to borrow his sister's phrasing, *redonk*.

(He thought it meant ridiculous, not that he'd ever gotten up the nerve to ask.)

Kevin was used to being, if not the most handsome man in the room, the most charming one. He could hold his own in any cocktail party with friendly jokes and a casual smile which made women feel comfortable. He could fend off some pretty serious lookers with nothing but his quick wit and kind gestures. Gorgeous male model types were somewhat out of his league. It threw him off his game. He tried to remember all the cute, sweet things he wanted to say to Nikki. He could still win this thing. Whatever *this* was. He'd kind of hoped for a meet-cute at the diner, but running into Nikki, this chiseled Nordic-looking guy, and a fluffy dog on the stoop was not in the script.

And what a dog! Such a fluffy, cute, cream-colored dog. Kevin was almost too charmed by the dog's big, pleading eyes to properly focus on getting Nikki's attention away from the handsome drink of water clinging to the pup.

With an effort, Kevin managed to get his head back on the real situation at hand: who was this guy, and did it mean he'd really spent too much time back in New York, time he could have spent down here with Nikki?

He had, and he knew it. Kevin was all too aware now that he'd wasted his time in the city. He couldn't fix the messes he'd made in New York. He didn't even want to. He just wanted to start over— in this beautiful place, in this quiet countryside, and who knew? Maybe even with this spitfire of a woman.

Who was now looking at him with an expression that was half shock, half anger.

He'd *definitely* stayed away too long.

Kevin ran his hands through his hair, pushing fox-colored locks out of his eyes. Now he figured his hair wasn't romantic-poet material; it was just too long. He should have gotten a haircut. He made a quip about interrupting their business, but neither Nikki nor the guy with the dog responded. Nikki still looked shocked to see him. The guy still looked desperate to—what? Get rid of him? Unload the dog, that looked kind of heavy?

The dog licked its nose and wriggled, tail wagging joyously. Well, at least the dog was happy to see him.

Well, they couldn't just stand here staring at each other. Someone had to say something, get a conversation going.

Kevin tried again, since no one else seemed willing.

"Hiya, Nikki," he said, aware even as the words came out that this was a seriously weak greeting after two months of silence. Well, might as well plow ahead. "Did ya miss me?"

His voice came out folksy, ridiculously so, and he sounded like he was making fun of the slight country accents people had in these parts.

Nikki merely pursed her lips, then went back inside the restaurant. The bells on the door jingled merrily, then silenced abruptly as the door hit the jamb.

Kevin looked back at the guy with the dog. They were both gazing down the stairs at him with something like pity. *Great. Even the dog thinks you lost.* "So, uh, what's with the dog?" he asked, to deflect attention from the serious rejection he'd just received.

"Found it along the road," the guy said. His accent was bland, almost unnoticeable. He didn't have the country note Catoctin Creek natives flavored their vowels with. Either he wasn't from here, or it had been educated right out of him. He was wearing riding boots and breeches, which Kevin found a little odd. "You like dogs? I need to find it a place to stay. But I'll be honest, I don't think his owner is coming back."

"Why? Whose dog is it?"

"We think it's a dead person's dog. He might need a home for good. Sounds that way, anyway. I'm new around here; I don't know all the ins and outs of folks here."

The dog scrabbled against his chest, suddenly anxious to come and visit Kevin. His tail, long and feathery, thumped against the guy's hip. Kevin felt drawn to that dog like a magnet. He hopped up the stairs and had his hand on the dog's soft head before he'd realized what he was doing. "No," he said regretfully, rubbing the dog's silken ears, aware that every move he made contradicted his words. "I don't live here. I can't take in a dog."

The dog tilted his head and licked Kevin's wrist. Despite the icy wind whistling past his ears, Kevin felt warm all over.

"Man." The chiseled guy shook his head sorrowfully. "I never shoulda picked up this dog. But I couldn't just leave him by the side of the road. We were miles from any house besides the O'Reilly place, and she swore he wasn't her dog. The Beerbaum kids must have left him. That's what we think, anyway."

Kevin's fingers were deep in the dog's soft hair. He had no idea who the Beerbaum kids were, but he definitely hated them. "That's a shame. A real shame. People are horrible. But, why can't you keep him?"

"Oh, I don't really have my own place. I live above the barn at Elmwood Equestrian Center. You know it? I just started as head of the lesson program. It's too soon for me to start asking for exceptions."

"Elmwood? I thought they just did therapeutic riding." Kevin had absorbed a fair amount of Catoctin Creek gossip in his visits, including Nikki and Rosemary's uneasy relationship with their old schoolmate Caitlin. He knew Caitlin sent adults who wanted to rescue horses to Rosemary for crash courses in horsemanship— Rosemary called these women Caitlin's "do gooders." He also knew all three of the women had a rather combative relationship. Or they had until Rosemary and Caitlin had started making nice earlier in the year.

"We do both," the riding instructor explained. "Volunteers do the therapy lessons. Then they end up wanting their kids to ride. So Caitlin hired me to expand the paid lesson program. Lotta new suburban families in the area. I'm Sean, by the way. Sean Casey."

"Kevin," he replied absently. The dog was licking his fingers. Kevin felt a surge of something warm and rich in his midsection, and he made a split-second decision he saw no possibility of regretting. He wasn't going back to New York, anyway. It was all decided. The dog? Preordained. Destiny. "You know what? I really like this guy. Let's stick him in my car. I'll take him with me."

"Are you serious? But you said you can't have a dog. What if it turns out he doesn't have a home? You won't take him to the pound, will you?"

"I would never. What I meant was, I couldn't manage having a dog back in the city," Kevin said. "But you know what I just remembered? I'm not going back there."

As Sean deposited the wiggling, licking, tail-wagging dog into the backseat of Stephen's car, Kevin glanced up at the plate-glass windows of the Blue Plate Diner. He saw Nikki looking out at him, a blank expression on her face. Kevin smothered a smile of relief. At least she was still watching him. She wasn't as indifferent to him as he'd feared. "I'm just going to go inside and see if Nikki will sell me a pie," he told Sean. "The car's still pretty warm, I think he'll be okay."

Sean nodded, brushing long curls of blonde dog hair off his jacket. "Where are you going to take him tonight?"

"I'm staying with the Becketts at Notch Gap Farm," Kevin said.

Sean's face lit up. "Oh, that's perfect! Rosemary doesn't have a dog."

"You know her? Oh . . . through Caitlin, I guess?"

"Yup. And you know Caitlin, too? Where did you say you live?" Sean peered at him.

"New York City," Kevin said. "Or, I used to. I'm moving here."

Sean gaped. "That's a big move."

"Just big enough. Don't tell anyone, though." Kevin gave him a friendly cuff on the arm. "It's all new still."

"Well, congrats, I guess." Sean couldn't hide his confusion. "It's a pretty small place, but it's nice if you don't mind that. And close to a lot of bigger towns. I've only been here a few weeks, myself."

Kevin nodded impatiently. He didn't need to be told Catoctin Creek was small, or nice. He had it all under control. "Listen, buddy, thanks for the dog. It's a nice housewarming gift. You should do that for everyone in town. Move in, get a dog! Great slogan, don't you think?"

"Sure, man . . . sure. Well, happy Thanksgiving!" Sean was beating a retreat to his car, his expression letting his real thoughts on the matter slip: this guy Kevin might be a little bit crazy.

*Well, sure,* Kevin thought, looking at the smiling face of his new dog through the backseat window. *I might be a little crazy. Or a lot. But at least I know exactly where I want to be.*

He looked over his shoulder, hoping for another glimpse of Nikki, but she'd disappeared into the depths of the restaurant.

"Wait right here," he told the dog, who panted and wagged his plume of a tail in response.

The bells on the door jingled again, and the slim young woman leaning on the hostess stand glanced at him, curiosity written on her face. "Did you want to sit down?" she asked. "Or is this more a to-go situation? On account of the dog?"

"Oh, you saw my new co-pilot?" Kevin joked.

"I don't think anyone's going to claim that dog, by the way," the girl said, shaking her head. Her name-tag read *Lauren.* "The Beerbaum kids were not here to socialize. I really think they left the old lady's dog by Mrs. O'Reilly's place and hoped she'd take it in. But Sean found it first! And here we are. I can't believe you just *took a dog* from Sean Casey. We barely know him."

Kevin cocked his head curiously. "If everyone knew Sean Casey, would it be okay to take a dog from him?"

"At least we'd know if he's doing this kind of thing on the regular or not."

"Ah, a serial dog-provider? Always coming into town with free dogs, taking advantage of city boys like me?"

She eyed him. "Something like that."

"I'm not making fun of you," Kevin said. "Promise. I just wanted to get a pie to take back to the Becketts' house. I'm abusing their hospitality in the worst way, and I want to cozy up to them with Nikki's famous lemon meringue. Rosemary's making every fruit pie in existence, but I know this is her favorite."

Lauren chewed at her lip and turned, trying to study the glass-sided dessert rack at the back of the restaurant. "Not sure we have lemon meringue left tonight. I'll just go and see." She crossed the dining room with long strides, leaving Kevin by the door. He scanned the room, but didn't see Nikki anywhere. She must have gone back into the kitchen.

Maybe that was for the best. She'd looked more angry than he'd expected, and he needed time to prep for this scenario. Kevin knew his tendency to leap before he looked was going to get him into real trouble one day—mainly because his mother had been telling him so at every opportunity for thirty-three years—but he had never really expected his impulsiveness to be what landed him in hot water with a woman. Didn't girls love an impulsive guy, the kind of man who showed up with flowers at the most random occasions, who didn't need any real reason to celebrate a silly anniversary or throw a dinner party? The kind of man who showed up without any warning and adopted a dog on her restaurant stoop?

The sort of guy who gave up his old life and started a new one in hopes she'd be a part of it?

That kind of guy would be *great,* Kevin thought. It was too bad he hadn't unveiled that side of his personality months ago.

Nikki would have welcomed him with open arms if he'd chucked his city life out the window back at Rosemary and Stephen's wedding. Now he was going to have to prove he wasn't a jerk who just vanished for months whenever he felt like it.

And that was going to take time . . . so it was a good thing about the dog. He'd need the company while he was working all of this out.

Lauren returned from the back, bearing a box of just the right height and width to hold a pie. Kevin had always found it kind of delightful that cakes could come in any size or shape, but pies were one universal size. He kept this to himself, however, because Lauren looked just a little no-nonsense.

"One left in the back," she announced. "Nikki was holding it for herself, but when I asked for it, she said it was just as easy to let you take it to Rosemary's place instead."

Did that mean . . . "Are you saying Nikki is having Thanksgiving dinner with Rosemary and Stephen?"

"Yup," Lauren said, tapping the cash register next to the podium. "Cash or charge?"

"Cash," Kevin replied absently, pulling out his wallet. Well, this was some luck. He knew Nikki's family didn't live in Catoctin Creek anymore, but they'd never discussed holidays and he hadn't expected her to be at Notch Gap Farm for Thanksgiving dinner. He couldn't hide a smile as he dropped his change into the tip jar. Thanksgiving with Nikki! Well, well, things were certainly looking up now!

"I guess the dog will be there, too," Lauren said, sliding the box into a plastic bag. "What are you going to call it? Gonna go minimalist and just call it The Dog?"

Kevin glanced out the window. The dog was looking at the restaurant steadfastly, waiting confidently for him to return. For a moment, he'd forgotten that he'd just adopted a dog. A dog with no name. And no collar, leash, kibble, or bowl.

"Should I name it? What if by Friday an owner shows up?"

"Trust me," Lauren told him, "that dog isn't going anywhere. And Mrs. Beerbaum probably called it like Honey or Dearie or something. She called her cats Sweetie-pie. All of them. Five cats. You'll have to name the dog yourself."

"I have no idea what I'd name a dog," he said slowly. "I guess I'll think of something on the way home."

"It should end in a *y* sound," Lauren advised him. "Something like Mikey or Doofy."

"Doofy?"

She smiled. "I don't know. Look at that face! He'd make a good Doofy."

"I'm offended on behalf of my nameless dog. But why the naming rule?"

"Dogs respond better to names that with a *y* sound. The sound holds their attention or something. Or maybe not." Lauren shrugged. "It's just something I've picked up listening to old men talk over their coffee."

"Ends in *y*. Well, I'll try. But he's not going to be Doofy." Kevin gathered up his bag. "Any sage wisdom on where to buy dog food on the night before Thanksgiving?"

"Trout's Market might still be open a few more minutes," Lauren said, glancing at the clock above the kitchen door. "Just down Main Street. You can stay parked in our lot, if you want. It's not exactly standing room-only in here."

"Perfect. Thanks, Lauren." Kevin rarely used the names he read on nametags, finding that kind of creeperish, but he and Lauren had shared some serious conversation and they knew some of the same people, so he considered it okay. Judging by her friendly smile, she felt the same way. He waved and ducked out the door. The pie went into the trunk of the car; he didn't trust the dog not to eat it while he was gone.

Kevin hustled past a few shuttered storefronts and found Trout's Market still open, its half-dozen short aisles mainly stripped of Thanksgiving staples like canned cranberry sauce. The pet food shelves were still stocked. Because Kevin's sole dog experience came from the fur-babies of Manhattan friends, he had a moment's panic about the dog's unknown allergies and medical history, then selected the most expensive kibble on the sales floor: a twenty-dollar, ten-pound bag of salmon and wild rice blend. He heaved the bag onto the rubber conveyor belt.

The teenaged cashier stopped popping her gum long enough to look mildly impressed at his selection. Then she flipped the bag over and skimmed the bottom.

"What's wrong with it?" Kevin asked, feeling a little harried now that his car (with the dog inside) was out of his sight. If someone broke a car window to give the dog air, he'd be in big trouble with Stephen. Worse trouble than just bringing home a dog without asking.

"Nuthin'," the cashier said, flipping the bag back over. "Just checkin' the sell-by date. We don't see this move real often."

Kevin felt a hot red blush overtake his cheeks. He tried to hide it by pulling up the collar of his coat, but the cashier spotted it and smiled. *Her* name, he noticed, was Jessa.

"You must be one of Stephen Beckett's friends," she said knowingly. "Down from New York City for Thanksgiving?"

"How did you know that? Are you clairvoyant?"

She tapped his open wallet. "I can see your ID, and Stephen's the only person in Catoctin Creek from NYC." She paused. "Also, the fancy dog food."

"Yes," he sighed. "I can see how that might give me away." Catoctin Creek struck him as more of an Ol' Roy kind of town.

"Well, I'd *love* to see New York City," Jessa said wistfully, swiping his credit card. She moved her gum from one cheek to the other and gave him a coy smile. "When you goin' back?"

"Not sure," Kevin managed to reply, a little overcome by the suggestiveness in her tone. He took the credit card back from her without touching her fingers, a massive effort as she seemed to reach for him, and shoved his wallet haphazardly into his coat pocket. Scooping up the bag in one arm, he fled the market before Jessa could insist he take her back to the city with him.

Clouds were thick overhead, their underbellies reflecting the orange street-lights, and as he opened his car door, fending off the happy advances of the dog—his new dog!—an icy drizzle began to fall. "Brr," he told the dog. "Get out of the driver's seat—go on, get back, now. Let's go someplace warm. I know a pretty little farmhouse where you'll fit in just fine. We can set up camp and make plans there."

The dog licked his cheek appreciatively.

Kevin clicked his seat-belt into place with some difficulty. "Okay, buddy. Sit over there—that's it. I need to be able to see the road if I'm going to get us there." A new thought occurred to him as he admired the fluffy dog's panting face. "I really hope Rosemary isn't allergic to dogs."

# Chapter 5

# Nikki

"I can't believe he took that dog." Nikki leaned on the back counter. She'd been rubbing at a smudge on the dessert case, but now she let the towel flop on the countertop. The slow evening had been perfect for helping her get ahead on her Thanksgiving cooking, but it had also awarded her all too much time to think about Kevin. Where he'd been. Why he'd made off with a dog. What she was going to say to him tomorrow. "What is he planning? He's going to take that Muppet of a mutt back to New York?"

"You should have said Manhattan," Lauren said absently, her eyes on her phone.

"What?"

"It would have been funnier if you'd said Manhattan," Lauren explained. "Alliteration is funny."

"I forgot you're good at English." Nikki craned her neck to peer at Lauren's phone. "What are you looking at? Shouldn't you be working?"

Lauren rolled her eyes. "The only person here is Ivan MacDougal, and you know he doesn't like to be bothered."

Well, she had Nikki there. Offer old Ivan from the lumberyard a coffee refill before he was ready for you, and he'd stiff you his customary dollar tip. Nikki shrugged. "Anyway, Kevin lives in Queens. A big tower in Queens. So the alliteration thing wouldn't work."

"Where do you think he's staying here? At Rosemary's place?"

"Probably at the old Beckett house." The house, which had been sitting empty since Stephen moved down to Notch Gap Farm, had been the source of some earnest conversation in the diner—when would he sell it, would he build something else on it, what if out-of-towners moved up there—because Stephen had initially gotten mixed up in Catoctin Creek land speculation, and no one had forgotten it yet. Farmers knew to be skeptical of a land dealer, even one who seemed reformed. "Kevin knows his way up there without getting lost, and it gives him some privacy. That's where he stayed during the wedding."

Ivan got up suddenly and stumped towards the diner door. A jingle of bells, and he was gone. A lone dollar bill sat next to his empty coffee cup.

"That's it," Lauren said. "It's seven forty-nine. Call it?"

"Call it." As Lauren headed to the front door to flip the sign to *Closed* and lock up, Nikki turned and propped open the kitchen door. Just inside, Betty was washing up the night's pots and pans, while Patrick scrubbed at the oven. "We're clear, guys."

"Yay!" Betty cheered, because she was an old dear.

"Finally," Patrick grunted, because he was an old crank.

Nikki watched the backs of their heads for a moment, feeling that familiar twist of affection and frustration the restaurant often gave her, and then headed up front to help Lauren count down the cash register. But the holiday eve had been so slow, she wasn't even needed there.

"Just confirm the totals for me and you can go home," Lauren told her, jotting down figures on a notepad. "I'll mop the floor and turn out the lights."

Nikki hesitated. Not because Lauren wasn't capable of shutting down the restaurant—it was hardly complicated—but because going back to her apartment would simply open her brain's floodgates. If she'd been low on distractions here, she would be completely undeterred from analyzing her entire life, and what she'd done wrong with Kevin, all night long.

"Seriously, I don't need your help," Lauren insisted. "Look, I'm literally done."

"Fine," Nikki sighed, taking the small wedge of cash Lauren was waving. "I'll double-count this and go home. Thanks."

"Happy Thanksgiving." Lauren gave her a pat on the back and started sorting credit card receipts. "Go cook something complicated for Rosemary."

Nikki turned the knob on her oven.

*Click, click, click.*

No hiss.

No *woosh.*

She sighed and leaned on the cold stove-top. "All igniter and no ignition, is that it?"

Nikki didn't need to tramp outside and gaze at the meter to know the gas was out again. This was a recurring problem in her apartment, an otherwise pleasant studio built into the brick garage behind Hazel and William McKinley's pretty Victorian house on Catoctin Street. Before it had been a garage on the little alley behind the Catoctin Street houses, it had been a carriage house with room for a buggy and two horses, which meant it wasn't huge, but roomy enough for one woman who did little at home besides sleep and cook.

The spacious studio and cozy loft bed had been home for two years now, and Nikki had kept the interior simple and unfussy. The furnishings were minimal but comfortable: a deep gray couch topped with lime green pillows, bookshelves with a dark cherry finish filled with cookbooks and fat paperbacks, striped gray and white curtains shutting out the pretty, if exposed, view of the McKinley's backyard from the front wall's French windows. The back wall was a long galley kitchen, with enough counters and cabinet space to satisfy Nikki's most complicated culinary demands.

All in all, it was a nice place, when the gas wasn't on the fritz.

Now, though, Nikki glared with some consternation at her cooking supplies. She'd planned to bake the sweet potato casserole she'd assembled earlier—it would be much better tomorrow if she baked it now and then let it sit in the fridge overnight, all the flavors intermingling, before it was reheated in Rosemary's oven for Thanksgiving dinner.

Well, there was always Rosemary's oven . . . which was almost certainly free right now. What could Rosemary be baking at eight-thirty? She was probably in her pajamas and drinking chamomile tea already. No one would mind if Nikki popped in and borrowed the oven for an hour.

"Looks like you're heading to Rosemary's house a day early, sweetie-taters." Nikki scooped up the casserole dish and headed outside.

She hopped into her little black Honda coupe, settled the casserole dish on the passenger seat, and headed out through the tiny grid of Catoctin Creek's residential streets. Catoctin Street, Brunner Lane, Main Street, Summit Avenue—there wasn't much more to the town than those four streets, and then darkness overtook her as the country roads curved sinuously through the sloping fields and forests outside town.

She turned at the leaning mailbox, Notch Gap Farm's only marker, and drove up the gravel driveway, watching the chilly moonlight shine through the skeletons of tree branches entwining overhead. The bridge over the creek rattled under the car's tires, the same rhythmic rattle it had been making since she'd first started visiting Rosemary as a little girl. For twenty years of their lives, Nikki had been a fixture at the farmhouse. Even now, with Rosemary happily married to Stephen, not quite so desperate for company as she'd been in years past, Nikki was here at least twice a week. She was practically a part-time resident of the farm. That was how she knew she could just show up and use their oven without having to check ahead of time. That was why she didn't even bother sending a quick text before she drove over.

That was why she didn't pause to rethink her plan when she noticed Rosemary's car, the one they used for trips to town, wasn't in its usual parking spot. Nikki figured they must have gone down to Frederick for dinner—Stephen was surprisingly happy with country life, but now and then his New Yorker's need for a little noise and color drew them into the nearest city for a few hours.

Nikki simply parked near the front porch, hoisted her casserole dish, and went around the back. They never locked the kitchen door.

Out back, the frosty grass crunched beneath her feet. A square of golden light fell on the ground. Nikki glanced up and noticed a light was shining in the back spare bedroom. For a moment her eyes narrowed, wondering if someone was staying here. But no— there was no reason for Kevin to stay here when he'd been at the other house on his last visit. Someone must have just forgotten to switch the light off.

She climbed the creaky kitchen steps and let herself inside. The kitchen was swathed in shadows, but Nikki could see the only lights that mattered: the little blue flames of the pilot lights under each burner on the stove. Amazing that a farmhouse two centuries old could have working gas, and the gas in her newly renovated apartment was constantly breaking down! Nikki really had her doubts about the work Ian Yingling had done for the McKinleys. He hadn't been reliable in school, and she saw no reason to trust him as a contractor.

But that was a complaint for another day. Right now, she had access to a perfectly pleasant kitchen and when Rosemary came home, they could have a nice gossip session. Nikki happily set the cooler on the kitchen table and pushed back the filmy curtains at the window. Moonlight flooded into the kitchen, and she saw no reason to flip on the light just yet.

Once she'd turned on the oven, Nikki busied herself putting away the dishes Stephen had left in the drainer earlier that day. She knew their routine: Rosemary cooked, and Stephen cleaned up. Such a nice partnership, sharing chores and doing nearly everything around the farm together.

*I'd love someone helpful in the kitchen to do my dishes,* Nikki thought wistfully, putting away the silverware. *Although I don't know if I'd like someone leaning over my shoulder all the time. Rosemary doesn't mind a clinger, but I need a little independence in a man.*

She smiled grimly at the idea. Not that it mattered what kind of man she wanted. Kevin had been the last person to show any interest in her, and if he'd been sold on her charms, he'd have come back before now. The dating pool for anyone her age in Catoctin Creek had dried up long ago. High school sweethearts had paired up for life, or at least until the kids were old enough to handle a divorce, and the more ambitious of her classmates had left their little hometown for bright futures in Frederick, Baltimore, Washington, even New York. She'd heard Lacey Wilkes had gone to San Francisco. That was the farthest any of them had flown, but Lacey was hardly the only one to say *see ya* to Catoctin Creek.

*I don't need San Francisco,* Nikki reminded herself. *I just need a decent kitchen, a little bit of a challenge, and someone to come home to at night.*

Was that such a big ask?

Seriously, even Ian Yingling was married, and he'd been a jerk through five years of elementary school, three years of middle school, and four years of high school—although he'd barely been around senior year, just taking his senior year of English and some shop classes to prep for the electricity and plumbing certifications he'd take once he graduated. Despite his being a total tool who had never really progressed beyond pulling a girl's hair and laughing when she cried, Katie Barnett had been more than happy to go with him to Homecoming and Prom, and since graduation day she'd given him three babies in between shifts at her physical therapy job down in Frederick.

How could Ian Yingling, terrible contractor and human, be married and successful while she, Nikki, talented chef and interesting person, was destined to continue running a greasy spoon alone for the rest of her life?

If only Kevin had really been interested in her. But no, he'd gone back to New York and forgotten all about her. All of those glances they'd shared, all of those flirtatious conversations, had just been to pass the time while he'd been playing wingman for Stephen, and helped get that whole Long Pond land debacle under control. He hadn't *really* been into her. And why would he be, when there was an entire city of fascinating, successful women to choose from? Look at him tonight, he shows up at her diner and it's to buy a pie. Nikki opened the fridge to get a drink and saw a familiar white box on the middle shelf.

There was her pie now, sitting in Rosemary's fridge.

Nikki closed the fridge door and then opened it again. She looked at the pie. "Wait a minute," she whispered. "The pie is here?"

Just then, Nikki heard the noisy fifth stair make its signature creak.

Her hands froze on the door handle.

The creaks continued down the hallway. They were coming closer.

*Who the hell was in this house?*

Maybe Rosemary had gone out alone, and it was Stephen slowly approaching her. If so, oh boy, she really hoped he hadn't gone to bed while Rosemary was out and she really, *really* hoped he wasn't a naked sleeper. She and Rosemary had never discussed this. Now Nikki was curious, actually. But she didn't want to find out this way. She did not want to see Stephen appear, nude, against the yawning darkness of the downstairs hall.

Nikki did what she had to do.

She flipped on the kitchen light, wincing at its brightness as the pleasant moonlit shadows vanished from the old kitchen.

There was a stifled gasp from the hallway, and the footsteps stopped.

Nikki took a deep breath. *Action plan.* First step: be logical. She'd seen Rosemary's car was gone. So, this had to be Stephen. Even if it was really, *really* out of character for Rosemary to go out alone in the evening. Could he be getting sick? Maybe Rosemary had gone to buy cold medicine.

She decided to take a chance.

"Stephen?" Nikki called. "Are you okay? I needed to use the oven, and I thought you guys were out, so I just let myself in."

A moment of silence stretched out into what felt like entire minutes.

Nikki bit thoughtfully on the inside of her cheek. She slowly reached across the stove-top and drew a butcher knife from its block. Best to be prepared for all eventualities. No one had been murdered in Catoctin Creek for thirty-some years, and she wasn't about to be the record-breaking body.

Then she heard a cough which sounded oddly familiar. It definitely wasn't Stephen, though. Nikki hadn't realized it until that moment, but different people had their own distinct coughs and apparently she knew what Stephen's personal hack sounded like.

She summoned up her loudest, scariest Restaurant Manager voice. "Okay, who is out there? If you don't want to be stuck with this knife I'm holding, you can just head right out the front door. I won't follow you. Just get out."

The next sound she heard wasn't a cough. It was a *laugh*.

Her hand tightened on the knife. She hazarded a glance back at the block, considered, and grabbed another one. Two knives were better than one.

Nikki's knees were slipping into a defensive crouch and she was wielding both butcher knives like a Ninja preparing for single combat when a familiar voice called: "Hey Nikki? It's Kevin. Can I come into the kitchen without getting stabbed full of holes?"

# Chapter 6

# Kevin

Taking a deep breath, Kevin entered the kitchen doorway with a dramatic flourish.

"Ta-da!" he announced, twirling, but he misjudged the width of the kitchen door and slammed his knuckles against the wooden frame. *"Gah!* Ouch." He gave Nikki a lopsided smile as he shook out his sore hand. "So, uh, hello again."

She cocked an eyebrow at him. He admired her cool reserve, even if he wished she'd show him just a *little* emotion. "You gonna want ice for that hand or what?"

"Oh, no. It's fine." Kevin realized he was cradling his abused fingers and released them, flexing his hands to show they were still fully capable. Man's hands. Manly, manly man's hands for all the country trials and tribulations he might face, and all the do-it-yourself needs Nikki might require. Although she clearly had self-defense under control.

In fact, she was still holding the butcher knives, one gripped in each ladylike hand. He eyed them warily. "Think you could put those down?"

She glanced down at her weaponry as if she'd forgotten she was armed. "Oh, sure. If you promise there's no one else in this house who doesn't belong here."

*Ouch.* Kevin felt another blast of the same icy gaze she'd turned on him at the Blue Plate. Nikki was making it really clear he'd messed things up. He watched her turn back to the oven, wishing he could figure out how to make up for his disappearance in the fall. How to explain that he had an awful way of fixating on problems, even the ones he couldn't solve, and he'd been so immersed in trying to fix his old life in New York, he hadn't remembered to nurture the new one he'd left in Catoctin Creek?

It was complicated, that was for sure. He tried and failed to think of a way to say all of it, then resorted to a foolish observation.

"Cooking, are we?"

She glanced sidelong at him as she turned to the oven, checking the temperature. "Can't hide anything from you, can I?"

Kevin raised his hands, wincing a little as he straightened his sore fingers. "I surrender! You wanted to kill me, and you didn't, and I thank you for that. But what brings you to Rosemary's kitchen at nine o'clock at night?"

"I could ask you the same thing."

"Where did you think I'd be? You saw me two hours ago."

"I just assumed you were at Stephen's old house." She paused. *"Especially* since you took a dog home with you without asking Rosemary first. And where is the dog?"

"In the barn, curled up on a pile of horse blankets. I asked Rosemary before I took them," Kevin added quickly, seeing the look on her face. "I realized on the way here that I'd better ask where the dog could go. Rosemary said something about her great-grandfather's hand-hewn floors and told me nothing came inside until we were sure it was housebroken."

"That sounds about right. I don't think there's ever been an indoor dog at Notch Gap Farm."

"Even the cat lives in the barn," Kevin said, eager to keep their conversation volleying along. "Also, the cat does not like the dog, but I think they reached a truce before blood was drawn."

"Rosemary will murder you if anything happens to that cat." Nikki opened the oven door and slid a casserole dish inside. "Where are those two, anyway?"

"Stephen took Rosemary to the Waterwheel for a romantic night out. He said he could only get her to go so late because I was here to do night-check on the horses." Kevin plastered on another comical grin and tried for a joke. "Say, do you know what it means to do night-check on the horses?"

Another sidelong glance, another annoyed expression. "You seriously don't know? Don't worry about it. I'll do it."

Another strike. Did he have any left, or was he out? Kevin was doing so badly tonight, he was losing count. "No, I know . . . I was just kidding. Rosemary showed me last time I was here. And she went over everything before she left. I have a list." Kevin realized he was sweating, and it wasn't just because the oven was heating up the kitchen. He felt like a comedian getting booed off stage. He kept trying to make her smile, and she kept making him feel like an idiot instead. It wasn't a pleasant sensation.

The thing was, Kevin wasn't used to feeling like an idiot. People were nice to Kevin. He was generally well-received. He was a Nice Guy. This was Kevin's greatest strength—he wasn't great at business, he wasn't creative, and he'd never had the opportunity to find out if he was good with his hands, so he got through life by being nice. It wasn't always the most rewarding course of action— for example, he got phone numbers from girls who gushed: "You're just so *nice,*" but they always ended up having something else to do when he called them for a date. Things like going to surprise engagement parties or having to attend a Drunk Painting class with their best friend, things which did not involve a Nice Guy they'd met at a bar or a business luncheon.

Of course, they always seemed like nice girls, too. Did he have a type? Nice Girl Who Doesn't Call Back? Was that something he should dig into with a therapist?

Nikki, though . . . she didn't seem like those nice girls. Sure, she could behave nicely, when she wanted to, but she was other things as well. Confident, gutsy . . . and a little scary, if Kevin was going to be completely honest with himself. He'd always known Rosemary had a strip of steel up her spine, but Nikki was solid.

He sat down at the kitchen table and watched her begin cleaning up the kitchen. Rosemary was pretty tidy, and Stephen was fairly organized. The kitchen was tidy enough. Nikki seemed to look at everything with the X-ray vision of a restaurant manager with the health department on the way. She lifted the pies Rosemary had made earlier and started whisking away crumbs from the countertop.

"So, what are you cooking?" Kevin finally asked.

"It's a sweet potato casserole."

"Oh! With little marshmallows?"

She gave him a stern look. "No. For God's sake. Are you a marshmallow fiend, too? This entire town, I swear to God . . ."

She went back to cleaning.

Kevin wondered what the hell he'd done wrong. "I just thought —I'm not saying I *want* little marshmallows, I just . . . I'm making conversation, Nikki."

"You don't have to. You can leave me here. It only needs to bake for forty-five minutes and then I'll be heading home."

He watched her work, mulling over the situation. Nikki was Rosemary's age—that made her close to thirty, if he wasn't mistaken. She was medium-height, slim, forever wearing skinny jeans with tunics or blouses which were just a shade darker than what most of the good housewives of Catoctin Creek would wear. He thought she looked like an artist. Actually, that added up: a chef was an artist who worked in flavors, after all.

"Tell me about this sweet potato casserole," he begged, hoping she'd quit cleaning and sit down with him.

Nikki glanced over her shoulder at him, still wielding a dishtowel. Her expression softened. "It's a new recipe I'm excited about," she replied, and her voice *did* sound enthusiastic, suddenly. So *excited* wasn't an overstatement for how food could make her feel. "It has a cinnamon-pecan crumble on top. So there's still a sweetness to it, but more of spiced flavor than just the sugar-onslaught of marshmallows. I think it's going to be sensational." She paused, setting down the towel. "If Rosemary isn't mad at me for skipping the marshmallows."

Kevin grimaced in sympathy. "Old family traditions?"

"Aileen Kelbaugh was a marshmallower. And Rosemary always had Thanksgiving with the Kelbaughs. This is the first time without them, actually. She thought they might come back for the holiday, but . . . you know how elderly people get in the cold.

They're down there in Florida being warm. They're not coming back here. Not ever, I'd say."

"Do *you* always come over for Thanksgiving?"

"Yeah, I have since my parents moved away."

He watched her face darken. "Where'd they go?"

"The desert sunsets of Arizona." Nikki sighed and started to sit across from him, then seemed to think better of it. She went back to the fridge and pulled out a bottle of white wine. "You want a drink?"

Kevin had already sampled that white wine earlier, from a local farmer who fancied himself a vintner, and found it seriously lacking. Still, he nodded eagerly. He'd drink anything she wanted, as long as she would sit and talk to him. "Yes, please."

She wiggled the cork free and poured. "My sister moved to Arizona and started a family there, so everyone else eventually moved out there as well. They take pictures of enormous cactus and send me Hopi clay plates to hang on my wall. Which . . . I mean, they're gorgeous, but I don't have that much room. My apartment is limited in decor space. So I have a box of decorative clay plates under my couch."

"Wait, you live in an apartment? In Catoctin Creek?" In his limited travels around the region, Kevin had only seen farmhouses, decaying mansions, some trailers, and generic brick ranch houses like Stephen's. There were no apartment complexes that he was aware of in this land of wide open fields.

"It's a garage apartment," Nikki said with a shrug. She sat down, sliding a glass across the table to Kevin, and took a sip from her own cup. He watched the flavor roll around on her tongue, and grinned when she winced. "Yikes. This is bad. Don't believe anyone who tells you Catoctin Creek has good grape soil." She took another sip anyway. "Anyway, I live in the backyard of Hazel and William McKinley's house. William McKinley is kind of like the town mayor. If we had one, he'd be the guy. I went to school with his youngest daughter, Jennifer."

"And where is Jennifer now?"

"Frederick." She rolled her eyes. "The bounteous golden city of Frederick. That's where most of us end up after high school. The ones who don't have the nerve to really head to a big city."

Kevin, a son of the big city who had until recently never considered leaving his hometown, was fascinated by the direction this conversation was taking. "But *you* stayed here. And so did Rosemary. Not everyone leaves."

Nikki looked at him. *"You* left."

He felt his lungs squeeze together. "I did. But only because I wanted to come back so badly."

She leaned back in her chair, gaze skeptical. "Make it make sense, please."

"I wanted to come back and stay. All I've been doing, the past three months away from here—from *you*—" He took a deep breath. "It's all been so I could come back without being dragged away so quickly again. All of that back and forth, stolen weekends? It's not good enough, Nikki. I needed more than I could have. I've been working, nonstop, just trying to get my freedom."

"Your freedom to come here."

"Yes."

Nikki eyed him as if he'd become a dangerous snake. But at least the skepticism was gone. He took a long gulp of wine, feeling as if he'd been incredibly reckless. "Well, that's as good an answer as any," she said eventually.

He had the feeling this branch of the conversation was ended, and he wasn't too upset about it. Some things were too raw to be discussed at a kitchen table, beneath the yellow glare of an old-fashioned ceiling lamp. This was a discussion for the dark, for candlelight, or perhaps only the glow of stars.

"Tell me why you stayed," Kevin said suddenly. "I want to know all about it."

Nikki looked into her glass. "Well, you know Rosemary. She would never leave this farm, not in a million years. At first I was here because my family was here, this was where I lived. And then when they left, Rosemary was still here . . . and it's beautiful . . . and I inherited the Blue Plate, so that kind of cemented the deal. You know how it is . . . some places are just too *home* to ever leave, I guess. Even if . . ." Nikki's voice trailed off.

Kevin found himself scooting forward in his seat. "Even if?"

"Oh, even if it's kind of boring, I guess." Nikki laughed ruefully. "Even if I can't have the things I want here, is what I was going to say."

Kevin felt a little rush of excitement. Nikki, confiding in him? Unprecedented. Before, she'd only wanted to push and pull, playing with him and teasing, keeping things light and tantalizingly combative. The stresses of Thanksgiving and bad white wine were taking their toll. He made sure his face was arranged in its most sympathetic lines when he asked, "What is it you want?"

Nikki tossed back the rest of her wine with *what the hell* flair. When she spoke, her words came quickly, as if she was trying to ride this wave of honesty before it fizzled out. "I want to create a gathering place that's as beautiful as this town. I want to change Catoctin Creek into a place that lasts, instead of a place people leave. I want . . . I want to cook interesting meals for interesting people."

Kevin was on the verge of suggesting she cook for *him*, but stopped himself with great effort. "Go on," he urged her instead. "I love the sound of this. Tell me more."

Nikki leaned onto her elbows, ready to level with him. "So, it's like the Waterwheel. The restaurant that Stephen and Rosemary are at, a few towns over. Locals don't really go there. It's for the tourists going to all the antique shops in the town. Catoctin Creek doesn't have that kind of draw. No one *comes* here. If they did, maybe we'd have someplace like the Waterwheel, someplace kind of adventurous, with new flavors and things."

Kevin's brow crumpled as he tried to follow her line of thinking. Nikki was the only game in town. Why would she want more restaurants here? "So you want tourists to come so . . . you have more restaurants in town? Competition for the Blue Plate?"

"No." Nikki rolled her eyes, looking like her regular self again. "Forget the Blue Plate. I want to run a *better* restaurant. I want to have a Waterwheel of my own. I want to be a chef, not the manager of a greasy spoon diner. There's a place for the Blue Plate, there always will be, but it's not the place for me. I'm only running it because my aunt gave it to me. If I could do more, believe me, I would."

Kevin sat back, astonished. Who was this ambitious person? He'd known she was driven, known she was a hard worker, but somehow, he'd never realized Nikki had *dreams*.

Now he realized how foolish that was. Of course she had ambitions and hopes. No one could have Nikki's energy without wanting something worthwhile to direct it all at.

He wished he had half her drive, even if she didn't see it going anywhere. Nikki knew what she wanted. Kevin still had no idea.

Well, he didn't know what he wanted to do for *work,* anyway. In terms of fun, on the other hand . . . he started to slide his hand forward, hoping to touch her fingers. She'd look at him searchingly, and he'd give her a deep, meaningful look which said *I understand you, baby,* and then she'd smile—

"It's not going to happen."

Kevin put his hand back on his wineglass, chastened. But it turned out Nikki wasn't talking about him. She was gazing at the timer on the oven, waiting for her sweet potato casserole to finish so she could go home to her own apartment. She hadn't even seen his tentative move.

Kevin sighed—half in relief, half in chagrin. "What's not going to happen? The restaurant? Why not?"

"Because Catoctin Creek couldn't support it, for one thing," Nikki told him. "And because I couldn't afford to rent a storefront to stick it in, for another."

"But you could add some dishes to the Blue Plate menu?"

"Nuh-uh. Not happening." She closed her eyes briefly. "Trust me, there's no changing the menu. For many reasons. Palates and tradition, just for starters. My ancient kitchen staff. No one would be up for it. Plus, my idea doesn't fit into a place with booths and a drop ceiling and cross-stitch samplers on the walls, you know? The Blue Plate works perfectly as it is. It even gets good press as a real country diner to stop at. But upscale? No. Fancy menu? Definitely not. Hey, who knows. Maybe something else will happen someday, and I'll get my wish." But she didn't look like she really believed that.

Kevin hated to think Nikki was living a life of hopeless dreams. It was jarring with the image he'd always had of her, this strong woman who manhandled Rosemary whenever that sweet girl didn't feel up to dealing with the outside world, always arriving at the best possible moment with bags of comfort food and reams of good advice.

He was on the verge of telling her he was going to stay in Catoctin Creek and he'd do anything to help her realize her dream, when the kitchen timer sounded a cheerful *ding!*

Nikki jumped up, all business again, and the conversation ended. To his surprise, Kevin found he was relieved. Because he really didn't know how he was in any position to help her. He was broke and trying to find his purpose. *You're the last person she needs right now,* he scolded himself. *Nikki doesn't need to take on your problems, too.*

His wishes for her would have to wait until he made a few of his own come true.

Nikki put the casserole on a trivet. "Well, that's that."

"Are you leaving?"

"That's all I was going to prepare tonight. I'll have to come back tomorrow to finish my other sides." She picked up her cooler. "Thanks for the company. And for being honest with me," she added, with a little smile which made his heart race. "I appreciate the explanation. It was hard, you know? Thinking you've hit it off with someone . . ."

She shrugged. She was nearly out the door. He couldn't let her go.

"Come and do night-check with me," Kevin blurted. "I could use an expert's opinion."

"On what, how full the horses' water buckets should be? Night-check is just making sure everyone has hay, water, and is breathing. You know that, right?"

"And you could see my new dog," he added.

She made a face.

"You're not a dog person?" Kevin held his breath. If Nikki wasn't a dog person, he'd made a pretty serious misjudgment tonight.

"No, I am," she sighed. "It's just really cold out. But if you really want to show me the dog . . ."

"I *really* want to show you the dog."

She shook her head. "Fine. I'll help you do night-check and admire the dog."

Kevin resisted the urge to skip all the way to the barn.

The dog stood up, stretched elaborately, and wagged his feathery tail as they slipped through the side door into the barn. He'd left the lights on earlier, and the horses were awake under the pale golden bulbs, eating their hay with that quiet, thoughtful sound he found so restful.

Kevin bent over the cheerful dog, pleased his new pet didn't bark. "How about that?" he demanded of Nikki, grinning as if he'd trained the dog himself. "Noise-free!"

Nikki rubbed the yellow dog's fluffy head and smiled. Definitely a dog person, Kevin thought. Thank *God.*

"He's cute," Nikki said. "Much cuter now that we're not freezing in the wind arguing over him. I'll call the humane society for you on Friday, but I expect you'll be keeping him."

"Who would abandon a dog like this?"

"People who think farmers are starry-eyed animal lovers," Nikki explained. "I guarantee you those kids thought if they left the dog near Mrs. O'Reilly's farm, fate would take over and he'd have a happy new home with the neighbor."

"Well, they were half right."

Nikki smiled at Kevin, and he felt so warm he had to take off his coat.

She sat down next to the dog and gave him a good ear-rub while Kevin checked the water buckets and hay supply the way Rosemary had shown him, tossing extra hay to the horses who had run through their piles already. Rosemary had run a horse sanctuary from her family's farm for several years now, and the eight horses who lived in the lower level of the old bank barn ranged from a demanding miniature horse to a tall, dignified black draft horse. Kevin found it fascinating that all of them lived in harmony and ate essentially the same things. He spent a little extra time patting Rochester, the big black Percheron.

When he finished loving on the horse, cooing nonsense, he realized Nikki was watching him. "I've always kinda liked him best," he explained, feeling a little foolish. "The day I met Rosemary, she fell off him and I was the one who chased him down and brought him home."

"I remember that day," Nikki replied. "She had a concussion and Stephen stayed with her. I was so suspicious of him! And *you* somehow ended up in . . . Shippensburg, wasn't it?"

"Just Gettysburg," Kevin laughed. "I missed his house and ended up in Pennsylvania. To be fair, it's not far away."

"Well, I guess you know your way around here pretty well, now." Nikki got up, brushing her hands off on her jeans. The dog kept his nose close to her hip, not ready to give her up. "And with a dog? Who knows? Maybe you really are going to stay this time."

"Maybe I am." *Of course I am.*

"What are you going to call this fella?"

Kevin had been wondering that himself. "I don't know. He's such a Muppet of a dog, isn't he? What would you call him?"

Nikki studied the dog, who was smiling up at her, pink tongue dangling. "Cute . . . fluffy . . . definitely a monster. I'd call him Grover." She glanced at Kevin. "What do you think?"

Kevin wanted to pull her against him and kiss her silly, that was what he thought. "Grover's perfect," he said, cheerfully discounting Lauren's *ends-in-y* rule. "Dog? Your name is Grover now."

The dog turned his head and panted happily at Kevin.

"I'll see you tomorrow," Nikki said. "Bye, Grover." She started for the side-door.

Suddenly, Kevin couldn't stand the idea of her leaving so soon. He chased after her, catching her just as she opened the door. A cold wind whipped around them, sending her dark curls into a frenzy. "This ridiculous hair," she gasped. "I should get it straightened. Tie it back in a knot like the girls at the diner."

Wild hair licked at his face, and he reached out, catching the loose coils without thinking, his fingers brushing her cheek. He pressed his handfuls of hair up against her throat, as if to tuck it all into her coat collar, but when his skin touched hers, he stood absolutely still, arrested by the sensation.

"Your hair is beautiful," he told her.

They were standing very, very close to one another. Nikki's eyes caught the golden gleam of the old bulbs burning above the horse stalls, and they seemed to glitter as she stared up at him.

Kevin swallowed, suddenly brimming with words he didn't know how to say. This was where he'd hoped the evening would lead . . . and now he was afraid to ruin it.

Her gaze slipped from his own eyes to his hands, still holding the rich spirals of her hair. He watched her swallow, watched her lips turn up in a coy smile as she recovered her endless supply of cool.

"Are you going to drag me back to your cave?" she asked, with a husky chuckle in the back of her throat.

He grinned. "Not if you come willingly."

She covered his hands with her fingers and gently squeezed. He released her hair without thinking. "I have to go," she told him gently. "See you tomorrow."

She slipped out the side door before he could say anything, leaving him alone in the warm barn.

Kevin sat down on the chair she'd left vacant and the dog licked at his hands, thrilled to have company again. "Sorry I have to leave you in the barn all night," he told the dog. *Grover.* "But I have to make nice with Rosemary, or else I'm going to have to drag you back to the city."

There was no place in the city for Grover, anymore than there was for Nikki. And so if Grover stayed, here Kevin would stay as well.

She wouldn't really straighten her hair, though, would she?

# Chapter 7

## Nikki

Nikki woke up with a headache and a general feeling of foreboding. She looked at the Parisian bistro poster hanging on the wall opposite her bed and thought, *What happened last night?*

She remembered. *Kevin.* Kevin was what happened.

Nikki closed her eyes and groaned as it all came back to her: the late evening in Rosemary's kitchen, Kevin appearing like a ghost of good feelings past, splitting that bottle of awful local wine, admitting to a slick New Yorker that she wished she could be a fancy restauranteur instead of the proprietress of a rural country diner, joining him for night-check and *naming his dog*—what could be more intimate than naming someone's dog, honestly— that charged moment in the barn doorway, and finally, *finally* coming home to wash away all of her feelings with a bottle of much better wine, this one sourced from Spain instead of western Maryland.

Hence the headache. Even good wine, when mixed with bad, could tax the brain.

She rubbed a hand across her temples, experimenting with how much pressure she could take. Not the worst hangover in the world, she decided. Just a wine headache and the aforementioned sense of impending doom, and that really could have happened on any morning. Today, though, she needed to get it together, and on the double. Thanksgiving Day was one of the Blue Plate's rare days of rest, but she still had plenty of work to do before heading over to Rosemary's house for the afternoon.

"Action plan," Nikki muttered, throwing back the covers. "First, address hangover." She forced herself upright and scooted out of bed. The bathroom was right below her loft; four steps down and she'd be pulling out aspirin from the cabinet and filling a glass with cold water. Advantage: studio apartments.

"Second, hair of the dog." A small dollop of vodka from the freezer went into her glass of orange juice. The sugar and alcohol would clear her up in no time at all.

Once she was in the kitchen, things proceeded at a normal pace despite her lingering headache. Nikki was used to working through discomfort. There wasn't any back-up at the Blue Plate on busy days or when they were short-staffed. Either she stepped up, filled the empty slots, and ran the show, or all hell broke loose. No in-between. Something about working in the kitchen gave her that same energy, even if she was alone at home with nothing more pressing than throwing together a few more sides for Thanksgiving dinner.

"Three, toast." She put a few slices of brioche into her shining red toaster, then pulled out a big pot. *Four, potatoes.* She'd boil water for mashed potatoes right away so she could get to mashing, and then she'd tackle the honey-bourbon carrots. She and

Rosemary switched off on root vegetable responsibility each Thanksgiving, and Nikki was determined to bring her A-game.

She sipped at the screwdriver as her bread toasted and glanced over her small, but excellent, wine collection. She'd bring a few bottles of decent wine to dinner, just in case someone had convinced Stephen to buy an entire case of that awful local stuff. Stephen was a nice guy. Not as nice as Kevin, but certainly nice enough to be a pushover when he was trying to shop the neighbors' small businesses. Nikki suspected he was still trying to make amends for nearly turning Long Pond, one of the area's prettiest and most historic farms, into a subdivision.

Of course, Kevin had been part of that debacle, too. She wondered if he felt any remorse, any need to make reparations to the community, like buying terrible wine. Nikki sighed at the general problem of Kevin. She wondered if she was still angry with him. That little confession last night—well, at least he'd been honest with her when she'd asked. Brief, but honest. Somehow, she knew to believe him. What did he say, the words that made her breath catch in her chest?

*I needed more than I could have.*

Nikki leaned her forehead against the cold steel of the refrigerator and sighed. "It would be better if you could stay mad," she told herself. "Make him work a little, prove himself." But who could be angry with Kevin? He could charm the birds out of the trees.

Or maybe that was just the effect he had on her.

They'd been really close to a kiss last night—a kiss which might have led to more. She planned on doing her best to resist his flirtations today, but now she knew for certain he'd come back from the city with his sights set on her . . . and she wasn't sure she had the strength to tell him no.

"So then he looks at the salesgirl, and she's fluttering her eyelashes at him, and they're covered with gobs of mascara so she looks like two caterpillars have taken up residence on her face, and that's it, Stephen says, *sure, we'll take a case of it,* and I could have screamed." Rosemary was cracking up with laughter, a bottle of Antietam Gold Reserve waving dangerously in her hand. "So now we have more of this stuff than I could ever cook with, and Stephen is forbidden from ever going into a winery again."

"So much for our Napa Valley trip," Nikki quipped, taking the bottle from Rosemary before she dropped it. "Don't even cook with that," she added. "It'll ruin whatever you're making. You can probably make it into floor cleaner or something."

Rosemary sank down to the kitchen table, still giggling. "On my great-grandfather's hardwood floors? No, we'll just make the men drink it. *This* looks much better." She held up one of the bottles Nikki had deposited on the table. "Oh, it's from Spain! Mmm . . . sounds sunny and warm." She glanced at the kitchen window, where a leaden sky sat above the brown fields. In the distance, the leafless slopes of Notch Gap were two frozen humps of bare trees. On a day like this, it was hard to remember they lived in the most beautiful spot in the world. "The coldest Thanksgiving ever, isn't it?"

"Well, *this* tastes like a summer afternoon," Nikki promised, pulling down glasses. She looked forward to the simple headiness of wine, the perfect accent to a perfect afternoon. The kitchen was warm and scented with holiday smells: sage, rosemary, cloves, that indefinable deliciousness of a roasting turkey just taking on its golden hue. A pan of cornbread was cooling on the wooden counter next to the farmhouse sink, and Nikki's casserole dishes jostled for space alongside it. The fruit and pumpkin pies had been taken to the dining room and placed on the antique sideboard to be admired while they ate dinner. In true holiday fashion, the men were nowhere to be seen.

Which was problematic for Nikki, as she had Kevin on the brain and was impatient to see him, even though she hated herself for turning around every time she thought she heard a floorboard creak. At least she had time to test his story against a third party.

"So tell me," she began carefully, setting a glass in front of Rosemary, "what on earth is Kevin doing here?"

Rosemary smiled like the cat who got the cream. Nikki knew that smile. It meant she found the situation between Nikki and Kevin *hilarious*, but she wasn't laughing out of a modicum of respect for her friends. "Oh, well, you know . . . Kevin's been having a rough time. He needed to get out of the city. The last time Stephen went up to the city for some meetings, he invited him down for Thanksgiving."

"I get that he needs a break from the city. But for Thanksgiving? The holiday of mandatory family time? Won't his mother miss him?"

"He has a huge family, apparently. Irish New Yorkers. They either live there or they all come into town and gather at his mother's house in Woodside. He says he won't be missed." Rosemary shrugged. "Anyway, Stephen and I thought you'd be happy to see him again. Were we wrong?"

"It's not that you're wrong, just . . ." Nikki considered the question. It was confusing, this little thing between her and Kevin. If *little thing* was a fair assessment. Was it just a crush? If so, how embarrassing it would be to admit it had devastated her when he'd disappeared . . . or the way she couldn't get him out of her mind now. Nikki decided to play it cool, even though Rosemary would surely understand if she told her the truth. "I don't think there's actually anything there," she said, as dismissively as she could manage. "I mean, I didn't hear from him for over two months. So don't get all matchmaker on me, okay? Let's not try to make something out of this. We flirted, sure. But it was a wedding. Everyone gets carried away at weddings."

Rosemary looked so disappointed, Nikki almost changed course. She *could* tell her to spend the entire day organizing meet-cutes between her and Kevin until one of them took, or until Rosemary got over her hopes, whichever came first. Maybe something *would* happen. But what good would it do? What she ought to do was stay good and mad at Kevin. She shrugged, taking the middle ground. "I'm just saying, since I haven't heard from Kevin since your wedding, I'm not really feeling it. Seems like if he was interested, he'd have been around more than that. Even if he does live three hours away. *Stephen* managed it."

"That's true. But about that—listen to this—"

Stephen appeared in the kitchen doorway, momentarily distracting Rosemary, who felt the need to hop up and wrap her arms around him. Well, they were still newlyweds, Nikki reflected. This sort of thing was to be expected. She threw back a swallow of wine and made a big deal of flicking on the oven light and checking the turkey. She loved the two of them, she really did, but today of all days she just wasn't up for all the public displays of affection. This was Thanksgiving, for God's sake. Not exactly a romantic holiday.

"I was just about to tell Nikki," Rosemary was saying to Stephen. "But where is he? It's his news, really."

Nikki's hand froze on the oven door. *Tell me what?*

"He's out in the barn," Stephen replied. "I left him on water duty. It's safe enough to leave him alone when the horses are out in the pasture."

Nikki turned around. "I thought you trusted him to do night-check last night?"

They both stared at her.

*Damn.* She'd miscalculated the importance of last night, all right. Kevin had just brushed it off. Didn't even mention she'd been there.

She must have imagined that moment in the barn doorway. Blown it up into something it wasn't. He'd just been annoyed her hair was in his face.

Nikki shrugged off their stares, determined to play it off as nothing. "Didn't Kevin tell you? I was here last night to make the sweet potato casserole. You didn't even notice it was in the fridge, did you? So yeah, my gas was out again." Nikki sighed theatrically. "I'm going to have to talk to William and get someone in to check those lines, and *not* Ian, either—"

"Wait, so you talked to Kevin last night *after* he came back from the diner?" Rosemary sounded disappointed. "Does that mean he told you? He must have told you. And I missed it."

"Told me what?"

"His big news! About staying in Catoctin Creek for a while!"

Nikki felt her knees go wobbly, and she sat down hard in one of the kitchen chairs. "Excuse me?" Privately, she thought, *Well, at least now the dog makes sense.*

Rosemary's face lit right back up. "Yes! He's staying on for a while. Taking a break from New York, from his job, everything. He's going to stay up in the brick house."

"We'll find something for him to do," Stephen added. "We can't let Kevin run around with no responsibilities or he'll make everyone crazy. He claims he's going to find a job here, although I don't know what he'll do."

Nikki was having trouble concentrating. Too much buzzing in her ears. "Wait . . . why is he doing this?"

Was it about her? Was this Kevin's big Stephen-style move to stay in town and woo her silly?

Nikki wasn't the romantic type, but she could get behind the idea of a big gesture from Kevin. Suddenly, their parting moment took on significance again. The way he'd looked at her, the way his hand had brushed her cheek—*Your hair is beautiful*—

Nikki tried to get hold of herself before someone noticed that her pulse was rising, her cheeks were warming, her breath was quickening.

"He needs to find himself, like someone else I could mention did," Rosemary said. She gave Stephen a brilliant smile, her entire face radiating so much love, Nikki's insides seemed to twist with jealousy. "He was having an awful time in New York. So this one is being generous and giving him the space he needs to get away and do some thinking about what he wants out of life."

Nikki's bubble burst with a spectacular pop.

"He needs to find himself?" she repeated.

"Oh, you know how it is. His job isn't fulfilling. He's lived in the city his entire life." Rosemary laughed gently. "It's time for him to take stock, see who he really is."

That was the problem with these city guys, Nikki thought, drumming her fingers on the table. Too much time thinking, not enough time doing. If Kevin was really here on some sort of *what does it all mean* journey, he was going to have to find his answers without her.

"Well, good luck to him," Nikki said finally.

There was a moment of quiet. Rosemary glanced at Stephen, and he excused himself, grabbing a few bottles of water out of the fridge and heading back outside.

Rosemary sat down across from Nikki. "Hey, is there a problem with Kevin being here?"

Nikki snorted. "Of course not! You do what you need to do, Rosie-marie. I'm good with whatever." *God, that sounded fake.*

Rosemary's forehead creased in concern. "Because I thought it might be nice for you—"

"Like I said, it's not really a thing. We're not going to be a couple. Honestly," Nikki went on, warming to her cause now, "a guy wandering around looking for himself is the last thing I need in my life. He already has a job! And a place to live! What else could he want? You know I'm not big on the whole *why am I here* nonsense." She realized her voice was pitched a little high and subsided, dipping back into her wine.

Sure, she wasn't into any "finding her purpose" mumbo-jumbo. *That's why I stay up late coming up with new recipes no one will ever pay me to cook for them, right?*

Nikki knew she was being contrary for no reason, but she decided against drawing back, possibly because of the wine. Doubling down, that was the Nikki Mercer way. "If he wants to come here and do a little soul-searching, consider me unbothered and out of the way."

Rosemary still looked unconvinced, but she was good enough to accept Nikki's stance. That was part of their friendship. Rosemary accepted what Nikki said at face value. Nikki dug into every nuance of Rosemary's words and made her come clean when she was fibbing. Uneven, sure, but they worked well together anyway.

The kitchen fell quiet, with just the low hiss of the oven and the occasional pop from the roasting turkey to break the country silence. The women sipped at their wine and, in Nikki's case at least, wondered what to say next.

*Why say anything?* Nikki wondered. *We've never depended on conversation to pass the time.*

Still, now the silence between them felt unusually heavy, as if both were busily thinking deep thoughts about one another. Nikki finished her glass of wine and poured another; it was only three o'clock, but she could make a pot of coffee and undo the sleepy effects. Just as soon as she was done with this glass, that's what she'd do. *Action plan: coffee.*

Nikki always felt best with a clear action plan.

Her head came up as an idea flooded her brain.

That was exactly what Kevin needed, she realized. An action plan. If she knew Kevin, and she thought she did, that loon hadn't even bothered to think through a move to the countryside. He was going to sit up at Stephen's house and watch the sunsets over

Notch Gap and walk his goofy dog and try to *think* the universe into sending him a sign, or a new job, or a purpose in life: whatever it was he wanted. He would wait for it, instead of going out and chasing it. Nikki was convinced of this. People as easy-going as Kevin just didn't plan well enough!

Well, she could fix his wagon for him. She'd just think it through, make a list of jobs he could do, talk to some folks around town and see what opportunities were out there. If he thought he wanted to be a Catoctin Creek man, she'd find just what his options were and lay it out for him. Fingers itching for a pen and paper, Nikki got up and started rummaging through the kitchen junk drawer.

Rosemary watched her curiously. "What are you after?"

"Something to make notes with." Nikki closed the drawer.

"Look in the desk in the living room."

Nikki retrieved a notepad and pen from the living room, where an antique roll-top desk stood against one wall. "Perfect, thanks."

Rosemary raised her eyebrows. "And what is this for?"

"This is Kevin's action plan," Nikki said simply. She wrote: *Good with numbers? Mr. Barr's tax service* and underlined it for emphasis.

"His *action* plan?" Rosemary got up and looked over her shoulder. "You think Kevin should do people's taxes?"

"It's an option."

"Nikki, I don't think you understand what someone means when they say they want to find themselves." Rosemary's voice was amused.

Nikki huffed a sigh. "When I hear that, I hear someone who isn't making a plan, Rosemary. And that makes me crazy."

"So you're going to fix Kevin's life for him?"

"Someone has to."

Rosemary went back to her chair. "I don't think Kevin wants that kind of relationship."

"What kind?" Nikki challenged her, putting down the pen. "Like ours? Like when I push you to do things and you do them and your life gets better?"

"Well . . . *yeah.*"

Nikki shrugged. "That's what I've got to offer. He can take it or leave it."

# Chapter 8

# Kevin

When Stephen came through the barnyard gate, Kevin was busy trying to sluice a flood of cold water out of the barn aisles. Since he was using a plastic-bladed snow shovel, he wasn't having a *great* deal of success, but some water was leaving the barn and Kevin had decided to consider this a plus.

He paused in his work as Stephen came to the edge of the muddy puddle Kevin was creating in the previously pristine barnyard. The little rectangular paddock in front of Rosemary's bank barn was always meticulously manicured, because Rosemary used the space to teach her monthly horsemanship lessons to novice land-owners hoping to take in rescue horses, and in these lessons she emphasized cleanliness and orderliness above all else.

Not exactly what Kevin was accomplishing right now.

"Kev?" Stephen's voice was amused. "You okay, man?"

Kevin shoved some more water towards the open barn doors. The blade bit into a patch of clay—the floor was partially stone, partially the hard-packed earth which had slowly swallowed up the old flagstones over the past two centuries—and arrested his push mid-arc. He winced and grunted as his elbow absorbed the shock. "Yeah, I'm fine. Why do you ask?"

"Just . . . the barn seems wetter than usual."

"The important thing is that the hose is definitely reattached to the spigot and there will not be *more* water joining the water currently on the floor."

"Ah. Well, that's great. Really great. Makes this seem redundant, though." Stephen waggled the bottle of water he'd brought Kevin.

"Believe it or not, I *am* thirsty." Kevin splashed through the puddle, ignoring the cold water as it soaked through the seams in his old sneakers. These shoes were trashed anyway. Maybe for Black Friday he'd head down to the Francis Scott Key Mall in Frederick and treat himself to some work boots.

Water pooled between his toes. *Waterproof* work boots. He took the bottle from Stephen with a bland smile. "Thank you, sir."

"So, uh, what happened?"

"Oh, I tugged too hard on the hose and it came right off the spigot." Kevin had watched in horror as the hose came flying towards him. He'd run as fast as he could to the other side of the barn, only to see the spigot gushing water all over the aisle. Next time, he would check to see what was catching the hose before he yanked on it. Lesson learned.

Stephen was eyeballing the hose, which was still wrapped around the wheelbarrow which had entrapped it. "So you left the wheelbarrow in the way . . ."

"I did."

"And you *yanked*—"

"I'm new to this."

"Kevin, man, you really have no instincts around the barn, do you? Good thing they're outside."

"How could I have instincts around the barn? It is the twenty-first century and my family moved to Queens in 1895. I'll bet no one in my bloodline has been near a horse since the last milkman route went mechanical."

"My great-uncle Will was run over by a milkman's horse when he was a kid," Stephen said thoughtfully.

"Really?"

"That's what they say. He wasn't killed or anything. But I always think about it when the horses are running around like crazy. *That could be my Great-Uncle Will under those hooves.*' Stephen guffawed. "Very dark, I know."

"Seriously, did that really happen?"

"Well, it's an old family legend. And Great-Uncle Will spoke really slowly. So, maybe."

"Right." They looked at the wet barn floor for a few moments. "I think it's going to dry up on its own now," Kevin said hopefully.

"Probably will. And if Rosemary doesn't come out here before it's time to feed dinner, she'll never know."

"Works for me." Kevin leaned against the barnyard fence. "I'm tired, man. All day out here in the chilly wind, doing farmer chores? It's wiping me out. I might need a nap before dinner."

"Now there's a good idea. Even better idea: a beer and then a nap. You in?"

"This is why we're friends." Kevin grinned at Stephen. "Man, I really appreciate this. Inviting me down here, keeping me busy all day, letting me stay in the brick house—takes my mind off how rough things have been back in the city lately. I feel like a new person already."

"And letting you keep that dog. That helping, too?"

Kevin laughed and glanced over at the horse stall where Grover was currently blissed out, sleeping on a fluffy horse blanket he was pretty sure was going to accompany them when they moved up to the brick house. The blanket had been chewed on by rats, and half the stuffing was already out, so Rosemary had been happy to donate it to Grover. But she still wasn't willing to let the dog into the farmhouse until she knew for sure he was housebroken. Kevin asked Stephen if he was worried about the dog messing up the carpets in the brick house, and Stephen had laughed and said if he had to replace those ugly old carpets, the dog was doing them all a favor.

"I really appreciate the dog thing, too," Kevin said now. "I didn't see Grover coming, but I'm really happy about him. He'll be good company up there. I needed a dog. Maybe if I'd had a dog in the city, I wouldn't have felt so lost." He considered the implications of a dog living on a high floor of a condominium tower. "Although taking the elevator up and down every single time the dog had to pee would really suck."

Stephen was already opening the barnyard gate, but he paused and looked back over his shoulder. "You know, I didn't realize things were that rough for you. You should have told me sooner. I was really sorry I couldn't help you get a job with my firm, but I figured there were plenty of companies out there looking for a guy with your experience."

"Well, I mean, it's tough . . . admitting things aren't working out. Especially after I razzed you constantly about coming down here and getting all wrapped up in the Long Pond business." Kevin didn't mention there *were* plenty of companies hiring, but his numbers just didn't make the cut. He wasn't, in the memorable words of one headhunter, a desirable candidate. Just more proof Kevin wasn't living the life he was cut out for. His purpose was here somewhere.

He looked back at the slightly damp barn. He felt good out here, doing chores, getting dirty. He'd helped Rosemary feed the horses breakfast and turn them out in the pasture this morning, and that had felt good, too. Despite his defensiveness about being from a horse-free family, there was something about the big animals which really spoke to him. Taking care of Rosemary's horses, in particular, felt like a worthy use of his time. They were all rescues, all horses who had been knocked around, hurt and frightened by humans. Kevin felt like he owed them a debt, just by being a member of his own cruel species.

He didn't say any of this out loud, though. He just closed the gate behind him, double-checked the latch as Rosemary had shown him—even though there weren't any horses in the barnyard, she'd said it was just a good habit to get into—and followed Stephen up to the house.

Their shoes crunched across the crisp November grass. The farmhouse was just a few dozen feet away, its rust-red brick walls glowing warmly in a late appearance from the afternoon sun, the white paint on its two long porches tinted golden. The sun went down later here than it did in New York City, a fact Kevin appreciated; any extra evening time was a bonus as far as he was concerned. They were nearly to the porch steps when Kevin paused, his gaze arrested on the little Honda parked next to Rosemary's car.

"Oh, man," he groaned. "Is Nikki here already? That means it's getting late."

Kevin wasn't nearly as disappointed as Stephen. A nap sounded great, but Nikki sounded fantastic. He remembered their parting last night like it was just seconds ago, his heart speeding up as he recalled the way she'd looked at him in the soft glow of the barn lights.

Then again, knowing Nikki, she'd had time to think it over and decide she was mad at him again. He hung back as Stephen climbed the porch stairs.

"What are you waiting for, man? Let's go grab a beer and bug Nikki. She'd love it."

Kevin followed him reluctantly. "I don't know if that's the right move for me. I told you, things were a roller coaster last night. She's on the fence about me. I think I should just take it slow for now. Make sure she's really into me, you know?"

Stephen held open the front door, gesturing for him to get inside. "Kev, my red-haired friend, who would not be into you? You look like a ginger Paul Rudd."

"I don't even know how to take that," Kevin complained as he stepped into the hall—and nearly ran smack into Nikki.

The grin she threw him was almost a smirk. "I'd say with a hefty grain of salt." She pushed her arms into a black wool coat.

Stephen laughed. "Unkind, Nikki. Listen, take that coat off. Whatever you need, I'll get it for you. I'm already frozen."

Nikki pulled off the coat in one quick motion. "In the passenger seat of my car, a box of serving-ware, be careful, it's heavy," she directed. She turned to Kevin as Stephen headed back outside. "Well, ginger Paul Rudd? That's quite a crown for that fluffy head of yours."

"My back is strong," he assured her. "I can carry this weight."

She flicked a skeptical eyebrow in his direction. "Want to come into the kitchen? I'm making a pot of coffee to see us all through dinner. You look like you could use a cup or three. And a shower."

"And dry socks. What time are we talking dinner?"

"Oh, six, I think. Just waiting on the turkey now. As usual." She sniffed the air. "Smell it, though?"

"Smells amazing. But I'll skip the coffee," Kevin decided. He'd give her space this afternoon, let her think about how much she liked him. Hopefully. Also, the warmth of the house was making him realize how tired he was. "This farm boy needs a  nice little nappie-nap."

Nikki burst out laughing. "Are you *serious?* God, you men."

"What's wrong?" Rosemary called from the kitchen. "What are they doing now?"

"They're going to take their widdle nappies," Nikki replied, fixing Kevin with an amused look.

"Oh, of course they are!" Rosemary sounded like she was standing right next to him. Stephen was right, that hallway *did* have some crazy acoustics. "We'll just keep on working, though! That's fine!"

"Well, we *have* been cleaning the barn all day," Kevin began, thinking he deserved some sort of credit for the work he'd put in. Now that he was standing still, he could feel things tightening up: his neck, his shoulders, his lower back, his thighs . . . "Ugh," he announced as he bent over to take off his wet shoes. "That hurts."

He felt Nikki's scornful glance raking him. "What does? Your back?"

"Everything." He looked up at her. "Is it all supposed to hurt?"

Her smile was mocking. He loved it, the way the corners of her lips turned up and the corners of her eyes turned down. The way her long lashes fell over her cheeks as she looked him over, raking him with a glance, turning him inside-out with a single look. "That's how you know you're doing it right," she told him.

"Doing what?"

Nikki was heading back into the kitchen. "Life," she called over her shoulder.

Kevin tugged off his wet socks and staggered into the living room. The stairs looked too imposing to handle right away. He settled into the cushions of the sagging old sofa with a groan. *Life,* he thought. What an answer! That was the problem with Nikki. She had amazing spirit, but she seemed to think life was a slog, or a battle to be won, he wasn't sure which. Either way, she definitely wasn't in it for the joy. That woman worked too hard and celebrated too little.

He'd love to help her have a little more fun. Maybe even chase down that dream of hers. He had the experience in buying and selling real estate, in finding investors and capital . . .

. . . But he'd already covered this, hadn't he? He had the experience, but he'd never been very successful. A just so-so track record wasn't what Nikki needed. If he helped her finance a dream which ultimately failed, he would just be the villain in her life, not the savior.

Stephen came back inside with a rattling box of serving-ware. He paused at the door and glanced in at Kevin. "You told them about the naps?"

"I took the heat," Kevin assured him. "Now I'm a big baby."

"Oh, come on," Stephen said. "We're both big babies."

"That's for sure!" Nikki shouted from the kitchen.

Stephen took off his boots and hoisted the box again. "I think we're living out some kind of Thanksgiving movie script," he remarked, and shambled off with his clattering delivery for the kitchen.

Kevin closed his eyes and listened to the clangs and bangs coming from the kitchen, which eventually quieted as the scent of coffee floated through the living room. Kevin breathed deep and closed his eyes. *Just a little nap, and then I'll face Nikki again over dinner.*

Maybe he could get through a holiday meal without making her mad. A Thanksgiving miracle? Was that a thing?

# Chapter 9

## Nikki

Nikki's cinnamon-pecan sweet potatoes were a huge success, even without the marshmallows. So were the orange-glazed Brussels sprouts with butternut squash, the honey-bourbon carrots, and the gruyere-and-caramelized-onion mashed potatoes (there *was* a little pushback initially on the Brussels sprouts, but once the men had tasted them and realized how fantastic Nikki's instincts were, all whining quickly dissipated in favor of shoveling the food down as rapidly as possible).

Even Rosemary admitted prior Thanksgiving dinners, celebrated with her former next-door neighbors the Kelbaughs, had never tasted as delicious as this one.

"I never would have thought of these flavor combinations," Rosemary sighed, patting her full stomach as she finished a second plate. "And not only that, but you were *completely* right about brining the turkey. Who knew! My mother always just basted it with butter and drippings. So did Aileen."

"Oh, don't put down our mothers or Aileen Kelbaugh," Nikki blustered, fending off compliments with the same energy she put into concocting her recipes. "They were working with the best they had. And those Thanksgiving dinners were pretty darned good, anyway. Aileen has a magic touch with stuffing, for one thing, and I'm thankful she gave you her recipe. And the cornbread you made, that was your mother's recipe for sure. Tasting it made me feel like she was in the room."

Nikki had vivid memories of Sunday dinners in this very dining room, with Rosemary's soft-spoken parents presiding over a platter of roast chicken and glasses of iced tea. She knew Rosemary did, too. She suspected these memories were why they were seated around the table facing one another, with no one at the head, where Mr. Brunner would have sat in the old days.

It was hard having her own family in Arizona, but Nikki knew Rosemary had it so much worse. Being orphaned suddenly at any age was a traumatic experience, especially for a woman who had been happy to live at home with her parents. Despite Nikki's best efforts, Rosemary had wilted on her own, shrinking into the farm. Thank goodness she had Stephen now!

Nikki wondered, yet again, if she'd ever have anything like what those two shared.

Without meaning to, she let her gaze shift to Kevin. He looked back at her and smiled, so quickly she suspected he'd been waiting for her to glance his way. Nikki's heart did a quick tumble, and she averted her eyes before her face could give her away.

Too late. Everyone was looking at her. She bit back a sigh, aware this level of investment in her personal life was simply the hallmark of deep friendships. Could she really complain?

She'd love to, actually.

"Well," she announced, pushing back from the table. "I do believe it's time for dessert."

"Oh, God," Rosemary sighed. "More food?"

"You can do it, sweetie," Stephen said encouragingly. "I believe in you."

"That's very kind, but I think this is more physical than spiritual."

"There's lemon meringue." Nikki began to pick up the dirty dinner plates.

"I didn't see lemon meringue!" Rosemary's demeanor changed entirely. "I just figured Nikki had sold the last one before you got there, Kev."

"I ended up hiding it in the cellar fridge last night." Kevin cast her a wicked grin. "I let you think your pumpkin and apple pies were the only stars of the show."

"Well, now I have no choice." Rosemary slumped in her chair. "I will just have to find the room."

"Mind over matter," Stephen advised her.

Kevin pushed back his own chair and hopped up to join Nikki. "Let me help you clear the table." He started scooping up flatware and dishes with enthusiasm.

Nikki feared for the longevity of Rosemary's china, but she couldn't exactly insist he sit back down. "Thanks," she said lightly. "I'll take these plates in and start slicing the pies."

She meant to come right back with pie for everyone, but the kitchen was looking a bit like a once-cozy bakery which had been hit by a hurricane, so Nikki decided to give everyone's stomachs a little breather and got busy cleaning. She was already filling the sink with dishes when Kevin came in with the rest of the salad plates and cutlery. "You can set those in the sink," she said, stepping out of the way.

Kevin obediently placed his armload of dishes into the big porcelain sink. It was large enough to wash a sheepdog in and took half the house's water heater contents to properly fill up, so Nikki turned on some water to get things started, reaching across Kevin to turn the tap. As she did, her chest brushed against his arm, and a warm rush of sensation sizzled across her skin. She bit back a gasp.

"Everything okay? You didn't burn yourself, did you?" Kevin asked, his voice fifty shades of concerned.

She shook her head, impatient with herself. "Must have pricked myself on the sharp edge of the sink," she lied. "Underneath the ledge," she added, when he looked skeptical. "Feel."

Kevin, forever amiable, pressed his fingers beneath the sink's edge. "Oh, right," he agreed, but she could tell he was just humoring her.

"It's nothing. Watch out and let me wash these dishes." She nudged him aside with the energy of a grandmother chasing out her interfering offspring. Nothing sensual about that, which she liked. *Let's keep it professional,* she thought wryly. As if there was any real chance of that! All of her senses were aware he was standing close beside her, so close she could take a single step and be in his arms.

Now *there* was an idea. For just a moment, her hands stilled in the wash-water. Imagining.

"Can I help you with something?" Kevin asked.

Nikki glanced at the pots and pans towering on the stovetop. There was at least ten minutes' worth of dishwashing here, according to her restaurant instincts. Not *too* bad, but she didn't want the folks in the other room falling asleep, either. "Can you make a pot of coffee? I think that would make everyone happy."

"I can do that! I'm actually very good at making coffee."

Nikki wasn't sure this was a life skill to boast about, seeing as how it involved putting a few scoops of ground coffee into a machine, so she just nodded and went back to scrubbing dishes. Then a squeaky cabinet door made her turn her head again. He was rummaging in the pantry. "What are you looking for? The coffee maker is on the counter and there's a bag of coffee right next to it."

Kevin tugged a small cylinder with a cord out of the cabinet. "Gotta grind the beans."

She raised her eyebrows. "Since when does Rosemary grind coffee beans?" That was an affectation she hadn't counted on. Nikki might have high standards when it came to food, but coffee was coffee. It was dark, and bitter, and you added plenty of cream and sugar to it, and it woke you up. What else did it need? There was no reason to complicate things.

"I don't know." Kevin took a small bag of beans from another cupboard—a bag that was noticeably *not* Folgers or Maxwell House or any of the other five brands sold at Trout's. "Probably Stephen bought the grinder, to be honest."

City coffee. Nikki rolled her eyes. "I promised my aunt that while I might become a food snob, I'd *never* be a coffee snob."

Kevin just grinned at her. "Okay, crazy lady."

By the time she'd finished the dishes, Kevin had made the coffee, poured mugs for everyone, and come back to help with the pies. She dried her hands on a tea towel and turned around, feeling a little pulse of pleasure when she saw him setting out dessert plates on the kitchen table. He looked so domestic and sweet, bent over the little willow-pattern dishes Rosemary's mother had loved to collect, that she nearly did something foolish, like cross the room in one step and plant a big, smacking kiss on his lips. Instead, she pressed her palms into the sink behind her, leaned against them, and kept herself as distant from him as possible. Not far enough. This kitchen was too small for the two of them. "Why don't we take the plates into the dining room and serve out there?" she suggested.

"Yeah, I think that's best," Kevin agreed, stacking the plates again. "As I was putting these down, I was thinking, this is extra work."

"We can't have that." Nikki heard her tone go dry, but she had to shrug it off. *Can't fight your own nature.* "Anyway, this will encourage seconds. I'll bet even Rosemary has a go at each kind of pie."

Nikki followed Kevin into the dining room with the lemon meringue pie before her like a trophy. He held the door for her with gentlemanly courtesy, a smile on his lips which went clear up to his eyes. Nikki felt another moment of pure domestic bliss, which was only heightened by the scene of her friends sitting at the tidied dining room table, the last of the evening's blue dusk spilling through the curtains and glowing amidst their hair as they held their heads close in some quiet tryst.

She glanced back at Kevin before she set the pie atop the table, eliciting gasps and cheers from Stephen and Rosemary. *This is homey,* she thought. *A girl could get used to this.*

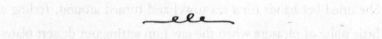

The helpings of pie eaten, the second pours of coffee cooling in their cups—it *had* been noticeably better coffee than her usual, much to Nikki's chagrin—and the darkness settling over Notch Gap Farm were all signs of a successful Thanksgiving feast. Stephen and Kevin eventually adjourned to the living room to watch a little football, after promising to go out and take care of the animals once they were sufficiently rested. Rosemary and Nikki went into the kitchen to finish cleaning up.

"Oh wow, you did a lot after dinner!" Rosemary looked at the dish rack, filled with clean dinnerware, pots, and pans. "I feel so bad! I was just out there talking about horses with Stephen."

"It's nothing," Nikki demurred. "Happy to do it. Dishes are part of my life anyway."

"Well, I'm sure you'd like a break from helping out in kitchens . . ." Rosemary wandered over to the coffeepot, gave it a little shake. "Empty. I'll make more."

"Oh, don't make coffee on my account. I can make us some nice hot toddies instead."

Rosemary put down the pot. "Now you have my attention. Another Nikki special?"

Nikki grinned. "Fetch me the kettle, my dear."

Rosemary handed over the teapot, and Nikki filled it at the tap. Her mind wandered as it so often did in the kitchen, when her hands were busy but the tasks were all autopilot. There was a faint sound of white noise from the living room, which she supposed was the crowd screaming at the football game.

"It's funny to think of Kevin and Stephen watching football," she mused. "They're so different from the usual guys around here.

Sometimes when they do something really male like that, it catches me by surprise."

Rosemary laughed. She was already picking at the edges of the half-eaten lemon meringue, Nikki noticed. "I know! It's terrible, but I feel the same way. And it's been crazy around here all day with Stephen teaching Kevin how to work out in the barn. I *never* expected Stephen to take to farmwork, let alone have him share it with his best friend like it's some kind of new hobby."

"Do you think Kevin likes it? I just don't see him being good with his hands." Nikki hated the way she immediately turned the conversation to Kevin. Why couldn't she have kept Stephen in the mix?

"I think he does." Rosemary pushed the pie away with great resolution. "I mean, he's really unfulfilled at his investment job. To be honest, I think Stephen just tolerates the work, too. I mean, I get it. How much satisfaction could a person really get just moving money around?"

Nikki nodded, pulling down the tea bags. How much, indeed?

As much satisfaction as running a family business a person had lost all passion for?

She had just poured her sweet-smelling brew into mugs when she heard the front door open and close. "Who was that?"

"I have no idea." Rosemary vanished down the hall. In a moment she came back to report that Stephen was asleep on the couch and Kevin was missing. "He must have gone out to check the horses and walk his dog." She sat down. "I *should* go out and help him."

Nikki handed her a steaming mug. "Go out and put the TV on something more relaxing. I'll go babysit Kevin."

"You don't have to do that." Rosemary's eyes were suddenly knowing. "Unless you *want* to . . ."

Nikki shook her head in mock exasperation. "Just let me do this for you," she said. "Try not to read anything into it."

# Chapter 10

## Kevin

Kevin felt a peace in the barn he'd never felt in the city—at least, not that he could remember. With his happy dog wiggling around his legs and the earthy smells of hay and horse filling the cozy space, he felt like he could fully relax. This was the opposite of the city, of that sleek tower in the sky where he'd put his things and tried to make a home.

"You're a good boy," he told Grover, who was busy trying to get in his way as he pulled down the hose. "But watch out, I have work to do. The water buckets need topped off." Grover pushed his nose under a stall wall and licked happily at spilled sweet feed a horse had left behind.

As he pushed the hose through the stall doors and filled each bucket, the horses stayed busy with their own pursuits. He liked the way they ignored him. Horses were so self-sufficient. Give them what they needed and stand back—they'd manage the rest. Right now, most of the horses were eating their hay, although the little miniature horse, Mighty-mite, was busily chewing at his own hind leg like a dog with an itch, and the graceful lady-horse in the back stall was sleeping with one leg resting, her eyes closed, her ears twitching gently as she dreamed. Kevin moved gently around the stalls, afraid if he made a sound he'd wake her.

They all needed a little more hay for the night—"Just toss them a few flakes," Stephen had told him, already speaking in the mysterious language of horsemen—but once they were watered, Kevin decided hay could wait a few minutes. He settled down in the scarred old chair by the feed room door and tipped his head back against the cold stone wall. The horses' breathing and big bodies warmed the surrounding air, and it was peaceful with the sound of their chewing. Kevin thought he'd never heard such a contented sound in the world. After a few moments, even restless Grover came to sit beside him, soaking in the calm atmosphere. Kevin rested his hand on his new dog's head.

*This is the life,* he thought.

If only Kevin was good at quiet time, it would have been a peaceful little moment. Unfortunately, Kevin's city brain wasn't conditioned for sitting calmly, drifting idly on contented tides. His mind wanted to run on overdrive, coming up with every problem he'd ever faced and zipping through every failed solution he'd tried. All the sugar and caffeine he'd just had at dessert probably didn't help.

*Sitting around a barn really is the best version of you, kinda sad.* Kevin's brain insisted. *Since you're a failure at your job. A failure at everything, actually.*

He wished his brain would shut up, but it *was* true—after all, why would his own brain lie to him? These were facts. He *was* a failure at his job. He had lost money for his clients with progressively serious magnitude over the past five years. This year would definitely be his last Christmas bonus; next year would probably be his last chance before he got fired. He was a failed real estate investor, too. What had he accomplished in New York City's hot market? He had bought condominiums in what was proving to be the least popular new construction tower New York City had seen in decades.

He probably wasn't great as a person, in general. He had skipped family Thanksgiving without receiving so much as a single reproachful text from his mother. And he hadn't been in love with anyone since high school.

Not to mention, no one had been in love with him.

He *had* to start over in Catoctin Creek, because there wasn't a single thing back in New York City for him to return to. No one to miss him. No clients to call him. No home to welcome him. Just failure, repeated over and over again in every measure which counted.

The sounds of the barn carried on around him. The horses rustled their hay. One of them snorted loudly. Another one seemed to react and banged one hoof against a wooden wall with a deep, hollow *thump*. Grover tipped his head up against Kevin's hand, pink tongue licking at his fingertips. None of the animals thought Kevin was a failure, and there was a lot to be said for that kind of silent support. He closed his eyes and sighed.

The main barn door slid open slightly, squeaking on its runners.

Kevin opened his eyes. "I wasn't sleeping," he said, expecting Stephen or Rosemary.

Nikki stepped through the doorway, and his heart lurched. He sat bolt upright. Grover turned in an excited circle.

She held up two steel mugs, steam escaping from their lids. "I thought you might want this to warm up." She looked around the low-ceilinged barn. "But it's actually kind of warm in here."

"It's the horses, Rosemary says. And all the loose hay covering the floorboards overhead." Kevin stood up and took the mug she offered him. Grover craned his neck, sniffing eagerly at their elbows. "It's nice down here. I was just listening to them chew, petting my dog a little."

*And counting my failures.*

"It really is nice. Too bad there's only one chair," she said, flashing him a heart-stealing grin.

"Please, sit down!" Kevin gestured gallantly to the chair.

"Ah, I'm just joking with you. I'm used to being on my feet all day, remember?" Nikki took a sip from her mug and her eyes widened slightly. "Mmm, that's strong, just the way I like it. Try yours and tell me what you think."

Kevin lifted the mug to his lips and was surprised to smell alcohol in the steam. "What is this?"

"It's a hot toddy. Special Thanksgiving edition, with cranberry vodka."

He took an enthusiastic sip. Warmth spread through him instantly, coating his tongue in a sweet-tart sensation of good feeling. "Wow! You are full of good surprises, Nikki. Did anyone ever tell you that? And—" he took another sip—"cranberry vodka? I've never heard of such a thing."

"Oh, that." She gave him a sidelong glance. "I made that myself."

Kevin was floored. "You know, you're right about needing your own fine-dining restaurant. You're really too good for the Blue

Plate. Maybe for Catoctin Creek."

She flicked her gaze away, and he immediately realized his mistake. "No. That came out wrong. I just meant—"

"It's fine," she said shortly. "Really. Anyone can make flavored vodka. It's not really that big of an accomplishment."

It wasn't the work, he wanted to tell her. It was the *idea.* She had all these incredible ideas. She was an expert in flavor profiles; she could easily pair up ingredients to complement and clash with one another in just the right ways. Kevin opened his mouth to explain it, but the words caught in his throat and he tipped back the mug again to cover up his silence.

Something about Nikki made it hard for his usual Nice Guy chatter to come spieling from his lips. Instead, she rendered him silent.

Nikki wandered past him and glanced into the nearest stall. "They need a little hay," she observed. "I'll help you throw some. Then, how about a little walk? I'm feeling all of that dinner."

"I'm feeling that third piece of pie," Kevin agreed, thankful for something easy to talk about again. He put down his mug on the chair and pulled the barn wheelbarrow out of a nearby corner. It was already stacked with hay bales from the supply in the upper barn.

Throwing hay was ticklish work; dust went up his nose and seeds clung to his fleece jacket. Kevin was soon covered with golden bits of hay, but Nikki held the square flakes away from her body, keeping her clothes mostly clean. He leaned over the wall of the pretty lady-horse in the back stall who had been sleeping earlier, giving her a rub on the nose, and she wriggled her lips on his wrist like a caress in return. Nikki came around the corner, a flake of hay balanced on her hand like a tray, and saw him laughing.

"What are you doing, you kook?" she demanded, a grin on her face.

"Just letting this lady-horse tickle me," Kevin admitted.

Nikki pushed the hose in the next stall and let it loose. "Lady-horse," she called over the roar of water. "Are you kidding me?"

Kevin shrugged. He couldn't remember what the horse's name was. Eight horses, all with their own names and personalities, was a lot for a newbie like him to take in. She was a horse, she was a lady, it was good enough for now.

He'd figure this all out eventually, he decided. Because he suddenly knew what he was going to do with his life in Catoctin Creek. He was going to work with horses. They were stunning, powerful animals who existed on grass and clean water, who exuded peace and solemnity; he felt he could learn a lot from horses.

Plus, anything he could do in a barn was better than pushing other people's money around. And that was really saying something, considering some of the things that happened in barns.

<hr>

The cold stars were gleaming over the farmhouse when they finally flipped out the barn lights and pulled the door closed behind them. Kevin had Grover at his side; he'd found an old leather collar in the feed room and fastened a lead-rope to it for a leash. "Ready for our walk?" he asked Nikki.

The dog danced around him, clearly aware of the word *walk*.

Nikki gestured at the sloping hill next to the barn. "Let's go up to the farm road. Have you been up the hill yet?"

"Just to bring the horses in from the pasture," Kevin said. There was a gravel driveway which wound behind the house and past the doors of the bank barn's big upper story, where the feed, hay, and ancient tractor were kept in shadowy splendor. The pasture gate was just across from the barn, but the driveway tracked on northward, finally disappearing into a clutch of pine trees growing along a steep slope.

"Oh, it's nice. The pastures on that side of the farm are all overgrown, and there's an old gate that leads into Long Pond. It comes out behind the Kelbaughs' house and barn. Come on, I'll show you."

She didn't have to ask twice. Even though the night was growing colder by the minute, Kevin scrambled up the hillside after Nikki, Grover leaping at his side.

Once they were on the gravel road, the starlight seemed to pick out their path ahead of them. Here and there round, creamy stones glimmered in the dim light; when he asked what they were, Nikki said they were just the local stone. She gave him a sideways look when he suggested they must have a name. "You know what all the stones in New York are, Kevin?"

"Well, sure," he said. "For one, New York's built on Manhattan schist."

"*Schist.*" She laughed. "Are you kidding me? I didn't expect an answer to that."

"I know a lot of pointless things," he assured her. "I could set you up with trivia answers for life."

"And yet you called that nice mare a *lady horse.*"

"Mare! That's the word. I swear the cranberry vodka knocked it right out of my head." Although he'd been calling her lady-horse before Nikki had ever arrived in the barn. Not important. "Someday I'm going to do something useful with all the pointless knowledge I carry with me every day."

"Oh, are you?" Nikki nudged him gently with her elbow. "Care to tell me what? Because I've been making a list of potential career paths for you in Catoctin Creek, and none of them include Trivia Captain."

He glanced over at her, taken aback. "You've made me a *list?*"

Her sassy smile faltered ever so slightly. "Well . . . yeah. I knew you were going to stick around, Rosemary said so, and I like to make plans so . . . I started working on an action plan for you. I figured they're not really your thing."

Kevin didn't know whether to laugh at his good luck or cry at her perception of him. She was right. Plans *weren't* his thing. It wasn't exactly a good look—not to board directors, not to clients, and not to high-energy country diner managers, either. "Well, thanks," he said eventually. He lifted his mug and sipped the cooling remnants of his toddy, hoping the alcohol would just take over, do his conversing for him.

Naturally, it didn't.

But the silence was companionable enough, and Kevin felt unusually peaceful as he walked through the night with Nikki at his side. The moon rose over the tree-lined hills to the east, a big golden doubloon of a moon, with a laughing face and an uncannily knowing air, and they watched it lift above the jagged edges of the leafless trees, shrinking as it climbed. Grover threw himself down on the dry grass along the road and chewed at a stick.

"A hunter's moon," Kevin said. "Isn't that what they call it, a full moon in fall?"

"That's October," Nikki corrected him. "This is a beaver moon."

Kevin couldn't help his snort of laughter. Nikki gave him a punch in the arm. "Ow, hey!"

"You deserved that," she told him, but she was laughing, too. "Be a grown-up, why don't you!"

"Not a chance. Never."

"Okay, Peter Pan," she said with a sigh. "I guess you're so full of sugar, there's no point in asking you to behave yourself." Her gaze wandered back over the countryside below them. Long Pond was sparkling with light, its still waters reflecting back the golden moon.

The moonlight glinted on her hair, a few long curls brushing against her cheeks. He was overcome with an urge to put his hands in it, feel those luscious coils as he had the night before, and suddenly he did it, reaching out before he quite knew what he was doing. He filled both hands with Nikki's wonderful, wonderful hair as she turned her head, her eyes wide and surprised.

Before she could do something Nikki-like, pull away or ask what he was doing or make a sarcastic joke, he leaned in and placed a soft, questioning kiss on her half-opened lips.

# Chapter 11

# Nikki

Nikki's first thought was, *Finally.*

Her second thought was, *What took him so long?*

Her third thought was, *Oh, no.*

Her attraction to Kevin had been instant: like a bolt of lightning the moment they'd met. But she really wasn't so sure they were . . . what's the word . . . *compatible*. The more she'd gotten to know him, the more she suspected they weren't compatible at all, not really. She was a person who made plans and took responsibility. He was a person who ran away to stay rent free at his friend's house to escape reality. To *find himself.*

That phrase really bugged her, in truth. Nikki had an idea people put too much stock into *finding themselves.* Reality was reality. A spiritual journey would not change simple facts of one's life. She couldn't go off to find herself and suddenly find she was running a successful white-tablecloth restaurant in the Schubert place.

No, it was much better to face facts and deal with them in a rational fashion.

Nikki couldn't help her annoyance with Kevin over his decision to run away from New York life . . . although she suspected a more normal reaction would be simple happiness in his staying. To accept he wasn't perfect and yet accept she was still attracted to him, still loved to be in his company, still wanted to spend time with him.

How could she just forget that he'd left her, though? He'd led her on, flirted with her, made her think they had something, and then he'd vanished.

And to think he'd chosen *now* to kiss her, after all of these months, right when he was starting to look like the sort of guy she could never be with . . . well, it just felt really *Kevin*, if that made any sense.

Like this guy's timing was permanently off.

Still, the romance of the moonrise, the light glimmering on Long Pond, the cheeky nip in the air, the mugs filled with strong liquor . . . she could see where her rush of desire came from.

Okay, *fine*. This was a good night for a kiss.

But that was all it was. A little moonlit magic; not a promise, not a harbinger of something bigger and real. He probably knew that already. He was probably way ahead of her. These city guys always had flings, right? Look at how Stephen had behaved before he and Rosemary had gotten together properly. Kissing her, then dragging around some ex-girlfriend, then back to Rosemary . . . yeah, city guys were up to no good. This was a fact.

Kevin was watching her, she realized, waiting for a response and looking a little freaked out as none came. Nikki checked herself. "That was nice," she told him, thinking he definitely deserved an

A for Effort. As far as nice, soft, sweet first kisses went, he came prepared to play. "Thank you."

Kevin grimaced. "Thank you?"

"What would you like me to say? *Kevin, run away with me?* Honestly," Nikki went on, warming to her subject, "what *is* the right thing to say after a kiss? Is there a social guide? I feel like as a big experienced New Yorker, you would know."

"The right thing is to kiss again," Kevin suggested. "No words necessary."

"Well, the *thank you* stands. I think it was nice and thanks for the effort. It was a good kiss."

Kevin, she could tell, was not doing well with this frank line of discussion. He was turning a little red—at least, she thought he was. The moonlight was not helpful for discerning colors. *Might as well put him out of his misery,* she thought.

"Okay, okay," she sighed, grabbing him by the collar. "Let's kiss again."

*❧*

Nikki woke up the next morning with her usual surge of energy. Mornings were her time to shine: she had ideas, she had lists to make, she had supplies to buy, she had flavors to discover. She enjoyed leaping out of bed and hopping down from her loft bed, landing just steps from her coffeemaker and a good, caffeinated start to her day.

So she was a little disconcerted to realize she had woken not in her own comfortable bed with its low ceiling and tiny window at the foot, but in one of Rosemary's guest bedrooms—to be precise, the front guest bedroom, with its swirling rose wallpaper peeling in the corners, and the four-poster bed where several Brunners had died while all of Catoctin Creek society gathered in the rooms downstairs to mourn their passing. A different mattress was on the bed now, of course.

Nikki blinked at the ceiling and tried to figure out why she was in the rose room. No one ever slept here. Too formal, and a little too much reputation in local circles as the room where nineteenth-century Brunners drew their last breaths. She usually slept in the back bedroom when she stayed over. It was more comfortable, and darker, with a view over the pasture slope and Notch Gap. Nikki tended to sleep late back there. The pillows were extremely deep and feathery. And no one, to their knowledge, had ever died in there.

*Oh,* she remembered. Kevin. He was staying in her usual room. She rolled her eyes and sighed as the night before came back to her in a wave of pretty memories.

The hot toddies, the long walk together, the moonlit kisses, the subsequent return to a freshly revived Stephen and Rosemary. There had been too much wine flowing for Nikki to drive home, and she'd been happy she'd thought to pack an overnight bag, just in case. She glanced at it now, on top of the Sheraton dresser between the two windows. *Nice work, Nikki.*

Well, she reflected, while she would have preferred to have woken up in her own little apartment, with her own bathroom and her coffeemaker, there *was* something to be said for Stephen's fancy New York coffee. She hated to think she might become a coffee snob, but the potential definitely existed.

Nikki sat up and pushed back the covers, feeling a definite chill in the air through her plaid flannel pajamas. The rose room's windows faced east, and a golden sunrise was peering through the frost-covered windows. "Yikes. It's way too early."

She shuffled across the uneven floorboards in her thick socks and wiped the steam from one window, peering through a patch of glass which had remained frost free. The morning was a soft gold-and-gray, sunlight creeping over the treetops as a ground fog clung stubbornly to the grassy lawn and wound itself through the black tree trunks of the front wood. "Nice view, though."

She heard creaking in the hallway, and listened as the footsteps went past her door and down the stairs. A few moments passed, then the front door opened and closed, and she saw Rosemary heading out to the barn, a red wool cap pulled over her wavy dark hair, her heavy black coat buttoned to her chin.

"Guess it's pretty cold, then," Nikki murmured. She pulled a black cable-knit sweater out of her overnight bag, pairing it with charcoal fleece leggings and thick woolen socks. Her coat was downstairs. If she needed anything else between breakfast in the kitchen and the drive back to her apartment, well, then she'd just have to freeze.

The kitchen was dark and didn't smell of coffee, to her disappointment. She supposed Stephen must be sleeping in and Kevin . . . well, Kevin *definitely* seemed like an over sleeper and he probably wouldn't wake for hours, sequestered in that dark bedroom. She didn't want to use the noisy coffee grinder while everyone slept, so she put the kettle on the stove and pulled a half-eaten pumpkin pie within easy reach while she waited for the water to boil. Her neck ached, and she pressed her free hand against it, trying to massage away the effects of sleeping in a new position.

Then she thought about Kevin sleeping on her pillows, and the intimate picture this painted was surprisingly sweet.

That kiss last night—well, *all* of those kisses, because they'd stood out on the moonlit farm drive and kissed for a solid ten minutes, until Kevin suddenly realized he couldn't feel his toes anymore and she'd dragged him back to the barn to put his dog to bed, although he had argued he didn't need his toes for kissing, or really anything, toes were overrated and he was sure he could get by without them—but that *first* kiss especially, so gentle and sweet, had stirred up all the feelings Kevin had first awoken in her when he'd arrived in Catoctin Creek with Stephen all of those months ago. She'd seen him and stopped in her tracks immediately; something inside of her had whispered, *"Oh, there you are,"* and while she'd never been able to explain that inner voice, she couldn't shake the memory of it, either.

Nikki knew she had to face facts: Kevin *was* someone to her, whether or not she was sure they were emotionally incompatible. He mattered to her. And he was here now, staying in her own town. Which meant she had to do whatever she could to help them move forward, right?

Even forgive him for leaving her without a word?

The kettle whistled; Nikki jumped and hustled to pull it from the lit burner, amazed her thoughts had been so distant she hadn't even noticed the rattle of boiling water.

Was this the kind of thing Kevin was going to just keep on doing to her?

She had settled back down with a mug of tea and the plate of pumpkin pie when Stephen came downstairs, bleary-eyed and momentarily surprised to see his wife's best friend seated at the kitchen table. "God," he said, staring at her from the doorway. "I forgot you were here and the kitchen's so dark, I thought there was a stranger at the table."

"Sorry," she laughed. "Just Nikki, not a mysterious stranger. I'll be out of your hair shortly. Just needed some caffeine to get the day going."

"You need something stronger than tea. I'll make coffee. There's no hurry, believe me. No one has any plans on the day after Thanksgiving, right?"

"Just the shoppers. You're telling me Rosemary isn't dragging you down to the mall for some Black Friday bargains?"

They eyeballed each other and then cracked up at the same time. Rosemary, in a crowd of people on purpose! The very idea was ridiculous.

"It is a little odd to have a Friday off, though," Nikki admitted. "My aunt never opened the Blue Plate on Black Friday, and I've just kept up the tradition. It lets the girls go shopping, if that's what they want."

"That's nice of you. And of her."

"Well, it was probably because no one was in town for breakfast. They were all in line down at the Francis Scott Key Mall," Nikki admitted. "My aunt was *very* savvy."

Stephen shook beans into the coffee grinder. "That's where you get it, then."

She couldn't answer right away; he hit the button and the rattle of the grinder took over the little kitchen for a moment. When it stopped, they both heard a creaking overhead.

"Welp, that woke up Kevin." He did not sound regretful.

"Do you two have plans for the day?"

"None. I guess we'll putz around the farm, maybe move some hay around or something."

"Sounds like fun," Nikki said absently. She was thinking about the action plan she'd written for Kevin. They needed to go over it together. She wanted to get him moving on it as soon as possible, or he'd just procrastinate. Wait for the universe to provide or some other city-bred nonsense. "Maybe we can have lunch together. I need to talk to him."

Stephen hit the button on the coffeemaker and turned around to face her, his expression highly amused. "You want a nice private lunch with Kevin?"

"Don't read anything into it! I've been writing him an action plan. He needs help figuring out what he's going to do next. We can go over it together. I think there are some really solid ideas . . . we can use his experience in the financial field to find something comparable here."

Stephen pulled a fork out of the drawer and sat down across from her, intent on helping her pick at the pumpkin pie. "You know," he said after a moment, "I'm not sure Kevin wants to go back to finance. I think he wants to try something new."

Nikki couldn't keep the skepticism from her face. "That's fine in theory. But really, what else has he done?"

"I mean, he wants to try something *really* new. That's why I've been teaching him his way around the horses. He's interested in farm work, like *manual* work." Stephen shrugged. "He says he wants to learn to work with his hands."

"Forgive me, but I don't really see Kevin being a guy who works with his hands."

"Well, I guess we'll have to see."

Stephen's lackadaisical attitude towards his friend's future annoyed Nikki. She put down her fork with a clatter. "We can't just sit around and see what happens. If he's going to be successful, he needs to have a plan that makes sense. You don't get anywhere in life by just letting your emotions take over. You're a businessman, you know that!"

Stephen regarded her with surprise, and she knew her quick temper had made things weird between them. She was really Rosemary's friend, not his, and that meant strong emotions didn't have a place at the table.

"Sorry," she said. "I didn't mean to get so . . . excited."

He held up his hands: *no worries.* "Nikki, I see what you're saying, but if I didn't let my emotions take over, I would have plowed right over Long Pond and we'd be building fifty custom homes on those fields. And neither you nor Rosemary would have ever forgiven me . . . or Kevin."

She nodded, conceding the point. "No, you're right. I didn't—I didn't mean it like that. I just want Kevin to think really clearly about what comes next."

She froze as Kevin's voice came merrily down the hall. She hadn't even heard him on the stairs, that sneaky little man! "You're right, Nikki, I promise to think clearly!"

Stephen winced and scooped up another piece of pie. "Crazy acoustics in that hallway."

# Chapter 12

# Kevin

K evin had slept like a top. There's nothing like a moonlit walk and a few good kisses to put a man in a good mood, and there's nothing like a fourth helping of pie after a heaping Thanksgiving dinner to put a man to sleep. The farm labor he'd been doing all day was just the icing on the cake.

He opened his eyes as the coffee grinder screeched beneath the bedroom floorboards, and his first thought was of Nikki.

*We had such a good time last night,* he thought triumphantly. He'd really gotten somewhere with her last night! That old beaver moon, it had been on his side. And then she'd stayed at the farm overnight, sleeping just across the hall from him! For a few minutes after he'd pulled the quilt to his chin, he'd thought of her, so close and yet so far away, but then his eyes had closed and he'd conked out for the next nine hours.

Now, though, he was refreshed and ready to come back at her, full throttle. He'd been as quiet as he could be, coming down the stairs, hoping to hear what she was planning on doing today. Whatever her plans were, he wanted to cancel them. He wanted her all to himself. He heard Nikki talking and paused at the foot of the stairs, standing in the front foyer where the hallway acoustics were at their most effective.

Nikki said, "I just want Kevin to think really clearly about what comes next."

He grinned. Oh, he was thinking about what comes next, all right! He did a little skip as he started down the hallway. "You're right, Nikki, I promise to think clearly!"

"Oh my God," Nikki said as he appeared in the doorway. "You came out of nowhere."

"I did! Good morning, good folk," Kevin announced expansively. He took a mug from the cabinet and poured himself a cup of coffee. "This smells delicious. Totally worth being woken up, when this is waiting for me."

"You were going to sleep all day otherwise," Stephen said wisely.

"So you're worried about me?" Kevin asked Nikki, who was avoiding his gaze. He sat down between the two of them and picked up a fork.

"How much did you hear?" Nikki asked, sounding miserable.

The truth was, not much. Just enough to know she had a plan for him and she was going to expect him to follow it. "I heard you caring about what happens to me," he told her. He took a bite. "Mmm! This is really good pie. Even better for breakfast."

"Rosemary made it."

"Right, I remember. Of course, *you* made the lemon meringue. Also really good. Is there any of that?"

Stephen gestured to the fridge. Kevin went to get it himself, partially as good will towards Nikki, partially because the fluffy texture of the meringue seemed particularly suited for breakfast.

Plus, meringue was eggs. Basically, it was an egg-white omelette with some nice lemon for a Vitamin C kick. The perfect way to start the day.

"I'm not actually going to stick around," Nikki was saying as he sat down with the pie in front of him. "Sorry. I just remembered a whole stack of paperwork I have to get through at home."

"Paperwork?"

"Accounting stuff." She shrugged. "You know how it is when you run your own business. Never off the clock."

"You need an accountant," Kevin suggested. "To give you more time to pursue your own interests."

"Interests? Like what?" Nikki almost, but not quite, snorted.

Kevin was beginning to feel sorry for her. The woman had no idea how to have fun. "Your *cooking?* Does that ring any bells? This amazing pie I'm eating did not bake itself. This flavor is incredible, by the way."

"I have plenty of time to cook," Nikki insisted. "I have a commercial kitchen at my disposal. And a very nice kitchen in my apartment, too."

"Good," Kevin said, deciding to be a little cheeky. "Cook me dinner tonight."

*"What?"* She had just enough outrage in her voice to sound adorable.

Kevin was feeling lucky, so he chucked her under the chin gently, something which he suspected might get him cuffed over the head if he timed it badly. Happily, her hands stayed in her lap. "You heard me, kid. Cook me a steak. With something exotic on the side. Black-pepper-crusted potato medallions or seaweed-relish empanadas or whatever pops into your head. I swear I'll eat it. Anything you make is bound to be amazing."

"*Seaweed relish—*"

"I was just putting random words together. You're the cook, you know best." Kevin threw back a bite of lemon meringue pie and watched her silently wrestle with how to take his words. He liked his chances at getting a meal out of her. And by meal, he meant date, and by date, he meant getting to know her properly alone, in her own home, where she would be comfortable enough to open up . . . and maybe not be so sarcastic and bossy all the time. Last night, she'd showed him two things: that she cared, and that she didn't want him to know it. He could work with both revelations. "I'll do some work around here and up at the brick house today, and I'll see you tonight. How's seven?"

Nikki shrugged as if she couldn't care less, but he could see the gleam in her eye when she answered, "Fine, you've yourself a dinner. I'll see you at seven." She pushed up from the table. "Guess I'll go to Trout's and see what the steak looks like today."

Kevin could barely keep himself from rubbing his hands together. He grinned at Stephen, who was regarding him with quiet surprise from across the table.

"You really got her to agree to dinner at her place? Just like that." Stephen shook his head. "Respect, my friend."

"It's her time to shine as cook," Kevin replied happily, "and my time to shine as a champion eater of good food. I can't wait to see what she comes up with for dinner."

"Is that all you can't wait for?"

"Well, she's very good at dessert . . ." Their eyes met, and they laughed.

Nikki's stocking feet had scarcely finished running up the stairs when the front door opened and closed again.

"What's the joke?" Rosemary asked, bringing a whiff of manure and cold air into the kitchen. She unwound her scarf as she sat at the table. "God, it's cold out there. Kevin, your dog is just fine, thank you for asking."

Kevin realized he'd completely forgotten he had a dog. Granted, he was only two days into this, but it was still a pretty serious oversight. "Crap, I'm so sorry. Did he do anything? Does he need anything? I'll go out right now." He was so embarrassed. His second morning as a dog-dad, and he'd already forgotten Grover existed.

"Sit down, he's fine. I gave him some of his kibble and let him sniff around the barnyard. He can't get around that no-climb wire. I bought it to keep dogs out, but it's working quite well to keep this one in." Rosemary shrugged out of her coat and let it slip to the floor. "Push that pie a little closer, will you?"

Stephen got her a cup of coffee and a fork while Kevin nudged the pie to the center of the table. "Thanks for taking care of him," he said gratefully. "It won't happen again."

"I know it won't, but it's really okay. If you stick an animal in the barn, I'll take care of it." Rosemary put a bite of pie in her mouth. *"Mmm.* Where's Nikki? She's not still in bed, is she?"

"Getting her things to go home," Stephen told her. "This one got her all worked up about making him dinner, so she has to go study her cookbooks and impress him."

Rosemary turned wide eyes onto Kevin. "You have a *date?*"

"That's right." He smiled, enjoying this.

"With Nikki," she confirmed.

"Correct."

Rosemary regarded him for a moment. Then she picked up her coffee mug and swirled it, looking into the dark depths. "Don't mess this up," she said finally. "I mean it."

Rosemary was a gentle soul, and Kevin had always adored her, but now her tone gave him a chill.

Kevin drove up to the brick house a few hours later, his bags in the back of his rental car, his dog panting out the sliver of window he'd opened, and a hopeful smile on his face.

The misty November morning had turned into a pretty winter's day. The fog had lifted, and a crisp blue sky overhead, shot through with icy feathers of cirrus clouds, made the perfect contrast against the black-and-brown branches of the bare woods. A flock of crows burst out of the trees when he paused at the end of Stephen's driveway to check the mailbox, shattering the peaceful morning with their raucous caws.

He pulled out a handful of mailers and dropped them on the passenger seat, thinking it was funny that rural Maryland mailboxes got stuffed with the same glossy junk as New York City postal boxes. Political mailers, coupons for oil changes—wait, here was one for a tree service and stump removal. He didn't get *that* in Queens. But no Chinese restaurant menus. He wondered how far away the closest Chinese place was, feeling a sudden pang of longing for some good cashew chicken. As for ramen, or drunken noodles, or Korean barbecue? It would probably be awhile before he tasted any of it.

Kevin sighed. Well, at least he had Nikki's cooking to look forward to. He wondered if she had any Chinese recipes in her repertoire, or knew her way around an Asian supermarket. There was probably one down in Frederick . . . Kevin grinned to himself. The county seat was regarded around here as the answer to everything, from jobs to dinners that didn't come with a side of fries, and he was already making the same assumptions all the locals did.

How long did it take to become a local in a place like this?

The driveway to the brick house was narrow and winding, the surface tarred in heavy black asphalt. The forest had grown up tightly around the driveway, and he drove slowly around the turns; Stephen had warned him these woods were full of deer who loved to spring out of the brush like booby traps, taking out unwary drivers. Then the trees ended very suddenly, cut away in a big circle around the little brick ranch house, which perched on its hilltop like a flattened toad. Its broad, staring windows reflected the yellow November sunlight. Grover gazed out the window, his tail wagging gently, evidently transfixed with his new home.

"You're an ugly house, but you'll do," Kevin said, parking the car out front. "Grover, *please* don't pee on the carpets."

He grabbed his bag, hopped out of the car, and unlocked the front door. Grover stayed close to his heels as he pushed inside.

A chilly, damp-smelling living room greeted him. "Oh, that's super."

Once he'd turned up the thermostat, Kevin threw his bag onto the bed in the master bedroom, which had a queen-sized bed covered with a patchwork quilt, a few sticks of farmhouse-style furniture, and a beige carpet which had seen better days. Grover busily sniffed every corner and leg of furniture. Kevin eyeballed him, hoping the dog would prove to be housebroken. So far, so good. No legs were being lifted, but that carpet would probably not show too much evidence of any crimes.

Well, he had some serious cleaning to accomplish. Dust coated every surface, and Grover was already sneezing. Kevin found some cleaning supplies in the hall closet and in the living room. He wasn't much of a maid, so he started with a dust-rag, wiping clean the living room's rather barren bookshelf. Stephen had gone on several online shopping binges while he had been living up here alone, trying to get over Rosemary with the power of credit cards and home delivery. While they'd been split up, he'd bought a few pieces of decor, furniture and knick-knacks. The improvement was significant, even if there were still a lot of bare spots on the walls and in corners. Kevin remembered the old plaid couch which had leaned against one wall and the mustard-colored, macrame *thing* that had once hung in the breakfast nook. Thankfully, those were gone now, replaced with a nice blue sofa and some black-and-white prints of snow-covered forests.

Those prints would look like photos taken just outside, Kevin reflected, if by some chance Catoctin Creek enjoyed a heavy snowfall.

"Now that would be nice," he told Grover, who was snuffling away with his head shoved under the couch. "Would you like snow?"

Grover's plume of a tail waved gently, probably more about whatever abandoned crumbs he'd found under the couch than the prospect of snow, but Kevin still took it as a *yes*.

He glanced out the front window, a big staring section of plate glass. The dull winter grass sloped down to the thicket of forest blocking the house from the road. He spotted a little movement in the trees and squinted until he could focus on the gray-brown shape of a deer picking its way along the edge of the wood. Suddenly, there were three—no, five—no, *six* deer moving delicately along the lawn's border, nibbling at the underbrush and nosing in the grass.

"Well, look at that," Kevin whispered, half-afraid he'd startle them if he moved, even at this distance. "My own little herd of deer."

Kevin slipped his hand into his pocket and pulled out his phone. He took a quick picture and sent it to Nikki. *Aren't they cute?*

The deer looked up as one, staring into the distance beyond the house, and then dashed back into the woods.

"Glad I caught them," Kevin told Grover, who had emerged from beneath the sofa and was now nosing around the front door. The dog looked up at him hopefully. "Outside? Not this way, son. I think you can go out back if you need a little outside time. There's a fenced yard. At least, I think it's fenced. Let's check."

He peered out the sliding glass door, which looked over the big backyard. For a moment, the view kept him arrested, forgetting he was checking for fencing. The full majesty of Notch Gap and the foothills leading up to the mountains spread out before him, the curving ridge so close he thought he could reach out and touch the twin peaks. The woods which covered the mountains actually started at the foot of the brick house's property.

The view was what had kept Stephen up here even before he'd met Rosemary, and no doubt it was what had captivated Stephen's father before him. It enchanted Kevin, too. He sighed and leaned against the chilly glass, taking it all in. The big, sloping backyard with its scattering of bare oaks and furry pines was dwarfed by the ancient, rounded peaks of the Catoctin Mountains.

Kevin loved the toothless old-man beauty of the Appalachians. The twin heights on either side of Notch Gap had just a few jagged rocks spearing upwards. They'd be invisible in summer, but now they peeked through the leafless trees.

"This will be good," Kevin said, sitting down at the kitchen table so he could enjoy the view a little longer. "I'll stay right here, figure out what's next, and enjoy the seasons." How many seasons? He really wasn't prepared to say. Kevin had no plan, and that was just the way he liked it.

His phone buzzed in his pocket. A text from Nikki!

*Don't let Grover see them.*

"Oh right, the fence! Sorry, Grover. My brain is like jelly." He hopped back up and took a good look around the perimeter of the backyard. There was a split-rail fence with wire set against it. Perfect for a dog.

"All clear, buddy!" he told Grover, who came padding over to join him. "You can enjoy the yard. Listen, can you be a good boy while I go to see Miss Nikki later on?" He rubbed the dog's soft ears, thinking of the evening ahead. He was hopeful he'd get the perfect date-night with Nikki: dinner, a lot of suggestive conversation, and maybe more.

# Chapter 13

# Nikki

*D*inner, Nikki was thinking urgently, *I need a plan for dinner.*

She had gone right home and flipped through the pages of six issues of *Saveur* and three of *Bon Appetit* before she found the menu she wanted to serve. Steak wasn't the nicest thing to cook in a one-room apartment, but a porterhouse seared in a cast iron skillet jumped off the page when she saw it, and as long as Kevin didn't mind opening the windows for a few minutes to let the smoke out, the pay-off would be delicious.

Of course, that was the other problem with steak: it had to be cooked while dinner guests were already prepared to sit and eat, because no one wanted a rare steak which had been sitting around waiting to be served.

Not exactly the best date night food, Nikki had thought more than once as she'd flipped pages, but of course Kevin probably had no idea these things needed to be planned carefully. He'd already proven he wasn't a planner. She rolled her eyes and got into her car, a list of ingredients shoved into her purse.

Naturally, Trout's Market didn't have an aged porterhouse, so she'd had to drive down to her favorite meat market in Frederick, and then drive another twenty minutes to a specialty market where she knew she could buy watercress for a salad—he'd made that crack about seaweed and she couldn't resist.

By the time she'd gotten home, stressed by holiday shopping traffic, she'd been ready for a nap . . . but now she needed to chop anchovies, garlic, and rosemary to season the steak with, and then she'd have to make the salad. Plus, of course, he'd want dessert. Kevin's sweet tooth had not gone unnoticed—that man could put away some pie!

She checked her recipes again, marking times on a notepad so she had a solid plan. The apricot tart she'd chosen supposedly needed four hours to cool to room temperature, and she'd need an hour to bake it, so if she started that right now, they'd eat dessert at eight o'clock. That should do the trick.

Nikki put on some jazz from the local college station and started chopping, feeling like everything was fine now that she had a plan. Dinner would be a snap.

The oven alarm was pinging repeatedly when Nikki sat up, dazed, from the sofa and looked around. *What's that sound?*

She sniffed the air, which smelled of rich, caramelizing sugar, and remembered the evening's plan with a speed that had her racing to the oven.

"Out you go," she told the tarts, pulling the pan out so quickly she scarcely had the oven mitts on. "No burning for you, not allowed!"

She took a deep breath once the tarts were saved. She couldn't believe she'd fallen asleep! It was so unlike her. Of course, the past few days had been nonstop cooking, working, and socializing, and she supposed the added stress of shopping around Black Friday bargain-hunters hadn't done her any favors. But now . . . time for a new action plan. She wouldn't write this one down. She'd just speak it into existence.

"Shower," Nikki said aloud. "Blow-dry hair, get dressed, tidy up apartment, make salad, open wine, open door to Kevin." She had two hours. That was plenty of time. *Plenty.*

Kevin's knock came at six forty-nine, a fact which a very startled Nikki confirmed by glancing at the oven clock. She heaved a sigh of exasperation. Hadn't he ever heard of being fashionably late? Here she was, still standing over the counter constructing the watercress-pistachio salad. Granted, this procedure was not complicated, but she hadn't planned on welcoming Kevin with a knife in one hand and a dirty apron covering her plum-colored tunic dress.

Or—maybe she did? Maybe starting off the evening by startling him with a knife was exactly what he needed? That could be their thing, their couple's inside joke. Knives.

*Maybe not.* She put down the knife and quickly unknotted the apron, tossing it over the back of a chair as she crossed the living room space to the French doors.

The door let in a gust of cold air she hadn't expected. Kevin's nose was pink. "Oh my gosh!" she gasped. "Come in, hurry! This cold isn't messing around."

Kevin stomped his boots on the mat she kept just inside the doors. "It is absolutely *freezing* out there! I was going to be leaning very suavely against the wall with a rose in my teeth, but that plan was out the window as soon as I walked out my front door and realized I'd accidentally moved to the Arctic tundra."

"Oh yeah? Where's this rose?"

He shook off his heavy wool coat and then reached into the breast pocket. "Right here, being kept warm against my heart." He waggled his eyebrows at her.

Nikki groaned and took the rose, which was in fact pretty warm. It was a gracious gesture, if a little over the top, but she was beginning to expect over the top from Kevin. He was cute and funny, but he did everything so jokingly, she wasn't really sure how much of it he meant. He could have pulled this rose stunt with her if they were just friends, too—she had no doubt about that. She opted for a casual response. "Thanks, sailor," she said, shoving it behind one ear, where it toppled dangerously alongside her cheek.

Kevin beamed at her. "That's a pretty color on you."

"It is?" Nikki had never thought of herself as a rose person, but maybe she was wrong. "Thank you. It was really nice of you to bring a rose."

"I also brought wine." He reached into the coat's front pocket and brought out a bottle. "Isn't this coat great? It's like a Mary Poppins coat. You can keep everything in the pockets."

"It's amazing. Here, let me hang it up for you." She put it on one of the free coat hooks near the doors. The apartment had no coat closet, so she had to make to do with the space she had. "There we are, sir. Present me with your ticket when you're ready to leave."

"Perfect. You're the best coat-check girl I've ever seen. But I don't have any cash on me! How can I tip you?"

Nikki turned around and found Kevin was standing right in front of her. She glanced up at his green eyes and felt a sudden pooling of warmth in her center. When she spoke, her voice was throaty. "You'll have to find some other way to make it up to me."

For a moment their eyes lingered on one another, and Nikki felt the air grow charged. Kevin's eyes seemed to darken, until they were the color of a stormy sea, and when Nikki realized she'd actually thought such a think, she blinked herself back to real life. *Let's not get carried away.*

She took the wine to change the subject. "Let's open this while I finish the salad. Come on, I'll give you the tour on the way. That's the living room, and up there is the bedroom, and here's the kitchen. Bathroom is that door. Pretty great, right?"

Kevin looked enchanted with her studio. "This is really nice! I love all the doors and curtains across the front. And it's really convenient having the kitchen along one wall like that! I always think it's silly to have the kitchen in a separate room. You can't talk to anyone, or watch TV, or anything."

"You won't think so in a few minutes," she warned him. "When I put this steak on the skillet, we're going to have to open the windows, and it's what, thirty degrees out there?"

"Something like that. But it's fine. I'm very tough."

"Sure you are. Hey, where's the dog?"

"Asleep on my bed," Kevin laughed. "Stephen's bed? Whatever. Turns out he's very housebroken, to the point where I can't believe he agreed to sleep in the barn on that old horse blanket. I'm not sure his paws have touched the ground since he discovered the furniture."

"That's too funny." Nikki could have guessed the dog was already used to houses. He was too tidy and polite to be a barn dog. "Just always remember to pull up the duvet, or you'll be sleeping in dog hair all night."

"That's good advice."

"I let the humane society know about him, by the way." She smiled sympathetically as Kevin winced. "Like I said before, I don't think you have anything to worry about. They haven't had any reports of a missing dog matching his description. I checked in with Mrs. O'Reilly, and the feed store as well. No one is looking for him."

Kevin's anxious face smoothed into calmer lines. "Thank goodness. Dogs are easy to get attached to, aren't they?"

"The worst," Nikki agreed, although she hadn't had her own dog since the family Labrador had died when she was twelve.

She thought Kevin would settle down on the sofa while she finished cooking, but he followed her into the kitchen. He took over the wine duties from her while she finished the salad, and he didn't even turn green when she explained that *stuff* was watercress. "Huh," was all he said.

"Did you ever have watercress before?"

"I have not. I kinda thought it was made up. I've only heard of it in old English novels."

"Well, tonight's an adventure for you." She topped off their wineglasses.

"That's what I was hoping for."

She smiled, feeling her heart thaw out. After being so coldly angry at him for so many weeks, it was a pleasant change. Having Kevin in her home, laughing at her jokes, ready to eat her food, was every bit as satisfying as she had imagined. Nikki raised her glass in a toast. "To new adventures, Kevin," she said.

He returned the smile as he lifted his own glass, tapping hers. "To new adventures, Kevin."

Aside from nearly freezing to death while the steak was cooking and the smoke was waved out the open windows, dinner was a success. Kevin was gratifyingly wowed by the seared porterhouse, which was bursting with flavor from the chopped anchovy seasoning she'd thrown over the top just after it came out of the pan.

"What do you call this?" He'd asked around a mouthful, sounding delighted as a man could be.

"*Bistecca alla Florentina,*" she told him, adding a little Italian trill to her letters.

"So . . . steak Florentine?" he drawled, sounding almost Texan.

"When you say it like that, it sounds like something gross you'd get in an old steakhouse, smothered in sauce. Be Italian. Everything's better in the mother tongue."

"That's true. I take it you're not a fan of, say, Peter Luger's."

"That's the famous old steakhouse in New York, right? Can't say as I've ever been." Nikki topped off their wine, feeling a little annoyed he'd bring up a fancy New York City restaurant. How could she ever compete with that?

"I could take you there sometime. Do you want to go to New York, have a restaurant tour? A chef like you must want to try some places in the city. We could spend a weekend trying whatever you want."

Nikki leveled her gaze at him. That was actually a really nice offer. And a big commitment, should she take it. A weekend trip was no minor act. "You know, you're not afraid to jump without looking," she remarked.

"And you love that about me," Kevin suggested.

"It makes me nervous. For you, not for me."

"Well, don't let it. I'm very capable. I moved all the way to Maryland by myself."

She was nice enough not to point out he was staying in a friend's house, rent-free. Kevin definitely got by with a little help from his friends. Could she see herself with a guy who had never rowed alone? Nikki shoved down the thought. She was literally sitting on a plan she'd created to help him figure out his life. So who was pushing Kevin along now? She was just as guilty as Stephen and Rosemary. Or rather, she was about to be.

Nikki smiled brightly at him. "Speaking of which . . . do you want to talk about the plan I wrote you? I think I can help you find work and get yourself in order."

"Oh, yes." Kevin put down his knife and fork. His plate, Nikki noted with some satisfaction, looked as if it had been licked clean. Grover couldn't have done a better job. "Can we do that right now? I'm so curious."

"I'll make coffee," Nikki said, getting up. "And then we'll go over your action plan. I think you'll like it."

"The coffee or the plan?"

"Both," she assured him.

Nikki took down the fresh bag of coffee beans she'd bought at the gourmet market and shook them into the grinder she'd picked up, at significant risk to personal life and limb, amid Black Friday crowds at Target. He'd like the coffee, she thought. And he'd *love* the plan she'd written for him. How could he not? She'd thought of everything.

She smiled to herself, thinking of how neat and tidy she could make Kevin's life.

## Chapter 14

# Kevin

K evin leaned back in his chair and put his hands on his stomach. He wouldn't have been surprised if a few buttons simply burst from his shirt, like in a cartoon. He was absolutely stuffed. Nikki had just served him the best dinner he'd ever had in his life, hands down. Those old boys at Peter Luger Steakhouse back in the city had *nothing* on Nikki's delicious steak Florentine, and the watercress-pistachio salad was a light, delicious accompaniment which put that famous creamed spinach of theirs to shame. He honestly couldn't believe she'd done all this cooking in this tiny little studio, with just a few hours to plan and shop.

One thing was for sure: Nikki definitely deserved better than the Blue Plate Diner. If the only thing standing between her and her dream of cooking interesting food for interesting people was a lack of confidence in her own powers, he thought he could set her on the right track. Nikki didn't have to wait for Catoctin Creek to catch up to her. She just had to cook her incredible food, and the people would come to Catoctin Creek for her. Why couldn't she see that?

He was still thinking about her potential as a chef as she came back to the table with mugs of coffee on a little tray, alongside china bowls of cream and sugar.

"Very elegant," he observed. "Almost too fancy to use on me!"

"I love this serving set, but I never get to use it," she said, sitting down across from him. "I like coffee black in the morning, but sweet at night. It feels like more of a treat this way."

He watched her ladle sugar and cream into her mug. The girl was not afraid of some calories in her coffee. He loved that. "We call coffee like that 'light and sweet' in New York," he told her.

"Really? I love it!" She beamed at her creamy coffee. "Light and sweet, perfect for dessert."

Kevin put one spoon of sugar and just a little dollop of cream into his mug. "I take my coffee 'regular,' as you can see." He grinned at her confused expression.

"Wait, so if I order a coffee in New York and they ask me how I take it, if I say regular, it's not coming out black?"

"That's right. Well, in a bodega or at a cart, anyway. In a fancy cafe or a restaurant? They'll probably speak like the rest of the country." He took a sip, rolled the coffee around his mouth. Dark, with very subtle hints of mocha and cherry. It could have been more rich and he wouldn't have complained, but there was decent flavor here.

Kevin decided against giving her a connoisseur's review, but he really knew his coffee, and she'd chosen these beans well. "This isn't half-bad, Mercer. I was expecting Folger's, after the way you reacted to Stephen's coffee."

Nikki shrugged, but a small smile tugged at her lips. "I bought it at one of the fancy little markets I went to today. It's called Illy. I figured Italians know coffee, so I couldn't go wrong, right?"

"There are so many layers of coffee culture, but I think Illy is a good place to start if you're learning about it." Kevin thought of the many small and trendy roasters of New York. None of the cafes he frequented would ever serve something as mainstream as Illy. But it was infinitely better than grocery-store coffee from a big plastic bucket.

Nikki was considering the flavor of her coffee with a puzzled air. "Tell me what I'm looking for in a good coffee. This is new to me."

"With *that* much cream and sugar?" Kevin laughed. "Wait until tomorrow morning when you drink it black, then tell me what you taste in it. I think you might be surprised."

There was a moment of silence while they each considered the following morning. Kevin knew he wasn't imagining the sudden heaviness in the air. Both of them were weighing their options, counting up the consequences and the benefits. He remembered the dog waiting for him at home and nearly groaned aloud.

"Well, here's your plan," Nikki said eventually. She unfolded a piece of paper and cleared her throat theatrically. *"One: Talk to local businesses about their financial services. Consider becoming independent financial planner for small local companies. Talk to funeral home, market, grain elevator, etc. Any company big enough to have investments, insurance, etc.'"*

Kevin was shocked into silence. This was what she thought he should be doing? He showed up for his big escape from his ordinary past life, and she wanted him to go do the books for a funeral home? Kevin took a gulp of coffee to hide his revulsion and nearly scalded his throat. *Should have added more milk.*

Nikki looked up at him for a reaction. Her face was anxious. She wanted to be right; she wanted to be helping him. He couldn't let her see how off-target she was. He'd figure that part out later.

Kevin cleared his throat and forced a smile. "Local companies. Got it. What's step two?"

"Okay. Step two is for if that isn't yielding results. This one says: *consider positions in financial firms in Frederick. Accounting, financial planning, retirement services.*" She looked up from the page, seeking his gaze again. He struggled to keep his face impassive as she explained. "There's a lot of wealth management to be done in Frederick. A ton of rich D.C. types live there. You could definitely find work in the financial sector and just commute back to Catoctin Creek. It's only half an hour."

Kevin felt a worried furrow cut between his eyes. This was more and more off-base. He wanted to let her down easily, preferably putting the job off to another night, but how was he supposed to answer her when she was looking at him so appealingly? "Nikki, I don't know—"

"Wait, there's a step three if that doesn't work. Listen. *Check online freelance options. Remote work seems like a great opportunity. Only downfall is not a lot of public Wi-fi in the area, so you'd be working alone.* Sure, the companies you've been talking to haven't made room for you. But there are smaller ones. You could downsize or try a new position. It costs so much less to live here, so that helps, obviously. And I know you're probably used to having coworkers, and living alone and working alone would be pretty lonely, but at least you'd be here, so you could visit with friends and everything . . ." She trailed off, her eyes searching his face. He watched her eager smile droop. "You don't like any of it."

"It's just . . . that's not why I'm here," Kevin said gently. He was touched she'd put in the work, but she didn't seem to get his motives at all. "I came to get away from all that, to learn to do something useful, something that *matters.*"

"These things matter! They matter to the people who need experts to help them. Jared up at Trout's Market could definitely use some help with financial planning. I happen to know he's wanted to expand out the back for the past two years, and he can't seem to make heads or tails of the financing. And Ripley Barr at the funeral home over in Walkersville needs to build new facilities because, I hate to say it, they put in a whole assisted-living community in right next door and it's doubled his business. He needs more viewing rooms, more facilities for—whatever they do there—but he doesn't know where to begin. The people around here could use an expert like you. Someone local they can trust. You could make a difference to people in Catoctin Creek." Nikki leaned back in her chair, her jaw jutting in a way he'd learned to respect. It meant she was secure in the courage of her convictions. It meant Kevin would find it very hard to make her see she was mistaken.

But she *was* mistaken, and he felt just a little impatient with her assumptions. Seriously, a funeral home consultancy? This was what she thought he'd left New York City for? "Catoctin Creek might need advice, Nikki. Fine. And the millionaires from D.C. with the historic houses they turned into Italian villas? They need help, too, right?" Kevin kept his tone even, but his pulse had jumped, and he was afraid his cheeks might be reddening. Still, he had to finish his point now. "Look, I've seen the real estate listings. I know about the excess wealth down there. It's as bad as New

York, and I'm trying to get away from people like that. I came here to escape these jobs, not just work on them from someone else's house."

Nikki's mouth became a thin line. "Well, don't fixate on the rich people when I just named two worthy local businesses who could use your help."

He sighed. "You're not wrong about that." He regretted the involuntary emphasis he put on the word *that*.

"But everything else? I'm wrong about all of it?"

Kevin saw the hurt in her eyes, and his stomach lurched. "Nikki, come on. I didn't tell you I'd come here to learn to work with my hands. It's not your fault. You didn't know." But she did know. Stephen had told her this morning. He'd heard it all, standing at the end of that echoing hallway. Stephen had been clear with her, and yet she'd still read him off this list of financial jobs, trying to help him make a future as Kevin the Investment Banker Part Two, without even acknowledging she might have made her little plan with some misconceptions about his interests.

As if she didn't even care that he wanted to change.

Maybe Nikki looked at him and saw a person who was finished, and finished in a good way, with a high-paying job which could give *her* the means to chase her dreams. Maybe she looked at him and saw a blank check, an excellent credit score, a steady income while she opened that restaurant she'd told him was just a fantasy. He didn't think so, didn't even want to imagine it, but the little sabotaging voice in his mind was working itself up from a whisper to a shout.

And the little voice had a point.

After all, Nikki wouldn't be the first girl who'd been interested in him for his money. Half the girls he'd dated as an adult had been more interested in his bank account than his face, which was not, despite anything Stephen said to the contrary, that of a ginger Paul Rudd. He was more goofy than handsome, more cute than rugged.

More average than anything else.

And Nikki? Just like those career-minded, brownstone-blinded, husband-hunters of Manhattan, who were looking for the partner to provide them with the right address, the best nanny, and the top-shelf stroller, she was willing to look past his less-than-movie-star good looks in order for the meal ticket his financial backing would provide her.

Kevin felt the weight of disappointment settle across his shoulders. This wasn't what he'd expected from this night.

This wasn't what he'd expected from Catoctin Creek.

Nikki sipped her coffee as the surrounding silence deepened. "Dessert," she said finally. "I made apricot tarts."

Kevin considered her carefully. Her own shoulders were sagging, and her curls were escaping their pins, slipping down around her pale cheeks. Her eyelids, cast down, were dark with exhaustion. A few minutes ago, she'd been vibrant and bright. Then he'd shot down her plans for him.

Maybe she wasn't a money-grubber. He thought he could give Nikki more credit than that—she was many things, fierce and resilient and strong, but she wasn't deceptive.

He could trust her.

But he couldn't get past the vision she had of his future: a dark, heavy thing which seemed to weigh on him even now.

"Kevin?" she asked, her voice thin. "Dessert?"

"I don't think so," he said regretfully. "I better get home and check on Grover."

# Chapter 15

# Nikki

Somehow, Nikki found the presence of mind to place two apricot tarts into a glass container and press them into Kevin's hands once he'd put on his coat. "Eat them with some whipped cream," she instructed, "or ice cream. Preferably later tonight. They won't keep very long. They'll go soggy."

He nodded and turned to the door. Nikki's heart wrung as she realized he was going to leave her without so much as a goodnight kiss. So what, this was his way of punishing her for writing an action plan he didn't like? He was just going to pretend nothing was going on between them? The walk last night, the kisses in the moonlight, that all vanished because she'd had the nerve to try to help him build a future here?

Nikki chewed on the inside of her cheek, a nasty habit which wasn't going anywhere, anytime soon, not when there were guys like Kevin in the world to make her crazy. She leaned out the French doors, watching him walk to his car, his path winding to avoid the dark ice patches in the driveway. She considered the back of his head, the tendrils of dark red hair which slipped from beneath his hat and over his coat collar.

If only there was snow, she thought wistfully. She'd scoop up a snowball and show him what fantastic aim she had.

"Hey, Kevin?" she called.

"Yeah?" he asked, looking over his shoulder at her.

She looked at him carefully, ignoring the stiff wind blowing around her, making him wait while she decided what to say next. She made up her mind. Maybe she didn't have any snow to hurl, but she could still aim a dart.

"Try not to be such a baby next time," she told him, and closed the door on his startled face.

Then she leaned on the door, listening for his car. After it had started up and driven away, she laughed until she cried.

Nikki would have loved to leave the dinner dishes on the kitchen table and crawl right into bed, but that was the problem with living in a studio: you can't close the door on a mess. So once she'd gotten all the tears out, she wiped her eyes, shrugged her shoulders, and cleared the table. After the table was wiped clean, the washing-up was calling her name, and by ten o'clock she had a perfectly clean kitchen to match the rest of the apartment . . . which she'd already tidied up in expectation of keeping Kevin's interest a little longer than she'd actually managed.

"Well, at least I got a clean apartment out of the deal," she said with a shrug.

Then, she remembered there was still half a bottle of wine to be finished.

She'd take it to bed.

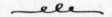

"You look tired," Lauren told her. "Take the night off and I'll run the place."

"Haha," Nikki replied, tying her apron strings. She'd slept late that morning and hung around the apartment most of the day, flipping through some magazines and pretending to get through some early Christmas shopping, although she really just ordered herself a new Le Creuset pan and some mixing bowls she'd found for a great deal. "You want to run the diner on a Saturday night after holiday shopping? We should have a line out the door by six-thirty."

Lauren glanced out at the empty parking lot, then looked rather ostentatiously at her phone, pointing out the time. "When does the big rush begin? We have an hour and a half to go."

"Trust me, they'll be here." Nikki walked around the empty dining room, looking for something to occupy her mind. The truth was, she'd been hoping there would already be a dinner rush, and she'd had a hard time hiding her disappointment when she saw there weren't even any early birds forking down peas or mashed potatoes from their favorite booths.

That was the danger of the holiday shopping season—as fewer stores were open in Catoctin Creek and the neighboring villages, people had to drive ever farther afield to do their shopping. When folks drove into Frederick to shop at the malls or the downtown boutiques, there was a decent chance they'd stay through dinner. Even if stopping at the Blue Plate had been a holiday tradition in years past, nothing fell faster than tradition when kids were hungry and fighting in the backseat of the car.

Sometimes Nikki really wondered if even the Blue Plate, venerable old institution that it was, could survive the constant change around Catoctin Creek.

And if she lost this place, what would she do? Who would she be without this diner? Where would she work?

Nikki imagined herself working at an Applebee's or a Chili's and couldn't stop herself from physically shuddering.

Lauren was eyeballing her. "Are you okay?"

Nikki shrugged, as if that's all she'd been doing before. "I guess I'm just tired, like you said."

"Go home," Lauren repeated. "You live two blocks away. If I need you, I'll call you."

Suddenly, all Nikki wanted to do was putz around in her own kitchen, maybe make something comforting like a spaghetti carbonara, put on comfy pajamas, and watch TV until she fell asleep.

"Okay," she agreed. "Thanks."

Lauren's eyes got very big. "Whoa—seriously? You're really taking me up on it?"

"What, did you change your mind the second it got real?" Nikki's fingers were on the knot of her apron.

"No, no, it's fine. Go home and rest, or whatever." Lauren was looking around the empty diner with a newly proprietary air. "I'll manage this place. Somehow."

A teen girl, one of the revolving cast of high school juniors and seniors who filled the evening server positions, wandered past the podium, her nose about an inch from her phone.

"Kassidy," Nikki said.

The girl looked up slowly. Her eyes came into focus after about a second—too long, Nikki thought, with an old-womanish glare at the girl's phone. "Hey, Nikki. What's up? Slow tonight."

"It'll pick up," Nikki sighed. "Lauren's in charge tonight. I'm not sticking around. Who else is here?"

Kassidy considered the question. "Misty," she said eventually. "She's in the back."

"Bothering Patrick?"

Kassidy nodded.

Nikki turned back to Lauren. "Keep Misty busy, or Patrick's going to yell at her and then she'll probably quit."

Lauren shrugged. "I could replace her in five minutes."

Nikki stared at her for a minute. Lauren had started working here a year ago as a blushing, shy high school senior. Nikki had figured she'd be in and out before three months were out, just like the others. Instead, Lauren had grown into a brisk, efficient woman. Nikki had been puzzling for a few weeks now about who Lauren reminded her of. Now she knew.

"I've been rubbing off on you," Nikki said, pulling her apron over her head. "We're going to have to watch that tendency."

~ 𝓮𝓵𝓮 ~

The early evening at home did her good. It gave her time to think properly. By the time her pasta had boiled, Nikki was beginning to believe that she and Kevin could patch things up. It was one little disagreement. Of course she didn't know him inside and out yet. They had barely spent any time alone together. They were bound to make mistakes.

So maybe she didn't quite understand Kevin as well as she'd first thought. Fine. There was no way to learn about a guy who didn't live in the same town, right? Now he did, so she'd just do a quick study. Get to know him a little better. She could still help him figure out his life, and they could pick up where they'd left off. Not with the arguing, but with the kissing.

After glancing at the clock to make sure it wasn't too late, she texted Rosemary.

*Plans tomorrow?*

Rosemary: *Horsemanship class at one. Just three students though. Are you free?*

*Lauren's running the joint on Sunday now.*

Rosemary: *Perfect. Wait, what happened with Kevin last night?*

*Ups and downs. Was he around the farm today?*

Rosemary: *Actually yeah. Played with Stephen all day. I barely saw him. Come help me tomorrow?*

*Very likely.*

Nikki smirked and tossed the phone aside. She could play teacher's aide tomorrow afternoon, fit in a little spying on Kevin . . . then stick around and have dinner at the farm. By the time Rosemary pulled a carton of ice cream from the cellar freezer, the two of them would be back on good terms. Maybe even romantic-walk terms, if Nikki could contrive it.

Pretty lucky that Rosemary had a horsemanship class, actually. Nikki enjoyed helping with those. While Rosemary was getting better at teaching, she still felt nervous around new people, and the people who came to her classes were generally outgoing: women who had held successful careers in their previous lives, and who thought classes should be filled with spirited back-and-forth discussion.

Basically, the kind of thing Rosemary absolutely loathed with every fiber of her quiet-loving being.

Luckily, Nikki had grown up taking riding lessons with Rosemary, and she could take over some of the class discussions, giving her introverted friend a break.

So this class would be the perfect excuse to hang out around the farm, see how Kevin was doing with his whole manual-labor education, strike up some friendly conversation, and eventually pull him aside for a quick *let's try this again* conversation.

Nikki threw some chopped pancetta into a pan with some olive oil and garlic. The rich, spicy scent flared up, filling her nostrils, and she closed her eyes to breathe it all in. Everything was going to be fine, she thought. Just fine.

# Chapter 16

# Kevin

K evin was pretty sure he'd never been so sore in his life.

Sore in mind, sore in body. He'd woken up from a nasty dream, something with dark fields, shouting voices, honking horns —none of it really seemed to match up. At the very end there'd been a weird, low drumbeat . . . he couldn't explain it.

Well, that made sense, he thought, giving up on parsing together the fragments of dream. Too many ups and downs in seventy-two hours. City to country. Farm chores. Friendsgiving. A date that ended in drama.

It could give any man whiplash.

Had he really already bungled things with Nikki?

Kevin rolled over, pulling bedclothes with him, and encountered something cold and wet. Grover's nose, pressed urgently against his arm. He heard a thumping sound, and realized the dog's tail was wagging steadily, smacking the bedside table with a rhythmic beat which exactly matched the drumbeat in his dream.

At least *one* part of his dream made sense now.

"Can I help you?" Kevin groaned.

Grover licked him right across the face.

"Oof! Okay, okay." He pushed himself upright, moving out of the splash zone, and rubbed his hands across his face and hair. The simple motion made his shoulders squeeze in agony. Farm work was brutal stuff. "Hang on, doggo. I'll let you outside as soon as I can figure out how to get my legs on the floor."

Kevin eventually managed to hobble his way to the back door, barely getting the sliding glass door open before Grover rocketed into the foggy backyard. He watched the dog tear through the wet grass, nearly disappearing in the swirling gray mist which seemed to have settled on the ground at the base of the hill, where the forest rose along the fence-line in a thicket of green fir and gray, bare branches. The sun wasn't up yet, but a pink blush was creeping across the sky behind Notch Gap. In a few moments, those leafless ridges would be bathed in golden light, and Kevin would feel breathlessly fortunate to be here, yet again. The sunsets over Notch Gap were famous, but the sunrises lit the mountains so spectacularly, he was surprised more people didn't rhapsodize about them, too.

Catching this sunrise was the only reason he didn't mind that Grover was clearly a morning glory.

Otherwise, he would *definitely* prefer to sleep until eight or nine. A long, lovely lie-in . . . just like any other grown-up human who suddenly didn't have a job to rush off to, a train to catch, coffee balanced in one hand as he rushed down the subway stairs . .

Speaking of coffee . . .

He left Grover to his doggy pursuits and set about making a fresh pot. He took down coffee beans, averting his eyes from the apricot tarts he'd so petulantly left out on the counter. He looked out the kitchen window as he filled the pot at the sink, watching the sunlight gild Notch Gap. For just a moment, Kevin had a moment of perfect contentment.

He turned on the coffeemaker and moved back to the sliding glass door. He'd just watch Grover play as the sunrise awakened the surrounding forest . . .

His eyes fell on a piece of paper sitting on the kitchen counter, and Kevin's heart fell.

It was Nikki's action plan, her crisp, bold handwriting outlining the prosaic new life she'd imagined for him. He'd taken it out of his pocket last night while he'd stood by the back door, watching Grover tear around the backyard under the glow of the porch light. He picked up the paper and looked over it. Maybe it hadn't been so bad. Maybe he'd overreacted, full of rich food and wine and a creeping exhaustion he hadn't even recognized yet. Judging by the way his muscles were screaming, he'd really overdone things the past few days.

His eyes flicked over the words and focused on her penmanship, on her forceful down-strokes, the fiercely jabbed dots over the *i*'s. Take away the disappointment he'd felt in what those dark letters spelled out, and he was left with a tantalizing reminder of the woman who'd written them: strong and forthright and utterly unafraid to run someone else's life according to her own specifications.

But he had to wonder if she'd ever take such liberty with her own life.

These few days in Catoctin Creek, ears and eyes open, had shown him Nikki wasn't living the life of her dreams—nor even her nightmares. She was just living the life she'd been given.

At first glance, Kevin couldn't understand how a woman so imaginative and remarkable could simply let her ambition pass her by. He'd thought he'd misjudged her. Nikki came across as a fiery spirit, but maybe she was just going through the motions . . . like so many other people he'd met, like so many others who had told him to keep his head down and carry on when he'd threatened to break free.

But now, eyes traveling over the page, he realized that in her vision of his life, she'd spilled her guts to him. She was the same person he had been. Living the safe life. Accepting reality. Chafing under harness, but not prepared to kick over the traces.

Until he'd finally gathered up the courage to leave New York, to insist that he could have something different.

Something better.

Grover pawed at the door and he opened it, barely noticing as the dog raced through the house with muddy paws and a stick shedding bark, experiencing a full-on case of the zoomies. Kevin put down the paper and ran his hands through his hair, barely noticing now how his muscles ached. He was too disappointed in himself to care what his body felt like.

He'd walked away from her after that fantastic dinner she'd cooked him, come home and left her tarts out on the counter, purposely letting them spoil, a move filled with spite which really only injured him. But imagine if she knew about it! Her feelings would be hurt, and for no reason at all.

He'd read Nikki all wrong. Especially when it came to the way she treated the people she cared about.

She deserved better than the silent treatment.

Grabbing his coat, Kevin plunged out into the golden morning. Grover followed him, still mouthing his stick. He walked the perimeter of the yard, as the cardinals began to chirp from the bare branches of the forest.

Grover sniffed his way along the back fence, the dog's tail waving over his back as he tracked the forest animals who moved through the yard in the night. What kind of animals? Kevin didn't know. Bunnies, he supposed. Raccoons. Porcupines? Did Maryland have porcupines? Kevin was almost overwhelmed by everything he didn't know about this place. He kicked at a few pinecones gathered under the fat little fir trees at the foot of the hill. The cold air nipped at his ears, and he imagined the entire property, firs and all, coated with a thick layer of pure white snow.

Too bad Rosemary swore up and down this region never saw snow before January. He felt ready for a snowfall, for enchanted forests draped all in white. He was ready for a little magic and fantasy to fill his life. He was ready for a holiday season of fireplaces and whispered secrets, hot toddies and stolen kisses.

Kevin was ready for a Hallmark movie to take over his life. He had the small town, he had the cute dog, he had the girl he wanted to woo—he just needed everyone to learn their lines while the set designer got busy shaking some snow over the scenery.

Eventually he tramped back up to the house, fed Grover his kibble and heated some instant oatmeal he'd found in the cabinet. He wanted to go to the farm, but it was too early to start bothering Stephen, so he tried to distract himself with Netflix. But why were so many shows these days about cooking and restaurants? It seemed like every hot new show featured some bright-eyed woman in a pretty flowered tunic who was going to cook him something fabulous.

Maybe the universe was trying to tell him he'd better fix things with Nikki, and fast.

His phone buzzed, rumbling across the coffee table, and he snatched it up with a quickness that belied his desperation for a distraction.

The message was from Stephen: *Exciting adventure planned for today!! Stacking hay - you in?*

Kevin lifted his eyebrows. Stacking hay didn't sound like a wonderful time . . . but he had nothing else to do today, and maybe Nikki would show up at some point. He quickly typed a response.

*See you in an hour.*

That gave him time for another cup of coffee before he went off to do some very manly work around the farm.

Oh, and to pop some NSAIDs. Kevin rubbed at his aching shoulders as he wrenched the lid off a pill bottle. How had farmers gotten through stiff, sore mornings in the old days, before highly effective painkillers were sold over the counter? No wonder they'd resorted to drinking cocaine in their soda by the turn of the century. Life must have been painful back then.

Kevin took his pills, glanced at the oatmeal box he'd left on the counter, and considered a second breakfast. A hard day of work ahead of him deserved something more than a packet of oatmeal, right?

Kevin cracked an egg into a pan, considered the cheerful dog panting at his side, and added another one. They both deserved a nutritious breakfast. He had a tough day of chores ahead of him, and Grover? Well, he had a tough day of being a good, good dog.

# Chapter 17

# Nikki

Rosemary was out in the barnyard getting her props ready for class when Nikki arrived, bearing a tray of brownies and a double batch of salted chocolate and caramel cookies.

Nikki could see the relief written across Rosemary's face when she realized Nikki had arrived. She smiled to herself. Rosemary was fully capable of teaching the horsemanship classes, but her friend had a way of working herself into a tizzy before each one, anyway.

"Oh, Nikki," Rosemary exclaimed, dropping a pair of buckets next to a hay bale. "Thank you for being here! You make every class so much better. And I'm running behind. The farrier was here earlier. But mostly just because you make classes better."

"You're just saying that because you love my triple-chocolate brownies."

"Anyone would," Rosemary conceded. "But the students are more attentive when they know there are treats on the line."

Nikki laughed. "You'd never know they're grown adults."

"Right? They get so whispery and giggly halfway through, every time. Gus said this morning I must have the patience of a saint to teach a bunch of city women how to take care of horses."

"How is Gus? Why'd he come on a weekend?"

"Oh, you know Gus," Rosemary said. "He's a good old boy. He said he didn't want to work on Thanksgiving, but that meant he was bored by Sunday, so he came over to do some hoof-trimming just to pass the time. He talked to Kevin a lot."

Nikki glanced over her shoulder. "About what?"

"Farrier work. Hooves and anatomy. Kevin was really interested in it all."

"Funny," Nikki said. "You never know what someone will like."

Nikki set up the treats on a nearby picnic table. She'd held back a few extra in the car, but there was still more than enough to go around a three-person class. She'd woken up early, couldn't fall back asleep, and spent all her nervous energy on baking.

She shed her coat and left it on the table as well. The bitter cold of yesterday had given way to a rather mild afternoon, with a bright blue sky and a crispness to the breeze that was more refreshing than chilling. "Nice day for a class. Everyone coming today is from Caitlin's?"

"Yup, her latest victims. All of them are volunteers from her therapeutic riding classes. All of them now want their own horses. I don't know how she does it. The parents buy ponies, the older women buy her so-called rescues." Rosemary laughed, shaking her head. "You know she has a deal with the auction in Greenville now? They send her their nicest horses and she sells them to her clients as horses in need."

"I mean, if they're at *that* auction, they really are, right?" The Greenville livestock auction was infamous for horses at the bottom rung of the ladder.

"Sure, yes. I mean it's good they're getting homes. She's just so —my father would have called her sharp, you know?"

"I know." Nikki had never liked Caitlin. Not when they were twelve, and not now. But she *was* finding horses new homes, and she *was* providing therapy to people who needed it. Was it just distasteful because she made money off all her good works? Nikki shrugged it off. What else could you do?

Rosemary settled a horse blanket over a bale of hay. "Oh, and there's a fourth now—a guy, if you please! Her new riding instructor, apparently. Caitlin wants him to see what I do, so he can sell my classes to more of the horse show moms she's collecting with her lessons."

Oh, the new riding instructor! Nikki could roll her eyes about Caitlin Tuttle's do-gooders and not feel bad about it, but Sean Casey? He was another story. Nikki wondered if that pretty boy knew what he'd gotten into when he'd accepted a job at prosperous Elmwood Equestrian Center. He'd probably expected some difficult parents and spoiled children, but was he really prepared for Caitlin? Nikki had her doubts.

Rosemary was eyeing her closely. "What are you thinking?"

"I'm thinking Caitlin's new riding instructor will file a sexual harassment suit by the spring 4-H show, if you must know," Nikki admitted.

"No! Do you really think so?"

"Have you met him yet? Or seen him?"

Rosemary shook her head. "Easy on the eyes?"

"Like, really, really ridiculously good-looking. And you remember what Caitlin was like in high school."

"She was a little boy-crazy," Rosemary remembered.

"A little!" Nikki snorted. "Ian Yingling and Martin Heinz got into a fight over taking her to Prom and she was so excited, she all but sold tickets to the match."

"I mean, isn't that on Ian and Martin?" Rosemary walked back into the barn and Nikki followed. "Plus, Ian fought with everybody. He's in anger management now, I hear."

"Really? You're probably right," Nikki conceded. "I've just never really loved Caitlin. You didn't either, as I recall. She was such a cat back when we all rode at Elmwood. And all her profiteering . . . I don't know. It's a tough business to make money in, I get that. I just wish it didn't look so conniving."

"Well, I've gotten to know her this year." From the feed room, Rosemary handed up Nikki a bucket filled with plastic baggies— samples of different horse feed. "Set this next to the hay bale? Thanks. And you know, she was dealing with a lot. Being a terrible rider when her own mother was teaching all of us to ride, never bringing home a blue ribbon while we hung ours up on the stalls, that was tough for her. She acted out at school a little, but can you blame her? She needed the win."

All of it was true. While Caitlin had inherited the farm and a love of horses from her mother, she didn't inherit any actual riding skill or teaching abilities. Even Nikki was a better rider than Caitlin, and Nikki had given up riding late in high school when she recognized she wasn't really that talented in the saddle.

When Caitlin realized she couldn't run the lesson and show program on her own merits, she'd made a move Nikki immediately recognized as strategic, beginning a therapeutic riding program. The program attracted donations and volunteers, and Caitlin made up for her lack of equestrian talent with a heaping helping of public relations know-how. She'd picked up so many paying students from the volunteers who showed up for therapeutic riding, hiring Sean Casey and expanding her lesson program had looked natural. But Nikki knew it had been her plan all along.

"You're right," she told Rosemary, who was coming out of the barn with a stack of supplement tubs. "Caitlin did need the win. And she's winning now. I shouldn't pick at her."

"And she's sharing the love," Rosemary said, looking over her little pile of equine supplies. "These lessons pay for a lot of feed."

The horsekeeping classes had been entirely Caitlin's idea. She said the region was overflowing with do-gooder moms and empty-nesters who moved to the country, had a bit of land, and eventually decided to adopt a horse in need, and *someone* had to give these folks basic horsemanship classes before they accidentally killed the poor things. Since Rosemary ran a horse sanctuary, she was just the person for the job.

Caitlin just breezed right past Rosemary's social anxiety, and eventually, Rosemary had managed to put aside her nerves as well —if only for a few hours at a time. Still, Nikki had to wonder what the first-ever male participant would do to Rosemary's anxiousness when she took center stage.

"Well, just so you know, I've met Sean a few times, and he's really nice. In fact, he's responsible for that dog who's been running around your place lately."

Rosemary laughed. "So I hear! Kevin admitted everything to me. I'm actually curious to meet him now. He sounds really sweet. And I'm getting used to having men around the place, now that Stephen and Kevin are nearly always in the barn. They're in there right now, you know. They're upstairs moving hay around or something. I hardly know what Stephen's up to these days. He reads things online and decides it's some vital chore which must be done immediately."

"I guess since we have a few minutes, I'll take them some cookies," Nikki said off-handedly, as if this wasn't her plan all along. "I brought extra." She'd brought an extra *two dozen*. Maybe she wasn't entirely on Kevin's wavelength yet, but she knew men responded well to baked goods. She'd figured the cookies would make a good apology, one she wouldn't have to say out loud.

"Go right ahead," Rosemary replied, winking knowingly. "I'll be down here finishing up my prep. The class starts at one."

Nikki took the extra tub of cookies and skipped up the stepping stones that had been placed in the steep slope next to the barn by one of Rosemary's forebears. She couldn't deny she was a little jealous of Rosemary's family homestead, since the Mercer family farm had been sold off for housing plots so many years before. Imagine if she had a property of her own! Imagine if she had a place like Notch Gap Farm—the possibilities at her fingertips would be endless. Nikki looked at the beautiful bank barn perched on its hillside and pictured a restaurant in its upper story. She fantasized about an echoing, thematic space filled with antiques and handmade tables and her own unique dishes. She'd seat diners from all over the capital region, and they'd rave about her talents as a chef and restauranteur.

For just a moment, her dream shimmered in front of her, and then a flock of crows startled from the hilltop, cawing as their black wings carved into the air in front of her, and she was back on Rosemary's quietly aging farm.

Well, Nikki supposed, some people got to inherit farms, and some people got to live in apartments, and inheriting the Blue Plate was still better than working in someone else's business. Dreams were just empty wishes to fill the downtime between all the thousand and one things that real life demanded. Nikki's sensible inner voice reminded her of this whenever she got a little too moony about her diminishing prospects as a chef. She shrugged it off and turned the corner, where the upper barn's big sliding doors opened onto the farm lane.

Nikki stopped short. Well, *well.* This was quite the scene.

Stephen and Kevin were both working away at stacking hay, pulling bales down from one high stack and moving them to another. It wasn't the task they were performing that was so surprising: rotating hay bales was a necessity of farm life—a thankless, time-consuming necessity. The hay sitting at the bottom of one big stack could slowly begin to mold and generate heat—a scenario which could ruin a lot of expensive hay at best, and cause spontaneous combustion at worst. Rosemary got her yearly hay delivery in July, and by late November, it was usually time to dig out whatever had been sitting on the bottom and use those bales up before they had time to go bad and spoil the lot.

What was arresting was how hard these two city-bred men were going at their hay stacking—and how good they looked in the process. Stephen had always possessed a physique which suggested regular weekly visits to the gym, something Nikki associated with city living, thanks to sitcoms and romantic comedies set in New York.

Kevin, on the other hand, had always seemed much softer to her. Although, Nikki reflected now, she had never seen him without a sweater or a coat on before. He had stayed away all summer, he'd worn a suit to the wedding, and he'd come back in time for the coldest Thanksgiving in years.

Now, though, Kevin's upper body was stripped down to one layer, a woven undershirt which clung to his back, shoulders, and chest, and gave Nikki a very impressive, very illuminating view of just how muscular Kevin was.

*Well, damn,* her sensible brain muttered, and she had to agree. *Didn't see that coming.*

Stephen glanced her way and gave a little wave, then went back to his task without breaking stride. Kevin, who was midway through shoving a bale onto its perch high above his head, was less successful at maintaining his focus. His face lit up at the sight of her, and he immediately lost control of the hay bale. He ducked and held up his arms as it rained down from above him.

Stephen burst out laughing. "Pay attention, Kev, or you're gonna get crushed!"

Nikki turned her face and smothered a smile behind her hands.

Kevin, a good sport, just sighed and picked up the hay bale again. He shoved it into place with one extremely forceful push, which seemed to be aimed at showing that hay bale just who was in charge. Then he brushed his hands against his jeans and walked across the hay-strewn floor to Nikki.

Having successfully choked back her laughter, Nikki held up the container of cookies and smiled alluringly. "Do you need snacks?"

His gaze bore into hers, giving her heart an extra flutter, but his smile was merely friendly as he replied, "Boy, I'll say."

Sweat had soaked through his shirt, and his friendly face grooved with lines from exertion, and dusted gently with tiny seeds and bits of hay. Without thinking, Nikki reached forward and flicked a little spike of grass away from his right eye. His skin was damp. "You should put a jacket on before you get chilled."

"Thanks," he said. "I'm a mess."

*You look fantastic.* "A sweaty mess," she agreed. "But it suits you."

He lifted his eyebrows. "How do you mean?"

"What can I say?" Nikki asked, feeling the hum of tension between them and loving it. "I am a simple country girl. I like a man who can stack hay with the best of them."

He grinned at her and took the container of cookies right out of her hands. "I'll be eating all of these now, thank you. When's the next holiday? I need to eat more to keep up with all of this farm labor."

"Christmas is next," Nikki said, lifting her eyebrows, "and it will be a *feast.*"

"Ah, a feast. That's exactly what I need." Kevin bit into a cookie, and his eyes widened. "My God, so *good.* Nikki, you're a wonder. You should be baking for the president. Or me. Bake for me."

"I think I just did," she teased, delighted their argument seemed to have faded away. Well, if Kevin wasn't bothered by it, she wouldn't be either.

As if he'd heard her thoughts, Kevin waved a cookie in the air to signal he had an announcement once his mouth wasn't so full. "I wanted to tell you, I got an interesting job offer this morning."

"This morning? That's amazing! What are you going to be doing?"

Kevin's grin was ear-to-ear. "I'm going to be the farrier's apprentice."

Nikki's smile faltered. Rosemary had said he was interested in hooves, but—"Kevin, you know what a farrier does, right? All day long? Bent over?" There was no way Kevin was prepared for a day in the life of a farrier.

"Yeah, he trims and shoes horses' hooves. It's awesome! He was here this morning to work on Rosita, that's the lady-horse by the way—" Did his grin really get even wider? Nikki thought it did —"and I watched everything he did, and finally I asked if he could show me how it all worked, and you know what? He let me get right under that horse, tuck her hoof between my legs, and do a little rasping! It was amazing. As soon as I started, I really felt like it was the right thing for me. So I asked him if he ever took on apprentices and he said sure, he could always use a guy to ride along and hold horses, and he'd teach me along the way."

Stephen came up, brushing hay off his shirt. "It was quite a performance," he said. "Kevin turned on the charm and then some."

"You were there?" Nikki stared at Stephen. She couldn't communicate with him wordlessly the way Rosemary could, but with her eyes she tried very hard to convey a message: *He's your best friend. Why didn't you stop this?*

Farriers did some of the toughest, most dangerous work in the entire farming community. Kevin was *not* ready for this.

He wouldn't last, he'd get disappointed, he'd go home, and she'd still be here, but this time she'd know how alone she really was.

Nikki felt her good mood dissolving.

———ell———

The first car was just pulling into the driveway when Nikki went back down to the barnyard. Rosemary gave her a nervous smile. "I always feel so sick when they start arriving," she confessed. "Every time is like the first session."

Nikki remembered the first horsemanship class, which had involved a little dry-heaving halfway through the lesson. She'd taken over the class while Rosemary ran behind the barn to get herself together. "None of them are like the first session. You're going to do great."

"Why does it always feel like I've never done this before, then?" Rosemary shook her head. "And it *will* be kind of weird with a guy here, I admit it. Of course—" her eyes widened as a figure approached—"of *course* he's the first one here!"

Sean Casey was dressed in buff riding breeches, tall black field boots, and a fitted black sweater. The warming day seemed to have conspired to help Sean show off his runway-ready good looks. "I'm telling you, she hired him for the eye candy," Nikki muttered.

"Okay, I see where you're coming from now," Rosemary agreed. "My goodness, what's a looker like that doing at a lesson barn in western Maryland? He ought to be down in Florida for the winter. Women will pay good money for a trainer like that to yell at them. Ugh, Nikki! He makes me nervous."

Nikki smothered a smile. "Don't worry," she said. "I'll still stay and help. But only to look at Sean."

Rosemary nudged her in the ribs. "You're so bad. Kevin is *right* upstairs. How many men do you need?"

*Just one,* Nikki thought. *One that will make good choices, and stick around.*

# Chapter 18

## Kevin

Kevin was still thinking about those cookies of Nikki's when he and Stephen finished with the hay project. "Suppose there's any of them left?" he asked as they walked out the barn doors and into the pale winter sunlight. Above them, on the slope of the north pasture, Rosemary's herd of rescue horses browsed through the browning grass.

Stephen led the way over to an old-fashioned iron spigot alongside the barn and lifted the handle. Icy water spurted out and he cupped his hands underneath, sloshing water onto his dusty face. "Mmm, that's better. How can I be so hot when it's like, forty-five degrees outside? The air's cold, but I'm roasting."

"Stephen," Kevin reminded him. "Cookies. Let's stay focused." He shoved Stephen aside to get at the water, feeling extremely masculine and strong after his hay-stacking session. But when he put his hands under the gushing stream, Kevin had to bite back a very unmanly scream. That water was *icy*. Straight out of the damn North Pole. His thoughts drifted back to snow. It was a good fifteen degrees too warm for a snowfall now, but something inside of Kevin still thought there was a chance. He just had a feeling about this.

As he mopped water from his face with his dusty shirt, he studied the western sky. But the sky above the mountains was a very innocent shade of blue.

Kevin dismissed the hope of snow and got back to the subject at hand. "Seriously, I must have more of those cookies."

Stephen wiped his face dry with the inside of his shirt. "We can go inside and see, but I'll bet she brought most of them for Rosemary's horsemanship class."

A light went on in Kevin's brain: here was a way to see more of Nikki, impress her with his horse-savvy, *and* get more cookies. A total win all-around. He made his voice casual when he said, "Hey, maybe I should join the class. The more I learn about horses, the better. You think she'd mind?"

Stephen shrugged. "Actually, that's not a bad idea. They probably only just started a little while ago. Go on down and see what you can absorb . . . and if there are any cookies when they're done, bring them in. I'm going to take a shower and get some work done in the office."

Kevin promised he'd bring any leftover cookies, without actually promising he'd leave any leftovers, and waved Stephen off to the house. Good for Stephen, getting some office-work done on such a pretty day! More power to him! Kevin didn't envy his friend his remote job anymore, not now that he had a new focus. Who wanted to sit at a laptop and squint at numbers all day?

Anyway, he'd learned Notch Gap Farm didn't have the fastest Wi-fi in the world. Just downloading email attachments here took so long, Kevin didn't think he could take the stress of trying to work out of Stephen's little office. Better to just be done with the whole thing. He'd always preferred a clean break to letting things drag on, anyway.

Kevin wandered down the slope alongside the barn, his jacket over his shoulders. The afternoon sun felt warm, but there was a little something in the wind, a reminder that yesterday had been below freezing and that kind of cold could come back. There'd been ice in the pasture water trough yesterday morning. Rosemary had shown him how to break the ice with an axe—the first time Kevin had ever held an axe. It was a very satisfying thing.

Rosemary's class was gathered in the barnyard, a smattering of middle-aged females in expensive L.L. Bean-type gear. Hanging in the back was a single tall, slim man in riding clothes. With a start of surprise, Kevin realized he was Sean Casey, the guy who had given him the dog. Grover was in the barn right now, relaxing in a clean stall until the class dispersed and Kevin had time to pay attention to him. He figured Sean would like to see the dog again. Once the class was finished, he'd take him over for a visit.

As Kevin carefully slipped into place behind the little cluster of students, he spotted Nikki standing a few feet behind Rosemary. She had the lead-rope of Rochester, Rosemary's massive black Percheron, and was keeping the horse amused by poking the rope's knotted end around his muzzle. He was trying to catch it, his lips making a popping sound as they smacked together. Meanwhile, Rosemary was using Rochester as a giant model, pointing out different spots that horse-owners needed to check every day for trouble. Kevin tried to focus. As a farrier's apprentice, he'd need to know all of this and then some.

"Now, Rochester usually has some soreness in his hips, which can be really hard to spot unless you're an expert," Rosemary announced, running her hands along the big horse's hindquarters. "But I'll give you an idea of how he shows it. Take a look at this jutting-out point right here. See that? It's the hip-point, and—"

Kevin watched Rosemary tap the horse's hips, remembering the day he'd met them both. That naughty old horse sure hadn't had any soreness in his hips *that* day. Rochester had dropped poor Rosemary on the ground and then run right across the Long Pond property. Kevin had dragged himself through what must have been a solid mile of muddy ground on the way to catch him and back, and then it had taken him a full ten minutes to get the horse's halter off once he had him back in this very barnyard. Nope, he'd been sound as a dollar that day.

Kevin smiled, thinking of it. The day everything had changed— the day he'd first come to Catoctin Creek, the day he'd met Nikki. If Rochester hadn't dumped Rosemary, Stephen wouldn't have stayed with her all day to make sure she wasn't concussed. If Stephen hadn't stayed with her all day, Kevin wouldn't have come back to Notch Gap Farm to pick him up. When he'd arrived back at the farmhouse that evening—after getting lost in Pennsylvania while he was trying to find Stephen's house—Nikki had looked at him like she couldn't decide if she wanted to kick him off the farm or tug him close for a fierce kiss, and he'd been utterly smitten.

He still felt the same way about her as he had that first day, and he suspected she felt pretty much the same way, too. Half-ferocious, half-titillated, *all* passion.

And there she was, holding the horse who had brought them together like a game show presenter while the host pointed out all of his attributes. *Give him a twirl, Nikki,* Kevin thought, and he chuckled to himself.

A few feet in front of him, Sean turned his head slightly. He saw Kevin and offered a half-smile before he turned his attention back to Rosemary.

The glance had been brief, Sean's expression entirely friendly. But it was enough to shake Kevin's composure.

*Good lord,* he thought. *That man's a Norse god.*

He hadn't realized it the other night, what with being tired from the drive down from New York, and the poor light in the parking lot, and Nikki glaring down at him, and the coats and hats and scarves and of course, Grover. Between the dog and Nikki, his attention had pretty well been taken up. And anyway, Kevin was used to ridiculously handsome men. He lived in New York City. It was like male model central up there. But those guys were carefully constructed versions of themselves, put together in front of a mirror each morning before they ventured out into the city.

Sean simply belonged in this setting, and his beauty was authentic.

Which made it a hundred times worse, Kevin thought ruefully. What did Nikki think of Sean? She hadn't seemed fond of him at the Blue Plate, but Nikki could be snappish with the people she liked. That was one of the things he liked about her—she was so sharp, so certain she was right, so ready to fight for what she believed. He remembered something his mother had told him when he was a lovelorn little boy of ten: *if she's being mean to you, she probably likes you.*

Maybe it wasn't true of every girl, but it had been true of Rebecca O'Leary, who had eventually stopped being mean to him long enough to peck him on the cheek, and he was pretty certain it was true of Nikki Mercer.

Kevin studied Nikki's face, waiting for her to notice him. If he could even be spotted behind Mr. Tall, Blonde, and Handsome. He took a step back. Maybe a little space between him and the back of the pack would help . . .

"Kevin, what do you think?"

He looked at Rosemary, who was gazing at him with a hopeful expression.

Had he just been singled out for audience participation? Unfair, Rosemary!

"I agree," he declared. "You're right."

The little cluster of students laughed, turning around to look at him. Kevin felt hot. "I'm sorry, Rosemary. I didn't even hear you," he admitted. "Ask again?"

Rosemary looked pleased with the diverted gazes. He knew she always felt better when she wasn't the center of attention. Nikki, on the other hand, looked a little annoyed. At him? He'd better pull it together.

"I was asking if you know why we call the left side of the horse *near*, and the right *off*. As in, 'the horse is lame in his near foreleg.' I thought you might have picked this up from working with our farrier this morning."

As a matter of fact, he *had* picked this up. Kevin brightened immediately. "The near side is where we do most of our work. We lead horses from the left, the buckles of halters and bridles are on the left, and we mount up on the left. The off-side we don't really do much with unless we're grooming or fastening up the girth on the saddle."

"And some people in a hurry don't even bother unbuckling the off-side buckles of the girth after riding," Rosemary added, "although I don't recommend this! Nice work, Kevin. You're learning fast."

Nikki favored him with a smile, and Kevin felt an absurd lift in his chest, as if a weight had been lifted. Was he the teacher's pet today? Maybe, but he really wanted to be the teacher's *assistant's* pet.

Was that a thing?

When the class finished, Rosemary took Rochester back out to the pasture while Nikki presided over refreshments, urging everyone to snack on the brownies, cookies, and a few bottles of lemonade set on the picnic table next to the barn. Kevin hung back, contrary to his initial plans. The seminar had been so good, he felt bad taking the cookies away from these earnest empty-nesters in their shearling-lined boots. So he waited it out, hoping there'd be some treats left. And so he had a perfect view when Sean swaggered up to Nikki and started talking to her . . . and when Nikki laughed, pushed back her hair, and *blushed.*

Well, this wasn't going to work. Kevin made his way into the fray. "Sean, how are things? I'm surprised to see you here. I thought you were already a horse expert."

Sean laughed, flashing movie-star teeth. "Caitlin said I had to come and soak up how wonderful Rosemary and her assistant are. I didn't realize her assistant would be our very own Nikki."

Nikki smirked at Kevin before turning back to Sean. "I certainly hope you learned something today."

"I learned what a talented group of women are running the equestrian community in Catoctin Creek," Sean replied smoothly.

Nikki rolled her eyes at that, which Kevin took as both a hopeful sign and a bad one.

Undeterred, Sean marched on. "I've been meaning to ask you . . . Nikki, is that short for Nicole?"

*Of course it's short for Nicole, you idiot,* Kevin fumed.

"No, it's just Nikki, actually," she replied. "With two *k*'s. I'm lucky, my mom wanted to spell it *N-i-q-u-i,* but my dad intervened."

*Oh.* Kevin rocked back on his heels, rather disappointed in himself for not bothering to ask her. He'd just assumed . . .

"I like it," Sean purred. "It's a very to-the-point kind of name. Nikki. *Nikki gets it done.*"

"That's so true! That describes me to a T."

Kevin lurched into the conversation with the grace of a car crash. "It describes you to a *Nikki,*" he quipped.

She glanced at him incredulously. He thought he could hear her asking, *Are you okay?*

He responded with a toothy smile. *Great, thanks.*

"Kevin," she said carefully, "can you please run to my car? There's an extra plate of brownies in there. I think we may need seconds."

"Or thirds," Sean was laughing as Kevin darted off.

He was only gone about thirty seconds, but seemingly no amount of time was too brief for Sean. As Kevin returned with the brownies, he heard Sean asking, "What about dinner with me tonight? I know it's short notice, but I'm usually busy with lessons every evening. This is a rare day off for me."

Kevin froze, waiting for her answer. He watched the back of her head, the auburn curls which fell in wild coils down her back. Surely she'd blow him off. He was too young for her, for starters—wasn't he? Sean looked younger than all of them, but that might just be his perfect genes.

Nikki shook her head. "That's a really nice offer, Sean. But I can't, I'm having dinner here tonight, with Stephen and Rosemary."

*And Kevin!* he thought triumphantly.

"Oh, they'd understand." Sean's tone had gone wheedling. "Just this once."

"No," Nikki insisted, her own voice cooling in temperature. "But thank you. Can you excuse me a second?"

She turned towards Kevin as if she knew he'd be standing there. In a few quick steps she was at his side, overwhelming him with her energy, her clean scent of minty shampoo. He wanted to wrap his arms around her and thank her for turning down Sean, but instead he just handed over the brownies, like a normal person. She took them with a quick smile. "Thanks for grabbing these. Don't worry, there's a secret stash for dessert later. You're staying for dinner, right?"

He gazed at her for a moment. She *really* wasn't mad, he thought incredulously, but he had to ask, anyway. "Nikki, you aren't upset about the way things ended last night, are you?"

"Me, mad? I chased you out of the house with a list of jobs you didn't want to do. I thought *you'd* be mad at me!"

His heart flooded with relief. "I thought I was, but I was just overwhelmed. The truth is, it was sweet. Misguided, sure, but sweet."

Her eyes studied him for a moment. "I have to get back to these guys and help Rosemary answer questions. Let's talk about it later, okay?"

"Later's good," he said. "I'll just go in and take a shower."

"Oh, even better." She winked at him and was gone. He watched Sean follow her over to the picnic table, and smiled when she turned her back on him, focusing on the women in the group instead.

After her enthusiastic greeting up in the barn, and this moment, he knew for sure there was still something between them. They could figure this out.

# Chapter 19

## Nikki

Nikki was watching a low white cloud stretch across the sky beyond the mountains. She'd been leaning on the kitchen sink for a while, peering through the window, and the angle was giving her a crick in the neck.

She heard Rosemary come into the kitchen behind her. "Come look at this," she said.

"What?" Rosemary asked, alarm immediately entering her voice. "Did a horse do something stupid?"

Nikki remembered that horses were always doing something stupid, either hurting themselves or destroying farm infrastructure. "No, no, they're fine. But . . . look at this cloud." She stepped back from the sink and let Rosemary take her place. "Does that look like a snow cloud to you?"

"It's too early for snow," Rosemary replied immediately, but she came over and looked, anyway. Nikki watched her face shift from skeptical to incredulous. "Well . . . I don't know what to say. It never snows in November. But that sure does look like a snow cloud. Was there snow in the forecast? It was so nice today. Chilly, but not freezing like the past few days."

"I haven't even had time to look at the weather," Nikki admitted. She rarely paid attention to the weather forecast. The restaurant was always open, come snow, storm, or sun. Since most of the staff lived within walking distance, she'd even opened the doors during the occasional ice storm.

For some reason, neither of them reached for their phones. They just pressed together at the sink, looking out the window at that glittering white cloud. Eventually, Kevin came strolling into the kitchen, bringing a smell of soap with him. "Don't mind me, I'm just here for cookies—hey, what are you two looking at?"

"We think we see a snow cloud," Nikki explained. "What do you think?"

Kevin peered over their heads. "You mean *that* cloud?"

"Yes! The only one there is."

He considered it while she waited for his judgment. Eventually he scratched his chin and said, "You know, I'm not actually sure what a snow cloud looks like."

"How can you not know that?" Nikki asked impatiently. "You're from New York! It snows there, doesn't it?"

"It does, but I don't actually see what clouds do the snowing. Just . . . clouds."

"Well, they look just like this." Rosemary frowned at the cloud as if she might scare it back where it came from. "Kind of like if a storm cloud was all flattened on top. Wispy at the edges and underneath. I'm going to go bring the horses in just in case."

Just as she turned from the window, Stephen appeared in the kitchen, waving his phone. "Hey, you won't believe this, but my weather app just dinged and—it says it's going to snow in fifteen minutes. How about that!"

Rosemary shook her head and hustled out of the kitchen, as if Stephen's announcement had sucked all the fun out of their cloud-watching. In a way, Nikki supposed it had. Snow meant extra work: the horses weren't wearing blankets, so they needed to come inside before the temperature dropped. And horses could get pretty goofy when the weather changed suddenly.

Stephen watched her go with mild surprise. Nikki figured he hadn't been here quite long enough to know what a chore a sudden storm could be when horses were involved. "So crazy, right? I guess this time of year anything can happen. What were you guys all looking at? Did the horses do something stupid?"

Nikki sighed. "We were looking at the snow cloud," she admitted. "But now I better go help Rosemary. If we hustle we can get the horses in and fed before it starts. Then we don't have to slosh out there in a snowstorm later."

"I'll help, too," Kevin chirped. "I know my way around a horse now!"

Nikki thought his excitement was nothing short of adorable. Too bad being a farrier's apprentice would probably squash all this enthusiasm in the first day. "Okay, farm boy," she told him. "Let's go divide and conquer."

The stalls weren't ready for the horses to come in yet. They needed hay, water, and in one case, a certain dog to be removed. "You know, he can probably go inside," Rosemary decided. "I guess he hasn't peed all over the brick house carpets. Grover? You want to go in?"

The dog bounced against the stall door, wagging his tail.

"There's your answer," Nikki laughed.

"I'll just run him in," Rosemary said, opening the door. "And then I'll start bringing horses in. Stephen, can you do water? Nikki, can you and Kevin do hay?"

"I'll throw down hay," Kevin volunteered, making for the ladder to the barn's upper story. Nikki followed him. She didn't need to go up. She just wanted to watch his unexpected brawn at work again.

The encore act of The Kevin Show didn't disappoint her—well, his muscles certainly didn't. By the time she put her head and shoulders through the trapdoor in the barn floor, he was already halfway up the haystack he and Stephen had made earlier, and was carefully dropping the uppermost bales to the floor a good twenty feet below. Nikki noticed he dropped the bales straight down, so they didn't burst.

"Who taught you to drop those the right way?" she asked, impressed.

"Stephen," Kevin said with a grunt, dropping a fourth bale. "Apparently he made a huge mess of hay the first day he helped Rosemary."

*He most certainly did,* Nikki thought, with a rueful smile. That was the day she'd first met Kevin, but before he'd shown up, she'd happened upon Rosemary and Stephen in the barn and thought she was witnessing a crime going down. She'd had her hand halfway into her purse, ready to pull out her phone and call 911, when Rosemary had told her she'd just fallen into a broken hay-bale Stephen had dropped. Action had progressed from there.

Funny, the way things turned out.

"Watch out now, I want to drop these down to the first floor," Kevin warned, climbing down from the haystack, and Nikki carefully dropped back down to the lower barn. She turned around, dusting the hay chaff from her hands, and saw Stephen watching her with a quizzical expression.

"What?"

"Are you two together yet?"

Nikki made a face. "Stephen, at least be subtle."

He laughed. "What's the point? We all know how this story is going to end."

*Do we?* Nikki wondered. For the first time in years, she wasn't absolutely certain that tomorrow was going to be the same as today. She didn't know *what* was coming next.

And she was starting to like the uncertainty.

The horses were milling around the gate, begging to be brought inside, and Nikki couldn't blame them. There was an icy wind whipping down from the mountains, and the fir trees above were roaring like ocean surf. Their mild day of chilly sunshine was vanishing quickly. Nikki had never seen anything like it.

"I waited for you guys because they're all off their heads with this wind," Rosemary said, passing out lead-ropes. "Let me handle the gate and we can try to get one horse at a time through. If they all get loose, I don't know that they'll go to the barn. Rochester looks ready to lead them to battle. They might end up in D.C. before he's done."

Nikki glanced at Kevin. "Are you ready for this?"

He grinned. "I've led Rochester before, remember? And he was being a dummy that day, too."

Nikki shook her head. "I doubt that was even close to what he's going to be like today. Have you ever flown a kite?"

"I have, actually."

"Okay, well, imagine the kite is eighteen hundred pounds and has hard hooves flailing around. I think you'd better take in Mighty-mite."

"Good idea," Rosemary said.

Kevin's face immediately took on an injured expression. Nikki had to stifle a laugh. "The *pony?*" he asked. "Really?"

"Miniature horse," Rosemary corrected automatically, slipping past Nikki. She opened the pasture gate just wide enough to sneak inside while letting no one escape, and pushed back some of the horses who crowded forward, pressing her hands against their broad chests. "Get back, get back!"

"Watch where she pushes them," Nikki told Kevin. "Horses have pressure points and they'll respond really quickly when you find the right spots."

"Is this the Advanced class?" Kevin asked.

"Extra credit."

He tossed her a brilliant smile, eyes sparkling, and she felt a flare of warmth in her chest. For a moment, she forgot they were rushing to get the horses in. They watched each other, neither wanting to look away first.

Then a few icy flakes of snow, barely more than flurries, flew straight into Nikki's eyes. "Oh, yikes!" she blustered, pawing at the ice left behind in her eyelashes.

"Nikki!" Rosemary called, "are you ready for horses?"

"We're ready," she confirmed, blinking hard. She glanced back at Kevin, who gave her a thumbs up. "Give us what you've got."

Rosemary hauled over Mighty-mite and handed the lead-rope over the gate to Nikki. "Pull him through while I hold everyone back," she instructed, and Nikki quickly opened the gate about a foot wide, just enough to let the mini horse scoot through the opening. She slammed it shut again as Rochester came hauling through the crowded herd, nearly taking everyone out—Rosemary included. Kevin jumped backward as the huge black horse stopped right before he collided with the gate, then leaned his massive head over, snorting like a dragon.

Nikki just shook her head and passed the mini's lead-rope to Kevin. "Take this kid down to the barn, please."

Kevin gave her a glance which plainly said he wanted a bigger horse, but he still obeyed, turning for the barn while the little mini trotted alongside, tossing his head so that his long dark forelock flew in the wind. Nikki watched them for a moment, reassuring herself that Kevin wouldn't lose control of the mini—Mighty-mite could be surprisingly tough, hence his name—then turned back to the chaos in the pasture.

Rosemary was dragging Rochester's head back so there would be room to open the gate. "*Move back, you big dum-dum,*" she grumbled at the horse. But Rochester kept shoving his chest at the gate, as if he had forgotten it opened inward. Maybe he'd never known. Nikki tried to remember if horses showed aptitude for things like that.

Suddenly there was a crash, and the gate was ripped from Nikki's stiff hands. It coincided with a tremendous gust of icy wind and a swirl of snowflakes, so that Nikki was never really sure if she actually saw what happened next or if it was all conjecture put together in her mind's eye.

What she *thought* happened was that Rochester reared up and got his forelegs over the metal gate, and then pulled backwards, bringing the gate with him. She heard Rosemary shriek as the metal groaned and gave way, and then the thunder of hooves as the other horses, panicked, turned and galloped up the pasture slope. She felt herself pushed aside by something big and hard—Rochester, of course—as the horse jumped over the wreckage of the gate and went thudding down the hill. She pushed herself up from the cold ground quickly, hoping Kevin was already in the barn.

He was standing halfway down the hillside, Mighty-mite tugging with frustration against the lead-rope, as Rochester went plunging towards them. Alarm bells went off in Nikki's brain. Rochester's ears were pinned flat to his skull. For some reason, this gigantic horse was about to take out all his aggression on the mini horse.

Unless Mighty-mite could out-maneuver him.

*"Let him go!"* Nikki screeched. *"Kevin, unsnap the lead and move!"*

There was so little ground to cover and Rochester's legs were so long, Nikki wasn't sure he could set Mighty-mite free and get out of the big horse's way in time.

But somehow he did. The little horse twisted and reared as the pressure on his head released. But the result was not what Nikki expected. Instead of running away, the mini ran full-tilt *towards* Rochester, his ears pinned against his head. He looked like a tiny demon.

Nikki had seen him behave like this before—every now and then, the miniature horse turned into a raging stallion and picked fights with Rochester, usually when a mare was in season—but she had no idea what brought it out right now. The stress of the wind, the falling air pressure, who knew? All she could think was that Kevin was safe. She couldn't be in the middle of whatever fight that tiny horse provoked with the biggest, most powerful horse on the farm. He'd get clobbered by a giant hoof, and that would be the end of him.

The fight didn't happen, though, because Rochester didn't stop to fight with Mighty-mite. He kept going, his ears pinned and his tail lashing, until he'd vanished around the side of the barn.

Nikki looked back at Rosemary, who was standing by the wreckage of the pasture gate, her face tired. "What on earth was that?"

Rosemary shrugged. "Who can explain horses? I guess he went into his stall after all. Stephen can shut his stall door."

Kevin approached Mighty-mite cautiously. The frustrated mini allowed himself to be caught, but he squealed and trotted all the way down the hill, still anxious for a fight.

"Well," Nikki said, "that was interesting." She brushed flurries from her hair and nudged the twisted steel of the gate.

"This is the third gate he's done that with," Rosemary said, disgusted. "This is why I always have to keep a spare in the barn. He just *loses* it sometimes. But that's how it is with rescue horses. You never know what they're dealing with."

Nikki admired how unflappable Rosemary was around equine disasters. If she could only remain this calm and contained in situations involving humans, Rosemary would have made an amazing president.

Behind them, Stephen and Kevin were coming up the hill; in front of them, the rest of the herd were trudging down the pasture slope, their eyes wide and their nostrils flaring. Snow was swirling around them, a white blur falling faster and faster, already clinging to blades of grass and the north-facing sides of trees. The horses switched their tails, annoyed at the weather and eager to come inside.

Rosemary held out her arms to stop the horses from coming too close to the mangled gate. "Nikki, can you go back down to the barn while the guys help me haul this gate out of the way? The others can find their own way down to the barn now that the troublemakers are inside, I just need you to shut the doors behind them."

"I'll come with you," Kevin said quickly. "In case they're still being trouble."

Nikki smiled at him. "That's very gallant of you."

"Well, I'll still need you to protect me if the little horse goes crazy again."

She bumped against him, laughing. "Miniature horses can be really dangerous! I didn't want you to get in the middle of something you couldn't easily stop. Thank you for listening to me and not being macho about it."

Kevin gave her a serious look. "Hey, I'm not here to get killed. I'm here to build a new life. If that means listening to you, consider it done."

"Whatever I say?" Nikki teased, flicking a snowflake out of his hair.

"Whatever you say," he replied, his voice dropping in timber.

That blazing fire returned to her chest, warming her through despite the frigid wind. "You know, Kevin, we might just be snowed in here together tonight." She stopped at the barnyard gate and glanced into the barn. No trouble, no rush. "And that pretty farmhouse can get cold on stormy nights."

With a suddenly masterful air which took her entirely by surprise, Kevin wrapped his arm around her and tucked her up close to him. His voice was husky when he replied, "Nikki, I promise you'll be warm all night."

# Chapter 20

## Kevin

Kevin was so excited, he was ready to leap into the air and click his heels together.

What a morning! The sun was shining, last night's snow was a glimmering white blanket on the lawn in front of the farmhouse, and he'd just had a phone call from Gus telling him they were still going out on rounds this morning. His very first morning as a farrier's apprentice! *Today* his life changed. *Today* a new chapter began!

It was the most exciting Monday of his life.

He'd still been in bed when Gus called, sure, and Nikki had looked over at him with sleepy eyes which quickly narrowed as she asked what the hell he was thinking, leaving his phone ringer on like that, but the promise of going out and starting his apprenticeship was so exciting, he just gave her a long, triumphant kiss in lieu of an apology. Nikki, apparently in an excellent mood despite the phone ringer, didn't even complain again. She just kissed him back, and it was possible things could have gotten out of hand if Grover hadn't woken up, jumped onto the bed, and licked them both until Nikki insisted, in a voice which brooked no argument, that he take the dog outside.

So he had, and found out Grover loved snow. Watching his dog leap through the thin layer of snow as the sun rose had felt like pure joy. He was still living on the happiness now, along with all of his other joys.

Imagine that! So much goodness in one morning!

*Yessirree,* Kevin thought, standing on the front porch and gazing over the snow-laced trees at the foot of the lawn. Things were going *fantastic* this morning, yes they were.

He was already bundled up for his day of blacksmithing, wearing jeans and hiking boots, a quilted flannel shirt over a thermal top, and a decent canvas coat which hadn't seen a lot of mileage in the fashion-conscious city. He'd borrowed some thick socks from Rosemary, who had promised him his feet were going to be cold all day—because apparently being a farrier's apprentice meant standing still for hours on end, holding horses who were standing on concrete barn floors, rubber-matted wash-racks, or even outside on the frozen ground.

And the ground was definitely frozen this morning. The temperature was twenty-nine degrees and everything outdoors had that glossy frozen sheen to it, from the cars and truck parked next to the house to the old red barn. The sky had that particular ice-blue color, too—something he knew well from the city—which promised an icy day from dawn to dusk.

The front door opened and closed behind him, and he turned to see Nikki, bundled up in sweatpants and a heavy winter coat, a knit cap pulled over her tumble of auburn hair. She was clutching a mug of coffee in both hands. "It's *far* too early to be dealing with this cold," she grumbled, not looking at him but instead at the thin layer of snow blanketing the lawn and forest. "One of the advantages of being a restauranteur instead of a farmer? Staying inside on freezing-cold mornings. You might want to reconsider your little farrier adventure."

Kevin tipped her chin up and gave her an appreciative kiss. "But snow is beautiful," he told her. "Especially here, where there won't be any piles of snow-covered garbage on the corners for months on end. No dancing through gray slush in the crosswalks. Snow in the country is so amazing compared to snow in the city! Can't we pretend it's not a pain and just love it?"

"Okay, Buddy the Elf. It's beautiful," Nikki admitted begrudgingly. "But I have to work at the diner tonight, and old farmers do *not* like driving in for their supper when there's snow and ice on the road. We won't make any money and my waitresses will be griping all night."

"Well, *I'll* come in and eat with you," he promised. He put his hands to his heart, going over the top and loving it. Nikki made him feel like he could be as goofy as he wanted, and all she'd do was roll her eyes at him. He *loved* it when she rolled her eyes at him. Why was that? He thought being mocked by Nikki felt like a hug. It was her own weird way of showing affection. Had other guys known this? Or was he the first to figure it out? She was making a face at him right now, and he wanted to kiss her silly. "If it's really that slow, you'll be able to take a nice supper break and sit down with me. It will be like a date."

"A date at the Blue Plate," she snorted. "Not even the high school kids will stoop that low, and we're the only game in town.

They'd rather get Cokes from Trout's and hide out behind the volunteer firehouse."

"It will be a date at your restaurant," he insisted, undeterred. "At your very own business, which you run so well. We'll start a new trend."

Nikki cast him a sidelong glance, then looked back out at the sunlit snow. "You don't need to flatter me, Kevin. I know exactly what I've got and what it's worth. I'm there five days a week, remember?"

Kevin hated seeing her expression darken like that. He wanted desperately for Nikki to be as happy about her job as he was about his. Well, as happy as he was about the job he was embarking upon this morning. He was starting a new life, and he needed everyone in it to be just as happy as he was. Nikki had confessed her actual dream to him, and he suspected now that she'd told someone about it, she couldn't quite put it aside again. Dreams were like that—you said them aloud, and the yearning to make them real grew even stronger.

Maybe starting a new life was a plunge they could take together —he could learn a new trade, Nikki could find a way to serve some of her creations, off-menu. Eventually it could blossom into a new business. He knew she couldn't just quit the Blue Plate and start something new, the way he'd done. Their circumstances were different. But the reasons for her to take a chance were just the same, and just as urgent, as his.

Kevin watched her eyes flick around the snowy yard, wishing he could find an answer for her. It was a puzzle. Well, he'd have time to think on it today. While he was holding horses and driving all over this beautiful winter wonderland.

"Look at the steam coming off the creek," Nikki said, pointing. "You could make a calendar today, with the right camera. Twelve perfect photos is all it would take."

"Only twelve? Perfect photos would be easy to come by today. You wouldn't even have to leave the farm." Kevin watched the steam rise, the golden light streaming through the trees, the blue patterns of shadows on the snow, and a sudden memory came to him. "Remember that old song—what is it—*over the river and through the woods?*"

"To Grandmother's house we go?" Nikki smiled at him. "Yeah."

"We sang that in school. And in my head, the song looked just like this. Riding in a sleigh through the snow, over the river and through the woods."

A light glinted on a windshield in the woods. Gus's truck made its winding way up the lane. It clattered over the bridge across Catoctin Creek and rumbled its way up to park behind Rosemary's truck. Kevin looked at the lines it had cut through the few inches of snow and felt a little imperfection creep into this beautiful day. Suddenly, he didn't want to climb into that cab and drive off with Gus. This was too lovely a day to spoil with roads and slush and mud. A snow day was a day to be cherished. Kevin had learned *that* as a young boy, running to the park the moment the school cancellations came crackling over the radio perched on the kitchen windowsill.

What he really wanted to do right now was take Nikki by the hand and go walking up the farm drive behind the barn again, nothing marring the lovely snow but their own light footprints.

They'd stay out all day, playing with Grover and building an army of snowmen.

If only the snow had fallen a day sooner!

"Well, I have to go to work," he said, a little sadly. "Will you take Grover for a little walk before you go to the restaurant?"

She smiled at him. "Of course I will. Now, you be careful out there, cowboy. It's a dangerous job, and I'd hate to have to nurse you back to health after some stupid horse stomps on you."

"Thank you for the words of encouragement."

"You're welcome. Oh, wait a minute." She turned, opened the front door, and retrieved a travel mug she'd left just inside. "You almost left without any coffee. Rookie mistake."

He took it with a smile. "You know, in New York I'd always leave enough time in my commute to stop and get a coffee."

"Well, in Catoctin Creek it's always BYOB. Unless you want gas station coffee, and somehow, I know better than that." She tilted her face up to his, and he had a glimpse of the gold flecks in her hazel eyes. "Go get 'em," she whispered, and gave him a goodbye kiss which put all the shine back in his morning.

❧❧

Gus wasn't as old as he looked. This revelation surprised Kevin. Gray-haired, portly, and sporting a beard which was leaning into Santa Claus territory, the farrier looked at least a decade older than his fifty-odd years. He had a permanent hunch in his back and a temporary splint on his wrist.

"From repetitive stress," he explained, waggling his hand at Kevin. "Physical therapy and everything. My daddy would've laughed at me, flexing those little do-hickies at the doctor's office, a nurse cheering me on."

"Your dad was a farrier, too?"

Gus squinted out at the shiny road. Either the snow hadn't stuck to the larger roads, or the meager traffic had been enough to melt it, but the wet blacktop was blinding now that the morning sun was reflecting off it. "And then some. He was a true blacksmith," Gus said. "He only worked with iron and a forge. He didn't just do horseshoes, he made barrels, signs, all sorts of things. I thought I'd be just like him, but things change. Folks learned their horses' hooves weren't as tough as they'd thought. Some other folks learned their horses' hooves weren't as *soft* as they thought. This work is always getting more specialized. Barefoot trimming, custom shoeing, you name it. I thought I knew it all just from working with the old man, but then I had to go to journeyman farrier school when I was thirty-five years old. I was the oldest man in the class. Care to guess how long ago that was?"

Kevin had not lived his entire life in New York City so that he could be tricked into an age-guessing game. "Absolutely not," he said with a grin.

Gus laughed. "Oh boy. That's not the worst answer I've gotten, but it's not the best, either. It was eighteen years ago."

Kevin did not put on his shocked face, and he was secretly proud of himself for such discretion. "Will I have to go to farrier school?"

"It's a good idea. Let's get your feet wet, first. It's a big commitment. You gotta move to the school for months, work long hours. Maybe you won't like this enough for all of that."

"Wow. Okay. And once you get through the school, do you have to go back for updates, that kind of thing?"

"You don't *have* to, but there's always seminars and new things to learn. It depends a lot on who you shoe for. Some folks don't care what you do as long as their horses' feet look straight and the shoes stay on for six or eight weeks. Some folks have a list of demands and want to see if they know more fancy words than you do. The show barns can go either way. You'd be surprised how much money some folks have and they don't want to spend it on their horses' feet."

Kevin considered this. One thing really stuck out in Gus's speech. "Let me ask you a really basic question, so I don't sound like an idiot: is it feet, or is it hooves?"

Gus laughed, his belly brushing the truck's steering wheel. "It's supposed to be hooves. But you find horse people say both. If you know all the clinical terms, you're allowed to use the slang, that's how it works. So horses don't really have feet, or ankles, or what-have-you. But we use those words all the time and we all know what everyone means."

Gus turned the truck into a driveway set between two elegant brick posts. A brass sign glinted on the right-hand post: *Elmwood Equestrian Center*. Kevin's eyebrows went up. This was the famous Elmwood!

Two big pastures lined the driveway, their rolling swells coated with white. Trim fences of black-painted boards met neatly at right angles and encircled the largest trees in the fields. A long, cream-colored stable drew nearer, seeming to nestle in the shadow of a tall box-like structure next to it. A traditional brick farmhouse, not unlike Rosemary's stood off to the left, half-hidden by a cluster of tall trees.

This was a wealthy place, Kevin could tell instantly. Notch Gap Farm, like most of the farms in the area, was in a state of gentle and picturesque disrepair. Elmwood was at the height of its powers.

"What's behind the barn?" Kevin asked. "It looks like a warehouse."

"That's an indoor arena," Gus explained. "For riding all winter. Elmwood is busy year-round. Riding lessons, boarders, horse shows, therapy riding. Caitlin's got forty-some horses and ponies here, and most of them are real expensive."

The stable had stalls running down either side of two long aisles; as Gus pulled the truck into the parking lot, a sliding door was open just enough to show the tidy aisle within, horses looking curiously over their doors. Gus backed the truck right up to the door, and a brown-haired girl in a sweater and jeans slid the door open wide enough for them to slip inside. "Cold out there," she said with a grin. "We're trying to keep the heat inside."

It *was* noticeably warmer inside, just like Rosemary's barn had been, although this vast horse warehouse was not nearly as snug and cozy as her little stable. Kevin was astonished at the idea of so many horses housed within one structure. It might take Gus *days* to get through forty-odd horses, he thought. How much time did he spend here?

"We'll be here all day," Gus said, as if reading his thoughts. He pulled down the tailgate and popped up the truck cap's window. Inside, the forge and a rack of shiny silver horseshoes waited. He tugged on each and they smoothly rolled onto the tailgate, made easy to access thanks to some ingenious runners. "Our one and only stop of the day. Nadine here will bring us the horses on the barn list."

"I'd love to," Nadine said apologetically, "but I've got to go pick up lunch for everyone."

"Lunch, already?" Kevin couldn't help but ask. It was only ten-thirty.

"We start work at six-thirty," Nadine said, winking. "And the cold makes everyone starving hungry by nine. Anyway, Sean's around. He'll get you set up. I think the first horse is Pumpkin."

"Oh, good. An easy one to start." Gus swung his arms, stretching. "I always like to start with a simple two-shoe reset."

"Hopefully he's easy," Nadine said. "When the temperature drops this fast, you never know."

Kevin lifted his eyebrows. "Why's that?"

Nadine grinned. "You're pretty new to this, aren't ya?"

Kevin shrugged. After a decade in one job, he'd forgotten how uncomfortable being the new guy could feel, but he was resolved to see this through. "I'm here to learn," he said finally.

"Gus'll teach ya right," Nadine assured him. "Well, I better go."

"Listen," Gus said, "while you're going to get lunch, can you bring back something for Kevin and myself? Saves us time goin' and comin' back later," he said to Kevin.

"Good idea," Kevin agreed, as Nadine nodded. He felt his back pocket, and then his coat pockets, and his heart chilled. "Oh, damn. I don't have my wallet."

"That's no problem," Nadine said. "You'll be back later this week."

"Every day this week, lookin' at Caitlin's list." Gus's voice was muffled; he was rifling around in the back of the truck. "Oh, damn."

"What is it?" Kevin craned his neck to see.

Gus turned around and leaned heavily on the tailgate, looking sheepish. "Nadine, you got anyone who's just trims, no shoes?"

"I sure do. Why?"

"Well, I meant to put the new propane tanks in the truck this morning, but the missus was talking my ear off about the grandkids' Christmas lists and . . ." Gus shook his head. "It went right outta my mind. Listen, there's an easy fix. Nadine, you're just going to Trout's for hoagies, right? Well, take Kevin along, and my credit card—here you go, Kevin—and he can go into the hardware store and exchange these old tanks for me." He pulled out some clanging gas cylinders. "Perfect solution. And I can do a nice easy trim by myself while you're gone."

Nadine nodded. "Works for me. You ready, Kevin?"

Kevin accepted the armful of mini-cylinders Gus thrust at him. The entire situation surprised him: being handed someone else's credit card, being bundled off in a young woman's car moments after he'd met her. *This would never happen in New York,* he thought, and then he smiled and shook his head. That was the whole point, right? To do things differently, to live a life outside his own narrow experience? He followed Nadine out of the barn.

"You all set there, buddy?" Nadine asked, buckling her seat belt. Her car was an ancient Subaru station wagon, not unlike something a Brooklyn mom would drive, although with a lot more hay and feed bags strewn around the interior than any conveyance in Brooklyn would ever have.

"I'm good," Kevin said. "I'm great."

# Chapter 21

# Nikki

As soon as Kevin was on the road, Nikki hustled back up to the front bedroom. She needed to straighten the place up before Rosemary could see the state they'd left the room in. The bedclothes were strewn across the floor, and so were yesterday's clothes. Nikki closed the door behind her, feeling embarrassed. They'd been quiet . . . but had they been quiet enough? Judging by the mess they'd left behind, things had gotten a little more heated than she'd intended.

Not that Rosemary would mind, of course. She'd been egging Kevin on; Nikki had heard her! But it was the *principle* of the matter. You didn't go to your friends' house, stay overnight, and immediately hook up with the other house-guest without at least attempting to be quiet and respectful.

Or without cleaning up your room afterwards. Nikki started dragging the sheets back into place, wishing the antique bed wasn't quite so high off the ground. She wasn't the tallest woman in the world, after all. "This bed was built for a giant," she huffed, tugging the top sheet up to the pillows. "Wait a minute . . . what do we have here?"

Kevin's nice wool coat had gotten tangled up in the sheets—she didn't even know why, and she was determined not to think too hard about it—and something bulky hit her hand as she pulled the coat free. She shook the coat and his wallet fell from a pocket, hitting the hardwood floor with a thud.

Nikki looked at it and sighed. "Oh, you dummy. Now I'm going to have to find you and bring you your wallet."

Then, a smile played around her lips. A reason to go and see Kevin? That was positively providential.

Yeah, she missed him already. How quickly he was getting under her skin! Maybe they could have lunch together. Gus had told her they were spending the day at Elmwood. She'd just take a quick trip over there and see what their lunchtime plans were.

Once this place was tidied up.

Nikki stuffed the wallet into the pocket of her jeans and finished making the bed.

Elmwood was on the south side of Catoctin Creek. Nikki knew the drive by heart. The equestrian center was just as beautiful now, resting under its blanket of snow, as it had been on those blue-and-yellow summer days when she and Rosemary had gone to pony camp together. They'd had so much fun on those long, hot days! Caitlin's mother had bred champion show ponies, and the farm was full of kids all day, all summer—kids washing ponies, riding ponies, brushing ponies, feeding ponies, taking ponies swimming in the farm pond, taking ponies for rides in the woods, tramping back on foot after ponies dumped them and ran home on their own.

Nikki had never been an expert rider; Rosemary had done the honors for the both of them at the annual county fair and in the 4-H shows every spring and summer, while Nikki had been happiest just putzing around the paddocks. Still, she'd learned a lot at Elmwood, and she was grateful her parents had let her ride there. She'd been less grateful for the presence of Caitlin Tuttle, but of course Caitlin had lived there, so that part couldn't really be helped.

Nikki turned her car up the drive to Elmwood, noting the new polish on the gleaming brass sign. Elmwood's shining evidence of success annoyed her just a little, partially because Caitlin had always annoyed Nikki, and partially because Caitlin had taken her family business and turned it into something bigger, while Nikki had only continued running the Blue Plate as if she was just managing the place for her aunt. The big barn and indoor arena dominated the center of the farm, their worth and prominence far surpassing any other farm in Catoctin Creek. Nikki supposed comparing the two businesses was pointless, apples and oranges, but it didn't change the general frustration that she felt around Caitlin's success.

Gus's truck was parked up against an aisle doorway, the door pushed open just wide enough for someone to slip in alongside the bed. Nikki pushed aside a rush of deja vu as she entered the barn; she hadn't been back here in years. In many ways, nothing had changed. If she looked more closely, though, she could see the fresh signs of prosperity in here: new brass nameplates on each stall door, leather halters hanging tidily where faded nylon had once been good enough, a spotless aisle and clean rafters which could only come from having a lot of well-paid help.

Closer at hand, Gus bent over the forehoof of a drowsing pony, peeling away at the overgrown sole with his sharp, hook-ended hoof knife. Sean Casey was holding the pony's lead and gazing at nothing. He was handsome even when he was practically drooling with boredom, Nikki noted with irritation. Sean jumped a little as he registered Nikki's presence, and the pony pricked his ears and fluttered his eyelashes, suddenly awake.

Gus sensed the change in the pony's demeanor and released the hoof, standing upright with exaggerated slowness. He turned around and spotted her. "Nikki Mercer, twice in one day! What brings you here?"

Nikki held up Kevin's wallet. "Your apprentice left this back at Rosemary's house. I just wanted to pass it on to him. Where is he?"

"Oh, wouldn't you know! He went back into town with Nadine. They were grabbin' lunch for the barn crew. And propane for my forge. If you wait around a little, they'll be back soon." Gus bent back over the pony's hoof, lifting it with large, sure fingers.

Sean gave her a welcoming smile. "Yes, stay and chat with me, please. Gus isn't very talkative."

Gus grunted. "*You* try talkin' with your head upside-down for hours."

Nikki slipped the wallet back into her pocket with a sigh. "I guess I have nothing else going on. I'm not needed at the diner until after two." She leaned against the stall closest to Sean and the pony, tipping her head back against the stall bars. The small pony inside came over to lip at her hair.

Sean looked ready to get his chat on. His face was open, his eyes bright. He was as handsome as ever, but Nikki thought he was looking a little pale today. He needed some sun. Too much indoor arena riding, probably. She liked a man with some color in his cheeks, like Kevin. Ruddy, red-headed Kevin. She smothered a smile, lest Sean think it was directed at him. "So, what's going on, Sean?" she asked, ready to do her part.

"Just lots of barn work today." He shrugged. "Lessons are all in the afternoon and one of the grooms was out sick, so I'm helping Nadine get through everything that isn't mucking out. I don't usually stand around holding ponies all day," he added, as if she cared what he did.

"There are worse things in the world," Nikki said drily. "I have to spend all evening in a diner, cracking the whip in the kitchen and making sure the grandparents of Catoctin Creek have enough gravy for their meatloaf."

"Hey, I've had the meatloaf at the Blue Plate! It's fantastic! Is it your recipe?"

Nikki imagined someone saying such a thing about any of her *actual* recipes. Someone besides Kevin. "It's my aunt's, actually," she replied. "And I don't even make it. Patrick takes responsibility for our meatloaf."

"Well, give my compliments to Patrick," Sean said grandly. "And your aunt. They're geniuses."

Nikki plastered a fake smile across her face. Inside, she felt herself shriveling up, the way she always did when people waxed lyrical about the diner's cooking. *Really, this is what you want?* she felt like screaming. *Just forty more years of the same old meatloaf?*

It wasn't that she wanted people to tire of the Blue Plate—after all, she didn't want the place to go out of business and leave her jobless. When she'd first taken over, she'd really appreciated all the compliments. For the first few years, she'd thought all that praise meant she was doing the right thing, that it meant she was giving the people what they wanted, which was a continuation of the many years her aunt had put into the Blue Plate, with no interruptions, as if her retirement to sunny Arizona had never happened.

Now Nikki was beginning to feel as if every compliment was another nail in her coffin, another reminder that things would never change in Catoctin Creek. No one wanted to know what she really had to offer. They were happy enough with what they already had from her. Could she blame them? Who would turn up their nose at really good meatloaf with a rich brown gravy, anyway?

Not even Nikki, truth be told. The meatloaf was delicious, even if these days she hated admitting it to herself.

Nikki pushed her fingers through the stall bars and tickled the pony's nose. Sean was from the outside, she thought. Maybe he would have a fresh perspective. "Say, Sean, if you could have any kind of restaurant added to Catoctin Creek, what would it be?"

"Are you opening something new?"

"Hah, not a chance." Nikki laughed chummily. "Just a little market research, to make sure I'm on the right path, you know?"

*The path to an early grave, more like.*

"Well, it's hard to say. If it was just me, I guess maybe Thai food? Or sushi."

Gus grunted at that. Nikki glanced at the farrier. He had moved to the pony's opposite hind hoof and was digging away at the sole as if he had heard nothing. But she knew better. If there was one thing the older members of the town were staunchly opposed to, it was sushi. Or as they would call it: *ugh, raw fish!*

"I don't think there's any chance of that happening," she told Sean.

"Maybe a bakery? Muffins, coffee, croissants, that kind of thing? Everyone likes a bakery."

She'd thought about a bakery before but dismissed the idea as too small. If you couldn't have anything new, she'd reasoned, why not dream as big as possible? She allowed herself to admit this logic might be flawed. "Honestly? Not a half-bad idea."

"Sure is better than sushi," Gus interjected.

Sean grinned. "Can you bake?"

"Can I bake? You ever seen the dessert menu at the Blue Plate?" Blondies, brownies, cakes, and pies: maybe they weren't gourmet bakery-level, but they were all delicious and mostly by her. She supposed a good dessert transcended class. *Everyone* wanted a brownie—the only real question was if they wanted the edges or not. "I can bake all right. Hey, who knows, maybe someday I'll open a bakery here."

"Well, I love that idea. I'd be your first customer." He smiled winningly.

*Too* winningly. Nikki frowned at him, just to make her position clear. "I bet you would be. The question is, would there be a second or a third customer waiting behind you?"

Gus picked up another hoof, and the pony shifted weight suddenly, dipping one hip as if he didn't want to stand up on his own another second. "Whoooo-ah!" Gus bellowed, hanging on a second too long. The pony slammed down his hoof, ripping it from Gus's hands. "Damn!" He shook his hand hard.

Nikki leapt forward. "Are you all right? Let me see that."

"Just caught me with the ragged edge of his hoof." Gus rubbed his palm against his jeans. "Sean! Pay attention, please. You can flirt with Nikki later."

*He's not really flirting with* me, Nikki wanted to say, but then she saw the guilty look on Sean's face and realized he was. Then she looked past him and saw why the pony had jumped. Kevin was back, standing in the narrow opening of the door with a surprised expression on his face.

*Whoops.*

"He didn't say anything about it?" Rosemary asked.

Nikki tucked the phone against her neck and looked around the bustling dining room. She'd been ignoring the business tonight, letting Lauren oversee the servers and make sure the kitchen was keeping up, but the place was pretty quiet. The snowfall must have kept some folks home, she supposed. Older regulars who weren't as confident driving on wet and slippery roads as they used to be.

"Not a thing," she said, leaning the phone against her shoulder and wiping some menus to look busy. "He just handed over the hoagies they'd gotten for lunch and then made himself busy holding horses for Gus, asking lots of questions. He was focused on the horses. So I gave him his wallet, and I left."

"Well, that doesn't mean anything."

"He could have looked a *little* jealous."

Rosemary laughed. "Is that what you want? You want a jealous boyfriend? That doesn't sound like you. Didn't you break up with Ernie Boswell in high school because he wanted you to call him and let him know what time you went to bed every night?"

"That was stalker-ish," Nikki protested. "That was truly psycho behavior. I just want Kevin to think another man is flirting with me and look *moderately* perturbed."

"Well, it's early days yet. You have plenty of time to make him jealous. And I think Kevin might be used to women disappointing him . . . he has a low bar for that sort of thing."

Nikki put down the menus with a slap. Several diners looked up from their meatloaf and their fried chicken. Mrs. Rooney, who had been her second-grade teacher, frowned at her in a way which made her want to fold her hands in her lap. "What makes you say that?" Nikki hissed, averting her gaze from the disapproving Mrs. Rooney. "What do you know?"

"I just know he hasn't actually been in love with anyone since high school," Rosemary whispered. "Stephen told me."

"Oh my God." Nikki leaned back against the planter that blocked the first booth from the diner's check-in podium. "Are you serious? What kind of a stat is that? He's what, thirty-five?"

"Have *you* been in love since you were in high school?"

Nikki considered this. "Does Chris Hemsworth count?"

"No. Come on. No one's good enough for you. Don't put Kevin in that hole, too. Because you guys are going to be great together."

"Well, now the pressure's on, Rosemary. Thanks very much for that."

"Blah blah," Rosemary mocked. "Go back to work, Restaurant Manager. I have to go."

"Bye-bye," Nikki sighed, putting down the phone. She looked across the restaurant and locked eyes with Mrs. Rooney again. This time, she held eye contact until the elderly woman went back to her meatloaf.

# Chapter 22

## Kevin

Kevin let himself back into the brick house shortly after sunset, more sore than he could ever remember being. He'd been working with Gus for more than a week, but this had been the toughest day so far. His feet hurt, his legs hurt, his back hurt, his shoulders—the list went on and on. He'd spent most of the day holding horses for Gus, just as Rosemary had said he would, but this afternoon, things had escalated. Gus had let him start trimming an easy hoof with the curved hoof-knife, and the creeping agony of being bent in half like that, while a horse tugged impatiently on his grip and he tried to concentrate on where he slid that very sharp blade, was going to take some serious getting used to.

He'd barely unfolded himself from the car, but Grover's sharp barks let him know he was wanted inside, urging him on. Having the dog was a real comfort. Every night, Grover greeted Kevin with rapturous excitement, barking and spinning in circles and spilling happy drool everywhere. Now he bounced around the house, licking at his empty food dish every he time he passed the kitchen, wagging his tail at Kevin.

"Yes, yes, supper is coming," Kevin sighed, tugging off his boots. "Some of us have to clean ourselves up before we can tramp all over the carpets."

Not that his dirty boots would have made much difference. The brown carpets couldn't really show any dirt. Kevin glanced around the little house without pleasure. Even with the new furniture Stephen had bought, the living room felt blank and empty. Kevin hadn't had a roommate since college, but now he felt he would have liked to have come home to another person.

Not just any person. He'd like to come home to Nikki.

He had seen her occasionally during the past week, usually when passing through Catoctin Creek with Gus. Three times, he had only glimpsed her through the plate-glass windows of the Blue Plate, working away alongside her teenage staff. Yesterday, he had gone into Trout's Market as she had come out. He'd stopped in front of her, keenly aware Gus was sitting in the truck behind him, watching everything. Nikki's eyes had flicked up to meet his, the golden flecks in their depths catching the winter sunlight.

"How are things with Gus?" she'd asked.

"They're fine," he said. "But listen—can I call you? I thought maybe you'd call me."

She'd cast her eyes down, then back up, as if she'd had to consider his request first. "You can call me," she replied. "I'm busy most nights, though. I only have off Thursday this week. Lauren's doing something with her sister."

"Let's skip the call. I'll take you out Thursday night," he'd said impulsively.

"I'll cook for you, if you want," she'd countered, astonishing him. "On my day off, I like to cook."

"You've got yourself a deal, Nikki Mercer."

Kevin had been living in a fever of anticipation ever since. Now it was Wednesday night, and he still had another day to get through before Thursday.

"Well, good thing I have you to keep me distracted," he told Grover, who promptly flipped over his food dish with a clatter. "Right, right. Subtle."

Kevin poured kibble into the dog's bowl and let him go at it while he checked the contents of the fridge, half-hoping some good fairy had delivered gourmet groceries to him. Nope, just the few things he'd picked up from Trout's: a pack of hot dogs, some yogurts, a pouch of sauerkraut. What he really wanted was hummus, but that apparently hadn't made it to Catoctin Creek yet. He supposed Rosemary and Nikki stocked their shelves from a grocery store closer to civilization. He'd have to figure that out, maybe in a few days when he returned his rental car and bought the used pickup he'd found cheap at a local car-lot.

A pickup truck, a house, and a dog: Kevin figured he should have been happy, but the truth was, he was only a few days into his brand-new Catoctin Creek life and he was already lonesome as hell. The empty rooms echoed back his words when he spoke out loud to cut the silence, and his bed felt big and cold at night. Grover had chosen to be a floor-dog, despite all of Kevin's entreaties for the dog to climb into bed next to him. Kevin put off bedtime and got up early, anxious to avoid the empty feeling in his chest when he sprawled across the center of the bed, pillows heaped to either side.

His loneliness made little sense, though. Was this about missing the clatter and company of city life, or was this about missing Nikki?

It had to be Nikki. He'd thought about her every day in the city, and now that something was finally happening between them, staying apart from her felt crazy. Not to mention, he was keenly aware he wasn't the only man in town who saw Nikki's potential. Maybe every Catoctin Creek local who'd ever had a shot with Nikki had already come and gone, but Sean Casey was new *and* very clearly interested. He'd seen the guy's face when Kevin walked into the Elmwood barn. Sean had been gazing at Nikki like she was the only woman in the world.

That was *his* look for her, dammit. The longer he stayed away, the better shot someone like Sean had at diverting Nikki's attention. Sean with his damned Norse God good looks.

"I should drive right back to town and see her," Kevin said aloud. His voice bounced back from the living room walls, and the echoes made him feel so hollow, he nearly turned on his heel to head right back out to his car. Luckily, he happened to glance down at himself. A day of working as a farrier does not do agreeable things to one's clothes. He sniffed the air experimentally, and found he had an atmosphere of hoof-smoke, which was a particularly vile singed smell he hadn't been prepared for.

Comprehension dawned on Kevin. "Oh man, I'm gross."

Grover finished his food and wagged his tail in gentle agreement. Kevin studied him for a minute, then glanced at the clock. It wasn't even seven yet. Early.

"Do you want to go to town, buddy?"

Grover parted his lips and panted. It looked enough like a smile to Kevin.

"Right after I shower," he told the dog, and headed for the bathroom.

It took him longer than he expected to get cleaned up. At eight-oh-two P.M., Kevin started rapping on the glass door of the Blue Plate. The *Closed* sign was hung neatly on the door, and the lights in the dining room were half-out. Kevin cursed the hot water heater in the brick house for the millionth time. If the damn thing had been running properly, he wouldn't have gotten here so late. Even so, he'd hustled down to town at a breakneck speed, and yet he'd *still* missed beating closing time by two lousy minutes.

Even if he'd made it before someone flipped the sign, he doubted he would have been brave enough to waltz in and order food from Nikki's staff with just a few minutes until close. All the stares from rude staff in New York could not equate the treatment he'd (deservedly) get at her hands in such a scenario. One does not simply order a meal five minutes before close and expect to be treated well in return.

Still, she might be persuaded to make him a little doggie-bag if there was anything left in the kitchen. He'd come rushing down to see her without bothering to eat anything first, and now he was absolutely starving. Grover was in the car, nose passed to the windshield, happily wagging his tail, but he'd eaten already. No wonder he was so cheerful.

The kitchen door swung open, and he saw her slim body silhouetted by the bright kitchen lights. Kevin's heart lifted in a way he had never felt before. *Be cool,* he told his heart. *Don't do anything I wouldn't do.*

His heart, thudding like mad, seemed determined not to listen to him.

Still, Kevin held it together as Nikki crossed the dining room and unlocked the front door. She opened it wide and hustled him inside. "It's cold out there!" she scolded him. "What are you doing here so late?"

He tried to imagine growing up in a world in which being out at eight o'clock was considered late. Nikki's life was so tiny and adorable. He wanted to put her in a snow globe. Right after he kissed her. "Can I kiss you?" he stage-whispered. "Will your staff catch us necking in the doorway?"

She shook her head disapprovingly, but she was smiling and he knew he had her charmed. "Okay, weirdo. You can kiss me. We've done worse, God knows."

Kevin made sure the kiss was very professional and work-appropriate. "How was that?"

"Freezing."

"I didn't want to embarrass you."

"No, I mean your lips were cold. Also, it's freezing in this dining room. I already turned down the heat for the night. But whatever, now you can tell me why you're here. *Not* that I'm mad about it," she added. "I just have to get back to the kitchen and make sure things are going smoothly. Also, you were supposed to come over tomorrow. You're a day early."

"I know. I just wanted to see you."

Nikki regarded him for a moment. Then she leaned against the podium and sighed. "Are you hungry?"

Kevin nodded. "I'm starving. Any chance you'll give me a doggie-bag of leftovers?"

She smiled and shook her head. "You deserve better than a doggie-bag. Go back to my place and preheat the oven. Three seventy-five, you got that? When it dings, take out the casserole dish on the top shelf of the fridge and shove it in to bake. By the time I'm home, we'll have a good supper waiting. Nice, warming food. You probably need it after working outside all day." She dug around in her jeans pocket, pulled out her key-ring, and detached the house-key from it. "See you there in about forty-five minutes?"

Kevin took the key from her, astonished. "When you say nice, warming food, what are we talking here?"

She gave him a twinkling smile. "That's a surprise. You like spicy?"

"Of course!"

"You'll like this, I promise."

Kevin didn't care if the entire conversation was double entendre or not. In fact, he was so hungry, he kind of hoped it wasn't. Or if it could be both, if it could be both a delicious, spicy meal *and* a delicious, spicy Nikki, he'd be a very happy man.

—☙—

Kevin and Grover both felt comfortable in Nikki's apartment. Grover settled down alongside the couch, while Kevin slipped off his boots and glanced around, feeling the warmth of Nikki all around him. The warmth was literal as well as figurative: the furnace was running full-tilt and the space was comfortable, but once he'd turned the oven on, he felt compelled to turn down the thermostat a few clicks just to keep from having to take his pants off.

Far too soon to be greeting Nikki wearing just plastic wrap, anyway.

He rolled back the foil a little on the casserole, found an impenetrable layer of cheese, and decided they were working with something Mexican in nature. Maybe enchiladas. *Yum.*

With the casserole safely baking, he next considered the bottles of wine stacked neatly in a little frame atop the fridge, but decided anything spicy and cheesy was really asking for beer. Luckily, Nikki had a good supply of that, too. He helped himself to a bottle and settled down on the sofa to look at his phone, one hand rubbing Grover's soft ears, periodically glancing up and gazing around the pretty room. He couldn't believe he was really here, waiting for Nikki, as delicious cooking smells filled the space.

She walked in just as he was setting the casserole dish on the stove-top. He took off the oven-mitts and turned around. "Well, hello!"

She grinned at him, pushing down Grover as the dog frantically greeted her. "Honey, I'm home!"

Kevin's heart did that thing again. It was a fast, frantic, fluttering motion, and he was having strong suspicions about what it all meant. "I'll have a cocktail made for you in a jiffy, my darling," he replied in his best mid-century accent. "Just you take off your things and come over here and kiss me."

"Gladly, honeybear," she laughed, tugging off her coat. "Oh! Get off me, dog!"

They tumbled into each other halfway across the room, which was conveniently where the sofa was located, and progressed through several layers of clothing before Kevin's stomach growled so loudly they both startled.

"I thought that was Grover for a second," he admitted.

"Oh my gosh, you need to eat," she chortled, pushing herself upright. "That casserole has to be cool enough to cut into. Let's have dinner."

Kevin looked up at Nikki, her spirals of hair escaping from its ponytail and coiling delightfully around her high cheekbones, and thought he'd never seen anything more delicious. "You're all I need," he told her. "Come back here and let me ravish you."

Nikki groaned, shoving at him as he tried to scoop her back up into his arms. "I'm not going to listen to that stomach incessantly while I'm trying to get my romance on. Come on, you've been working a big tough man's job all day, come have a big tough man's meal."

Kevin followed her to the kitchen, taking the plates from her as she pulled them down from the cabinet. "What would you feed me if I wasn't working a big tough man's job?"

She considered him for a moment. "Soup," she decided.

"I like soup."

"*Canned* soup," she amended, with the air of someone announcing there was poison in the wine.

"I grew up eating canned soup," Kevin protested.

"We all did, but those were different times and we are different people." Nikki rolled back the foil on the casserole dish. "Mmm, this looks fantastic. That cheese is bubbling in all the right places, if you know what I mean."

"I love what a food snob you are." Kevin kissed Nikki's ear, just to make her squirm. "You're almost a food bully. What would you do if you came up to the brick house, and I served you canned soup?"

"I'd be offended," she told him seriously, "and rightfully so. Put a little effort in for your girlfriend, man!"

Kevin pulled her close, nearly dropping the plates. They clattered on the countertop. *"Are* you my girlfriend?" he breathed.

She laughed against his cheek. "Of course I am," she told him, her voice a husky whisper. "What did you think we were doing? Don't play your city games with me. I'm no pushover, and I'm done waiting around. Now, you play by *my* rules. You're in my house, you're cooking my food, you're setting my table? Look at yourself! I'm training you, Kevin. I'm making you the perfect boyfriend."

"I should feel emasculated," Kevin grumbled, "but you're such a superb cook, I don't even mind."

His joking words were just a brave front. Kevin was only barely keeping his head above the waves; the surge of emotion overwhelming him was almost too much to handle. It was *frightening,* gripping this whole other human so closely, pulling her close to him with such intensity, realizing that skin-to-skin was as near as she could really come and yet he wanted *more,* somehow, to absorb her right into his being. He closed his eyes against the onslaught of feeling, wanting only to feel her, to bask in her, to be part of her.

"Kevin," she whispered. "Are you okay?"

He didn't know how to answer that. He nodded, his face still pressed against hers.

"Good." There was a pause. "Kevin? Dinner's going to get cold."

Her earnest practicality—that was just one more thing he loved about her. Oh, God! He was in love with her. That was what this was. *Love*—for the first time in his adult life, love. He'd watched Stephen fall for Rosemary, and wondered when it would happen for him, and all the while he'd been falling for Nikki and hadn't even realized it.

He was an idiot.

"Kevin, baby." Her arms tightened around him in a quick, reassuring squeeze. "Whatever it is, you'll feel better after you eat something."

He let her go and leaned back, gazing at her with wide eyes, seeing her with the full shimmer of love sparkling around her face. Her smile was hesitant at first, then pure and full.

*She loves me back,* he thought. *But I know she won't admit it.*

If there was one thing to be certain about with Nikki, it was that she'd make him earn every move up the ladder. Nothing would come easy with this spirited girl he'd fallen for.

Kevin could live with that.

"Okay," he agreed. "Let's eat."

# Chapter 23

# Nikki

K evin's phone was ringing. Nikki looked up groggily. Her
eyes sought out the clock on the oven. *Ten-thirty!* Who the
hell was calling someone's cell at ten-thirty at night? And why did
he persist in leaving his ringer on? Nikki thought she'd made her
position on being woken from a dead sleep by his phone very clear.
She kicked Kevin, and he grunted in response.

"Get up," she demanded. "Your phone is ringing."

"What? Sorry. Hand it here."

She reached out and took the phone from her little nightstand.
"Don't make this a regular thing," she growled, but he was already
answering on the line.

"Alice? What's going on?"

*Alice?* Nikki was suddenly wide awake. Who on earth was
Alice? And why was she calling in the middle of the night? Well,
close enough. No, Nikki wasn't usually asleep by now, but the
principle remained the same: it was too late to be calling people
unless there was a genuine emergency. Kevin could make a new
outgoing message on his voicemail: *Sorry, I keep country hours*

*now. Please leave a message and don't call after nine o'clock in the future.*

Kevin was sitting upright, talking quickly into the phone. "No, I'm not there—why didn't you tell me you were coming? A *surprise?* Who told you that was a good idea?"

Nikki got out of bed, climbed down from the loft, and stalked into the kitchen. She took down a bottle of whiskey and a cut crystal glass, and poured herself a little measure. She did not take down a glass for Kevin. He could get his own whiskey, after he told her exactly what was going on and who Alice was.

"I mean, I can be up there in . . . fifteen minutes, I guess. No, more like twenty. It's late, and I had a couple of drinks . . . yeah, I'm out tonight, what about it? I have my own life down here, Alice."

*Yup, he has his own life, if I don't end it for him in the next five minutes.*

"Great, just . . . oh wait, you know what? There's a key under the mat. Yes! Seriously. See it? Look again. See it now? Good. Go inside. Make yourself at home. I'll be up in a few. Yeah. Uh-huh. Bye Alice!"

Nikki felt the whiskey burn in her throat. "Alice?" she asked casually.

Kevin put down the phone and rubbed his face with both hands. "Oh my God, Nikki. I cannot believe this. She just shows up out of the blue. Why are people like this?"

"Who is she, Kevin?"

He must have registered the sharpness in his voice, because he suddenly snapped to attention. "Oh, Nikki, don't get the wrong idea. No—Alice is my cousin."

She raised her eyebrows. "Your *cousin?* Why would your cousin just show up?"

"Why would anybody do anything in my family? Listen, your family is . . . it's small, it's spread-out. You let each other live their own lives. Mine is a big Irish family. It gets messy sometimes. They want to know where everybody else is, all the time. I'm guessing my grandmother sent Alice down here to check on me. It's the kind of thing they do."

"They just appear randomly at doors?" Nikki thought such an arrangement sounded terrible, and this was with the full awareness that she missed her own family very much. Well, at least Alice wasn't a girlfriend. "How close a cousin is she?"

Kevin laughed. "*First* cousin, weirdo, and anyway New York's not like Catoctin Creek, we don't marry our cousins, no matter how distant."

She snorted. "I read enough Edith Wharton in high school to know that's a *very* recent policy change."

"Edith who?"

Nikki rolled her eyes. "So what, now you're leaving?"

"I can't just let her stay all night up there at Stephen's house. She'll be scared to death. Alice lives in a tiny little studio on the Upper East Side. She's never been more than six feet from another person in her entire life."

"Sounds like it might be an edifying experience for her," Nikki said drily. She downed the rest of her whiskey as Kevin climbed down from the loft. When he and Grover were gone, she poured herself another measure. This was just what she should have expected from letting a man stay over. Broken sleep and a lot of unnecessary stress.

—————

Eventually, the whiskey did its job, and Nikki slept deeply that night. When she woke up, the sun was shining, the snow was melting, and the enchantment of their early winter seemed to be thoroughly over.

*All gone, as if it never happened at all,* she thought, tugging the curtains closed so she wouldn't have to see the snowmelt pooling into muddy puddles outside the French doors. She supposed it wouldn't snow again until February, if then— Maryland was too far south for reliably snowy winters, and in recent years, they'd gotten more chilly rain and ice than anything else.

"Snow and romance," she murmured to herself, looking around her apartment. It felt a little smaller this morning, as if the walls had crept in on her overnight. "Two things I don't see much of. Maybe this was some kind of Thanksgiving fantasy." She spied some muddy paw-prints by the door and grinned ruefully. No, it had really happened. She had the mess Grover left behind to prove it. Anyway, there was no such thing as a Thanksgiving fantasy. She was getting ahead of herself this holiday season.

"Maybe by Christmas he'll come back," she said wryly.

Her voice seemed to echo in the lonely room.

She looked at her coffeemaker, the bag of Illy beans sitting next to it, and then tugged on a wool coat and duck boots. Nikki needed caffeine *and* distraction, and that meant a walk to the Blue Plate.

She stepped out into the crisp morning air, took in the sea of mud at her doorstep without enthusiasm, and then squelched her way along the two blocks to the diner.

At the Blue Plate, Doris and Phyllis were presiding over the messy remnants of the breakfast rush, which was down to two elderly couples still dining and several tables in need of bussing. Nikki resisted the urge to head straight to the dishwashing sink and grab a bussing tray. Instead, she picked up a warm ceramic mug from the tray next to the beverage station and poured herself a cup of coffee. The staff were more than capable of doing their job without her butting in. Her long, untroubled relationship with the morning crew relied on Nikki's knowing her place.

The more dour of the two waitresses made her way over to greet Nikki, her lips pulled back in a vinegary smile.

"Mornin' boss. You want some breakfast?" Phyllis asked, tucking her pencil into her blue-gray cap of curls. "Bobby made waffle batter. He could toss some in the iron for you."

"Really? Why would Bobby make waffle batter on a weekday?" Waffles, made from scratch by morning cook Bobby, were only served on Sunday and school holidays. They were regarded as celebration food in Catoctin Creek. Every other day of the week, pancakes were good enough.

"Oh, wouldn't you know that Ellie Baughman wanted waffles, and Bobby makes Ellie whatever she wants. I think he's going to ask her to dinner one of these days." Phyllis delivered this news of late-blooming love with no discernible pleasure in her face. The waitress had grimly watched love come and go as she'd presided over the Blue Plate dining room across the decades. Nikki found it doubtful Phyllis could believe in the emotion at all, after the many post-prom breakups and fraught families she'd seen in these booths over the years.

Nikki was not yet so jaded, although she could see herself heading in that direction if things didn't pan out with Kevin. She pushed back the thought of him now, trying to concentrate on the Blue Plate gossip rather than wondering what Kevin was up to without her. "Ellie and Bobby, huh? My goodness, we could have a Blue Plate wedding reception. Wouldn't that be cute?"

"Adorable." Phyllis pushed open the kitchen door. "I'll tell Bobby to make you some waffles."

Nikki sank onto one of the round seats facing the back counter. The diner counter saw little use these days, except for after-school theatrics from a few local tweens with an allowance and nowhere else to spend it. Most of the restaurant patrons were old enough to prefer booths, and a few were so opposed to the hard-backed chairs in the center of the restaurant, they'd always choose to stand at the door and scowl at anyone lingering over their decaf if a booth wasn't available the moment they walked in.

Just part of Catoctin Creek's charm, she thought wearily, a population of people so stuck in their ways they couldn't even change their seat, or the day of the week they ate waffles. She bet if she *did* try to open a bakery, no one would even come. Maybe Sean, since he'd asked for it. Everyone else would still tramp right over to the Blue Plate for their morning coffee and muffins, or their evening decaf and pie. "Why go somewhere new?" they'd ask. "Why go somewhere fancy? That's for out-of-town folks."

The doorbells chimed, and a little gust of cold wind made its way through the diner and whisked around Nikki's ankles. She shivered, wishing she hadn't shed her coat by the door, and was reaching for the sweater she kept on a nearby hook when she realized the new guest had settled down next to her. She spun back around on her stool, surprised. When she saw who it was, she nearly smiled—but stopped herself just in time. "Well, Sean."

He grinned at her, and she marveled at how he could live so unguarded, with his movie-star smile, with his twinkling blue eyes. Despite his charm, Nikki's heart did not melt, which she knew was more evidence she was firmly, almost troublingly, in Kevin's camp. "Heya, Nikki."

"No barn chores today?"

"All the grooms showed up this morning, so I was off the hook. I thought I'd wander down for a little breakfast before lessons start up later."

Phyllis burst out of the kitchen, the door swinging behind her. She glanced at Sean, then at Nikki. "Coffee for your friend?" she asked, and started filling a mug.

"You're having coffee," Nikki informed him.

"Coffee is perfect," Sean assured her.

"It's far from perfect, but it's hot and caffeinated."

Phyllis put down the mug with just a little too much emphasis. "What, now you don't like the coffee I make?"

"No, it's fine. I was just . . . ." Nikki was flustered. She was afraid she must be developing impossibly snobbish tastes if she was putting down her own coffee in her own diner.

But it wasn't her choice, this coffee; it never had been. She just kept on ordering what her aunt had ordered. The brew in Phyllis's pot was really her aunt's coffee—just like everything at the Blue Plate had been her aunt's choice. The biggest change Nikki had ever made here was training Lauren as an assistant manager. Her aunt had never had one until she'd brought Nikki on.

"What's your favorite place to get coffee?" she asked Sean, once Phyllis had stalked out of earshot. "Like, really good coffee. Do they have that in this part of Maryland?"

"Oh, there's a lot of places. This area has some nice cafes, I'll say that. Let's see, there's one up in Pen-Mar, there's a good place in Walkersville . . . but favorite? I guess I really like this place down in Frederick, on Jefferson Street. It's called Sunflower Coffee Roasters."

Nikki hated touchy-feely names like that. *Sunflower* and *rainbow* and *golly-gosh-gumdrops*—they made her nuts. She swallowed her annoyance along with a gulp of bitter coffee. "Oh, that sounds . . . cute."

"It's so cute," Sean enthused. "Super-cool farmhouse vibe, everything is fair trade, they make the most ridiculous chocolate croissants, and they roast their own coffee, which is why it's so good. Coffee has to be *fresh,* you know?" He took an experimental sip of his coffee now.

Nikki watched his nose wrinkle ever so slightly. *Snob,* she thought automatically, but she knew he was probably right. Someone used to drinking coffee from freshly roasted beans would not like the ground coffee she bought in twenty-pound foil bags from a restaurant distributor, which then sat in a Bunn industrial coffeemaker for hours. That wasn't snobbery. That was just having working set of taste-buds.

"I'll have to go there sometime," she said, hoping he didn't think that was a come-on. "I need to broaden my coffee horizons. As you probably now know."

"Yeah, I could take you if you want."

She forced a smile. "Maybe. But you know how it is . . . I'm only free at odd hours. I'll probably have to just visit when I'm in Frederick for restaurant supplies or something."

"No problem," Sean said cheerfully. "Keep me in mind."

Phyllis stalked by. "Waffles should be done," she announced, heading into the kitchen.

"Oh, we're having waffles," Nikki informed Sean.

"I love waffles!"

"These are pretty decent. Bobby makes the batter himself, so it's not some goop from a carton. Apparently he's using them to woo one of the merry widows here, so you know it's good stuff."

"So they're love waffles," Sean said appreciatively. "See, it's things like this that make a small town so filled with character."

"Are you from a big city? I would have thought a riding instructor your age would have grown up on a farm or something."

"I'm from Middleburg," Sean said. "The one in Virginia, not Maryland. So the town's a decent size, just with horses everywhere."

That explained his farm-to-table tastes, Nikki thought. Middleburg was pretty fancy. A place where *Country Living* meant horses and high-end SUVs, not cows and mud.

The waffles landed in front of them on heavy ceramic plates, along with a sticky glass bottle of pancake syrup. Nikki pushed the syrup over to Sean, but he held up a hand. "That's okay. Just butter for me. Once you go with real maple syrup, it's hard to go back."

Nikki sighed. "You remind me of Kevin, you know that?"

"Kevin is a diehard maple syrup fan?"

"I have no idea. But I feel like he would be. I feel like . . . oh, I don't know, like I'm straddling this line trying to make two different types of people happy, and it's going to make me crazy." Nikki didn't know why it felt okay to open up to Sean. He just had that kind of face. A friendly, listening, empathetic kind of face.

Which was a little befuddled right now. "This isn't about syrup, is it?"

She dumped the pancake syrup over her waffles. "Nope, Sean. It's not."

A bitter wind whistled around her neck, despite the mild day, and Nikki plucked at her coat collar as she gestured to the Schubert house. "This is the one," she told Sean, feeling resigned to her fate even as she showed off her fantasy. This house was too elegant, too grand, too special, to ever belong to Nikki. "I daydream about this house all the time. This is where I'd put a cafe and restaurant, if I had the money." *And the clientele.*

Sean, standing next to her, tipped back his head to take it all in. "Wow," he said eventually. "This is pretty classy for Catoctin Creek, if you don't mind my saying so."

"No, it totally is. The family who built it made a killing with their farm, and they showed off. My grandparents *hated* the Schuberts. Said they were stuck-up and put on airs. I don't even care. I just want the house. Look at that big wide porch, and see how you can look all the way through, from front to back? All that space would make amazing dining rooms. Imagine having breakfast on the porch, or an elegant dinner inside." Nikki could just see the warm, golden light of old-fashioned globe lamps hanging over her tables, reflecting off the polished wood of original floors, as black-clad servers bent over their guests, taking orders and recommending their favorites. Where was she? Oh, in the kitchen, running herself ragged and loving every minute of it.

Sean pushed back his knit cap and rubbed at his hair. "Well, it's sitting empty, and that's not doing anyone any good. Why don't you go for it? See if they'll lease it to you?"

"If I thought it would do the business, I'd try. But, honestly, Sean, there's no chance. I know you're from a country town with a lot of nice businesses, but Middleburg is a lot richer than Catoctin Creek. They're not even in the same universe. Do you honestly think the locals would even go to a place like this?"

Nikki could scarcely believe she'd opened up to Sean about her fine-dining dreams. It had just come up naturally, talking about country living and country tastes, about the differences between a thriving, wealthy town like Middleburg and a decaying backwater like Catoctin Creek. Somehow, she'd ended up walking with him down the wet sidewalk until they were standing outside the last house on Main Street, the brick Queen Anne she'd give anything to own.

"I think people would come because of you," Sean said thoughtfully. "Because you're one of theirs. And I also think if the food is good enough, people will come from out of town. You could help the town turn over a new leaf. If there are folks driving through who stop and eat, they'll want to stop and shop, too. Someone might open an antiques shop, or an art gallery. There are plenty of storefronts on Main Street waiting to get spruced up. I think that's how it happens . . . that's how country towns come back. Someone has to start it."

Nikki nodded. Part of her felt the same way. The other part? Well, that part thought she'd lose her shirt, and the Blue Plate, and be left with nothing. "Thanks, Sean. I appreciate you walking down here with me."

He gave her a friendly hug, wrapping one lanky arm around her shoulder. "I'm glad to help. It's nice to get to know you! I know you went to high school with my boss, too, so maybe you can give me some pointers on dealing with her. She's really tough, you know."

Nikki laughed and shoved him off. "Your ulterior motives are showing! This was never about me, was it?"

They staggered back down the sidewalk, still laughing, and Nikki knew neighbors would peek out their windows to see what all the noise was. That was okay; they knew her well enough. She couldn't imagine anyone in Catoctin Creek would think anything of Nikki walking down the street with Caitlin's new riding instructor.

But the last thing Nikki expected was for Kevin to go driving by.

# Chapter 24

# Kevin

"Why didn't you ever tell *me* about this house?" Kevin asked. He was keeping his voice down, acutely aware Alice was a few feet away, chatting amiably with Sean. Bless Alice! She'd taken one look at his face when he pulled up at the Blue Plate parking lot and known instantly there was something wrong. When he'd explained to her that the auburn-haired woman they'd passed was *the* Nikki he'd been talking about, she'd nodded gravely and said she'd leave him alone to talk with her.

"I'm sure it's perfectly innocent," she'd added as she got out of the car. "Don't go making any accusations, Kev."

Kevin had just shrugged before he walked down the street to meet Nikki. He hadn't liked the red blush on her cheeks as she'd greeted him, or the coldness of her lips when he kissed her. Never mind that the air outside was still chilly. The weather had changed, the snow had melted, and Nikki was horsing around on the street with that handsome young man from Caitlin's. Something was up, and he wanted to know where he stood.

Apparently, not very high, judging by her explanation. Kevin's feelings had been stung. He'd known she wanted to start a new cafe or restaurant, but he hadn't known she had the spot picked out. That was *important*. Why hadn't she told him? He had to work to keep the hurt from his voice when he said, "I don't understand why you're down here telling Sean your hopes and dreams, and you didn't share this place with me."

Nikki was looking past him, as if the little cluster of storefronts on Main Street were very interesting all of a sudden. When she spoke, her voice was tense, steeled for a fight. "I didn't plan to tell anyone. It just *came up*. Sean is from a place that makes a lot of money off being a country town. Maybe we could have something like that here, I don't know. I thought his opinion might be valuable. We were having breakfast, and we started talking about Catoctin Creek, and we ended up here."

"What about *my* opinion? I'm literally in investments. I know how to work with real estate, and find seed money. That's my job."

She glanced at him then. "Are you sure? I thought you were a farrier's apprentice."

Kevin felt his face turn hot and red. "So you *don't* think much of that idea. I thought so! You really think I ought to be doing the accounts for some shopkeeper here, don't you? Want me to head over to the funeral home now, ask how I can help them expand the old morgue? Or maybe I ought to be doing *your* books, would you like that?"

"Excuse me?" Nikki's eyebrows came together. The distant look was gone now. Kevin knew she was seeing him clearly, and she didn't like what she saw. He couldn't blame her. "Excuse me, but I think it's pretty rude to taunt someone for trying to *help* someone else. I worked with the information I had. I didn't know you wanted to become a laborer. At the time, I thought you *liked* working in an office. You told me I was wrong, and I accepted that. I haven't mentioned it since, if you haven't noticed. You want to be a farrier? Do that. You want to invest? Do that. You can do whatever you want."

"Because you don't care," Kevin blustered. Even as he said it, he knew it was ridiculous, knew he'd gone too far. Why couldn't he stop himself? Because he was still mad, because he'd seen the way Sean looked at Nikki, because he'd seen the way other women looked at Sean, and he didn't want to think of Nikki turning her gaze on him in that feral, hungry way. Had she ever even looked at Kevin that way? Come to think of it, he didn't know that she had. She looked at him fondly, she looked at him scornfully, she had even looked at him appreciatively—but there hadn't been many hungry, lascivious glances which bespoke pure heat, at least none he could recall.

He was being ridiculous now, and he knew it. He wished someone would come and stop him. He wished Alice would appear and drag him away. He wished anything would happen—a blizzard, a tornado, an out-of-control dump truck—to stop him from fighting with Nikki.

No one else came. Instead, Nikki was walking away from him, her shoulders high and tense beneath her wool coat.. His heart lurched. "Wait, Nikki. I'm sorry. I'm *sorry,* for God's sake. I was just jealous . . ."

Nikki stopped and looked at him, her eyes piercing. He could see the gold flecks in them sparkling, seeming to dance with anger. "You might have been jealous, Kevin, but I don't think that's what this is about. This is about *you* and your relationship with yourself, not your relationship with me."

He stared at her. What did that even mean? "I'm sorry. I don't understand."

She sighed and came back, putting her hand on his arm. He resisted the urge to pull her close, kiss the argument away. She had something to say, and drowning her out wouldn't help his cause. "I made you a plan. You didn't want it. You said you wanted to work with your hands. I let you go do that, fine. But when I wanted advice on starting a new business, I went to someone else. Because you said you didn't want to do your old job anymore. And now you're mad, because you lost your position of authority. You gave up what you had, and you don't know how to deal with it."

He considered her words. "That might be right."

Nikki tilted her head and gave him a look he'd seen on his mother's face many times, gazing up at his father's face: a look of exasperated affection. "Trust me, Kevin. I'm right. I know this feeling all too well. Because I'm afraid to do it." She glanced back at the Schubert house, and he thought her eyelashes looked wet. "I'll never give up what I have. I'm not that kind of person. You're braver than I am."

"If you want to open a restaurant in that house, I can help you," Kevin said urgently.

Nikki's face softened, and her fingers pressed into his arm in one quick, reassuring squeeze. "I appreciate that. But I don't really want to. Not badly enough, I mean. It's just a silly dream." She glanced over his shoulder. "Alice is up there waiting. Take her to the Blue Plate and tell Phyllis to make you guys the last of the waffles. They're really good."

"Where are you going? Come sit with us." He clung to her as she turned to leave. "I want you to meet Alice."

"I just have to run back to my place," Nikki said. "I need to get you guys some maple syrup."

She headed off smartly, moving at such a clip Kevin couldn't even ask her what on earth she meant. He just stared at her back, her hair bouncing over her shoulders, feeling utterly befuddled. They'd just had a fight, which was unfortunate, but they'd made up, which was great—it was the maple syrup thing he couldn't quite follow.

Sean had been dawdling nearby, and he ambled over as Kevin watched Nikki walk away. "Sorry I got things confusing, man," he offered. "We were just talking about farm-to-table and antiquing and stuff. It wasn't flirting or anything."

Kevin sighed. "It's fine. I'm sorry I took it so far. But now I'm just trying to figure out why she thinks I need maple syrup."

Sean's eyes widened a little, and then he laughed. "Maple syrup? Oh man, she's going to do it. Trust me, she's going to do it. It's just a question of time."

"Do *what?*" Kevin thought he might be losing his mind. Maybe country living just wasn't for him. The people were all crazy, for starters.

"She's going to open that restaurant she's dreaming of," Sean said. "Maple syrup is just the beginning. It's a slippery slope, my man."

He took Alice back to the brick house after their impromptu waffle brunch. She said she was tired after the drive down from New York, and she hadn't slept well in his quiet little house.

"It's spooky here," she told him seriously. "Places should not be this quiet."

Kevin had spent the night in Alice's tiny studio before and knew first-hand the way every sound traveled through its cardboard walls. She was used to living with the sounds of other people: their arguments over dinner, their lovemaking afterwards, their breakfast conversation the next morning. Kevin had lived with other people as a soundtrack for his entire life, too, but he'd felt very ready to change that record.

He could understand why Alice, five years younger, wasn't there yet. But she'd catch up, eventually.

Probably.

"You get used to it," he said. "The quiet can be very refreshing."

Alice made a face which said she doubted it. "Anyway, I'm only here to make sure you come back home. Grandma is worried about you. She missed you at Thanksgiving. She said you aren't allowed to miss Christmas."

"Grandma noticed I wasn't there?" Kevin was touched. "What about my mother?"

"I heard her say something about it," Alice said vaguely. "She was really busy, though. With dinner and everything, you know. It gets so crazy at holidays. Uncle Kenny fell off the garage roof again, did you hear? But Rudy Guglielmo had parked in the backyard even though your mom said not to, and it was lucky because he landed on Rudy's car instead of the concrete patio."

Another normal family holiday in Queens. "Did he break anything?"

"The windshield." Alice shrugged. "But insurance covers that, and Rudy said he needed a new windshield anyway. He said the old one leaked. But that was like, one little thing in a weekend full of crazy. So you can see why your mom didn't have a lot of time to notice you were missing."

"Sure." Kevin turned up the driveway to the house. There was still a little snow left on the ground between the trees, and he noticed dainty hoof-marks from the resident herd of deer, little diamonds cutting through the lacy film. "I get it. Hosting Thanksgiving is a big deal. I guess I could fall through the cracks."

He glossed over it, but he couldn't help feeling a little hurt. Even though it had been his choice to leave New York before the holiday, couldn't his family at least miss him? Couldn't his own mother at least wish he'd been there?

No, his grandmother was the one who noticed and sent a delegation after him.

"It *is*, Kevin," Alice insisted. "Anyway, how long are you going to be here? Can we go home together? I want to go to a friend's party on Saturday and it's all the way up in Hamilton Heights so I have to like, stay overnight, but it's a really big place so it's cool. You should have moved up there. You can get so much space in upper Manhattan, and you don't have to cross the river. And the buildings don't sway, because they're old. They're built better. You should sell that Excelsior condo and buy something pre-war."

"Maybe the old buildings sway *because* they're old," Kevin suggested, but Alice was getting out of the car already, not listening to him. Rightfully so, he figured, because he had no point. There was no doubt moving to the Excelsior had been a huge mistake.

Unless, of course, you counted that move as a galvanizing factor in his life which would eventually make him come *here,* to escape the city he'd called home his entire life and the job he'd hated his entire adult life, to find a new calling and a new life and a new dog and maybe even a woman who loved him . . .

Kevin had begun using the word *love* in his mental wanderings and he had to admit, it was kind of addictive. The only question was when he would use it out loud, with Nikki.

And what she'd do when he said it.

He wasn't ready to think about that, though. Far too soon. Sure, they'd been eyeballing each other since early in the year, even as Stephen and Rosemary met, fell in love, and got married in the same span of time. But Nikki wasn't impulsive. She was cautious and thought everything through . . . to a fault. If he moved too quickly, she'd shut the door in his face.

He had to take his time with this one.

Alice was already on the stoop, tapping her foot at him. He got out of the car, listening to her complain about the little house.

"Why do we have to go back together?" he asked, unlocking the door. "You can't go alone? It's your party. From what you said, I only have to come back for Christmas."

That was doable, he thought. Even if he'd rather be here for the holiday.

Grover jumped off the sofa and headed over to greet them, wagging his tail furiously. Kevin started his usual browse for messes, but so far Grover had proven to be housebroken. "You're such a good boy," he told the happy dog, who nearly flipped over with excitement at this praise. "I'm so glad no one wants you but me!"

"Wow, that's so weird," Alice said.

"We've had a sign up at the feed store and Rosemary calls the humane society every day," Kevin explained. "Imagine if someone wanted him back? I'd be a wreck."

"It would just like, be easier," Alice said, continuing her original conversation. She pulled back the vertical blinds on the sliding glass door. "I'd just return my rental and we could split the drive back. Oh, wow, this is *some* view!"

"You didn't notice it before?"

"No, I was too tired. And then I was too hungry. Look at the mountains all covered in snow! I love it. This is so nice. It's like a retreat. It's like a monastery, like my friend Dylan Burgh went to stay at that one time."

"That's exactly what it's like," Kevin agreed, cutting off a long story about Dylan Burgh. "And that's why I'll be staying longer than the rest of this week. You can stay or you can go, Alice, but I'm not in a hurry to get out of here. I'll come back for Christmas. Tell Grandma that and see if that's good enough."

"Is this about that girl?" She let the blinds fall, closing off the winter wonderland in the distance. "The one with the dark red hair? Because she's kind of scary. Like, really intense. And I think that blonde guy liked her."

"He doesn't. That's Sean. He's harmless."

"Then why were you guys yelling?"

"A misunderstanding."

"Hmm." Alice did not seem convinced. "He was *really* hot. I know you're like, seeing her, but maybe keep an eye on things there."

Kevin bit back a groan. Well, he didn't need to get her on his side with Nikki. He just needed her on his side about Catoctin Creek as a whole. And he thought he could work that out. "Alice, you love Central Park, right?"

"I *love* Central Park, and you know it."

"The Ramble?"

"The Ramble is amazing."

"Perfect," Kevin said. "Then this weekend, you stick around and let's go on a little hike in the woods. You can see how beautiful the mountains are here. Like the Ramble, but bigger."

"The weekend? I had that party, remember? Why not go for a hike tomorrow?"

"I have to work."

Alice rolled her eyes. "The horse job? Kevin, come on. You're just messing around with that."

"Alice," he said warningly, "did I make fun of you when you ran that blown-glass bong gallery?"

She narrowed her eyes at him, but he knew he had her. Everyone in the family had had an opinion about that gallery job, and the boyfriend who had owned the place, but Kevin had just told her to have fun with it. And she had, right up until the lease ran out and the place became a frozen yogurt shop. The boyfriend had gone to Colorado, where people were more appreciative of bong art, in his opinion. Alice had gotten a job at a college friend's non-profit, answering phones and setting appointments.

Where she should probably be right now, come to think of it.

"Okay, fine. Keep your horse job. I guess I can stick around for a couple days. Kayla's parties usually end with the police, anyway.

Can I take a nap now? I'm like, really tired. And we ate all those waffles."

"Of course. Nighty-nite, cuz."

Alice went back to bed, and Kevin sat down in front of the television. Grover joined him, his tongue hanging from his mouth. Kevin rubbed Grover's silky ears and sighed. "Family can be really difficult," he told the dog.

Grover panted up at him.

"You're really cute. I'm surprised Alice hasn't figured out that if I adopted a dog already, maybe I'm not planning on going back." Dogs were allowed in the Excelsior, of course—being a dog parent in New York City was extremely fashionable—but taking Grover up and down the elevator every time the dog had to pee sounded like a total nightmare for everyone involved. He didn't think Alice would ever put herself out like that.

Strategically, the hike was a good idea. Alice could head back to New York full of stories about how gorgeous she'd found Catoctin Creek. Everyone would come around to the idea of Kevin living in some kind of natural wonderland. Sure, western Maryland was no New York City, but there were other ways to live besides the grind and the grid.

A walk in the woods would be the perfect way to show off his new life. He'd call Rosemary and see if she was available—she'd be sure to know some local trails. Would Nikki be able to come? He didn't even know if Nikki *liked* hiking, but she should be there, too. So Alice could carry home tales of his beautiful and thoughtful girlfriend. Grandma would be thrilled.

Kevin flipped on the television and turned it to the weather, happy Stephen hadn't shut off the satellite service. "What do we have this weekend," he muttered, and he could barely contain his happy squeak when the forecaster announced that tomorrow, western Maryland would once again see snow.

# Chapter 25

# Nikki

"**A** hike?" Nikki asked blankly. She glanced at her phone, confirming she was, indeed, talking to Kevin. "You want to hike?"

"Yes, let's go on a hike!" Kevin replied. "I want to take Alice."

She wondered if he'd been reading some website about how to live better and it had suggested communing with nature. This sounded like something Kevin would do. Nikki was not a big nature-communer, but she wasn't about to tell other people they couldn't do it.

"You go for a hike and have fun," she told him. "Show Alice the woods. I have to work this weekend."

Kevin's sigh was so enormous, she could practically feel the gust of breath over the phone. "Come on, Nikki, take some time off and come with me. Lauren can run the diner. I've seen her in action. You deserve some time to yourself."

"I take time to myself. But I can't just take off all the days because you want to play." She regretted the edge that had come into her voice. "Sorry. Look, I'll make plans next weekend for

Lauren to cover a close and I'll come with you then. Can it wait until then?"

"No," Kevin said. "I want Alice heading back to New York early next week. Filled with tales of Catoctin Creek's splendid hiking trails and wide-open spaces. That's my plan, anyway. And I wanted her to tell them all how great you are, too, which means I need you with me."

There was a moment of silence between them. Nikki felt frustration welling up in her. She had a *job*. She worked on weekends. She couldn't just take off and leave the way Kevin could. Okay, fine, he was a ride-along with the local farrier, but he had given up his career to do that. He couldn't ask her to do the same.

"I have to work," she said again.

"You work too much."

*So fancy-free,* she thought, her jaw tightening. She understood he wanted to find himself, but at what cost? He just what, wasn't going to go to work when he didn't want to? Was that his thing?

Nikki didn't think she could get used to that kind of attitude. It felt like a non-starter to her.

The realization made her sad.

"Nikki," Kevin murmured, "go look out your window."

"Kevin, please don't be standing outside my window."

"No, I'm not! I just—go look, okay? I want to see something."

She didn't bother pointing out that *she* would be the one seeing something out her window. Instead, she stalked across the apartment and pulled back the curtains on her French doors. Before her fingers even touched the heavy fabric, she realized the light had changed.

Heavy, fat snowflakes were falling past the glass, landing on the ground in fluffy piles that were already heaping over the little path to her front door. "Oh my goodness," she breathed. "More snow? How did you do it?"

"I told you, I love snow," Kevin said teasingly. "What's it like there? It just started a few minutes ago up here, and the grass is already getting covered."

"I guess the same here. There's a thin layer on my sidewalk—maybe a quarter inch? I don't know. Well, we can't go out *now*, we'll get stuck somewhere."

"It's supposed to stop this afternoon. But it's going to stay cold. Nikki, come on. Play hooky Saturday. We can go for a nice hike in the snowy forest. Doesn't that sound amazing? Rosemary is going to show us an easy trail that goes back behind the house and up the mountainside."

She felt herself nodding slowly and was suddenly grateful he couldn't see her. Was the snowfall putting her under some kind of enchantment? She already felt calmer, more acquiescent. She let the curtain fall, blocking her view of the snow. "It's still the weekend. If the roads are clear enough to drive, people will be coming to the diner," she said. "I really can't."

"Nikki," Kevin said. "Come on."

She sighed. "I'll let you know."

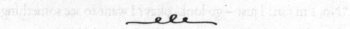

The Blue Plate held no charms for Nikki that afternoon. Patrick was in the kitchen when she arrived, slamming lids onto pots and heating up the oil for the flock of fried chicken that would be served that night. She pressed her fingers to her temples as he dropped a vat of mashed potatoes into the steel steam table, where it would wait to be called into action.

"What's the matter with you?" He looked back over his shoulder at her. "You look like yesterday's oatmeal."

"Thanks, Patrick. Very thoughtful of you." Nikki glanced over the sides he'd prepped for dinner. They all looked vile. Green beans swimming in the water they'd been canned in, lima beans which would taste only of the salt and pepper patrons doused them with, biscuits . . . well, actually, the biscuits looked buttery and delicious. She plucked one from the tray and bit in. Hot and fluffy, the way her aunt had taught her to make them.

Aunt Evelyn should have been a baker. Her diner's cooking might never have been high cuisine, but everyone could appreciate a well-baked biscuit.

The savory flavor of the biscuit on her tongue brought her back to her conversation with Sean that morning, and all the daydreams that had been flitting through her head since then. She was having her visions again, more clearly than ever, but refined with the bakery concept: the Schubert house with golden light streaming from the first-floor windows, happy customers on the porch eating biscuits and cookies, sipping coffee and tea, while inside she prepped a handful of tables for the select dinner service she'd offer that night: just a few seasonal dishes, a menu she selected and prepared with her own hands.

Things didn't stop with her imaginary restaurant, either. She conjured up a rejuvenated Main Street, bustling with a string of thriving antique and vintage shops, maybe an ice cream parlor reopening in the old Happy Dairy space, where she'd gotten cones with Rosemary right up through their high school days. She imagined Catoctin Creek as a more vibrant version of itself: with the same storefronts, but busier. With the same patrons who came in for fried chicken and meatloaf, but healthier. With the same people who had always lived here, but thriving.

Nikki finished the biscuit and as the last buttery flakes melted on her tongue, she suddenly knew she couldn't possibly spend the evening here, doing the same old jobs she'd been doing for years, watching the same old people she'd watched for years. She needed a change. They all just needed a change.

She'd be the first to take it.

Nikki brushed the crumbs off her hands and went into the dining room to find Lauren.

Elmwood's barn and indoor arena were lit up against the early onset of evening, and there were parked cars jammed into every inch of the parking area in front of the barn. Nikki had to struggle to find a topsy-turvy spot alongside the driveway, the car's right side tipped up against a small snowbank. She hoped the snowfall wouldn't get heavier, or she'd have a tough time getting out later.

Inside the barn, well-dressed children in breeches and boots, sweaters and puffy vests, were dashing around, grooming ponies and horses. At the end of the aisle, she could see horses flashing past a gateway, trotting around the indoor arena. A few adults were clustered near the arena entrance, wearing thick coats and hats, expensive boots with shearling lining spilling over the tops. Nikki took her place near them and glanced at their faces, but she didn't recognize a single person. The parents of Caitlin's students were not Catoctin Creek natives, and they didn't eat at the Blue Plate.

Nikki squared her jaw.

In the center of the arena, Sean was walking in small circles, facing the pack of riders as they trotted around him. He was explaining some facet of riding in a pleasant, carrying speaking voice, but Nikki didn't pay attention to his words. She was too busy rehearsing what she'd say to him once he was done, as soon as she could get his attention.

He glanced past the trotting horses as they drummed by the gateway, and his gaze fell on Nikki. She saw him go still for a moment; then he raised his hand in hello. He quickly turned back to his students, but Nikki knew he'd come looking for her as soon as the lesson was finished.

It took him a few minutes to get past the parents and kids, who all seemed to adore him and wanted to ask him constant questions, but Sean finally made it over to Nikki. She was leaning against the horse stall nearest the arena, idly playing with the whiskers of the tall, lop-eared gray mare who lived within. "This one's cute," she said as he approached, hoping to dampen the anticipation in his eyes. "I used to ride one just like her when I was a kid. Twenty years ago," she added, hoping to remind him she was older, not really his type.

"Juno's really nice," Sean agreed, his glance barely taking in the gray mare. "What's up? I sure didn't expect to see you here."

"It's about the bakery idea," Nikki said. "Can you keep a secret?"

Sean nodded, his blue eyes serious. "To the grave."

"It won't be for that long, I promise. But I want to do it. I want to find a way to open the bakery cafe. It's not *everything* I want, but it's a start. It's a step in the right direction. Will you help me?"

Sean stepped closer, testing boundaries. She wished her back wasn't against a wall. "Of course I'll help you. With anything you need. But—" his brow furrowed. "What can I do?"

Nikki supposed those were the deepest wrinkles that baby's-bottom face had ever known. "I could just use some help figuring out what works in other markets. I know you go out more than me—maybe you could collect me some menus, take some pictures of the bakery displays, that kind of thing, while you're out?"

He nodded, his forehead smoothing. "I can do that, sure. And what about some menus and things from the places down in Middleburg, you want those?"

"That would be *amazing,*" she told him, more enthusiastically than she'd meant. Sean took a step closer, and Nikki put her hand against his chest. "Easy there, buddy. Kevin already had one fit about you today."

Sean immediately stepped backwards. The folds returned to his forehead, and his eyes were positively tragic. He looked like a sorrowful hound dog. "I'm really sorry, Nikki. I didn't mean—I talked to him, too, you know. I told him there wasn't anything but—there's a *little* something, Nikki. For me, anyway."

Nikki wondered what she'd done to deserve this. "I know, Sean. I'm sorry."

He shook his head. "It's okay. It's not on you. Just, keep me in mind if you and Kevin—"

"Don't you say it," she warned him, shaking a finger.

"Sorry. Menus. You got it, Nikki."

"Thanks." Nikki looked up and down the barn aisle. "And listen, can you talk to these moms? All the ones in shiny new L.L.

Bean? Find out what they like, and if they ever come into downtown Catoctin Creek. I'll need them for this to work."

# Chapter 26

# Kevin

"**R**osemary's here!" Kevin called.

There was no answer from the guest bedroom. He sighed and stalked over to her doorway.

Alice was fast asleep in bed.

This had pretty much been his cousin's state of being for the past two days. As much as she'd protested the quiet of Catoctin Creek, once her ears had adjusted to the silence, her body responded by simply switching off. Alice had been napping half the day away before turning in early, then sleeping late. Yesterday, she hadn't even changed out of her flannel pajamas, and he'd barely seen her for dinner before she shambled back to her bedroom, yawning hugely.

Despite the sudden-onset narcolepsy, Kevin wasn't really worried about her—he doubted she'd slept this deeply in years. After all, no matter how much a person protested they loved the hustle and bustle of the city, the human body was only set up to withstand so much noise around the clock. And her apartment really was like living in an 24-hour bowling alley.

"Alice," Kevin hissed, although he was none too hopeful he'd wake her with anything less than shouting in her ear, or maybe a brass band. "Wake up so we can go hiking with Rosemary."

She didn't move.

"Oye." Kevin went back to the front door, Grover hot on his heels. Rosemary was coming up the walk as he opened the door to her. "We may have a slight delay on our hands," he said apologetically.

"Make me coffee and I'll forgive you." Rosemary looked cheerful. "We're all out down at the farm and I could use a cup before we go thrashing around in the woods. Hello, you," she told Grover, who was sniffing ecstatically at her jeans. "Yes, I've been in the barn this morning. You miss the horses, don't you?" She glanced up at Kevin. "I actually heard back from the Beerbaum grandkids."

Kevin felt his heart contract. "What did they say?"

"Oh, they don't want the dog, if that's what you're worried about. Sorry to scare you. They claim that poor old Mrs. O'Reilly said she'd handle finding the dog a home. I guess they know I'm not going to chase down an old widow and demand why she left a dog out to starve, so there's no chance I can dispute it. But we both know that's not what happened. Even if she'd agreed to handle things, which I know she wouldn't have, Grover wouldn't have ended out along a highway on cold night."

Grover panted up at her, his face aglow with love. Kevin wanted to get on a plane to Boulder and give those Beerbaum grandkids a piece of his mind, and by mind he meant fists. "Why are people like that?"

She shook her head, her hands still buried in Grover's luxurious coat. He'd gotten even softer and silkier since he'd moved up to the brick house and ate two square meals a day of that expensive salmon and rice kibble. "I mean, go ask my horses why people are so terrible. Every single one of them probably has a different reason to hate humans. Luckily, animals are capable of a lot of forgiveness."

"More than we are," Kevin said. He shook his head, aware the mood had taken a sudden nose-dive. "Sorry about that! Thanks for figuring out the whole thing. It's been kind of worrisome at the back of my head. I was a little afraid someone might show up and try to claim him. Let's get you that coffee."

Rosemary slipped off her snowy boots at the door. "By the way, they told me his old name."

Kevin waited, but she just brushed off her hands and smiled at him. "Are you going to tell it to me?"

"No," she said firmly. "I'm not. It would just confuse him now, and make you feel guilty for changing his name. But I'll tell you what—Grover's a *much* better name."

⁓

They were each on their second cups of coffee when Alice emerged from the bedroom—wearing jeans and a bright red sweater, Kevin was gratified to note, instead of her flannel pajamas. She rubbed her eyes and sat down across from them. "I've never slept so much in my life," she said in a gravelly voice. "It's like a cleanse. A sleep cleanse, is that a thing?"

"It should be," Rosemary said, highly amused. "Are you going to be able to stagger outside for a walk in the woods?"

Alice glanced past them. The vertical blinds were open, and the white expanse of the backyard, churned up by Grover's paws during his daily zooms, glimmered under a pearl-gray sky. "Yeah," she decided. "Just let me caffeinate a little." She pushed back from the table and went into the kitchen for a mug.

Kevin cast Rosemary a rueful grin. "I really hope you weren't on a tight schedule today."

She shrugged. "Not me. No seminar today, and Stephen is working on some client thing all day, so I just had to take care of the horses and feed dinner later. I'm surprised Nikki couldn't make it, though."

Kevin averted his eyes.

Rosemary sighed. "What's going on with you two now?"

"Nothing serious." Kevin heard the double meaning and almost laughed. Not quite, though. "I asked her to take the day off to come, and she yelled at me."

"Sparring so soon?" Rosemary didn't sound surprised.

"Seems that way."

"Nikki's work ethic is her biggest fault," Rosemary said. "I realize that sounds crazy, but—"

"No, I get it. She doesn't take time to relax."

"And she probably never will. But she needs to be working at the right thing. I don't feel like the diner's making her happy."

Alice came back, coffee in one hand, bag of grocery-store croissants in the other. "Are these any good?"

Rosemary glanced at the bag. "No."

Kevin grimaced at her. "They're the finest croissants Safeway has to offer."

"You're not going to find any good baked goods within forty-five minutes," Rosemary informed Alice. "We go to Frederick for pastries."

"Someone should have told me that before I uprooted my life to come here. Bread is important to me."

Alice flicked the bag's twist-tie at him. "You won't come back to make Grandma happy, but croissants will change your mind?"

"I said I'm coming home for Christmas," Kevin reminded her. "I just have to remember to clear the freezer first, so I can stuff it with New York contraband when I come back."

Alice worked her way gloomily through the croissant and then shuffled back to the bedroom to finish getting ready. Kevin leaned back in his chair and picked at a pastry. They were very dry and left crumbs everywhere. If it was possible to make a croissant without butter, this would be the result. Rosemary, he noticed, didn't even touch them. She just sipped her coffee and gazed out the window, apparently riveted by a pair of cardinals zipping their way around the backyard.

"Nikki should open a bakery," he said eventually, just to see what Rosemary would say.

Rosemary glanced at him, her lovely eyes curious. "She should. Has she been talking to you about that?"

"Not me. But I think it's on her mind."

"Well, don't push her," Rosemary warned. "Wait for her to tell you about it. If there's anything to tell."

"It has to be her idea, right?"

"Kind of. But Nikki's careful. *Too* careful, sometimes. She has to move slowly, and I think you're . . . well, you're impulsive, Kevin.

If you get too enthusiastic about something, it could scare her into thinking it's a bad idea."

Kevin knew he was too impulsive for Nikki's slow, deliberate way of doing things, but on the other hand . . . he wasn't sure he liked what Rosemary was saying. "You're saying that if I like the idea, that's an automatic red light?"

"I wouldn't take it personally." Rosemary tipped back the rest of her coffee. She was so gloriously unconcerned, Kevin thought wistfully. She had always had a certain quiet presence. But now, with Stephen's strength at her back, she had grown less fragile, less ethereal. She'd come into her own: a wise woman. He remembered back on the first day he'd come back, watching her bake her pies, thinking she was like a good witch. She gave him that impression again now. Rosemary knew what she was talking about.

"Nikki isn't going to move without a solid plan," Rosemary continued. "She needs time to reach her own conclusions and take her own steps. She knows—because you told her—that you're not a guy who needs a plan to shake things up. That's all I'm saying."

Kevin nodded slowly. He wanted to fix things for Nikki, set her all up with the new business of her dreams and watch her soar. But if Rosemary was telling him to back off, he knew he had to listen.

He'd like to change it some day, but for now, no one knew Nikki better than Rosemary.

Once Alice finally emerged, they went tramping through the backyard, leaving wet footprints in the soggy snow as Grover tore around in frantic circles around them, utterly thrilled to have company. The day was gray but still, and the temperature was hovering right around freezing, so no one felt too chilled once the exercise of walking had warmed their blood. Rosemary knew just where the little gate in the deepest, darkest corner of the backyard was, and she brushed snow off the latch with her gloves before pushing it open, the hinges creaking with disuse. A little snowy path darted off in either direction, roofed with the dark limbs of leafless trees.

"It's just like the Ramble!" Alice exclaimed. "But wilder!"

"How did you know about the gate?" Kevin asked Rosemary.

"When Stephen's father lived up here, the whole town used to come for his party on the Fourth of July," Rosemary reminded him. "And someone's dog would always find this gate and push through it. I'd always join the search party and help find the dog. We never lost one for long!"

Kevin looked the gate over anxiously. He'd put Grover on a leash, and the dog was straining against his collar, trying to get into the underbrush on either side of the path. "I'd better take a look at it later. If Grover gets out, we'll never find him."

"Well, the snow is keeping it firmly closed now," Rosemary pointed out. "I think you have time. Come on, let's get this hike on the road. We only have a few more hours of daylight, and I want to take you right up the side of Notch Gap."

Alice glanced back at Rosemary. "So you're saying we won't get back in time for a nap?"

# Chapter 27

# Nikki

S he showed up late, but at least she showed up.

That was what she told herself, anyway.

The cold, gray day wasn't the kind of weather which brought in diners, and she'd noticed a definite slip in sales over the past few weekends since Thanksgiving. It confirmed her worries that people were staying in Frederick for dinner after their holiday shopping. But instead of obsessing over how to bring in customers to fill her empty tables (a fruitless task since there was no magical way to conjure up cars or passersby on Catoctin Creek's lonely Main Street) Nikki settled into a back booth with a cup of coffee and her laptop.

She spent some time going over the websites of small-town cafes located all across the country, noting their prices and menu items. After a slow lunch gave way to a dead mid-afternoon slump, she rubbed her eyes and closed the laptop. Lauren looked her way as the computer clicked shut. Then she said exactly what Nikki expected her to.

"Go home, Nikki."

Nikki stood up and stretched. "Okay," she replied. "That's what I'll do."

She was rewarded with a look of pure astonishment from Lauren.

The snow under her feet was slushy but still hanging on, so she sloshed back to her apartment and changed into a pair of warm duck boots, slid a lining of silky thermal underwear under her jeans and sweater, and tugged a wool cap down over her ears. She looked at herself in the bathroom mirror, which was really only useful from the neck up. The dry air had loosened her usual curls, leaving her hair a little lank and lifeless, so she pulled a flat brush over the waves until they slowly straightened.

"There," she told her reflection. "Now you look like one of the teenagers right after they've flat-ironed their hair into submission."

She had to admit it was a pretty look.

Was she going for pretty?

"Of course you are," she snorted, and with a grab for her keys and purse, she was out the door.

By the time she'd made it up the steep driveway to the brick house, the afternoon was half-over, and she was pretty sure she was on a fool's errand. Still, she parked next to Rosemary's truck and walked up to the front door. No one answered the door, and when she peered through the narrow window lining the door, she saw a dark, shadowy house. Well, that's what she'd expected. They were off on their hike. The question was, could she catch up with them?

Nikki crunched through the snow heaped around the sheltered side of the house and let herself into the backyard. She immediately spotted the hiking party's footprints, tracking from the back patio down the sloping yard. She gazed to the trees in the distance, marking the yard's boundary. She imagined she saw a flick of red in the bushes. A hat? Was someone there? She saw it again, fluttering to a new branch this time. No, just a cardinal.

Nikki felt a wave of desolation wash over her, a strong sadness she hadn't experienced since missing the school bus in second grade. She was alone! Everyone had gone without her! The street had felt so empty, it was as if everyone in the world had vanished at once.

That day, she'd run into the house and been rescued by her mother, who hustled her to school, just beating the bus. Crisis averted.

Today, though, who would save Nikki?

She'd have to save herself.

A kind of madness took over then, and she went running down the sloping backyard, slipping and sliding in the wet snow, desperate to catch up. She was sure she could follow their footprints, figure out which way they'd gone and join them. They'd all have a laugh, and Kevin would congratulate her on having the ability to leave the diner to Lauren. He wouldn't even know it was because she was suddenly sick of the sight of the place. He'd think it was his own influence, and she'd let him, because for ten minutes this afternoon Nikki just wanted to be *happy*.

She slipped through the gate and found the hiking trail leading off in either direction. Her eyes skimmed the footprints—would they have turned left, or right?

Her heart sank as she realized the trail had seen a busy day.

There were footsteps leading both ways. She felt like an army must have been using this path today, marching down the path towards Catoctin Creek or up into the mountains, or both—

maybe they'd gone back and forth, just to trample into oblivion any tracks she'd wanted to find. In truth, it might have been just a few people who had taken the path and returned by the same route, but the damage was the same: she didn't know which way Kevin and the others had gone.

She had been left behind.

*Again.*

The word came to her in a rush of sadness, and she clung to it like a life preserver. *Again.* Everyone left her. Everyone moved on. Catoctin Creek slowly emptied, one by one, the people she had gone to school with, her friends, her family—nothing was left but Rosemary, who had Stephen—and the Blue Plate.

And just now she felt like the Blue Plate was eating her soul alive.

Nikki looked around at the white-coated world, the canopy of ice-laced trees shimmering overhead, the gray dome of the sky pressing above them like the lid of a pot. She felt utterly alone. She could have phoned them, she could have asked which way they'd turned, if they'd linger for a few moments while she scrambled to catch up—but no.

She wouldn't.

Nikki turned and walked back up the slope to the brick house, hoping they wouldn't come back until after dark and would miss her extra set of footprints, pointing in the wrong direction. She'd made her choice, and everyone had moved on without her. What else could she possibly expect?

"Sean was here," Lauren said when she walked into the diner.

Nikki was thankful Lauren didn't ask where she'd gone, or why she'd come back just two hours later. A few more of the tables were filled, and there was a gentle buzz to the dining room which soothed her spirit. "Did he want anything or are you just sharing?"

"He dropped this for you." Lauren held up a big manila envelope. It was clipped shut with a metal brad. Nikki took it from her, feeling the hard card-stock of menus inside.

"Did you open it?" she asked, plucking open the brad to peek inside.

"Did I open your personal mail?" Lauren was affronted. "Yes, I rummage through all of your special deliveries. Obviously."

"I was just asking because maybe he said what it was, I don't know. It's nothing private. Not from Sean. Jeez." Nikki was rambling now. She closed her mouth, peered into the envelope, and flicked through the menus. It looked like Sean had made a special trip into Frederick and gone to every bakery and cafe he could find. One of the menus was even laminated. *Stealing for me, how thoughtful.* She'd have to return it once she was done with her research. "There's no need to get worked up."

Lauren pointedly drew a washcloth across the stack of menus heaped on the podium. "No one's worked up. Oh, and we're out of blondies, if you feel like baking something."

Nikki let the envelope fall closed. "That's exactly what I feel like, thank you." She smiled at Lauren, causing the younger woman to peer at her suspiciously. "Or maybe I'll make something special, test out a new recipe. How about that?"

Nikki felt calmer as soon as she had all of her ingredients sitting in front of her. The kitchen was hot and Patrick was playing the classic rock station, her least favorite soundtrack for baking, but at least she could measure and sift and mix to her heart's content, letting her mind slow to the rhythms of the task at hand. It was a welcome break from the world of worry she'd been dealing with. While her brain was thinking out a fresh new recipe, she didn't have any space left to think about new cafes, her old diner, or what was going to happen between herself and Kevin. She just had to follow the simple, safe rules of baking.

Patrick was crashing his way through a country-fried steak and several hamburgers when she slipped a pan of brownies, nestled on a graham cracker crust, into the oven. He threw a lid over some burger patties to steam them and eyeballed her baking station. "What are you mixin' up there?"

"S'mores brownies," Nikki replied, taking down a bag of mini marshmallows—leftovers from the Thanksgiving weekend, of course. "Just an idea I had."

He lifted thick eyebrows. "Lauren was supposed to tell ya we were out of blondies."

"She did. I just wanted to try something different." Nikki watched Patrick's brow furrow as he tried to comprehend this entirely new sentiment. The watchword of the Blue Plate kitchen had always been to change nothing. If she could switch up the dessert menu, he was probably thinking, what might she do to his dinner menu?

But when he spoke, he surprised her. "You know who will like these? Bobby. He told me today that Ellie Baughman loves brownies. And I know for a fact she likes marshmallows, because she ate my sweet potato casserole back on Thanksgiving weekend."

Nikki gaped at Patrick. "Are you serious? So Bobby's really going for it with Ellie?"

"They're going on a date tonight. I think the waffles did it. So now they're going to start seeing each other, and who knows? Bobby and Ellie Baughman. Lovebirds." Patrick spoke solemnly.

As well he should, Nikki thought. Love was solemn business. It made a person do crazy things.

Like run through the snowy woods, hoping to catch up with a man who had been on a hike for hours already, and was likely miles away.

Nikki was certainly glad she hadn't let things go *that* far.

Thank goodness she was sensible enough to stop at the gate.

# Chapter 28

# Kevin

K evin got into the truck alongside Gus and rubbed his hands together. "Another cold one," he said.

"Mmhmm." Gus wasn't generally talkative first thing in the morning, Kevin had noticed. You got to know a person, driving around winding country roads together, wrestling with bad-tempered horses together. And that's exactly what he'd been doing since he packed Alice back to New York City with instructions to tell everyone how happy he was in Catoctin Creek.

Driving. Standing. Bending over. Rinse and repeat.

A farrier's life.

You got to know your companion, but you got to know horses, too. In just a couple of weeks, Kevin had absorbed more information on equine personalities than he ever could have believed existed. They all had their preferences, and it was up to a handler to figure them out. Some horses liked to have their noses rubbed almost constantly, while some would bite you for even trying it. Some horses would lean on the farrier, grateful for the chance to rest one of their legs; some would suddenly drop their weight completely and then lurch to one side, leaving Gus to scramble for safety while Kevin hung on to their heads like mad.

He had become Gus's bodyguard, learning to watch equine body language and warn him with a sharp word before a crafty horse did something dangerous. Gus said Kevin had a sixth sense about horses, and often repeated that he didn't know how he'd managed without Kevin's help before. "Of all the holders I've had, you're the quickest to catch a horse at some foolishness," Gus told him.

Kevin blushed under the compliments and wondered who would be his bodyguard when it was *him* under a horse someday.

He'd already been under quite a few already, actually. More than he'd expected when he took on the job. Every day there was at least one horse who was considered a simple job, who just needed a quick trim, or whose hooves could offer a little anatomy or diagnostics lesson. Gus liked to run open-and-shut cases past Kevin, showing him how to spot telltale signs of hoof and leg problems.

Just yesterday, Kevin had been presented with a horse who was "three-legged lame," as horse-people put it. The poor thing was literally hobbling down the concrete barn aisle, and Kevin would have sworn the horse had a broken leg, but in less than five minutes, Gus had shown him where to find the abscess which had been making that horse's life miserable.

He'd carefully cut away the sole above the abscess with a hoof knife, let it drain, and then stood back as the owner competently balled the hoof up with a baby diaper and sugared iodine, finally wrapping it all up in duct tape. The hoof looked like a Christmas present from a mechanic when the young woman was through.

"These things are common, huh?" he'd asked, watching the horsewoman spool the horse's foot up in padding with impressive speed.

The horsewoman had rolled her eyes, more at the horse than at Kevin. "I'll say."

"Especially when we get wet spells," Gus said with a nod. "All of this wet snow and muddy thaws turns a horse's hooves to mush. One little crevice gets some dirty mud in it and wham, you've got an infection."

They were delicate, horses, even more so than he'd realized while watching Rosemary work with her little herd or while helping Stephen with barn chores. They walked on hooves so strong they could absorb the shock of a pounding hammer and wear shoes made of steel, but they could also wilt at the least change in weather, the slightest slip-up in their schedule.

All in all, Kevin found horses fascinating, and a very good distraction from the ongoing problem of Nikki. She wasn't talking to him again. At least, that's what it seemed like. He hadn't talked to her since she'd turned down his offer of a hike. The days had piled up since then, and she hadn't called. Hadn't texted. Hadn't given him any indication she was still thinking about him.

At least when he was working, he didn't have time to wonder what on earth she was doing to him. The drives could be problematic, though. Hopefully today they were going to a nearby farm.

"We got a decent drive to work this morning," Gus said, pointing the truck's bumper north and driving towards the curving spine of the Catoctins. "Gonna look at some Standardbreds today. You ever heard of 'em?"

"Can't say as I have." Horse breeds had not been covered in New York City's public education system.

"They're trotters. They race 'em. You know, harness racing. You've seen that. The Meadowlands, up in New Jersey, is harness racing. And Yonkers, that's in New York."

Kevin considered it. Come to think of it, he *had* known about harness racing, somewhere in the most cobwebbed recesses of his brain. He had seen the word *Yonkers* on the back pages of tabloids read by old men on the subway, and on the occasional poster scattered around the city. "Yeah, I know what you mean. So they only trot, they don't gallop, is that it?"

"They *can* gallop, but they've got a real mean trot and they're taught that's what comes first. And plenty of 'em pace—they move both legs on either side at the same time. You'll know it when you see it."

"Dogs do it," Kevin realized.

"Some dogs do it, yup."

"So do they have different hooves, different needs, that kind of thing?"

"They've got honking enormous hooves," Gus said with relish. "Built like iron. I love 'em."

Any horse Gus loved, Kevin resolved to love. He tilted his head back and watched the snowy countryside pass by. Dairy farms, stubbled corn fields, empty expanses which would be planted with soy in the spring: all of it was swaddled in fresh white, reflected in the pearly sky above. Every time the truck rounded a curve, it was like seeing another painting in a gallery of landscape art. An Andrew Wyeth, he thought dreamily. Just farms and plain living, as far as the eye could see.

Gus shook his thermos and sighed. "We're stopping in the next town," he announced. "I need coffee."

A gas station was approaching on the right, the lonely sentinel of a little crossroads. "I imagine they have coffee," Kevin suggested, not so much because he was in a hurry for gas station brew but because he knew Gus liked coffee from Exxon stations, Mobil stations, and rickety mom-and-pop no-name stations with equal enthusiasm.

"Not when we're this close to High Rock Coffee Company," Gus said, shaking his head. "One advantage of doing work on the other side of the mountains. Man, I dream about this stuff."

Kevin lifted his eyebrows. "Sounds fancy!"

"Nah, it's not fancy. I don't need nothin' fancy. But it's real good."

They crossed over the Catoctin Mountains in a criss-cross of ascends and descends, and the broad plain of a vast new valley, a patchwork of farms which stretched to the horizon, appeared before them. "Wow," Kevin said with appreciation. "What are we looking at here?"

"This here's the Cumberland Valley," Gus told him. "That's Pennsylvania right up there. That's why the next town is called Pen-Mar."

Close to the foot of the mountains, a little town of about the same size as Catoctin Creek seemed to cling to the two-lane road. As the truck entered the town, Kevin immediately noticed this village was more prosperous, and apparently visited by tourists. Main Street boasted a couple of outfitters, a knitting shop, and some galleries with watercolors hanging on display. There were also a few gift shops, with lots of swirling letters painted on their plate-glass windows, evidently waiting to welcome summer weekenders.

Kevin thought Catoctin Creek could look like this, with just a little paint and a few new ideas.

Gus slowed and turned into an alley jutting off from the road. He parked the truck behind a tall white Victorian pressed into the jumble of storefronts and narrow houses. "This is the place. We'll just run in and grab a cup." He hopped out of the truck and led the way to the building's back door.

Inside, a narrow hallway led to a warm, coffee-scented cafe. Kevin felt like he could have been somewhere back in the city. The floors were of honey-colored wood, scarred with decades of hard use but still polished and limber. A shining mirror, surrounded with gilded trimming last popular in the nineteenth century, hung behind the espresso machine and assorted coffee ephemera, and there was a bake case filled with every sort of deliciousness behind its glass, from cookies to croissants. Everything looked hearty and warming, and like it would pair perfectly with a winter's day.

A server looked up from a table he'd been wiping down. "Hi folks! Be right with you!" He paused, then his customer-service smile widened into something real. "Oh, it's Gus! Didn't recognize ya, all bundled up in that coat. Last time you were here, it was still kinda nice out."

"I only pass through every six weeks," Gus admitted. "Damn those Standardbreds and their perfect feet."

"You need more clients on this side of town," the server told him. He tucked his towel into his apron and walked behind the counter. "We have the reserve blend today. You want two?" He winked.

"One for here and one for the road, right?" Gus laughed. "Nah, I'll take one large and my friend here—" he looked at Kevin —"Well, you know your way around a menu, get whatever you want. But I recommend the reserve blend, black as night. You'll feel like you can pick up one of those Standardbreds and spin 'em around on your pinkie after you finish."

Kevin laughed. "Sounds great."

"This is the perfect place for an 'I'll have what he's having,' decision," the server assured him. "Gus is a coffee connoisseur."

"Aww, stop that," Gus scolded, but he was grinning as he handed over cash, and tucked a hefty tip into the mason jar by the register.

And Gus wasn't kidding about the reserve blend, black. Kevin was delighted with the flavor of the coffee, and the smooth aftertaste on his tongue . . . but what was really on his mind as they left the cafe was the perfect way that little business had blended its on-trend menu with the aesthetic of the pretty little town . . . and how a gas station coffee drinker like Gus happily paid extra for the taste of a good roast.

There was potential here.

The farm where the Standardbreds lived was impressive, and Kevin found he really did enjoy working around the large-boned horses, who were generally much more calm and accepting of work done on their feet than he would have expected of a racehorse. He could do a couple of trims on easy horses, and the rest of the time he stood in the handsome aisle of an elegant barn, wiggling the lead-shank under the nose of horse after horse, while Gus got the dirty work done.

The downtime and the easier horses gave Kevin plenty of time to think. If he'd been dreading the quiet time earlier, now he had plenty to peruse. First and foremost, he wondered if Nikki had ever driven over the mountain and visited that cafe. Surely, if a little town the size of Pen-Mar could support coffee and surroundings like that, Catoctin Creek could, too. And, just as she'd said that morning on Main Street, a bakery cafe was a perfect little jumping-off point to a small restaurant. Despite what she thought, Nikki didn't really have unattainable aspirations, he realized, his excitement growing. Nikki could have what she wanted.

She just needed someone good with money to help her make it happen. And maybe Kevin hadn't been the best investor in Manhattan, but he still knew how to operate all the levers and systems that made the money machine go. Anyway, surely a mediocre Manhattan investor was plenty capable enough for a rural Maryland cafe. You didn't exactly need Warren Buffett to get a concept like this off the ground. You just needed passion and a local touch—something Nikki had in spades.

He resolved to put together a plan and then bring it to Nikki— kind of like she had done with her action plan. No—*exactly* like she had done. She had been so generous with her time, and he had been less than gracious in turning it down. He'd make up for it with a plan she could really put into place, a gesture he knew she'd appreciate more than a bouquet of roses.

Before they left the Standardbred farm, one of the grooms came up and whispered something to Gus. The two men glanced back at

Kevin, and Gus nodded. Kevin, who was hanging up the lead-rope from the last horse he'd put away, watched the groom approach with some nervousness. "Everything okay?" he asked, hoping he hadn't done something wrong with one of the racehorses. They were probably worth gobs of money, judging by the grandeur they lived in.

"Yeah, of course, I just have something you might want to see." The groom smiled mysteriously and took Kevin down the long row of stalls, past a tack room filled with gleaming harness, and through a side-door.

Kevin gasped.

They'd entered some kind of carriage house, a space that was half warehouse, half museum. There were wheeled conveyances of every type sitting in the half-light: a stagecoach, a dairy wagon, a circus wagon, complete with bars for whatever animal had been paraded through the town streets. The groom wove through the collection and then stepped aside as if he'd found what he was looking for. "I heard you talking to Gus about how much you liked all the snow we've been having," he explained. "I do, too. Look here. This is my favorite thing about working here."

He was standing before a gleaming antique sleigh.

The sleigh was gorgeous, a confection of dark red paint and shimmering gilt. It sat on smooth, sinuous runners, their slanting gleam giving the impression of motion even though it was confined to this crowded room. It was positively Santa-worthy.

The song he'd mentioned to Nikki, that first morning together, came back to his head.

*Over the river, and through the snow . . .*

As a child in Queens, surrounded by bricks and pavement, that song had been pure magic. It had conjured up a world outside of rattling subways, roaring buses, the exhaust and the car horns and the broken mufflers on dollar vans, puttering past his window at all hours of night and day. The sleigh bells seemed to ring louder than every other sound, creating a buffer between Kevin and the crashing gears of reality.

Now, looking at this sleigh, Kevin fell in love. He felt like he'd been missing this sleigh his entire life and hadn't even known it before. Was he a sleigh enthusiast? Was this his life now? It seemed very possible. Maybe there would be a headline in twenty years: *Catoctin Creek Man Amasses World's Largest Sleigh Collection.*

"This is the most beautiful thing in the world," he sighed, shaking his head. "Do you take it out? Does it get used?"

The groom nodded. "We do take it out! You need hard snow for it, though, and Maryland's not known for a nice thick snowpack like they get out west, or up north. But this might be our year. With all that snow out there this early in winter . . . who knows? We have two horses trained to pull it, and they absolutely love to go out and pace through the snow."

"I'd love to see that," Kevin said. Just the idea gave him goosebumps. The beauty of horses—the beauty of snow—the beauty of this sleigh: what a combination! "Is there any way? Do you take it out in public?"

"Sometimes, but it's tough. We're hoping this year the Pen-Mar Winter Festival will have enough snow to bring the sleigh out. We'll do rides, demos, that kind of thing. I got to do it about six years ago and it was unbelievable. People love it."

"Is that soon? It must be, right? Christmas?"

"It's in January. There's a better chance of snow that time of year. Come out and see us at the festival. I'll make sure you get a ride and show you how to hold the reins."

Kevin's heart did a flippity-flop. He imagined this beautiful sleigh gliding noiselessly through the white landscape, being pulled by a dark horse with perfect, enormous hooves. He remembered winter days in Queens, turning the pages of his songbook and savoring the pictures. *Mom,* he'd called more than once, *why isn't it like this when we go to grandmother's house?*

*Grandmother's house?* She'd asked. *You mean your Grandma's apartment?*

*Over the river and through the snow, this says. To Grandmother's house we go. I want to go that way.*

His mother had given him a sidelong smile; even now, he could remember it. Her "Oh Boy," smile, he'd learned to call it. The one that meant: "Oh boy, this kid's got an overactive imagination."

But this is what he had wanted. His entire life, Kevin realized, he had been longing and longing for the pages of those storybooks.

He just hadn't known they could exist in real life.

And what about Nikki, he thought, walking slowly back down the barn aisle. What was her storybook?

The cafe, the beautiful restaurant, the thriving town?

Could that storybook exist in real life, too?

# Chapter 29

# Nikki

Nikki smelled like fried chicken.

She always smelled like fried chicken on Wednesday nights, and she had made her peace with this several years ago. Blue Plate fried chicken was legendary, and half the town seemed to show up for the thick hunks of buttermilk-brined, deep-fried thighs and breasts and drumsticks that Patrick made so reverently, batch after batch sizzling in the fryer, the oil popping so loudly that no one in the kitchen could even hear each other without shouting. The restaurant was always full from five o'clock to eight, dinner hours, and in good weather folks would even show up for takeout containers which they'd eat from in the parking lot, leaning over the hoods of their cars or sitting in the backs of their pickups, creating impromptu community picnics which the servers, Nikki included, eyed with longing as they toiled away in the increasingly hot, close, crowded restaurant.

Cold weather killed the parking lot crowds, but there were still enough hungry patrons to fill the booths inside. Nikki stood by the back counter and watched the restaurant turn around her, the plate-glass windows softly lit with strings of colored lights woven around artificial garland, jangly Christmas pop playing through the old speakers along the ceiling, gaudy sweaters and brooches brightening the usually dull wardrobes of her farmer clientele.

Christmas had crept up on her with unusual stealth this year. Nikki was used to Thanksgiving giving way to a wave of holiday decorating, invitations to cookie-decorating parties at the VFW community hall, requests for donations to school fundraisers, and her own childish pleasure in the holiday. This year, all of that had faded into the background. Kevin's arrival at Thanksgiving had thrown her usual life into turmoil. She wondered if Lauren had handled the donations, or if the PTA just hadn't called this year.

Lauren might very well have done it. Look at her now, swooping in with a coffee pot in one hand and an iced tea pitcher in the other, filling glasses while the other girls are grabbing orders. Look at her slide between tables, nodding and smiling, taking requests as if she's their server. Look at her swiftly depositing the pots back on the beverage station before wiping her hands on her apron and ringing out two families who are just now ready to pay up and leave. Look at her gracious smile, look at her efficiency!

Nikki looked, took it all in, and realized she wasn't needed anymore.

At least, not like they used to need her. Lauren was everything the restaurant needed, good with the old and young customers alike, and managed the state of the kitchen with a judicious eye. She was diplomatic with servers and impatient diners when food was coming out of the kitchen late, she was kind when their resident widows and widowers like old Mrs. Wesley in the corner booth here were in no hurry to go back to her quiet, lonely house and just wanted to linger over coffee and an empty pie plate.

*Lauren won't stay forever.* The thought hit her with the force of a freight train. Lauren was young, intelligent, confident. Eventually, in six months or a year, she'd decide her time in Catoctin Creek was over. She'd leave, maybe for Frederick, maybe for college or a restaurant job in a city farther afield, and Nikki's chance would be gone.

She was going to have to promote that girl, and step out of her way, or risk losing Lauren too soon. Before she'd had a chance to make her move.

If she was really going to make it.

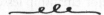

The brightest spot in her evening came when Nadine and Caitlin appeared in the doorway. Caitlin rarely ate at the Blue Plate, having decided in her mid-teens that she was "allergic" to grease and embarking on a lengthy and boring (to her friends) phase in which she only ate side salads dressed with vinegar. Nikki realized now that Caitlin had probably been dealing with an eating disorder. Looking back at high school these days was full of uncomfortable realizations about the things they'd glossed over, or even teased people about.

Tonight, though, Caitlin had looked bright and healthy, and she'd brought her nice little assistant, that dark-haired young woman Nadine, whom Nikki occasionally saw driving around town in a rickety old hatchback or the much nicer, glossy Elmwood pickup truck. They'd ordered fried chicken and even though Caitlin had carefully removed the skin from hers first, they cleaned their plates and asked for pie afterwards.

"Come and sit with us," Caitlin said cajolingly. "Let's catch up. You can take off a few minutes, right? I see Rosemary all the time, but I barely ever get to talk to you."

Nikki had looked around the buzzing dining room. Everywhere she turned, people were either smiling at their servers or smiling at their plates. Lauren zipped around like a dragonfly at top speed. The Blue Plate was truly a well-oiled machine tonight, and Nikki wasn't even one a cog. "Yeah," she decided. "I can take a little break."

They ate slices of lemon meringue pie and caught up. Caitlin gushed over Rosemary's horsemanship lessons. "I know we started them to help people take in rescue horses, but I've had three horse sales in the past two months to grads of her seminars! People are learning so much, they're really taking the deep-dive into horse ownership!"

Nikki lifted her eyebrows. "And they're boarding them with you, right?"

Nadine smothered a smile and concentrated on her pie.

"Well, yes. I still have an indoor arena and Sean to teach them," Caitlin said comfortably. "So they stick with me for the better facilities. But it's so much better to have boarders who know how to take care of their own horses, even if they don't *have* to do it."

"That's true," Nadine said, looking up again. She was pretty, Nikki thought, with tan skin even in the dead of winter, dark hair and dark eyes. She probably wouldn't stick around very long; Caitlin's assistants were chronically overworked and had a tendency to burn out after six months or so. Then again, she'd first seen this one at the spring fundraiser back in March, so Nadine had already lasted longer than the average suggested she would. "And the people who are moving into the area are really interesting. They want to show, but they're much more civic-minded than just chasing ribbons. They want to get involved with grassroots organizations to preserve farmland, or increase diversity in the show-ring, things like that. I really like them."

Caitlin shrugged. "As long as everyone gets along, I'm fine. And as long as Sean doesn't keep running through the prettier ones like a raging stallion."

Nikki's eyebrows made another swift lift to her hairline. "Excuse me?"

Nadine looked back at her plate.

Caitlin put a bite of pie in her mouth and smiled.

"Oh, it's like that?" Nikki leaned back in the booth and laughed. "Young Sean, the Expert Trainer, offering private lessons on proper seat position? Where to put one's legs? A little help with mounting?"

Caitlin guffawed and nearly spit out her pie.

"It's like that," Nadine said, her voice barely audible. "He's a pig, honestly."

Caitlin rubbed her assistant's back with a motherly air. "As coworkers, I'm afraid Nadine and Sean have their ups and their downs. Today was one of their downs. That's why I thought fried chicken was in order."

"Coworkers can be tough," Nikki said sympathetically. "Especially when they're slutty boys."

"How's *your* boy?" Caitlin asked, smoothly changing the subject in that schmoozy way she had. "I've seen him with Gus a few times. Looks like he's really settling into the farrier life."

Nikki considered the question. How *was* Kevin? She hadn't seen him much of him recently, or of anyone, really. She'd been holed up in her apartment, going over menus and clicking through the websites of small town bakeries, trying to parse out the secrets of their success. Trying to decide if she could replicate it here. The s'mores brownies had been a huge hit with customers. Tomorrow, when she had a little extra time, she was going to try her hand at lemon-raspberry bars. She was testing the sales of new items versus the regulars and recording the results.

"Kevin's good," she decided. "Adjusting to a new kind of lifestyle, I guess. It's tiring, standing there holding horses all day, digging out hooves, driving all over creation. It wouldn't be my first choice in a job, anyway."

Caitlin regarded her with an amused smile. "You don't approve?"

*Oops.* Anything she said to Caitlin could and would make its way around Catoctin Creek, and definitely back to Elmwood, where Kevin would hear about it from Sean . . . what a tiny little world they lived in! Nothing but the concentric lines of a spider web, woven around and around and around them . . .

"No, I *definitely* approve." Nikki smiled, showing her teeth. "It's good for him to learn something new, and he's enjoying being around horses and out in the fresh air, doing things with his hands. Guys need that. Look how good it's been for Stephen. He's like a new man."

"Stephen is still working in investments," Caitlin pointed out. "He's just doing it remotely. Why doesn't Kevin do that?"

"He wanted a change," Nikki said stoutly. "Sometimes we all just want a change."

Caitlin laughed. "I'll bet! We all just do what we're given to do, though, don't we? Me with the farm, you with the Blue Plate. Nikki, do you ever imagine you'd been born in a different town? Somewhere with a little more, I don't know, *style?* Catoctin Creek can barely support your diner, as good as the food is, but I bet you'd rather be cooking something different from fried chicken, wouldn't you?"

Nikki shook her head, letting her hair swirl around her face. At least it would cover the pink in her cheeks. "Catoctin Creek's home, Caitlin." The words seemed to pull from somewhere deep inside of her. "There's nothing wrong with our town. Even if it makes us mad sometimes."

Caitlin's eyebrows were eloquent arches. "Anywhere else, and you and I both would have been free from the start. But here we are, living our family's legacies for them. Come on, Nikki, you know what I mean. We were the improvers once, remember that? And they handed us our improvement and told us where to stick it."

Nikki knew what Caitlin was getting at. The woman sitting across from her was no horsewoman, but she was throwing everything she had at making her late mother's equestrian center a success with the gifts she'd been given. Nikki was a born chef, and she was giving her days and her nights to this diner. They'd tried to change Catoctin Creek, once upon a time, and the town had pushed back. Hard. They'd been put back in their places.

*And here we remain.*

She cast her gaze around the dining room, at the happy couples eating their dinners, and realized for the first time that she, Caitlin, and Nadine were the youngest people in the room by decades.

At that moment, Lauren power-walked past their booth. She was smiling tightly, the hard-won smile of the customer service professional who is trying not to let anyone see her sweat through a problem. She looked capable and strong. She looked like she was running circles around the place and she liked it. She looked like she was ready to take over the Blue Plate, and Nikki wondered if she would, if offered the chance.

She barely heard anything else Caitlin or Nadine said until they said goodnight and disappeared. Or anything anyone else said until Lauren had turned the sign around, cashed out the register, and made her customary demand of Nikki.

"Go home."

Nikki said goodnight to Patrick and Betty as she went out the kitchen door, but she didn't turn her feet towards home. She kept walking down Main Street, sidestepping the slush slowly turning to ice at every intersection.

So now here she was, in the cold, moonless night, standing in front of the Schubert place and smelling like fried chicken. *Start with a bakery,* Sean had urged her, with all of his tourist-town wisdom. So she'd gathered her menus, and she'd played with her first new recipes.

But could she ever really turn this old house—or any space in Catoctin Creek—into a cafe? The Blue Plate's business was down on the year before. Yes, even on fried chicken night. This was no time to start a new venture. She'd never even get the loan to make it happen. The starlight glinted on the dark windows. They'd stay dark, until the roof began to leak, the ceilings came crashing down, and the house was nothing but a shell.

Everything she was doing? It was a waste of time.

"It's not going to happen, is it, old house?"

The house sat quietly, its empty windows staring blankly into the night.

Kevin was standing by her front door, looking forlorn in the darkness. Nikki, who had been dawdling, her head down and her eyes unfocused as she mourned her the end of her fantasy, stopped short when she saw him there.

"Kevin," she gasped finally, forcing her feet forward. "It's a little late for you to be out, isn't it? Go home and get your beauty sleep."

His laugh was so familiar and comforting, yet it made her heavy heart ache to hear it. She wasn't ready to be cheered up; she wished she hadn't made a joke at all. She should have just told him to go home, put an edge to her voice so he'd know to obey. He was a tough guy now; he could take it.

"I still haven't adjusted to country hours," he admitted. "I'm up until midnight every night like I still live in the city, so I'm setting three alarms to make sure I get out of bed in the morning. Luckily, Gus doesn't start too early. He says he's mellowing out in his old age and likes a nice long cup of coffee and his newspaper every morning. Gives me a little extra time to sleep."

"I'm glad it's working out for you," she said, meaning it sincerely. She unlocked the door and stepped inside. The familiar warmth of her apartment wrapped around her, scented slightly with chocolate from some baking she'd done that morning, and she felt a little better just for being inside. She decided she could handle Kevin's presence, after all. She beckoned for him to follow. "Come inside, warm up, and tell me what you're doing out here so late."

She slipped out of her coat and snow boots, and walked over to the kitchen to put the kettle on. It felt like a tea kind of night. When she turned back around, Kevin was pulling off his coat. Her breath caught in her throat—his shoulders and arms had grown more muscled over the past few weeks, and now they pressed at the confines of his checked flannel shirt.

Maybe a hot toddy, instead of just tea. Nikki wasn't sure she was up to all of those muscles sober.

He noticed her staring and grinned, obliging her with a flex that nearly popped the buttons off his chest (and Nikki's eyes out of her head). "Not bad, right? I've been working with the hammer and the anvil, and it's wild how heavy that thing is. Not to mention all the holding up hooves and scraping away with the knife . . . it's better than body-building in some gym, that's for sure."

Nikki nodded, her eyes still wide as she took in the new Kevin. He'd always seemed so soft to her, a soft city boy who couldn't be asked to fend for himself, and while she'd been pleasantly surprised that day in the barn, *now* he looked like a mountain man who had come down from his cabin to carry her off. She swallowed, pushing back some very vibrant fantasies she hadn't even known her brain was harboring. "You look great," she said, aware the word was ineffectual. "Really . . . healthy."

Kevin laughed. "You do, too." He flopped onto the couch and patted the cushion next to him. "Come sit with me. I want to tell you about something."

She ran her hand through her hair. "I smell like fried chicken."

"I love fried chicken. It's fine."

She hesitated, then went for it. Surely they'd been through worse together than a scent of fried chicken? "Okay, Kevin. I'm here. What's up?"

"Have you ever been to Pen-Mar?"

"On the other side of the mountains? Sure I have, everyone goes there at some point. They have a cute little winter festival. Lots of tourists in summer."

"Have you ever been to the High Rock Coffee Company?"

Her brow furrowed. "No . . . it sounds a little familiar, though. Maybe it's just the name 'High Rock' that's ringing a bell, though. That's an overlook up on the mountainside."

"Okay. Well, Gus took me there today. You have to see it. I think you'd really be inspired."

"Inspired? What are you talking about?"

"I heard you talking to Sean about it. That day—the day after Alice got here. You said you wondered if people would buy coffee and cake from you, and he suggested you start a cafe. He's right. I *know* you could do it, Nikki! And this place in Pen-Mar proves that the town could support it. Maybe not just Catoctin Creek, but people in the area or passing through. Weekenders. Sunday drives. Antiquers. Those kind of people. You could build a beautiful cafe that would put Catoctin Creek back on the map."

Kevin was talking faster now; Nikki was struggling to find a pause where she could interject, tell him she'd been working on something, but that it wasn't ready yet—it might never be ready. His words should have excited her, telling her they were on the same page, but instead they were just making her feel more and more nervous. If Kevin thought she should jump, Nikki thought, that was surely a sign she should take a step back.

He was still going, though. "Who knows? Maybe it would turn this whole town around! Wake up the businesses on Main Street, give people some spending money and the impetus to fix up the storefronts. Maybe Catoctin Creek has some life in her yet, Nikki, and you could be the one to bring her back!"

He paused at last, almost out of breath with the force of his excitement.

Nikki stared at him. What was it, about people from other places who wanted to fix her town? The presumption got her back up. It was one thing talking to Sean about this sort of thing, but for a *New Yorker* to tell her Catoctin Creek wasn't good enough— Nikki jumped directly into defense.

"Kevin, what on earth are you talking about? Catoctin Creek doesn't need brought back to anything. Catoctin Creek never *was* anything! It's just this—it's a little town where two roads meet and a big crick goes through on its way to the river. It's a place for a feed store and a grain elevator. It's where the volunteer fire department and the post office are based. That's *it*. This was never some bustling county seat or something. Don't go looking for former glory where there isn't any."

Kevin gaped. "But, Nikki—"

"And anyway, what makes you think you can show up here and start listing ways this town needs to be fixed? Do you think that's what the people here want, for some New Yorker to show up and start chattering about how they ought to paint their front doors and straighten out their windows and sell some trinkets that tourists might like? Don't be that person, Kevin. Don't be that person who thinks they know best when in fact they know absolutely nothing."

She took a breath.

He stared at her, his ruddy face gone pale, and she felt horrible.

Nikki waited for him to get angry, to tell her he'd only been trying to help, to storm out. For this—for their little play at romance—to be over. Because she'd just proven she wasn't the kind of person who could turn down her crazy enough to be a good partner. Kevin hadn't said a word she hadn't believed on her own. The only crime he'd committed was saying these things out loud.

She opened her mouth to apologize, and waited for words to come out.

Before she managed to say anything, he drew in a breath of his own, and when he spoke, his voice was soft. "That's a lot of defense for Catoctin Creek, Nikki. And I know the town doesn't *need* to change. But you have to admit everyone would benefit from a little more business. And I notice you didn't say one word about yourself, or the cafe idea."

"What do you want me to say? Do you want me to tell you I don't want it?"

"I wouldn't believe you."

His quiet assurance stung. "Well *believe* it, because I don't! I was just being nice to Sean, he's new here and he said he wanted to know more about the town—"

"That's not true."

"How would you know?"

"I work with Sean every week, Nikki. We talk."

"About *me?*"

"About you, sometimes. Sean thinks you're a genius and you deserve the chance to prove it. And so do I. We believe in you."

She pushed away from the couch and walked around the little apartment, hugging her arms to her chest, wishing she had somewhere else to go. The perfect little space had suddenly grown tight, the walls closing in on her.

"And I know he has been looking into it for you," Kevin continued mercilessly. "What's stopping you? You're not mad at me. I'm not the problem."

He was right. He wasn't the problem. Catoctin Creek wasn't even the problem. *She* was the problem. She didn't have enough; she didn't know enough; she wasn't enough.

She'd known it the entire walk home from the Schubert house. She'd known her dream would not come true. With every step, she had been more certain of it. All her research had led her to this point: to giving it up.

She wasn't even going to let it sit and percolate. She was going to just watch it disappear. With just a few subtle words, Caitlin had reminded her of what had happened the last time they'd tried to change Catoctin Creek. Kevin didn't know about it. Sean didn't know. They had no idea what could go wrong.

"I can't have it," she said finally. "I can't have the house, I can't have the cafe. There's no money, and there's no hope. You don't even know how much work—"

"How could I know, Nikki? Look, you have tried to help me since the first day I got here. I understand that now. I misunderstood you at first, and I'm sorry. I don't want to do the same thing to you. But I do want to help you achieve this dream.

And I think you can help the whole town while you're at it. Even if you don't think anyone wants it."

"It's not that I don't *think* it, Kevin, I *know* it!"

"How, how do you know?"

She dropped onto her bed and put her head in her hands. She didn't want to talk about it. She didn't want to relive it. But because of him, she would, all night long.

"Go home, Kevin."

# Chapter 30

# Kevin

Kevin bent to pick up the little white pony's hoof. Glowworm was a good pony with good feet, making him one of the handful in Caitlin's barn that had been designated as Kevin's projects. His goal was simply to keep the pony's hooves healthy and trim through all the hazards of winter, and so far, he'd been doing pretty well. Until today, when Glowworm had thrown a shoe during a ride.

The shoes were only two weeks old, far too soon for them to be loose or overgrown, and Kevin was embarrassed.

"It's not your fault," Gus told him, leaning over to get a look at the bare hoof. "Look, see where the nails pulled through the hoof wall? See the scrape here on the heel? He stepped on himself and pulled it right off. It's the pony's doing, not yours."

"Is there anything I can do to prevent that?" Kevin asked. "Set the shoe a little more forward?"

"If you can," Gus said with a shrug. "Smooth out that ragged edge with a file and see what you've got."

Kevin set to work, running the hoof rasp's sharp edge along the torn section of hoof. Glowworm drowsed above him, or rather next to him—the pony was so small, Kevin felt like he had to hike the little guy's hoof up unnaturally high just to pin it between his knees.

Caitlin came wandering down the aisle to watch. She leaned against the wall next to Kevin. "Nice job," she said after a few minutes. "You're getting good at this."

"Just a few years left to go and he can work on his own," Gus said cheerfully. "And I can retire. I'll sell him my route, like a paperboy."

"Then we have to convince Catoctin Creek to accept a new farrier," Caitlin laughed. "And that will only take another decade."

Kevin's ears pricked. "That's the second time I've heard this town doesn't react well to change, Caitlin. Is there a story there?"

"Oh boy," Gus said, just as Caitlin snorted and said: "A *story!*"

"I'll take that as a yes."

"It's less a story, more a cautionary tale that everyone in town repeats whenever someone wants to try something new," Caitlin said. "Basically, about fifteen years ago, some high school kids decided to start a town improvement society. I think they got the idea from some book."

"You think, or you know?" Gus interrupted. "Because I seem to remember you were there."

"Fine, whatever, Gus. Make me look bad in front of the new kid. I was there. I was part of it. We had big ideas about fixing up Main Street, sprucing up some of the more ramshackle houses, adding a beautiful *Welcome to Catoctin Creek* sign on the way in and *Thanks for visiting, come back soon* sign on the way out, the whole civic improvement bit. It was a nice idea!" Caitlin looked a little outraged over how excellent their plan had been.

"So what went wrong?" Kevin adjusted Glowworm's hoof between his knees and pushed the rasp across the ragged edges of the pony's hoof wall. Tiny shavings of hoof curled away and snowed down on the old leather farrier chaps he'd bought from Gus. It was very satisfying.

"No one wants to be improved, that's what," Gus supplied.

Caitlin laughed ruefully. "That's the gospel truth. And the entire town went on a rampage against us. People actually took screws out of perfectly straight shutters and pulled them crooked. The kid who mowed the grass along the verge outside of town was paid to *not* mow. And some sticklers boycotted the Blue Plate because it belonged to Nikki's aunt, and Nikki was one of the group leaders. One guy took his smoker, put it in the parking lot of the firehouse, and served burgers and pork sandwiches just to stick it to the Blue Plate."

Kevin's mouth dropped. Glowworm wiggled, tugging to get his hoof free, and he gave the pony his hoof and stepped away. Every horse needed a break from standing three-legged too long. Kevin's back needed the break, too. "I never heard any of this."

Caitlin shrugged. "It's kind of an ugly chapter in the town history book. People just got so contrary, and they overreacted, and then they were embarrassed with the way they acted. It really only lasted a couple of weeks, maybe a month, and then the society disbanded and everyone went back to their own business. And the local Moose Lodge did eventually raise money to put up a pretty nice *thanks for visiting* sign, so we got that anyway."

So this was it, Kevin thought, shaking his head in wonder. This was why Nikki was refusing to even consider opening a cafe. She didn't just think there would be no customers . . . she'd thought she'd get shut down, boycotted. She could lose the support of the town for both restaurants—just like she'd lost the support for her aunt's diner. He wondered how much money her project had cost her aunt. She would have regretted every lost penny. "So people really do hate change here."

Gus shook his head. "I don't think it's so much about change as it was about being told they had to change. Like I said, people don't want to be improved. But they don't mind when something is improved *for* them."

"We were heavy-handed," Caitlin admitted. "I can see that now. We were a bunch of teenagers, what did we know about anything? And they taught us a valuable lesson. Even here, I've had to go slow, make changes very gently, to avoid hurting the feelings of anyone who has been here since it was my mom's place."

Kevin picked up Glowworm's foot again and held up a shoe to it, trying to gauge where the curving metal would have to be reshaped to fit the hoof. He was having a hard time concentrating on the job at hand. All he could think about was Nikki, and the lesson she'd learned as a teenager: the *wrong* lesson. It wasn't that Catoctin Creek couldn't accept change . . . it was that Catoctin Creek wanted to change on its own terms. Adding a cafe to the Schubert place wouldn't force the town to change its character. It would simply give them something they hadn't had before. A new choice. And everyone liked choices.

If the people of Catoctin Creek chose to follow Nikki towards a brighter future, wouldn't they be improving the place on their own terms?

He looked up from Glowworm's hoof one more time. "Caitlin, what do you think about a bakery in Catoctin Creek?"

Caitlin smiled.

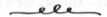

He couldn't find the Schuberts.

It had become the only hole in Kevin's plan. Over the course of a week, he spent his evenings at the kitchen table of the brick house, researching contractors and requesting estimates on kitchen renovations. He had everything sent back to an anonymous email address he'd set up for this venture. If it didn't work out and no one ever found out how much work he'd put into this business plan, that would be sad . . . but it would be better than explaining the failure of yet another Kevin McRae investment attempt.

The only problem? The house. He followed every trail of documentation he could find, but it all seemed to lead in circles. There was no contact information for the owner of the old Schubert house. The only thing he could conclude was that the Schubert children had sold the house to a private business. Their own, for tax purposes? That was anyone's guess.

But Kevin kept going, setting his disappointment about the Schubert place aside. The house was only the first obstacle, and it wasn't even the biggest one.

If he was going to get Nikki's buy-in, he had to treat her like a reluctant investor—build a proposal that showcased the project, the cost, the risk, *and* the community support. Then he had to present it, convince her, and get her to sign on the dotted line. He had to prove to her, beyond any doubt, that she was a bet worth taking.

"One more time into the fray," Kevin sighed, opening up Excel and cracking his fingers. "Let's build a business proposal no one can ignore."

Rosemary met Kevin in the barnyard on a crisp, cold Saturday afternoon, just a few days before Christmas. A fresh blanket of wet snow had fallen the day before, and she'd scraped a clear patch in front of the barn so Kevin had a day place to work. "You're sure about this?" she asked, giving him one more chance to escape. "I know Gus said you can handle it, but I don't want you to feel like you have to do a trim without him yet."

Kevin was holding a canvas bag of farrier tools, some new, some purchased from Gus's impressive supply. Rosemary had called yesterday, needing work done on Bongo, the chestnut Belgian gelding she'd rescued several years ago. He was a little overdue for his regular trim and had somehow knocked a sizeable chunk from the side-wall of one of his massive front hooves. The snow had them so behind schedule, Gus had looked at the picture Rosemary sent and suggested Kevin go fix it himself on Saturday.

"You've got everything you need to get the excess hoof trimmed away and round off those nasty edges," he'd told Kevin, who was too surprised to speak. "And Bongo's an easy horse. A little kid could trim that horse."

"I'm sure," Kevin said to Rosemary now, digging deep for a reserve of confidence to see him through. He'd been working on hooves for a month now, after all. Which didn't sound like a lot, but he and Gus could get through a lot of horses in one day, and so by this time he'd probably trimmed thirty horses by himself, and shod nine or ten. "As long as Bongo doesn't decide to sit on me, we should be good to go."

Rosemary smiled. "He's been known to lean on Gus, but I'll do my best to keep him off you. Let me grab him out of his stall." She went back into the barn, and Smoke, the gray barn cat, streaked out.

Kevin leaned down to give Smoke a pet—the cat didn't have much use for him since he was usually accompanied by Grover. But Grover had gotten himself good and soaked in the wet snow this morning, and Kevin decided to leave him at home in the warmth of the house. "Nice kitty," Kevin cooed. "Big brave mouser-kitty."

"Hardly," Rosemary laughed, bringing Bongo out to the barnyard. "He hasn't caught a single mouse in months. Smoke is a freeloader."

Kevin straightened and looked over Bongo. The horse seemed to have grown since the last time he'd seen him. Or he'd just forgotten how huge a Belgian was. Bongo seemed to be three times as wide as the sleek ponies and Thoroughbreds at Elmwood and the other riding academies in the area. And his hooves! Like manhole covers. Kevin wondered if he'd made a mistake.

But there was no turning back now. He gathered up the canvas bag again and set up next to Bongo's right front, where a section of hoof wall about two inches wide was flipped up obscenely. Gus had been right—he'd fixed hooves like this before, nipping the broken part out and using the rasp to make a beveled edge around the chipped area, broadening the area which contacted the ground.

He picked up the big hoof and started scraping it clean.

"Have you seen Nikki lately?" Rosemary asked.

"Not for a few days. I talked to her over the weekend." Kevin picked up his nippers, but Bongo was already beginning to lean on him. He gave the horse a nudge in the ribs to make him stand up straight. "She's been a little bit of a hermit lately. She doesn't seem mad at me, which is good. Just distracted."

Rosemary sighed. "I think she's got something big on her mind. But she won't let me help. Every time I ask, she says it's nothing."

*Oh, it's something,* Kevin thought. "Between you and me, I've been working on something I think will cheer her up."

"Is that right? Stand up, Bongo." He heard the jingle as Rosemary shook the lead-rope. "Nothing too grand or public, I hope."

"Goodness, no. Something to help her business along."

"That's good. She could use it. The Blue Plate doesn't seem to be as busy as it used to be. I think she's worried about money, honestly."

Bongo leaned against him again. Kevin stood up, letting the horse's hoof fall to the ground.

"Sorry," Rosemary said. "He must be testing you because you're new."

Kevin clapped his hand against the Belgian's thick neck. "Be nice to me, old boy."

"So the thing you're working on . . . it's about the bakery, right?"

He looked at Rosemary. She was smiling, a genuine smile. "I think I have everything figured out. It's the action plan of her

organized dreams. I just have a few pieces left—community
support, mainly. How do I poll this town?"

"Door to door," Rosemary said. "The old-fashioned way."

Kevin picked up Bongo's hoof again. "I was afraid you'd say
that."

"Why? You don't like canvassing?" Rosemary grinned, as if
she'd ever knock on a stranger's door.

"I don't know these people well enough," Kevin sighed. "But
I'll find someone who does."

# Chapter 31

# Nikki

Christmas Eve arrived with an early morning flurry of fresh snowfall and a promise of ice to cover it all that night. Standing by the front podium, Lauren peered out the window of the Blue Plate as a fiery sunset burned behind the snow-covered mountains of Notch Gap. The streets were quiet, just a few cars swishing through the slush on Main Street. Christmas lights blinked on the storefronts across the road, but everyone had closed up already, save Trout's Market and the Blue Plate. And the Blue Plate might as well have been closed.

"We should close up," Lauren announced, turning back to the warm, mostly empty dining room. Nikki was leaning on the back counter, absently drumming her fingers along with the chorus of Wham's *Last Christmas*. There was no such thing as Whamageddon when you worked with the sounds of Mountain Lite FM playing in the background all day, every day. She'd lost that game on the Saturday after Thanksgiving. "People are taking the ice storm warning pretty seriously."

Nikki straightened up with a sigh, pressing her hand to her back. When had the act of leaning over for more than five minutes turned into a backache-inducing offense? Getting old sucked. "I guess you're right. I'd rather you guys were all home safe before anything starts up, anyway."

Mrs. Wesley looked up from her mug of decaf. "I'm going home, dear, so don't stand around on my account."

"Oh, Mrs. Wesley," Lauren said affectionately, "I'd stay here all night if that's what you wanted."

The old woman smiled, wrinkles creasing across her face. She was wearing a red sweater and had a distinct Mrs. Claus vibe. "Don't you worry about me. My daughter moved back to Frederick. I'm going to have a family here for the holidays again." Her smile grew broader, somehow. "And there she is!"

A woman of about Nikki's age came into the Blue Plate, bringing a gust of cold wind with her. "Phew!" the woman announced, shaking off her scarf and hat in the doorway, taking care to stay on the thick doormat that absorbed snow and slush all winter. "I should have stayed in California!" She looked up, and Nikki felt a shock of recognition. The woman's hair was the color of ocean sand instead of mouse-brown, and her tan spoke of warmer climates. But that was definitely Amber Wesley, her tenth-grade biology partner.

"Amber!" Mrs. Wesley exclaimed. "Come and say hello to your old friend Nikki Mercer."

Nikki wished she could disappear behind the counter. What if she just slowly lowered herself to the floor and stayed there? No, Amber would definitely notice. It was too late to hide. She came around the counter and joined Amber at the hostess stand. "It's crazy to see you again," she said honestly. "I never thought you'd come back."

"Neither did I," Mrs. Wesley interjected.

Amber laughed. "Well, neither did I, honestly. But San Diego's *expensive*. And I was ready to buy a house. My partner and I want to start a family."

"I'm going to be a grandmother," Mrs. Wesley announced.

Nikki's eyes widened. "Are you—"

"Oh, not me. My wife." Amber grinned. "Dodged that bullet."

Nikki laughed. "Wise. Very wise."

"And you're—"

"Still here," Nikki finished, smiling to hide the sting. "Just running the best little diner in Catoctin Creek."

"It looks great," Amber said, looking around the dining room. "Nothing's changed."

"Nope," Nikki replied. "Not a thing has changed."

"I'm really sorry to cut this short—I promise to come back! But I want to get Mom back to my place before it storms."

Mrs. Wesley began the slow process of climbing out of her booth, and Amber moved to help her. Nikki, who usually stepped into assist the elderly woman, stood back with Lauren and watched Amber get her mother upright, bundled into her coat, and safely out to her car. Then she turned to Lauren. "Close. Right now. Before anyone gets any ideas."

She just wanted to get out of this place. This diner where time stood still, while everyone else outside kept leaping ahead of her.

Lauren went about her usual evening procedure, flipping the sign, locking the door, opening the cash register to count out the till. Nikki made sure the servers were doing their clean-up duties, and then she went into the kitchen, expecting to see Patrick and Betty in an advanced stage of wrapping up for the night.

Instead, she saw a flood of water sitting across the floor, already an inch deep and growing worse by the second. She turned astonished eyes on Patrick and Betty, who were both leaning over the dish sanitizer, urgently turning knobs.

"What happened?" Her voice was sharp, and the kitchen staff turned as one, their faces alarmed.

"It wasn't me," Betty said urgently. "This old thing wasn't switchin' on, so I went to reset the do-hickey in the back and it just started hissin'—you'd have thought there was a snake inside—and Patrick said to open the door—"

Patrick ran a hand over his bald head and looked at the water pooling around his ratty old kitchen shoes. "The door *shouldn't* have opened," he said petulantly. "It should've been locked if the water was runnin'."

"Oh God." Nikki stared at the water streaming from the sanitizer. She should have known what to do, but her mind, still sluggish with the Christmas Eve slowdown, wasn't registering the solution. She felt water creep into her shoes. It was warm.

Footsteps slapped the tiles behind her, and then Lauren was shoving her aside, splashing through the kitchen and out the side door. She heard a wrench of screaming metal as cold air rushed inside, filling the kitchen with steam, and then the water turned off abruptly. The sanitizer shook once as the pipes emptied and then sat quietly.

Lauren came back in, propping the door open behind her. "Go and grab your coats, it's going to get cold while we push this water out." She pushed past Nikki again, gathering the other servers.

Grumbling, the girls put on their coats and took the mops and squeegees Lauren passed them from the cleaning closet. Nikki reached for a mop, but Lauren shook her head. "I'll manage this," she said. "And then I'll call Ian Yingling to look at this thing. You go and count the till."

Speechless, Nikki turned and did as Lauren told her.

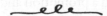

She'd planned on driving to Rosemary's on Christmas Day, but with the ice storm forecast so dire, Nikki just stopped home for a few things and then hopped into her car, heading for Notch Gap Farm before the weather could turn nasty. As it was, the roads were already dotted with dark icy patches, and she took twice as long as usual on the winding country road between town and the farm, all too aware of the yawning drop-offs along some of the tighter turns.

Rosemary came out onto the porch to greet her. The house was looking particularly festive—Stephen had been a little over-the-top with his first opportunity to go all-out with holiday decorations, and there were lights on both decks of the porch, lining the lower story of the bank barn, and twinkling along the barnyard fence. A big fat fir tree sat inside the living room, its tiers of colorful lights glinting through the front windows.

Rosemary tucked her arms close to her chest as Nikki shouldered her overnight bag and crunched through the frozen snow to the porch steps. She was ready to settle down for the night, make a drink or two, and sit around with her friends. She could really use someone to talk to after the evening she'd just had. The way Lauren had taken charge, while she'd frozen in place! Ian

Yingling had been in the kitchen before she'd gotten the night's cash deposit into the safe. Everyone had gone home more or less on time, and Ian had fixed the sanitizer with a couple cranks of his wrench.

Nikki had been entirely unnecessary for the first time in years, and the realization was making her wonder if she should move up her timeline. Give Lauren a promotion and a raise. Step back from the restaurant's daily operation.

Craft a plan for her bakery.

But she could see immediately that her problems would have to wait. Rosemary wasn't her usual serene self.

"Have you heard from Kevin?" she asked before Nikki could even make it up the stairs. "He was supposed to be here already, but he isn't and he hasn't answered his phone."

"Kevin's coming?" Nikki asked, feeling dazed. "I thought he was going back to New York for Christmas."

"He wanted to keep working with Gus, and they're supposed to get all that snow from this storm system, so he managed to put it off." Rosemary shrugged. "But now I'm worried about him. You don't think anything could have happened to him up at the brick house, do you?"

———— *ele* ————

Half an hour later, nerves shot from dealing with the slick roads, Nikki was getting out of her car at the brick house. She'd told Rosemary and Stephen to stay put—she'd handle finding out where Kevin was. But as she approached the brightly lit rancher, the blinds still open in the front window as if it was midday, not eight o'clock on a cold December night, she wished she'd accepted their back-up. Something was wrong. Grover wasn't looking out of the window, uttering the occasional bark and pressing his wet nose to the glass. And when Nikki looked inside, she could see right through the house and into the backyard through the open vertical blinds.

She ran around the back, letting herself into the yard, and almost immediately saw Kevin's phone, lit up in the darkness. She scooped it out of the snow. Rosemary's number was on the screen.

"Hey," she said, leaving it on speaker as she walked into the backyard. "I just found Kevin's phone in his backyard."

"Oh my God," Rosemary breathed. Her voice spilled across the frigid yard, the snow lit yellow by the back porch light.

"I'm sure there's a good reason," Nikki said, fighting the panic in her chest. This was Catoctin Creek. No one was murdered here. No one was robbed. Nothing happened here, ever. "I'm going to look for him, okay? I'll call you from my own phone."

"I'm sending Stephen up there," Rosemary said. "You can't be up there alone."

Nikki had to agree with this. "You stay there, okay? In case— just in case."

She put Kevin's phone in her pocket and took out her own. She needed the flashlight function now, as she trudged farther and farther from the lone lightbulb at the back of the house. She swept the beam of sharp white light across the snow in front of her, training it on the single set of footsteps leading to the back gate.

# Chapter 32

# Kevin

Kevin had been standing in the cold backyard, calling Grover, for more than five minutes. And as the sun set beneath the lowering clouds in a sudden burst of red and gold, he realized the dread gradually rising in his chest was turning into terror.

Grover was definitely gone.

He'd let the dog out after he'd gotten home from rounds with Gus. It was Christmas Eve, but horses always needed their hooves taken care of, and so even though appointments had been light, emergency calls to tack on lost shoes or deal with abscesses had still taken up extra time. Their goal of finishing at lunchtime had turned into a regular day, culminating with a stop at a show barn near Pen-Mar. That meant grabbing coffee at High Rock Coffee Company, an action which had a particular blend of elation and despair for Kevin. He'd taken in the holiday decorations and special treats in the bake case with special attention. He was still going to sell Nikki on the cafe of her dreams—and on him, in the process.

It was just going to take a little more time. He had to get everything right. Leave one blank spot, one *TBD*, on the business plan, and she'd put her back up, refuse to look at it, tell him to forget the cafe already. Rosemary had been right when she'd said his eagerness would be an instant red flag. Nikki needed everything in apple-pie order before she'd approach a new venture, and he was determined to prove he could provide just that.

He still had time, he'd told himself on the drive back. He still had time, he'd told himself as he let Grover out and started packing his overnight bag to drive down to Notch Gap Farm. He still had time, he'd told himself as he called and called the dog's name, listening to the syllables vanish into the frosty dusk.

Now he was out of time. Kevin bundled up—he'd been outside all day, but the real cold was just descending, a bitter breeze picking up ahead of the coming storm front. He'd scarcely made it into the snowy yard when he thought he heard a noise around the side of the house, by the trash cans. He ran over, his coat half on, and saw bright eyes blinking at him. He shouted, waving his coat, and the animal vanished over the fence. Whatever it had been, it wasn't Grover. And that meant it wasn't worth his time. Kevin took off down the hill, yanking his coat on properly as he ran, his heart full of misgiving.

He was still twenty feet away when he saw a drift of snow had pushed the gate at the foot of the yard open. Not much—but enough for a slim dog like Grover.

Kevin suddenly couldn't catch his own breath. He just stood there for a moment, staring at the open gate, feeling like a vise had tightened around his chest and locked him in place.

*Grover was alone in the woods.*

On a cold night, with an ice storm forecast to hit within a few hours.

Sweat was popping on his forehead, and he felt as if his skin was burning hot and cold. For just a moment, Kevin wondered if he might simply pass out from the awful reality.

*Man, you really don't know how to handle an emergency, do you?*

The words were inside his own head, but the voice was Nikki's. He looked back and forth wildly, half-expecting to see her appear from around a bend in the trail, or emerge from the woods, snow-covered and laughing at him, Grover dancing at her side.

Of course, there was no one out there—he was alone in this. Alone in everything. *No*—he couldn't panic. Or rather, he had to stop panicking. He had to get out there and find Grover.

Luckily, the fresh snowfall had been just enough to show new footprints. And he could see where the dog had gone. Kevin took off running down the snowy trail, the deep blue of the sky just after dusk slowly fading into darkness.

At first there was a cold, yellow moon shining helpfully through the leafless branches which wrapped over the trail, and Kevin thought he had a chance. But there was no sign of Grover, and time was ticking by. He reached for his phone to check the battery. He'd need as much juice as possible, just in case.

Just in case of—what? Kevin didn't really know, but he strongly suspected he didn't have the woodsman know-how he ought to if he was going to be running around the Catoctin Mountains after dark, in the dead of winter. So he was leaving it at *just in case.*

He reached into both coat pockets, feeling for his phone, and his breath came a little more quickly as his hands encountered emptiness. He checked the pockets of his jeans, and his footsteps slowed to an unsteady halt. He unzipped his coat and reached into the pockets of the sweater beneath, and as a fresh realization fell over him, Kevin's vision swam.

Kevin couldn't remember the last time he hadn't had his phone on him. No—that wasn't quite true. He *could* remember. He'd been about seventeen, and he'd taken the N train to Coney Island to meet up with some friends, and he hadn't been able to find them. He'd accidentally dropped his phone off the side of the elevated train platform near his apartment a few days before; in those days, you could live without a phone for a few days, so he hadn't gotten a new one yet. Anyway, he had been trying to get a decrepit payphone at the Coney Island subway station to work when he looked up and realized a group of teens he didn't recognize had been following him around, waiting for him to let his guard down. Kevin had looked around for help and discovered one of those rare New York City moments in which absolutely no one else is around. He'd given up his wallet without a fight, but they'd bloodied his nose for him, anyway.

He'd had to jump the turnstile to get back onto the subway platform so he could get a train home to Queens.

It didn't seem likely he'd get jumped by a gang of teens in the deep forest of the Catoctin Mountains, but Kevin still didn't like the feeling of having no phone. The lifeline the phone represented had grown from existential to very real in the past decade, anyway. Without it, deep in the woods, he was truly cut off from the world in a way he had never experienced in his life.

But phone or no phone, he still had to find his dog. Grover came first, safety second. Kevin glanced back at the faint light of his own yard one more time. Then he took off in the opposite direction. There was no going home without Grover.

With the help of the rising moon, Grover's fresh footprints were pretty easy to follow for the first half hour or so. Kevin tramped along, half-enjoying himself as he took in the shimmer of moonlight on the snowy underbrush, the trail of silver running ahead of him, the deep-blue shadows pooling beneath the trees. There was something bewitching about the sleeping forest, and he wished he had thought to come out here under better circumstances, maybe bringing Grover out for a moonlit walk, or to stroll this path with Nikki on his arm, letting the stars overhead and the sparkle all around them work their little magic until even his tightly wound lady-love learned to relax for a little while. Or was that too optimistic? Kevin allowed himself a little smile.

Then the moonlight vanished.

He stopped, looking up at the sky. High clouds had finally rolled in, blowing eastward with the rapid clip of some unseen atmospheric gale. The brilliant stars winked out, not one by one but dozen by dozen, swallowed up by the layer of cloud. The moon glimmered silvery behind the gauze of clouds for a few moments more, and then it was blanked out completely.

The woods were now only lit by the soft luminescence of the snow.

Kevin felt panic rising in his chest again. "Grover!" he shouted, his voice hoarse now from hollering. *"Grover, come on!"*

The woods glowered silently at him, as if his voice was breaking a sacred silence he had no right to profane.

Kevin turned in a slow circle, looking back the way he'd come, then at the trail ahead, where the paw-prints he'd been following still led merrily into the darkness. Where had Grover been going? Was there a way to head him off? Where did this trail even go? When he'd come out hiking with Rosemary and Alice, she'd led him on offshoots and down forks and pointed out cut-offs. He never could have navigated all the trails in these woods alone, even with a very good map. Without her guidance, he was stuck on this single main pathway—what if he turned off of it by mistake in the darkness?

All the what-ifs crowded into Kevin's brain until he felt paralyzed by indecision. He needed a plan, and instead there was nothing but a clamoring insistence from every side—go forward, go back, *maybe just shout some more?*

"Kevin?"

The voice came from behind him, distant and silvery on the icy wind. Kevin whirled and peered into the darkness.

He saw the dog first.

# Chapter 33

## Nikki

N ikki had only been on the trail a few minutes when she heard a crunching noise in the brush to one side. She knew there wasn't anything too dangerous in the Catoctins this time of year, but she still held her breath as she flicked her phone's light back on and pointed it into the woods, sweeping the beam through the ghostly branches of the snowy trees. Hopefully, she'd only see a startled deer staring back at her, two wide eyes framed by a pair of enormous pricked ears.

Nothing.

"Hmm." Nikki didn't exactly want to shout into this quiet night: after all, who knew what answer a person might get from a moonlit forest? Ghosts, ghouls, especially hardy hikers—she didn't want to run into *any* of that alone, thanks. There was another crack in the brush—closer this time. She drew in her breath, but the voice which came out was barely a squeak. "Grover?"

A crunch and a crackle. She tried again, managing a proper shout this time. *"Grover!"*

A whine, a crack of breaking branches, a sharp yelp—and then there he was, bursting out of the thick tangle of shrubs and vines lining the path. The dog leapt up, his front legs balancing against Nikki's hips, and he smiled up at her with his big laughing mouth.

"Oh my God, *Grover,*" Nikki cried, wrapping her arms around the dog. "You big goofy dumb-dumb idiot, what are you doing out here alone?"

He panted at her, his breath steaming into the moonlight. She thought she'd never been so happy to see someone in her life. But Grover was alone—which presented a new problem.

"So if you're here, where is Kevin?"

———*ele*———

The answer was in the snow at her feet: his boots kept on walking, deeper into the forest. Nikki shivered as a fresh gust of wind whistled through the woods. She'd really only been dressed for the drive and quick run into Rosemary's house, not for a hike on a subzero night. Her wool coat was warm, but she could have used a couple of extra layers underneath it. And her feet? Best not to even discuss how numb and wooden they were beginning to feel. Grover seemed pretty chipper still, but she suspected he was going to wear out soon. At least there was a moon—

—Nope, cancel that. Nikki looked up at the high layer of cloud racing across the sky. The precursor to the approaching front that was meant to bring a layer of ice to the entire area in just a few hours. She wondered if she should call 911 and tell them there was a man lost in the woods.

Maybe she should have done that a long time ago. Nikki's gloved fingers curled around the phones in her coat pocket. If only he hadn't lost his! He must have been in such a rush when he realized Grover wasn't in the yard . . .

"Grover, buddy, what should I do?"

The dog looked up at her, his teeth glinting bluish white in the darkness. He was staying so close by her side, even without the benefit of a leash; she knew he must have serious regrets about the way his night had unfolded.

"You want to go home, don't you? Me, too, buddy. But if we don't find Kevin—"

Her mouth was suddenly too dry to continue.

Had she really said those words? Had it really come to that? She'd been walking for only half an hour; surely they were only two miles or so from the brick house. The Catoctin Mountains weren't exactly a vast wilderness, either. To say they were lost out here, to say they couldn't locate Kevin now, was absolutely ridiculous.

And absolutely terrifying.

Nikki needed Kevin to be okay. *Needed* it more than she needed warmth for her frozen feet or air for her burning lungs. *Needed Kevin,* more than she needed pride or self-reliance or common sense or any of the other boring columns she'd built her adult life upon. When she found him, everything would be different. She would be more flexible, she would be more open, she would let him in and let him help her. No one understood her like Kevin, but she just kept pushing him away. Finding excuses to rage at him. Poking holes in every argument he made. Arguments he'd made to improve *her* life.

She would tell Kevin she was sorry, and that she needed him.

When she found him.

He had to be just around that bend up ahead. And she'd prove it, too. Nikki opened her mouth to shout.

Beside her, Grover made a strangled sort of whine. She felt his tail beat against her leg.

"Kevin?" she called into the night, her voice catching in her throat.

Grover took off running, hurtling forward, his light-colored fur capturing the gentle glow of the snowpack. With a shout of terror, Nikki stumbled after him, forcing her cold feet to obey her fear. If he got away from her—if he saw some animal that might attack him—

She rounded the curve in the trail, a bend which would have been beguiling and promising on a spring afternoon, and was simply a terrifying camouflage of what was waiting in her future on this frozen night, and stopped short. Grover was leaping up on someone—his tail was hammering the icy air—

"Oh God, *Kevin,*" Nikki cried.

# Chapter 34

# Kevin

He didn't want to let go of her. Not ever.

But with Grover still trying to climb up his legs, and the cold gusts of wind reminding him that an ice storm was growing closer and closer with every passing moment, Kevin reluctantly released his bear-like grip on Nikki. She tipped her face back, her cheeks red both from cold and from pressing into his shoulder, rubbed by the rough, icy canvas of his coat. Her eyes seemed to sparkle even in the half-light surrounding them, as if the snow itself was enough to pick out the gold which hid in their depths. Kevin was seized with one of those overwhelming, heart-grasping moments of love which caught him more and more often these days. For a moment he could only gaze back at her, his thoughts and motion arrested while he grappled with a surge of overwhelming feeling.

"I needed to find you," she whispered. "I was going crazy."

"I'm right here," he whispered back. "It's okay. We're fine."

"We're fine," she repeated. "Kevin, listen, I'm so sorry for the way I acted."

"Don't apologize, please. Just—"

"Yes?"

"Let me help."

She pressed a soft, cold kiss on his lips. "I will."

Then she was turning, tugging at his arm, and he felt himself following her, his cold feet rising one after another to crunch through the snow crusted on the trail.

"We have to get back," she told him in a more normal tone, though her voice was hoarse with cold. "I want to tell Rosemary I found you, but I can't even use my fingers to type at this point."

"Voice activation?" Kevin suggested, and was immediately impressed with himself for having such a novel idea when a moment ago he'd have been hard-pressed to tell her his own name.

"Oh, good idea." She dug into her pocket and came out with something. His phone! Kevin took it back greedily and gave it a look he knew was entirely too affectionate. It was just a glass and metal box. But being without it had been truly frightening.

So were the number of notifications on the screen, including the one from his weather app, which read: *Light rain will begin at 9:35 p.m.*

The current time was 9:26 p.m.

He almost told Nikki they needed to hustle even faster to beat the beginning of the storm, but decided against frightening her. They *were* hustling, after all. Nothing short of breaking into a run would get them home faster, and he didn't want to twist an ankle and end up on the ground, crawling home in an ice storm because the Life Flight helicopter couldn't get to them through the howling winds.

Gosh, he was getting good at imagining worst-case scenarios.

Kevin barked a few commands at his phone, which behaved sluggishly in the cold, and got the job done. "Okay," he told Nikki, "Stephen and Rosemary have been advised."

She looked over her shoulder at him. "And what do they say about all this?"

He glanced back down at his phone, which was just lighting up with a response. "Rosemary says hurry back, she has chili waiting to warm us up."

"Mmm," Nikki sighed. "Rosemary's chili is absolutely unbelievable. And I'll bet there'll be cornbread. Did she mention cornbread?"

"No," Kevin said, putting his phone back into his coat pocket —the inside one, this time. It was amazing that they could be rushing back over the same trail he'd just been stumbling down a little while before, but instead of experiencing utter terror over his lost dog and the feeling of being a small man in a big forest, he was having a mundane discussion about the dinner awaiting them at a friend's house. He had just spotted a light through a break in the forest—a yellow glow which was his own back porch light. They'd be back safely in just a few minutes, and then they could hit the road for Notch Gap Farm.

"Ouch!" Ahead of him, Nikki slipped, and he just caught her before she tumbled to the ground. She looked accusingly at the slippery patch that had caught her mid-step. "That's *ice,*" she said, in a different tone. "It wasn't icy there before."

He ran his toe over the silver sheet, where earlier there had been a sloppy, slushy puddle. The top cracked under his gentle pressure, sending a bubble of water over the surface. "You're right. It froze while we've been out here."

They looked at each other, and Kevin thought of the rain warning on his phone.

It was already below freezing.

They'd missed their chance to get to Rosemary and Stephen's house.

The rain hammered down with the intensity of a summer storm, wind gusts sending it streaming against the big plate-glass living room window. Kevin pulled Nikki a little closer to him on the sofa, and she snuggled her head against his shoulder. Grover was stretched out at their feet, completely passed out. Kevin had a feeling the dog would sleep through the night after this evening's excitement, and it was a good thing, too. There would be no going outside for a little late-night sniff and pee. He wasn't exactly sure what the dog would do in the morning, either.

Ice was already gathering on the trees and stretching in a clear, solid carpet across the lawns. If a snowfall was a lovely, comforting thing to enjoy from the warmth of a well-heated home, an ice storm was a lengthy terror, watching as the world was coated in a slick, unrelenting layer of heavy enamel—which would certainly bring down trees and power lines, and keep them pinned here for days. Hopefully with electricity, but there was certainly no guarantee.

They would have been better off at Notch Gap Farm, where the house sat in a hollow sheltered from the wind, and there were plenty of fireplaces, even an old wood-stove to keep them warm should the electricity go out. But when he'd said as much to Nikki, standing in the doorway as the rain pelted down, she'd reminded him that being at the farm also came with a few hitches.

"We'd have to slide out to help with the horses," she said practically. "Here, at least, we can stay inside. And the furnace is propane, right? We have nothing to worry about. We won't freeze to death for a couple of days while the world tries to thaw out."

She shifted now, sitting upright and shaking her head. He looked over at her, eyes greedily taking in her flushed cheeks, her drooping eyelids. "You fell asleep!"

"I guess I did." She brushed at her face, running the back of her hand across her lips. Kevin felt a fire smoldering within. "Still raining like crazy, though."

"It's supposed to rain all night," he said. "I've been watching the weather while you dozed."

"We'll be alright," she reminded him. "I know it feels weird to be cut off from the outside world, but nothing bad will happen to us."

"How do you know that?" Kevin asked, more to prolong this moment: her intense eyes fastened on his, her warmth pressed close to him. "Prove to me nothing bad will happen. You can't do it."

She leaned forward and her eyelashes fluttered down on her cheeks. "Only good things," she whispered, and she kissed him.

"Only good things," Kevin replied softly, and it was like a pact between them.

# Chapter 35

# Nikki

The world outside was a sparkling diamond of unparalleled clarity: too blinding to look at, but too spectacular to ignore. Nikki stood at the back door and gazed out into the frozen wonderland. The backyard was one sheet of crystal; the trees surrounding the property were shimmering with icicles, and the woods beyond, stretching all the way into the mountains, glittered in the morning sunlight. A fresh blanket of white snow sat atop the twin peaks of Notch Gap, and the sky behind the mountains was so clear, it must have been the same shade of azure as in the days when the world was young and new.

And it was cold out there. A breath of icy air seemed to emanate from the sliding glass door, as if the glass was permeable. Nikki tugged at the neck of the flannel robe she'd snagged from Kevin's closet, pulling it more closely around her. Even with the heat running full-tilt, the house's unsheltered position on its hilltop meant the windows and doors were susceptible to drafts from every direction. If Nikki bought her own house someday, she hoped it would be more like Rosemary's farmhouse: old-fashioned and filled with character, and snuggled into a hollow or wrapped with old trees to provide natural cover from the winter winds.

Grover panted against her leg.

Oh yes, and she'd have a dog-door and a plan for icy days.

"Hey, bud, what am I going to do with you?" She leaned down and gave the dog a rub. The world outside was in a deep-freeze, but Grover had to pee, at the very least. "Give it a shot," she told him, wrenching the frozen door open with difficulty.

Grover went outside like a shot, skidding on the heavier ice in the house's shade, before he found a patch of grass which had softened in the morning sunlight. Nikki watched him from the kitchen window as she set up coffee. Kevin had bound the gate tightly shut with wire after they'd passed through it last night, but she would not forget their night in the woods in a hurry. Grover was going to be under her beady eye until he came back inside for his breakfast.

Kevin came out of the bedroom just as the coffeemaker pinged, sniffing the air like a bloodhound. Nikki took down mugs and poured him his first cup, smiling at the easy domesticity of it all. Their relationship thus far had been a series of zig-zags, and she wished it could always be like this: just two people in an iced-in house, drinking coffee in the kitchen.

She supposed she was ready to skip ahead to old married couple status, bypassing the rest of the drama in their way.

But first—she laughed as Kevin pulled her close, dropping a series of kisses on her bare neck, which made her shiver with delight. There were years left before they were an old married couple, she decided.

If they could just hold it together. If she could be open, and if he could be understanding.

"It looks pretty frozen out there," Kevin said later, peering out the window. "Are we trapped up here together?"

"At least until tomorrow, judging by the forecast," Nikki said, joining him. "And Grover has petitioned for indoor bathroom rights." The dog pressed his nose against her hand as he heard his name. His fur was still cold from his short trip outside.

"Poor guy. I wouldn't want to go out there either, buddy."

"So, it's Christmas at the brick house." Nikki tilted her head against Kevin's shoulder. "Too bad, because Christmas at Notch Gap Farm is like something out of a storybook."

"This is pretty close to a storybook," Kevin told her, giving her a wicked smile which made her body flush with heat. "All alone in the frozen wilderness with me. I like this story."

She laughed as he squeezed her closer. "Why do I feel like I'm locked up with the big scary bear?"

"*Grrrrr!*" Kevin growled, his teeth nuzzling at her throat, which might have sent them stumbling to the bedroom if Grover hadn't panicked and started barking at the top of his lungs, dancing around the pair of them until Nikki had to push both of them off.

"Sorry, buddy, sorry, sorry." They apologized to the dog in unison, showering him with pats until he calmed down and retreated to the living room sofa, where he watched them reproachfully.

Nikki grinned at Kevin. "I think we better take it easy in front of the kid."

He grimaced. "Well, now what are we supposed to do?"

Nikki looked around the bare little house. "Too bad we don't have any decorations, or we could play with those. This place could use a little Christmas makeover."

Kevin stared at her for a minute, and then his face lit up. "You're not going to believe this. C'mere."

She followed him into the guest bedroom, a plain affair with a quilt stretched across a double bed, a pine chest of drawers, and not much else. "This is not doing much for my Christmas spirit," Nikki joked.

"This will." Kevin opened the closet door and tugged some boxes out of the back corner. He popped them open in front of her. "Ta-da! Holiday spirit, as requested."

Nikki couldn't believe it. The boxes were glittering treasure troves, stuffed with tinsel and garland, lights and ornaments. There was even a long, slim box housing an artificial tree. "Amazing," she breathed. "I think our morning is set!"

They spent the better part of the day decking the living room, dining room, and kitchen with everything in the Christmas boxes. Stephen's father had had a corny streak a mile wide, judging by the number of waving Santas, fat old-fashioned colored bulbs, and metallic silver and gold garland in the boxes. The day went quickly —even with breaks to take the obligatory Christmas Day phone calls from their parents. By the time they were finished, the brick house's plain common areas were bursting with color and light— which was perfect, since the clear, brittle blue sky had clouded over once more.

Ever mindful of impending meals, Nikki dug around in the fridge and freezer until she'd found the ingredients for a Christmas feast of sorts. Pork loin, orange-cranberry relish, and green beans dressed in a vinaigrette made it onto her menu. With dinner off her mind, she accepted a glass of wine from Kevin and they sat in the living room, looking around at their holiday wonderland. She felt like she was simply buzzing with happiness.

"This is like a Christmas out of a kid's book," she told him, snuggling close. "My parents weren't big on decorating. This is absolutely perfect."

"There's a good idea," Kevin said. "Tell me one Christmas fantasy. Something out of a book that you always wanted to see come true on Christmas. Then I'll go."

Nikki thought about it. "Okay," she said. "I always wanted a goose for Christmas dinner. Like in Charles Dickens. We usually had a ham. My mom told me no one ate goose anymore. And I guess she's right, because it's pretty hard to find. But someday I'm going to have a huge Christmas dinner and there will be a massive roasted goose on the table."

"That sounds amazing. It could be a full Victorian Christmas."

"Yes! We could do it at Notch Gap. Wouldn't Rosemary's dining room look amazing lit with candles, nothing but pine garlands and holly for decoration?" Nikki felt like she was unearthing an old love of the holiday season, something she'd buried under practicality when her family moved away. For the first time in years, she allowed herself to imagine a big family Christmas dinner. Only it wouldn't be with her parents as the family sitting around the table . . . it would be with Stephen, and Rosemary, and her own children . . .

Nikki shook her head quickly. Where had *that* thought come from?

Kevin didn't seem to notice. He was already thinking about his own Christmas fantasy. "It kind of plays right in with mine. Which is good, because it makes mine less cheesy." He laughed at himself.

Nikki gave him a little pinch. "Oh, come on, I said a Christmas goose! What could be cheesy about yours?"

"Okay, okay. I want a sleigh ride."

"A sleigh ride!" Nikki was surprised. "You know, I've never even seen a real sleigh."

"I saw one a few weeks ago, but it was in storage. I want to see it out, on the snow. I want the jingle-bells and everything. Like a Christmas song come to life. You know the song, about going over the river and through the woods? Like that." Kevin shook his head, grinning. "Isn't that silly?"

"No." Nikki wrapped her arms around him, touched by the sweetness of his fantasy. "It's lovely. I think it's lovely."

Kevin turned to her with eyes brimming over with emotion. "*You're* lovely," he whispered.

*ele*

The next morning came with a sound of dripping water—ice melting, drops of water falling from the eaves and the trees. A south wind was blowing, and as quickly as they'd been iced in, Nikki and Kevin were free to go back into the world.

And as sorry as Nikki was to leave their little Christmas wonderland, she knew she had too. For one thing, Christmas had come and gone. Today was the 26<sup>th</sup>, and the Blue Plate was scheduled to reopen for breakfast at eight o'clock.

Nikki didn't wake up Kevin when she slipped from bed. Grover padded after her and she let him out the back door, noting the relative warmth in the breeze. Even the snow would be gone by afternoon if this trend kept up. She supposed it was for the best, although she'd miss the snow. Well, the season was young yet. They'd probably get more before spring. This had already been the snowiest season on record. No reason to believe that would end before January even began.

With the coffee percolating, Nikki sat down at the dining room table and flicked through her phone, glancing over her email. She'd ignored it the past few days, but now she noticed a few holiday offers had come through from restaurant suppliers. Spotting a deal she wanted to take advantage of, Nikki reached for a legal pad and pen which had been left on the table. She unfolded the pad to look for the first unused page, and then she spotted her name, written in Kevin's loopy handwriting.

She put down her phone and drew the pad closer. It wasn't snooping if it was your own name on the page.

# Chapter 36

# Kevin

The notepad was the first thing Kevin saw when he came out of the bedroom. It had been left on the table, a pulled-out chair in front of it, as if the person sitting there had leapt up in a rush. The house smelled of fresh coffee, but there was no mug to be seen and when he pulled out the coffeepot, he saw it was completely full.

Unbothered, Grover wagged his tail and nosed at his empty dish. Walking like a man in a daze, Kevin poured a cup of kibble for the dog and then went to the front window. The water ran in rivulets down the front window, draining from a faulty gutter, but he could see the empty spot where her car had been.

Kevin cursed.

It was always something with Nikki, he thought later, drinking the coffee she'd made, sitting in the chair she'd left pulled out from the table, the notepad she'd been reading still open to the page titled *Nikki's Action Plan: Bakery*. It was always hot and cold. They were together, then they were fighting. They were happy, and then they were mad. He was offended. She was insulted. Then the other way around again.

Maybe it wasn't supposed to be this hard.

Kevin thought again of Stephen and Rosemary—the happiest couple he knew. The path to their wedding had not been strewn with roses. And two people, at their age, would not be instantly compatible. He *knew* this. He came from New York City, where serious relationships and marriages came later than maybe anywhere else in the world. The stresses of education, and struggling up a career ladder, meant coupling had to come later— when people were formed, their edges hard and inflexible.

He knew he could learn to be flexible. He needed Nikki to do the same.

When Kevin's phone buzzed, he snatched at it eagerly, hoping Nikki would be on the other end. But it wasn't her voice that greeted him.

"Hey, Gus," Kevin said weakly. "What's up?"

"I know I said we'd take a few days off," Gus said apologetically. "But Caitlin has a few who need done, and I'm bored. You feel like heading out to Elmwood with me?"

Relief flooded through Kevin's veins. Work, instead of sitting here wondering where it had all gone wrong with Nikki? "I'll be ready when you get here," he said.

Caitlin had gone all out on Elmwood's holiday decorations, with garland, white twinkling lights, and even Christmas stockings for all the horses, pinned to their stall doors next to their name-plates. The barn radio was still tuned to the all-holiday station, and Bing

Crosby was crooning away about a white Christmas as Gus and Kevin set up the truck for horseshoeing. Nadine wandered down to see them, wearing just a hoodie and jeans instead of the layers of winter gear she'd had on lately.

"So much for our white Christmas," she said, kicking at a little pool of meltwater forming by the barn doors. "It's going to be fifty degrees today."

"Might as well go out and get a tan," Kevin suggested, checking the propane tanks. "I heard there might be more snow for New Year's Day, if you like that sort of thing."

"I like it okay," Nadine said thoughtfully. "Especially since I started working here, and there's an indoor. Last winter I worked at Hinkley Sporthorses up near Pen-Mar, and most of that job was outside. I seriously almost moved to Florida."

"And we're glad you didn't." Caitlin seemed to appear out of nowhere, popping inside the barn with a smile on her face and one of her handsome pointers on a leash at her side. "I need you here, not in Florida. Gus, can you imagine life without Nadine?"

Kevin knew Nadine handled all the scheduling and payments, so he wasn't surprised when Gus chuckled and agreed that the young woman was indispensable. Apparently whoever she'd replaced hadn't been quite so efficient.

Caitlin tugged at her dog, who was straining to get to Kevin. "Sit down, Herbie," she scolded. "Listen, Kevin, can I talk to you really quick? In private? It won't take a minute."

Kevin exchanged surprised glances with Gus. "Of course."

They walked down the aisle a short distance, leaving Nadine to get out the first horse for Gus. Caitlin paused by the wash-racks in the center of the barn. "It's about Nikki," she said, her voice low.

Kevin's heart pounded. "What? Did something happen?"

"No! No, it's—I was talking to Sean, and he told me about her bakery idea. Says she could really do something for the town with it, start a ball rolling. And I think he's right." Caitlin looked up and down the aisle. "Here's something no one knows—the Schubert house? That's mine."

He stared at her. *"Yours?"*

"Yeah. I bought it from them over the summer. I was thinking of restoring it, maybe starting a bed-and-breakfast—" Caitlin sighed and ran her hand over her dog's speckled head. "I can't spend all of my energy here. This place is running great, but I have good people in every position now. I'm ready to try something new. Something that's *mine.*"

Kevin thought he understood. He didn't know Caitlin's history like Rosemary and Nikki did, but he'd absorbed enough. Caitlin was doing her best with someone else's legacy. Just like Nikki.

Was there something in the water of this town that made the women so damn loyal to their past?

"But here's the thing," Caitlin went on. "Catoctin Creek isn't ready for a B-and-B. It needs something like Nikki's bakery to get it started. This town needs a lot more than a coat of fresh paint, but once the D.C. types start stopping off for breakfast while they're heading north, and showing up on weekends? They'll notice. Things will start to change. If this place takes off for her and we get tourists, I'll buy another house and fix that up, instead. I can wait."

Kevin's mind was already racing, thinking of the ways Catoctin Creek could grow more polished. Welcome more visitors. The sleeping town didn't have to wake up much—just enough to stretch and show off a little. He was thinking about loans and investment and finding capital for small businesses when he realized Caitlin was talking again.

"—If we could find a way to make a lease work, without making Nikki feel uncomfortable, that would be great."

*No,* he almost said. *I'll buy it for her.* But that was going too far, too fast.

And anyway, he was still sitting on two condos in Queens.

"I'll talk to her," he promised. "We'll make this work."

Knowing he held the key to Nikki's dream in his pocket made Kevin's day incredibly difficult. He felt half-awake throughout the morning in the barn aisle, holding pony after pony as Gus worked his way through the shoeings. At one point, Gus had a mouthful of nails—a moment when Kevin was generally extra-attentive to keeping the horse still—and nearly swallowed one when the horse jumped at a shifting shadow and reared up, getting away from Kevin.

"Well, that's enough wool-gatherin' from *you,*" Gus grunted, spitting the nails into his hand.

Kevin, settling the horse back down, felt himself blushing with embarrassment. "I'm so sorry. I'll pay more attention."

Gus leaned against his truck and surveyed Kevin with an amused gaze. "Looks to me like you got too much on your mind to be a proper assistant. We'll cut after lunch, anyway. Think you can help me survive until then?"

"I can do that," Kevin promised, but his head was already back in the clouds. After lunch, he thought, he'd go and find Nikki.

## Chapter 37

# Nikki

Nikki was walking the streets of her little town, peeping in windows to look at Christmas trees, admiring the droop of garland on wide porches, watching children play with new toys in their soggy backyards. She'd gone in and opened the diner that morning, but the morning crew was more than capable of dealing with the slow after-holiday crowd. Breakfast hours during the week between Christmas and New Year's Day were typically quiet. Nikki's aunt had always said this was a traditional time for moms, home from work on a rare extended break, to make lavish pancake breakfasts. For the entire family to sit around the house in their pajamas until late in the morning, simply enjoying each other's company.

They'd tire of each other later, Aunt Evelyn would laugh knowingly, and that's why lunch and dinner would pick up.

Nikki had always believed in her aunt's business wisdom. How else to explain the sheer longevity of the Blue Plate? But maybe the Blue Plate had simply been running on familiarity all along—and now, Catoctin Creek was changing.

The realization was startling. All around her, Nikki saw strangers. The familiar faces of her childhood were giving way, house by house. You could see it in the restorations: the new windows, the freshly painted porches, even gleaming copper gutters on one lucky house. You could see it in the clothes: fewer Carhartt jackets and clunky boots, more L.L. Bean and shearling-lined booties. You could see it in the cars: luxurious SUVs and sleek new sedans, many bearing dealership logos from northern Virginia suburbs.

There were new people in town. Everywhere.

When had this change begun? And how had she not noticed it? She'd been spending so much time closeted indoors, either in her kitchen or at the diner, that she hadn't seen the new faces in town.

Because they weren't coming into the Blue Plate.

Now, she saw strangers doing the things her friends' families had once done. She saw weary parents drinking coffee on their porches, robes pulled close against the chilly air, while their kids squealed and played. She saw beaming grandparents getting out of cars bearing boxes from the donut place down in Walkersville. She saw aimless adults like herself, wandering the quiet streets, looking for something to do with themselves in their tiny town, and finding nothing.

As she stood at the corner of Brunner Lane and Summit Avenue, a gleaming sedan she didn't recognize pulled up in front of a trim, pretty brick house she'd last recalled belonging to the Sadler family, who had moved away months ago. A family of five spilled out of the car and went up the front walk, letting themselves in. Nikki didn't know them, which gave her a moment's disquiet. But what stuck with her even more? The coffee cups in the parents' hands.

They had the sunflower motif of that cafe down in Frederick, the one Sean liked so much.

They'd driven their young family all the way into town for breakfast.

Nikki's breath came quicker as she registered all the signs she'd missed—and what she could do with it! She could give all of these wanderers, these lost souls from the suburbs and cities, something they'd know and appreciate. Artisan coffee on a wide porch, with heaters lit in winter to chase away the chill, ceiling fans in summer to stir the languid air. Fresh pastries and muffins from her oven to take home to their families, tied up in neat brown boxes. Conversation and camaraderie in a warm, cozy cafe, an escape when they were tired of their own four walls. Country charm, adding its own special flavor to the experiences they'd been left craving, which turned Catoctin Creek from a place they'd moved to, a place they called home.

For the first time, she realized Catoctin Creek was a real, living place outside of her memories. There were more people here than she had thought, and not just the strangers from out of town but also the people she'd gone to school with, who had come back with good jobs and decent income and started fixing up the houses where they'd grown up.

Catoctin Creek was *younger* than she'd realized, younger than the day-in day-out regulars of the Blue Plate belied.

She wondered if maybe she would have a chance out here.

Her footsteps took her back to the Schubert house, and she rocked back on her heels, once again seeing the house transformed to her vision. If only there was some way she could afford it!

On New Year's Day, Nikki woke up early and couldn't get back to sleep.

Luckily, she hadn't been up late. Rosemary and Stephen had encouraged her to come over, but she couldn't be bothered. She knew Kevin was up in New York, anyway—he'd sent her a text letting her know he was going home as he'd promised, and she'd replied *okay, have fun.* No emojis, no avowals of love or missing him. Nikki wasn't sure how she'd flubbed things so constantly with Kevin, but it seemed part and parcel of this entire holiday season. From Thanksgiving to New Year's, she'd watched her business decline, her dreams spiral in and out of reality, and the relationship she'd wanted for so long turn into a roller coaster she just wanted to escape.

Nikki was tired. Mentally and physically wiped out.

Which made waking up so early annoying, but at least she had some really nice coffee waiting for her.

"That was a good change I made in my life," she told herself, pushing back the covers and swinging down to the first floor of the apartment. "If nothing else, at least I upgraded my coffee."

The bag of coffee sitting on her kitchen counter had come as a surprise in the mail. She'd looked for a card, but it seemed to have been forgotten, or maybe it had gotten lost. She'd been intrigued by the pretty red bag and the golden lettering, especially when she realized it was from a small town on the other side of the Catoctin Mountains. Now she picked it up. "Okay, High Rock Coffee Company," she said. "Show me what you've got."

She poured beans into her coffee grinder, relishing the scent of the freshly ground coffee afterwards. It pooled through the apartment and wafted around the edges of the room, a spicy scent filled with character that her old canned grounds had never offered. She wondered what some of the other houses in town smelled like this morning, if the new prosperity she had observed extended to things like fresh-roasted coffee and shiny new coffeemakers which promised the perfect brew at the perfect temperature. She flicked on the radio for company while the coffeemaker rumbled to itself.

"And a very happy New Year's Day to you, Frederick County," the host was saying cheerfully. "It's thirty-four degrees, but the temperature is expected to drop a few degrees as a front moves through the area, and yes, folks, we are talking about more snow . . ."

Well, that sounded promising. Nikki had been planning to stay inside and do some work, but she was already feeling in desperate need of a walk to clear her head. Or at least to attempt to clear her head. So far, she'd been failing—stuck on the subject of a place to put her cafe she could actually afford, stuck on the subject of what to say to Kevin, stuck on whether they were really meant to be together.

But Rosemary had said long walks always helped her think through problems, and so walking Nikki would go. And if it snowed on her, so much the better.

She decided to walk up Summit Avenue and through the little wind of narrow streets atop Copper Hill, a forested ridge which rose up on the east side of Catoctin Creek. There were a few pretty houses up there, and she wondered if they still had their fancy Christmas decorations up. Coffee in travel mug, snow boots donned, Nikki headed out into the cold first morning of the year.

She was dawdling halfway down Summit Avenue, looking at the new copper gutters on the old Langhorne house, when she heard voices from across the street. Nikki looked over her shoulder and saw two men chatting on the porch of the ramshackle Queen Anne across the street. The house had always looked held together by paint in Nikki's high school days; today even the paint was gone. But the man in the doorway was wearing overalls daubed with paint, as if he was working on renovations, and the other man was—

It was Kevin.

She immediately looked for somewhere to hide. The thorny hedge growing up beside the Langhorne mailbox presented itself, and she dove behind the shrubbery, kneeling down and hoping neither Kevin nor the man inside the doorway had seen her. Why?

Well. *Why* was a good question. Nikki looked at the melting snow pooling between the toes of her boots and considered her position with Kevin. What was it, exactly? Were they dating? Were they on a break? Were they broken up? Were they in love?

Nikki realized it could be almost all of those things, which was problematic at best. She'd like to say they were dating—she'd like to believe they were in love—she had to admit they were on a break—she was afraid they might be broken up.

And even if she defined their relationship one way, there was no telling if Kevin would come to the same conclusion.

"That's your whole problem, Nikki," she whispered to herself. "You sit on the surface of things. You take everything for face value. The Blue Plate is old and broke, so you think the town is old and broke instead of looking for the real reasons. Kevin has been quiet, so you think he's sick of you. But maybe he misses you just as much as you miss him!"

Well. That had been worth speaking into the cold morning air. Just saying the words made them feel real. "He misses me," she repeated. "He misses me." She left out the *maybe* on purpose. Maybe was for hemming and hawing. Maybe was for the Nikki who stayed on the surface, who hung out at the edges.

It was time to start *doing*.

She stood up, emerging from behind the hedge with so much force her hat fell off.

Kevin, who had been crossing the street in her direction, jumped at her unexpected appearance and fell back . . . splashing right into the slush-filled puddles of Summit Avenue.

"Oh, no!" Nikki shrieked, running to pull him up. Kevin was grasping at a leather briefcase, trying to hold it over his head with one hand, since the rest of him had tumbled into a cold puddle. She read the situation quickly and grabbed the briefcase from him, hoisting it to safety while she let him save himself. Once he'd pushed himself upright, he looked down at his sopping wet pants, then at her, and shook his head. He wasn't smiling—or was he? Was that a hint of a smile in his eyes?

She held out the briefcase sheepishly. "I'm so sorry."

He took it from her and slipped the strap over his shoulder. "Were you hiding behind a hedge, Nikki Mercer?" he asked cooly.

"I may have been," she admitted. "Please don't ask why."

He sighed. "I won't. But can you at least let me dry off at your place?"

"Oh, of course you can. Come on, come back and dry off, have some coffee—" she grabbed him by the arm and started dragging him up Summit, trying to ignore the glaring windows of the houses on either side of the street. Lovely to look into after dark, but on a bright sunny day like this, all they offered her imagination was the potential for dozens of prying, mocking eyes to watch her make yet another mistake in front of the entire town.

Nikki was starting to understand why Rosemary never wanted to leave her farm.

Luckily, the apartment was just two blocks away, and the last bit of that was the quiet, tree-lined alley between backyards. She let Kevin in and took his briefcase again while he wriggled off his soaking boots. They looked at his wet trousers in consternation for a minute. Then Nikki remembered some flannel pants she'd gotten for Christmas last year. They were entirely too large— Nikki had no idea what her sister had been thinking—but they'd work just fine for Kevin.

"Here you go," she said, rooting them out of the bottom of her dresser. "I'll put your pants in the dryer, if you want."

"That'll be fine, thank you." Kevin tugged on the flannel pants. "Cozy. Now, is that some seriously good coffee I smell?"

Nikki brightened. "It is! Wait until you taste it. Sit down, I'll bring it to you." She hustled over with a mug. "Someone mailed this to me. It's made in Pen-Mar, apparently." She saw Kevin's expression and her eyes widened. "That was *you?*"

"You don't even remember when I asked you if you've ever been to the cafe in Pen-Mar?" Kevin took the mug from her with a shake of his head. "Honestly, woman, do you hear anything I say?"

"I don't listen to anyone," Nikki whispered. "That's something I've been thinking about a lot lately." She paused. "Hey, you're supposed to be in New York."

"I went up two days ago. I came home last night."

"On New Year's Eve? You could have been killed by a drunk driver!"

"I know. But I wanted to talk to someone, and he told me this morning was best."

She wanted to know more, but he wasn't volunteering and she decided she wasn't in the best position to dig into his business. "Listen, Kevin, I want to apologize. I keep pushing back at you whenever you try to help me, and that's an awful habit of mine that's just gotten worse. It's not just you. I . . . I guess I haven't been listening to *anyone* lately." She laughed ruefully. "Lately? I mean, ever. Rosemary could probably back me up on that. Lord knows I've never really listened to her."

"She does say you're the pushiest person she's ever met," Kevin admitted. "But she loves you for it."

"Without me, Rosemary would never do anything." Nikki knew she wasn't bragging. It was the truth. "She wouldn't have Stephen." She paused. "I wouldn't know you."

He reached out and took her hand. "Maybe you would, if you wanted to enough," he told her. "You're a pretty strong-willed woman. I think the universe might know it has to bow to your commands every once in a while."

A warmth spread through Nikki's chest, and for a moment she thought about just leaning forward, kissing him, and letting the whole conversation dissolve into the morning light. But no. She had spent enough time ignoring what Kevin had to say—what whole crowds of people had to say or thought about her ideas. She could give him this time—it was the least she could do for him, after knocking him into a puddle with her own foolishness. Had she *really* hid behind a hedge like a little kid?

"So Kevin, why did you send me this coffee?"

"I wanted you to know what this town can support," Kevin said. He pulled out his briefcase. "And that's the same reason I was talking to one of your old classmates back there. Yeah," he added, as Nikki's face registered surprise. "That was Doug Clifton. I met him at Caitlin's—his daughter has a pony. Apparently you took German together?"

"I don't remember *any* of it. Rosemary took Spanish, that was wise of her."

"Well, you and Doug have something in common. That and living in your hometown. And appreciating good coffee." He winked at her and handed her a notebook.

Nikki took the notebook uncertainly. "What's in here?"

"It's a little market research he did for me leading up to our meeting. I wanted a local to do it. Take a look."

She opened the notebook and started paging through. Handwritten, in tidy print, Doug had recorded the support for a bakery-cafe as part of a restoration project on the Schubert house. There were dozens of entries. Nikki felt her throat clog with a suppressed sob. She ran her fingers down the names. Most were unfamiliar, but a few jumped out at her: old classmates, old friends, old enemies. Still here, just waiting to support her.

She finally looked up at him. "Kevin, this is . . . I don't know what to say."

"Say you're going to start a cafe."

Nikki laughed, but her heart was falling all the same. "I can't afford to, even if everyone in Catoctin Creek swears they'll come and support it."

"Ah, Nikki." He tugged a portfolio out of the bag. "Take this."

"And what's *this?*"

"It's your action plan."

She opened the portfolio with a sense of disbelief. He'd finished it! From those scrawled notes on the legal pad which had so infuriated her, he'd somehow put together a full proposal, with charts and numbers and notes, which outlined how she could start her business. At the end there was a little addendum of good wishes from the people who believed in her the most. Rosemary, Stephen, Caitlin, Sean, even Lauren had all jotted down their encouragement for her.

She touched Sean's name softly—he'd written, *I promise to be your most loyal customer!*

"He started this," she said. "I guess I'll have to give him free coffee for life or something."

"Him and Caitlin," Kevin replied, flipping back a few pages. "Read that."

Nikki read the incredibly generous terms Caitlin was offering her for a lease on the Schubert house, and she felt tears spring to her eyes. "What did I do to deserve these people?"

# Chapter 38

# Kevin

The Pen-Mar Winter Festival was a little smaller than Kevin had expected, but its heart was in the right place. He looked at the little town's Main Street, which was sparkling under the glow of twinkling white lights, and lined with bright tents. Couples sipped steaming hot cider as they strolled down the wet street, and kids played in the snowdrifts heaped at the corners. He glanced around a few corners, hoping he might see the Standardbreds and their sleigh. The guy from the farm hadn't contacted him, but he supposed that could be an oversight. With all this great snow and the below-freezing temperatures, surely the sleigh would be here.

Beside him, Nikki quivered with anticipation. "I can't believe I haven't come to this since I was a kid! It's amazing!"

He kissed the smooth hair pressed against her cheeks. She'd done something to straighten her curls, and he missed them, but Nikki was cute whether her hair was sleek or in spirals. "You've been working so hard, I almost feel bad convincing you to start a new business. You deserve some time off. I should have built a business case for spending the rest of the winter in St. Bart's."

She laughed. "You'd have a lot harder time getting that one past the board. So, where are we meeting Rosemary and Stephen?"

"Oh, later, for dinner at this place called The Farmstead. I think you're going to love it."

Nikki made a face. "Sounds pretentious."

"That's what you're going to be saying about your own cafe, if you don't let go of this prejudice about nice things!"

She laughed. "I know, I'm just kidding. But in the meantime, I really want something warm to drink. Or just to hold in my hands. I swear, this is the coldest winter we've *ever* had."

Kevin smiled. "I know just the place."

He stopped outside the plate-glass window of High Rock Coffee Company and let her take in the spectacular warmth glowing from within. The golden light spilling from the cafe's antique globe fixtures seemed to draw patrons like a magnet, and there was a line out the door. They joined the queue and Nikki began hopping to keep her feet warm. "I can't believe how busy it is! And there is coffee and cider at a ton of different tents out here, with no wait at them."

"People will choose atmosphere over convenience," Kevin said. "That's a lesson New York taught me years ago. Hide an intriguing restaurant down a dark alley, and it will do twice as much business as a boring bistro on a boulevard."

Nikki laughed. "Lauren would give you five stars for that alliteration." She looked back at the cafe's welcoming window, the gold paint on the plate-glass and the old-fashioned filigrees swirling around the words *Coffee - Baked Goods - Conversation.* "I can't get over it. This place shouldn't look authentic. It shouldn't belong here . . . but it does."

"It adds to the town's aesthetic, instead of trying to be something all its own."

Nikki's face clouded, as if an unwelcome memory had suddenly swept over her. Kevin, watching her expression, had a feeling the town improvement society story was about to come out. He waited, not wanting to give away that he'd heard it already. He was sure she wouldn't want to know her story was being told around town. They stepped up another place in line, and a waft of coffee and spice drifted from the cafe door as it opened and closed.

"You know," Nikki began, "when I was in high school, my friends and I tried to do something about the way the town looked. We kind of had this idea, I think—we thought people would like a more picture-postcard sort of atmosphere for the town. But we went about it all wrong. We tried to change the people who were already running things. We should have just started our own business and proved to them that this way works."

Kevin's arm tightened around her shoulders. "That sounds like the kind of lesson that's hard to learn as a kid," he said. "I'm sure you meant well."

"We did," she agreed. "I think the town knew that, too. I mean, they came back to the diner afterwards." She shrugged, and he felt a stiffness leave her body. Kevin thought she might finally let go of that memory.

*Progress,* he thought, as they finally stepped into the welcoming glow of the cafe, and the cozy scent of fresh-roasted coffee greeted them.

"You're going to do this, you know," Kevin told her. They were seated at a little table near the cafe's plate-glass window, looking over the festival tents and fairy lights on Main Street. Occasionally someone ran by pulling kids on a big sled, and he'd jump at the motion, thinking it might be the sleigh. He was holding out hope they'd find it out there. His own little storybook fantasy, shared with Nikki . . . wouldn't that be something?

"I'm still scared," she said, looking at him over her coffee mug. "You understand that, right?"

"Of course I do. I was scared to move to Maryland." He stroked her hand, still warm from her discarded gloves. "But the pay-off was going to be so worthwhile—assuming it all worked out—that I knew I'd never forgive myself if I didn't go for it."

"And it did work out," she suggested, smiling at him in a way which made his heart beat faster. "I think it did, anyway."

"Are you kidding me? Look at us." Kevin gestured around the warm cafe. The line was still out the door, and the baristas were running off their feet, but everyone was smiling. No one was in a hurry. The atmosphere was just as they'd promised in the window, just as Nikki was hoping for in her own cafe: conversation and community. Strangers were talking to each other, neighbors were calling out to one another. "We're on the brink of bringing all of this to Catoctin Creek," he said. "And as for us, well . . . I'm happy. Are you?"

It wasn't a dangerous question anymore. He knew the answer; it welled up in her sparkling eyes before she even spoke. "I'm happy."

A jazz band struck up a tune outside: young men and women in fluffy coats and hats, gathered close around a heater, began to play *Sleigh Ride*. Even though Christmas had been weeks ago, the jolly sounds of the winter anthem gave Kevin a happy, anticipatory feeling, as if he was a kid waiting on Santa Claus again.

And in a way, he was. Everything that had happened in the past year: coming to Catoctin Creek, meeting Nikki, giving up his life in New York, discovering his true calling with horses, finding his way into the community, helping Nikki take the lease on the Schubert house from Caitlin—all of it had just been improvements upon improvements, like opening a small gift to find an impossibly larger one inside, again and again and again. Kevin's life had grown outwards, gotten so much larger, since he'd left the big city for a small town. He could hardly wait to see what the next gift would be.

He had a few ideas about what he wanted, but he knew the rules.

*No peeking.*

— ele —

They were passing the last of the festival before Kevin realized they'd run out of tents and crowds. "Hey, we should go back," he said, tugging at Nikki's hands.

"Nope," she told him, smiling. "Come over here." She turned down an alley, and they walked between quiet old houses, their windows darkened. The entire town seemed to be back on Main Street.

"Where are we going?"

"Surprise," Nikki said.

Kevin raised his eyebrows. He thought he was the one with surprises. What could Nikki have up her sleeve?

The alley spilled them onto a quiet field behind the town, blanketed in white and luminous in the darkness. Kevin's gaze followed Nikki's eyes, and he gasped.

Trotting towards them were two big horses with manes flying like flags. They were drawing a sleek, silent sleigh through the snow—the gilded, grand sleigh from the Standardbred farm.

"It's magnificent," Kevin whispered.

"Over the river and through the woods," Nikki said. "Are you ready for your first sleigh ride?"

"How did you know?" He was overcome.

"Kevin, I run a diner. You think people don't run to me to tell me everything they hear about you?"

"Gus?"

"And Sean. And Nadine, actually."

"That's so kind of them."

Nikki smiled up at him. "You're one of us now. Maybe you're more suited to Catoctin Creek than I ever was. Wouldn't that just be typical?"

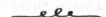

"Hey, man." The groom from the Standardbred farm hopped down from the sleigh once the horses were standing before Kevin and Nikki. He held firmly to the reins as they tugged, eager to be off again. "Things were busy at the farm and we weren't going to do the sleigh this year after all. But someone convinced me to give a private ride. I'm glad she did. This is a test ride for the route we came up with for the rest of the festival."

Kevin looked at Nikki incredulously. "How did you do this?"

She just smiled. "Everyone in the horse business knows everyone. I just used the horseshoe telegraph."

Bells jingled as the horses stirred restlessly. "Let's hop in, everybody!" The groom climbed back onto the sleigh's low box. "Time for a ride!"

The whisper of the runners, the jingling of bells, the muffled thudding of the horses' hooves, the stars shining overhead as they crossed a broad field and left the town lights behind: Kevin absorbed it all with a happiness so huge, he didn't know where he ended and the surrounding experience began. "This is incredible," he whispered.

Nikki turned to him, the plaid lap robe tugged up to her chin. "Hmm?"

"This is incredible!" he shouted, and pulled her close. "You're the sweetest, most darling, most thoughtful, most wonderful—"

"Mmhmm," Nikki murmured, enjoying the show. "Go on."

"Most beautiful, most terrifying, most determined, most enraging—"

"Okay, loverboy, I think you've hit the end—"

"Let me finish! Most beloved, most perfect, most amazing girlfriend in the world."

She looked almost startled by the end, as if she'd thought he was going to end on a tease and not with the truth. But he needed her to know how he really felt. Their faces were almost touching—the sleigh bells were a serenade—the moon was rising in a cold orange crescent over the mountains—

"Nikki," Kevin whispered, his lips just inches from hers. "I need to tell you—"

The sleigh dipped and swung, and the horses' hooves suddenly made a new, echoing sound. They turned, startled, and saw the sleigh was traveling over a wooden bridge, the surface draped with fresh snow. A creek bubbled and frothed on either side, its swift current evident in the starlight.

He looked back at Nikki. She grinned. "Over the river," she said.

The bridge receded behind them and then a strange light was sparkling ahead, twinkling and winking as it grew nearer. Kevin's breath caught in his throat. The horses trotted right into a forest somehow strung with white fairy lights, thousands and thousands of white fairy lights, as if they'd entered a star-field hung with the black lacework of the leafless winter trees.

Nikki pressed her head against his shoulder. "And through the woods."

Kevin, overcome, could only wrap his arms around her, holding her as he meant to forever, so tightly this fascinating, unpredictable woman would never slip away.

# Chapter 39

# Nikki

Nikki dusted paint chips from her hands, stretching her back. She desperately needed a break. Scraping old paint from walls was no one's idea of fun, but it had to be done.

She walked across the creaking floorboards of the drawing room and looked out through the big front windows. The view never ceased to give her pleasure. What a dream, to be on this side of the glass at last!

From its commanding position on its hill at the end of town, the Schubert house looked down on Catoctin Creek's storefronts to the south, and across a pretty field with thickets of fir trees, their green branches laden with snow, to the north. Cardinals were flitting in the trees which stood around the house, picking through the seed she'd tossed out for them earlier. With this much snow, even the winter birds needed a little extra help.

It was hard to believe all of this snow, a full winter of snowfall like Catoctin Creek had never seen, and there would be more in a few days, according to the weather forecast. As Nikki and Kevin had started the long, slow clean-up of the Schubert house, the lawn, trees, and front walk had all slumbered under impenetrable layers of ice and snow. They hadn't even bothered trying to shovel the walk clear, just tramping to the porch steps through every fresh snowfall, making a hard-packed pathway with their boots.

But in a month's time, the meteorologists on the morning shows would talk about spring thaws, kids would be out looking for the first snowdrops on hillsides protected from the north wind, and the breakfast chatter in the Blue Plate would be about plantings and gardens. The world outside would warm up and begin to blossom as Nikki's work inside grew more intense, until by summer, she would spend most of her time here at this house, serving coffee in this big, paneled formal drawing room and out on the wide verandah.

There was a quick banging sound from the kitchen, then a burst of mocking laughter. She put down her paintbrush and went into the plastic-sheeted, plaster-daubed world of the kitchen renovation, where Kevin, Stephen, their contractor Mike, and his assistant Bertie were looking at a broken thingamajig with a blend of consternation and hilarity.

"Oh God," Nikki sighed. "What did you break this time, Kevin?"

"It's nothing," Stephen said quickly. "Just a cabinet handle."

"A fifty-dollar cabinet handle," Mike specified.

"What? You're kidding!"

"He is," Kevin said, rolling his eyes. "More like ten. And I didn't *mean* to break it. I think it was defective."

"When do you go back to work with Gus?" Nikki asked pointedly.

"Not for another week," Kevin said. "Just as soon as he gets back from West Palm Beach. The trainer who flew him down wants him to stay and do their horses' shoes for another week of the circuit down there."

Nikki glanced at Stephen. "Can this place survive another week of Kevin?"

Stephen gave Kevin a friendly shove, and they all started laughing again.

Nikki left the men to it and walked back out to the relative serenity of the drawing room. She loved this space—its mellow hardwood floors, the carved marble of the mantelpiece, the tooled mahogany around the broad fireplace, and the plaster scrollwork on the ceiling. Once she was finished stripping the old floral wallpaper and faded white paint from the woodwork, she planned to paint the walls a deep burgundy to accent the wood and absorb the morning sunshine that would come pouring in the broad windows from spring to fall. In a week, the tables and chairs would arrive, and she wanted to be finished with the painting by then, right down to cream accents on the window-sills and mantelpiece.

It was going to take a lot of work to finish in time, but she figured once she had the drawing room done, she'd really feel like the house was transforming.

Of course, this meant the rest of the house was a mess. She'd renewed her lease on her apartment with hardly a second thought —this place would be unlivable for a while yet. Upstairs, she and Kevin had staked out the rooms where they'd live someday, once they had the time and the funds to fix the drafts whistling through the windows, turning the second floor into an icy winter palace. For now, though, the first floor was their domain: the drawing and dining rooms, where she'd serve coffee, croissants and muffins in the mornings, just as Sean had suggested. In the afternoons, there would be cookies, cakes, dessert bars. And on occasional evenings, a select, experimental dinner service. Just to see how things went. Just to see what people thought. Just to see what Catoctin Creek really wanted.

Just to see what they could do together—she, and Kevin, and the town where she had lived all of her life.

The front door opened, and Rosemary came in, bundled from head to toe in black wool. She looked like a witch. Nikki vaguely remembered Kevin saying something about that. "Hey, lady," she called. "What brings you to the Money Pit?"

Rosemary laughed, pulling down her scarf. "Don't call it that, Nikki. The bathtub hasn't fallen through the floor yet."

"Only because we haven't tried the upstairs pipes. But don't worry. It's too cold up there to bother with the bathtub."

Rosemary sighed and looked around. She had a big tote bag over her shoulder. Nikki hoped that was lunch. "It's a lot of work for a lease," she said eventually. "I know I've said that before, but it's getting more apparent all the time."

Nikki grinned. She had a secret to share. "Didn't I tell you?" she asked casually. "Caitlin's going to sell us the place after all. And Kevin's stupid condos finally sold. Some Russian oligarch bought up every vacant condo in the tower. So we can really go in on this together—the business, the house, everything."

Rosemary gasped and dropped the tote bag. A couple of cans of Coke rolled out and picked up speed, rushing down the warped old floor. "Oh my gosh," she breathed. "That's incredible. And— wow, I hate to say this, but this floor is *really* crooked."

Nikki laughed, snagging the escaping Coke cans with one foot. "It's all part of the charm. I can't wait to watch Grover slide across it—right before I refinish the hardwood and banish him from the downstairs rooms forever. So, what else do you have in that bag?"

"Sandwiches by Bobby," Rosemary replied, making Nikki's day. Bobby's new lunchtime offerings were fat deli-style sandwiches bursting with flavor. He'd started making them for Ellie Baughman, who had told him the thick hoagie rolls from Trout's were too much for her teeth. Lauren made an executive decision while Nikki was working on the bakery, putting the sandwiches on the menu, and they were now boosting the Blue Plate's lunchtime traffic by a sizable margin. Plus, Ellie came in for Bobby's lunch break every day. The two of them were adorable. "And his hand-cooked chips. There's enough for everyone."

"Rosie-marie, you're a queen," Nikki sighed. "I'm *starving.*" She reached into the brown paper bag of chips and snagged a few. The chips had been Lauren's idea, too. They were cut fresh, fried, and dusted with herbs and salt before serving. Nikki would have thought they were too posh for the Catoctin Creek crowd, but they were actually addictive, and so far no one was immune to them. Patrick and Betty even insisted some be left over for them to eat on their dinner breaks.

They set up a picnic on the scarred old dining table that had been left behind by the Schuberts. Nikki was already thinking of asking Ian Yingling to refinish it—he was terrible with gas and electric, but the man knew his way around furniture. Maybe she could give him some business and sort of push him in that direction as a full-time gig. There was plenty of old, battered furniture to be found in western Maryland—and the newcomers flooding the area wanted it for their beautiful historic houses.

"Anything good going on over at the Blue Plate?" she asked, setting out napkins.

Rosemary gave her a conspiratorial smile. "Nadine popped in to take back lunch to Elmwood while I was there."

"Oh yeah? How's Nadine?"

"She said she was buying lunch for everyone but that lying snake, Sean."

Nikki laughed and shook her head. "Sean got over his crush on me pretty fast, didn't he?"

"He's just a boy," Rosemary said, rolling her eyes. "But Nadine takes everything he does pretty close to heart."

"Oh!" Nikki stopped what she was doing. "So you think it's like that!"

Rosemary shrugged, but her eyes were twinkling.

The men came tramping into the dining room, lured by the rattle of butcher's paper wrapped around sandwiches. Kevin came up behind Nikki and pulled her close, his soft whisper warm in her ear. "Your dining room is looking magnificent."

"Better than your kitchen?" she joked.

"I'll go get another cabinet handle tomorrow," he said, still using the same seductive whisper.

Nikki laughed and whirled around so they were face to face.

Kevin smiled down at her. His eyes were bottle green, his hair was falling into his face. His grip around her shoulders was strong, his fingers calloused. He was a new man in many ways from the one she'd first met last year, but in others he was exactly the same: a sweet, funny guy who had attracted her the moment she'd laid eyes on him.

"Happy?" he asked.

"So happy," she promised.

Kevin's kiss was light and promising. "Only good things," he vowed. "For you and me, I see only good things."

*The End*

# Springtime at Catoctin Creek

Go riding at Elmwood Equestrian Center! Nadine came back to Catoctin Creek without much hope of ever fitting in there. Her goals? Work a steady job as barn manager at Elmwood Equestrian Center, keep an eye on her mom, and keep her head down. Three things which would be easier without the constant annoyance of the riding instructor and her next-door neighbor, Sean.

Sean Casey never meant to stay in Catoctin Creek for long. His heart is on the big horse show circuit, along with his friends, and he's going back on the road as soon as he can. Assuming he ever finds someone with deep enough pockets to fund his dreams. As the riding instructor at Elmwood, he has his pick of rich older women to con into sponsoring him. It's a task which would go a lot more smoothly if that workhorse Nadine would get off his back.

Nadine is counting the days until Sean finally leaves Elmwood; Sean is exasperated with Nadine's grinding work ethic. Both have been going out of their way to avoid working with each other. So when spring brings the challenge of working together on Rosemary Beckett's sales horse, they're surprised to find they aren't the worst of colleagues, after all . . . and not bad neighbors, either.

With an enemies-to-lovers romp through the beautiful small-town setting of Catoctin Creek, a dash of daring horses, and spring in bloom all around, Springtime at Catoctin Creek is a charming, cozy romance perfect for your next lazy-day escape.

Read the first chapter now!

## Springtime at Catoctin Creek
### Chapter One: Nadine

A sweet breeze blew across the Maryland countryside, perfumed with blossoms and bearing an appealing message from the sunny south: spring was on its way.

Nadine turned her nose up to the cool air and let it waft over her. That floral scent! The entire morning was saturated with it! She'd never learned much about flowers, their names and all that, so she couldn't guess what bouquets she was sniffing on the steady west wind this morning. She just knew the fragrance was enlivening her senses, making her feel chipper when a full mug of coffee had not, and giving her the energy she needed to get on with this day. She pushed locks of waving black hair back from her cheeks, tucking it behind her small ears, and turned her face full into that fragrant wind.

A thought, unoriginal but nonetheless sincere, ran through her mind: she simply loved springtime.

The idea made her laugh to herself. Loving springtime, what a concept! Who didn't, really?

Maybe Sean Casey. He was so contrary, he probably didn't like sunshine and rainbows, either. But Nadine had decided to not to worry about Sean Casey's opinions anymore. His likes, his dislikes, the women he flirted with. None of it was her concern. Sean was a coworker, and that was as far as things were going between them. She'd already wasted more than enough time on that man. Nadine closed her eyes briefly and put Sean out of her mind.

Of course, she was going to see him shortly, when he came downstairs to get to work, but for the moment, at least, she would live Sean-free. His pretty face could just go—vanish!

Behind her, a symphony of whinnies broke the morning quiet. Nadine opened her eyes and turned around, her hands immediately going to her wild hair as the wind pushed it over her face, and watched the little herd of ponies galloping across the fenced pasture. Beneath their hooves, the rolling landscape shone with green, looking as if someone had laid Easter grass across last year's beige stubble. The nimble ponies flowed across the slopes with all the grace of a flock of migrating birds.

Nadine's heart crept up into her throat and stayed there as she breathed deep, thrilling herself with the sight of those spirited ponies. All that was left of the once-famous Elmwood herd, these six ponies were treasured members of the equestrian center's therapeutic riding and lesson programs. She could name all of them: that was Pumpkin, in front for once, then the gleaming alabaster coat of Ghost—

"Well, that's cute."

Sean's voice made Nadine's pulse jump as well as her feet. She put a hand to her chest, willing her heart to calm itself. Why was he always sneaking around and spooking her like that? Why couldn't he just stay in the barn—or better yet, up in his apartment under the rafters?

Bad enough she had to listen to Sean thumping around at night on the other side of her living room wall, bad enough she had to work with him in the afternoons, when the onslaught of riding lessons descended on the barn. Did he have to come down and bother her before breakfast, too, when hardly anyone was around and she could just soak up the beauty of one of Catoctin Creek's most beautiful farms? She was lucky to live here, lucky to be back in her hometown, lucky to be manager of this gorgeous equestrian center...so it would be nice if she could just enjoy a moment of downtime without Sean once in a while.

"What do you want?" she asked, working to keep her impatience from her tone.

"The ponies?" Sean said, looking down at her. "They're very cute."

"The ponies are magnificent," she retorted sharply, because calling Elmwood's priceless pony herd *cute* failed to take into account how majestic, how elegant, how sought-after these ponies were in the upper echelons of the horse show market. For decades, Elmwood ponies had taken pigtailed girls and serious-faced boys to championships, their pricked ears and soft dark eyes emanating professionalism as they jumped around manicured courses, laying their polished hooves into the soft footing just so. Elmwood ponies were many things, cute included, but she wasn't going to let

Sean Casey get away with demeaning them with just one word of praise. They deserved dozens. "These ponies are *way* more than cute, Sean. Open up your eyes."

She glanced sidelong at him as she spoke, unable to resist taking in the view through her thick lashes. And it was a good view, as always. Sean was blessed with the looks of a Swedish prince. Or so Nadine had heard. Nikki down at the Blue Plate Diner had once told her Sean looked like a Nordic male model, and that was the source of all his problems in life.

Nadine had found it hard to sympathize. Her pale skin didn't win her any marks in the beauty department, especially paired with her wispy black hair that had to be pounded into submission with a round brush and an elastic band every morning, lest it puff up from her ponytail and get in her eyes while she was leading horses or mucking stalls. She had good green eyes, dark as forest leaves in midsummer, but no one else noticed them enough to remark on them, so she supposed it was probably just a personal preference, her own little vanity. Sean's eyes were a particularly shimmering ice-blue. Not that she ever looked at them, and—

He was grinning at her.

*Grinning* at her? He ought to be frowning at her. Why couldn't he just wake up and realize when she was insulting him? So frustrating. It was so difficult to throw Sean off his game. He was cheerful, chipper even, through the most challenging days on the farm. Even when their boss, Caitlin was being her usual chaotic self, Sean just carried on as if she wasn't making them crazy at all...

"I know they're good ponies, Nadine," he replied now, his voice amused. "I rode an Elmwood pony when I was a little kid, you know. Elmwood Bowtie. She was a leadline champion at Devon."

She hadn't known that. If she had, she would have hated him a lot more by now—something Nadine didn't even think was possible. Because oh boy, did she *hate* Sean Casey. Even if *hate was a strong word,* as her mother used to chide. Fine, Mom. She couldn't stand him. Did that get across the point?

Such a lying snake. Lying, flirtatious, cheap, lazy, good-for-nothing—just like every other man Nadine had been forced to work with. Ten long years of trying to make a career for herself as a professional horsewoman, and when she finally had the plum spot she'd always wanted, her boss had to go and hire Sean.

"You did not have an Elmwood pony," she huffed, turning her back on him and the landscape behind her. She hated to leave behind the galloping ponies, the flower-soaked breeze, but it was time to head back into the barn. Time to work. Anyway, the first blush of the beautiful morning had passed. There were high, icy clouds taking over the blue sky, and that lushly floral wind was growing a bit stiffer, too. There was a cold note to it which gave her the shivers. "Stop lying about your ponies. I'm going in to work on stalls."

"I'll help you." Sean tripped after her, taking care that his polished black field boots found all the dry spots in the muddy parking lot. "I have nothing else going on this morning. Just a couple horses to ride this afternoon before lessons."

Nadine kept her eyes resolutely forward. The big barn complex, with its double aisles and massive indoor arena attached at one end, loomed in front of them like an airplane hanger. "I have Richie and Rose to help me," she reminded him. "Three people's plenty to get stalls cleaned. Go do something else. Go polish your saddle."

"Three's plenty. Four's even better. Just let me get out of these boots."

She eyed his beautiful riding boots. Nadine was deeply covetous of those boots, which Sean kept in perfect condition even when the rest of his tack could sometimes fall into deplorable condition. She knew it was his best pair, not his everyday boots. "Why are you even wearing your good boots out here?"

"I was going to ride the new horse first thing this morning, and Caitlin was coming to watch with the owner. You know she likes to see me turned out all polished for clients. But it turns out he isn't coming until this afternoon, so there won't be time to ride him. All dressed up for nothing."

"Oh, right. Rosemary's horse. I'd literally forgotten about it." Yesterday, Nadine had prepped the last empty stall in the back aisle for Rosemary Beckett's incoming sales horse. Then a million other things had happened, in the course of a normal barn afternoon, and the new horse was crowded out of her brain. "Caitlin shouldn't have asked you to ride him as soon as he arrived, anyway. He should have time to settle in. I wouldn't ride him before Wednesday, at the earliest." Today was Monday; two days would be plenty of time.

Sean shrugged. "Caitlin said Rosemary wants him sold quickly, so the sooner I know what we're dealing with, the better. He could be very green, y'know? Rosemary gets her horses from auctions, so he doesn't come with any history."

"That's an even better reason not to push the poor horse." Nadine stopped in the barn entrance and peered down the front aisle, wondering if Richie and Rose, the grooms, had started mucking out yet. The big barn took several hours of hard work to clean each morning. They always started on the front aisle—so-called because it was the main barn aisle, lined with stalls housing the boarders, the paying customers. The "back aisle" was a little shorter and less trafficked, home to the farm horses and ponies, and dead-ending into storage below Nadine's apartment, while the front aisle led directly to the indoor arena, the barn offices, and the tack rooms.

She narrowed her eyes at the condition of her barn. The front aisle was a mess this morning. Blankets needed rehanging on their bars—Nadine liked them hung with hospital-like precision in perfect rectangles, their buckles tucked away out of sight—and that lovely spring wind had scattered hay everywhere. A bit of a mess while cleaning stalls was acceptable, but this was beyond normal limits. If Caitlin came down before they'd finished morning chores, she'd have a mini-meltdown. Nadine decided to ask Richie to use the leaf-blower to clear the aisle before they did stalls, while she fixed the blankets.

Assuming Sean went away. Why was he still hovering alongside her? Barn work wasn't his problem. He rode horses and taught riding lessons, and right now he didn't need to do either. Instead, he was still bleating at her about the new horse. The one who wasn't even here yet.

"I'm not going to push the horse, Nadine. Maybe have a little faith in me? Have I been hard on any of the other horses I've trained here?

Maybe he hadn't, but none of those horses had been challenges. Nadine knew tough horses, but she wasn't so sure Sean did. He rode with a stiff, elegant posture which told her he was more about theory than practice—more about looking pretty than riding effectively. Just the opposite of Nadine, as he was in every way imaginable. She sighed and turned back to him. "I'm just saying, you don't even know this horse. He could have been bouncing from barn to barn for months. He might be tired and miserable."

Sean raised a lazy eyebrow at her. "It's touching to see what faith you have in me. Nadine. I promise to be good to this tired, miserable, pathetic horse-tragedy you've built up in your mind. But, I still have to get him going. Sales horses are my responsibility, and I can't just waste time when Caitlin wants me selling, selling, selling—"

"Of course, you're very busy," Nadine agreed tartly. She turned on her heel, heading into the barn.

"I am very busy," Sean countered, chasing after her. "Wait, Nadine. Why are you mad at me now? I wanted to help you guys this morning!"

"Just go change your boots," she snapped. "If you come into a dirty stall in those boots, I'll kill you for boot abuse."

"I'm going to change them, we are literally walking towards my apartment where my other boots are—but listen, Nadine—" His hand rested on her arm, a soft gesture asking her to wait, to give him a chance.

Nadine froze. He'd touched her like this before, and more— giving a leg-up, steadying her while she dealt with a spooky horse, things like that—but they'd been buried under winter coats for most of the time he'd been here. Now, with his fingers pressing through her thin thermal shirt, she could feel those—feelings— again. The same feelings he'd set off with his casual touch when he'd first arrived here, six months ago. When Sean had first come to Elmwood to take on the riding instructor job, and she'd been such a foolish victim of his smile and his charm. She'd let him touch her arm, and felt the warm thrill his fingers gave her skin, and wanted more of it.

That first touch was burned into her brain—as was her reaction. She remembered the silly grin spreading across her face as she'd looked at him, but she didn't remember what she'd said. Or even what he'd asked. Probably something stupid and innocent, like if she knew where he'd left a pony bridle or if she could get a horse's mane pulled. Nothing which matched the magnetic reception she'd felt with his hand on her arm.

And then, after he'd taken those warm fingers away, she'd watched him march right over to Vonnie Gibbons, a middle-aged adult student who drove an Audi and dressed in perfectly matching riding outfits, right down to her thousand-dollar boots, and flash his movie-star smile at her.

Nadine's heart had sunk as she realized their connection was all in her head. The smiles, the charm, the soft touches, the thrills rippling through her at his touch: none of that meant anything. Sean Casey was just a big old flirt.

That's when she decided to hate him, and it had served her well ever since. Except, of course, for the whole working-together thing.

Now she tried to take a step back, flick away those burning fingers, but her feet didn't want to take her away, and her eyes didn't want to jerk from his. So she stood there, seething with a strange mixture of emotions, and let him talk as if anything he said mattered to her.

"Don't you want to stop fighting all the time?" he asked, his low voice charmingly pleading. "Wouldn't it be easier if we got along? I don't know how long I'll be here, but—"

"What does that mean?" Nadine interrupted, momentarily distracted. "You don't know how long you'll be here? Are you looking for another job?"

Sean dropped his hand to his side, his expression rueful. She missed the connection immediately, but at least she had the freedom to take a step back, as if those invisible magnets were slowly giving up their force. "No, I didn't mean to imply I'm looking for a new job, but, you know how it is. If the right thing came along..."

"Wait a minute. How could this not be the right thing?" Nadine was aware she should be encouraging him to apply far and wide to new jobs, preferably in California, or perhaps Germany, but she felt an irrational surge of loyalty to Caitlin and to Elmwood. She'd worked here a year now. She was proud of her work. And this place did things that mattered. Sean did things that mattered. "You have a good job. You're a riding coach with dozens of students, you have sales horses to ride and commission when they sell, you have access to a truck and trailer so you can go to shows, you have an apartment right up there—" she pointed up at the pair of barn apartments, their small windows overlooking the stalls and aisles. "I don't understand what else you could want."

Sean gave her a sideways smile. "I think you mean you don't understand what else you could want," he told her. "We're used to different things."

Nadine's lips slammed tight together. That did it. She was done talking to Sean for the morning. Arrogant, entitled, selfish...

She stalked up the aisle, mud flaking from her paddock boots with each step. It didn't matter if she made a mess now. She'd ask

Richie to get out the leaf-blower and scour this aisle clean. Then they'd muck out, and he'd blow the aisle again to clear up their mess. By eleven o'clock, this barn would be spotless—just the way she always left it, six days a week.

She was aware of Sean's tread as he climbed the creaking stairs to his apartment, the involuntary slam of his front door as he pulled it tight in the swollen old frame. Then she knew he was on the little linoleum pad just inside his door, unzipping his field boots and tugging them free. She knew where he was, what he was doing, in part because her apartment was a clone of his, in part because when the barn was quiet she could hear his steps on the floorboards, and in part because, for some annoying reason, when Sean Casey was around, Nadine always knew it.

"Well, maybe he'll leave," she muttered, taking down a manure fork and tossing it into a wheelbarrow. "I bet we'd all be a lot happier without lazy Sean Casey in the barn."

*Springtime at Catoctin Creek is available now from your favorite retailer or bookseller!*

# Also By Natalie Keller Reinert

The Eventing Series

The Alex & Alexander Series

The Grabbing Mane Series

The Show Barn Blues Series

The Catoctin Creek Series

The Hidden Horses of New York

Learn more at nataliekreinert.com

# Acknowledgments

I had so much fun writing this one!

Thanks to everyone who loved *Sunset at Catoctin Creek* and asked for more. This little town has become a getaway for me, and I plan to visit much more often in the coming years.

Thanks to my Patrons, who read the first drafts and send me so much good advice: Heather Voltz, Cindy Sperry, Rhonda Lane, Princess Jenny, Emily Nolan, Lindsay Moore, Brinn Dimler, Tricia Jordan, Lori King, Megan Devine, Sarah Seavey, Cheryl Bavister, Zoe Bills, Liz Greene, Diana Aitch, Orpu, Kathy, Rachael Rosenthal, Karen KC Monaco, Kathi LaCasse, Mary, Liza Sibley, Kathi Hines, Kaylee Amons, Cyndy Searfoss, Heather Wallace, Ann H. Brown, Dana Probert, Claus Giloi, Jennifer, Di Hannel, Sarina Laurin, Risa Ryland, Silvana Ricapito, Emma Gooden, Karen Carrubba, Thoma Jolette Parker, Annika Kostrubala, Christine Komis, Peggy Dvorsky, Katy McFarland, Amelia Heath, Andrea Parker, Kathlynn Angie-Buss, Alyssa, Harry Burgh, Amy Flood, Jessie Chouinard, Mel Policicchio, Nicola Beisel, Linnhe

McCarron, Leslie Yazurlo, Sherron Meinert, Susan Cover, Jean Miller, and Genevieve Dempre.

This list gets longer and longer with every new book, and I'm so thankful for all of you! Your daily support, comments, and suggestions are what makes my increased publishing schedule possible.

Special thanks to Susan Cover, Liz Greene, and Jean Miller for beta reading the second draft over the holidays and making some serious contributions to the story. I'm so grateful to you all!

# About the Author

I currently live in Central Florida, where I write fiction and freelance for a variety of publications. I mostly write about theme parks, travel, and horses! I've been writing professionally for more than a decade, and yes...I prefer writing fiction to anything else. In the past I've worked professionally in many aspects of the equestrian world, including grooming for top eventers, training off-track Thoroughbreds, galloping racehorses, working in mounted law enforcement, on breeding farms, and more!

Visit my website at nataliekreinert.com to keep up with the latest news and read occasional blog posts and book reviews. For installments of upcoming fiction and exclusive stories, visit my Patreon page and learn how you can become a subscriber!

For more:

- Facebook: facebook.com/nataliekellerreinert

- Group: facebook.com/groups/societyofweirdhorsegirls

- Bookbub: bookbub.com/profile/natalie-keller-reinert

- Twitter: twitter.com/nataliegallops

- Instagram: instagram.com/nataliekreinert
- Email: natalie@nataliekreinert.com

CPSIA information can be obtained
at www.ICGtesting.com
Printed in the USA
LVHW090428170323
741772LV00003B/541